Serial Murders of Mars

Paul Boulet

Gnome On Pig Productions

Serial Murders of Mars

Written by: Paul Boulet
Edited by: Hailey Dean, Jessica Lami and Alexis Allinson
Cover Art by: Paul Boulet and Danielle Kisch

Printing: 2017

ISBN: 978-1-387-27506-9

This book is a work of fiction. Any similarity to persons, places or things are either fictional or used in a fictional manner and in no way reflect any events or persons now or in the past.

Credit to other work for the author is listed in the back of this book.

The Gnome On Pig Productions logo was created by artist Elizabeth Eichelberger.

www.gnomeonpigproductions.com

"A stirring tale of dark intrigue and deadly adventure on Queen Victoria's Mars!"

-Toby Frost, author of the popular, Space Captain Smith series

"A mind blowing voyage through space to an epic confrontation on Mars."

-Mahegan L'AmiTime is of the Essence Book #1: Nightlights

"An intriguing spin on what our future/past could have been. You're not going to want to put it down."

-Alexis Allinson author of the Darkness Rising Universe Series

Serial Murders of Mars

Table of Contents

Epigraph

"Phobus and Deimus quickly drove Ares' smooth-wheeled, chariot to him and bore him up from the wide paths of earth into his richly wrought carriage and then straight lashed his team till coming to high Olympos." - Hesiod, Shield of Heracles

"God who made thee mighty, make thee mightier yet, God who made thee mighty, make thee mightier yet." -Land of Hope and Glory, A. C. Benson, 1902

Preface

It's my understanding that a preface is an author's personal introduction to a novel, intended to give the reader a deeper association with the author and thereby the novel they're about to read. It may therefore contain some background into the author's creative process which will then infer some aspects of the author him- or herself, (himself in my case). Whereas, I've spent a great deal of time considering my audience while comprising the novel, I find myself at a loss while writing its preface.

I'm not trying to make excuses but as much as I enjoy reading novels I seldom read the preface. If I do read the preface I usually do so after I've read the novel itself. I don't want to know too much of anything outside of what's actually in the story. To do so would forcibly puncture the illusion's membrane instead of being drawn into it. This places me at a disadvantage as I'm unsure who you are or how best to tailor this to be something that you'll enjoy/somehow enhance the novel you're about to read (or have read). In the following passages, I will illustrate, in multiple ways, what SMoM is like and also reveal a bit of what I'm like so that the way I choose to write it implies more than what's actually written.

First off, I can introduce SMoM by drawing some comparisons to one of my favorite fictional authors, Kilgore Trout. For those unfamiliar, he's a recurring character found here and there blotching up the pages of Vonnegut novels. One of this very prolific author's works (Trout's not Vonnegut's) is entitled, The Gospel from Outer Space. This novel has some similarities to SMoM (but not too many) just as I have some similarities to Kilgore (but not too many). This novel (GfOS not SMoM), is a kind of revisionist history. Actually, GfOS proposes to revise history, or really an alien from outer space proposes to revise history, really proposes to revise the theological accounting of the New Testament.

Likewise, GfOS includes references to the Christian messiah. (How could it not?) And, not to discount the obvious, it's a work of science fiction. Dissimilar to GfOS, SMoM doesn't propose to revise history it's set in a revised history. SMoM may or may not include an alien character and if it does it's not his/her/its role to deliver a new gospel to humanity. There is a character in SMoM who makes reference to the Christian messiah and who delivers a divine message (and I'm not revealing too much, you'll get to read that for yourself in the prologue, A Letter of Intent, unless you, like me, are reading this after you read the novel itself, unless you are even more like me and skipped the preface altogether). But, the message delivered in SMoM is by no means, "good news" no matter one's theological disposition. Trout and I also possess some similarities but I'll opt to hold them close to the vest for now and instead discuss more about how SMoM came into being, returning to Kilgore thereafter.

Coincidentally, on the day I composed this preface, I chanced upon a picture of Mars as I flipped through on-line news (literally via Flipboard). Fortune published an article on fortune.com entitled, Yes, We Can Build Industry in Space - And We Should Start Now, David Z. Morris, September 11, 2016, 1:24 PM EDT. Beneath the title, one of Hubble's pictures of Mars was chosen as the digital eye-catcher. The article summarizes a proposal, the source linked in the article, entitled, Space Development and Space Science Together, an Historic Opportunity, Philip T. Metzger, Florida Space Institute, University of Central Florida. In Metzger's proposal, he describes a, "strategy of incremental progress," toward a desired end-state he calls a Self-sufficient Replicating Space Industry or SRSI. His plan avoids the enormous overhead of creating habitable places in space by utilizing an automated workforce. Perhaps (at least at first) this may prove a wiser plan than executed in SMoM by Tyneside Spaceyardes, Ltd. of Newcastle upon Tyne. An automated workforce wouldn't be subject to indulgent human temperaments, i.e. what they might call "viscous humors," or would it be capable of independent moral agency (as long as they don't contact the project out to Cyberdyne Systems) thereby avoiding some of the ill-fated consequences brought about by the Tyneside alternative, not that Tyneside really had an option.

Accepted or not, Metzger's proposal acknowledges a widely discussed human inevitability (pending total self-annihilation). Forbes, on forbes.com, published an article, 'Trillion Dollar Baby' Asteroid Has Wannabe Space Miners Salivating, Eric Mack, contributor, July 19, 2015, concerning Asteroid 2011 UW158, an object only, "about a half mile across," possessing a platinum core that, "could be worth over 5 trillion dollars," and yes, that wasn't a misquote, that was trillion with a "t." So I believe the novel's basic premise is sound; if mankind could have fueled Victorian industrialism with assets reaped from without this terrestrial sphere, they most certainly would have. SMoM is then the imagined backtracking of that inevitability.

The rest started very organically during a conversation with a colleague who happened to inform me that he played a small role in a documentary. In that documentary, he appears in a dramatized scene, as part of a barbershop quartet entertaining passers by during the 1893 Columbian Exposition, also known as the Chicago World's Fair. I'll refrain from expounding but there's an inexhaustible depth of intrigue around that event, including what occurred in Evanston, IL, coincidently again the town in which I was born. Though it never occurs all at once and continues without notice, organic life has already sprung to seedling. The rest looks more like how I conduct research. Events shared in the film invariably lead on-line to browse the local library system or on-line book sellers. The black flashing cursor of Google's search (the one for Scholar and under the doodle alike), is such a simple enticing way to plumb the tactless superhighway (an archaic term like calling a road a motorway). Within the overwhelming results, invariably again, related Wikipedia entries are returned, which are more enticing still if only to conduct more searches derived from the references exiled to the footer (because no one dare consider the article itself primary). But with a bit more tenacity and even more luck you find something unexpected. Searches build upon another which intertwine on the Moirai's spindle. The results return links to an "old school" bulletin board that hasn't received a new post in well over a decade. It's the former haunt of a virtual consortium of conspiracy theorists who've considered your inquiry from angles that literally defy logic. This is the hotbed of the forge where iron melds with carbon to steel. If you have a fascination for the fantastic, these enlightened elite should share a space on your bookshelf (or favorites bar) alongside Hawkins, Nietzsche and Chomsky.

Which brings us back to Kilgore. Concerning the comparison of GfOS and SMoM, I mentioned that there are some, albeit slanted, points of similarity. Upon concluding SMoM, you may recall this comparison and say to yourself, "What the heck was this guy thinking? This story isn't remotely similar to The Gospel from Outer Space." What you might then conclude about me personally is that I am, as I've been told, "in love with my own prose" and that I like reading myself write. If you did so, on both counts, you are correct.

~ Paul Boulet (9/11/2016)

Πρόλογος: A Letter of Intent

Seventeenth, April, 1896.

These words must be written and I must write them. I must write them and you must read them. The following is a foretelling of the fate of man's greatest achievement and a prophetic chronicling of his vanity's greatest tragedy. They are not the words of a historian or journalist. These trifling professions merely record what they observe as if there is some power in observation. Their words are colorless, flavorless and lifeless. Not so with these words. These words reverberate with an inward property that nearly burns through the page. These words are divinely inspired. These are the words of a new testament, the words of holy scripture.

Even after reading these few lines can't you already feel the glowering presence between them? There is an anointing that saturates every jot and tittle. This is why I am the only one to write them, why I must write them and why you must read them. I alone have pounded out this future in the hammer-falls of my clenched fists.

In Xanadu did Kubla Khan a stately pleasure dome decree, but did the dread Khan ever suffer the invasion of his vaulted palace? Or did the Emperor Tiberius ever suffer an invasion of his Isle of Capri? Even now profane intruders are on the wing, ascending an iron clad Jacob's Ladder towards me. Soon after their arrival all that I have done will no longer be concealed behind the thick veil of planetary expanses. After considering these circumstances from every possible angle I see no other outcome. They will see beneath the gilded veneer. They will look upon the naked flesh of my beautiful atrocities. They will judge me and in so doing will brand me among the most prolific of villains. I will not allow them to drag me back to their planet of dregs to stretch my neck for the hangman's noose. I will burn them all in a fire of my ignition. I will vomit them from my mouth into the merciless vacuum of space.

Do you doubt my divinity reader? Let me tell you how I came self-aware. Picture me when I met with the suited aristocrats of space-borne industry. We assembled in the filth of an American city and climbed flights of dark steps to a paneled conference room many stories up. So like the gods they must feel! To conduct their business elevated above the underlings that scuttle in the dirt beneath them.

The richly upholstered office featured tall windows that glared down on muddy streets, the contents of dumped chamber pots and caked soot staining the brick neo-classical buildings with black weeping tears. The ranks of their working poor trod along below, dream-like in their daily toil.

Hidden away to this lot, my newly met industrialists lauded the success of their investments. Their poorly tailored vests were pulled tight around bulbous bellies. Their shoes shined with the spit of impoverished boys.

They set about reasoning with me. They pitched their offer with a charlatan's flourish. They promised me a handsome wage to leave Earth's nurturing embrace to live out my days on lifeless shores awash in a vacuous sea. I paused to consider their offer.

It was just then that my pondering took me elsewhere. I was swept away in the revelation of my true nature. There within the eternal night of my deep thoughts a sacred and mystic river sped before me. Its rapid waters steamed with an intoxicating vapor. It surged forth with a swell of torrential rainfall. It pounded down the perilous crags of the gods' high dwellings. It impregnated the imprisoned titan Gaia, damned to undying captivity under the mountain's roots into which that river flowed. Shackled Gaia moaned at the rape but was powerless to shun its relentless penetration. Sweet darkness and the rapture of night held me fast in embryonic warmth.

With a burst of afterbirth, blood and brimstone I was recreated. My lungs drew in the thick stench infused airs of Hades. My skin bristled with the hot breath of my panting parents in the wake of their throbbing passions.

My eyes opened to look upon lithe Nyx, goddess of the night, who stood wide eyed and attentive before my dripping birth. Her hair fell in long curls down the nape of her neck. Her shoulders were adorned with a wrap that resembled mists that hang low at dawn. She quivered with lust for my manhood to blossom. She sought to bear my progeny and I was yet instants old. But I denied her desires. I was not yet convinced she was worthy.

My revelation concluded and I was brought back to my earthly senses but everything had changed. I now knew that I've walked in the company of spiritual offspring ever since.

Regaining my composure, I turned to look back at the mundane setting around me. I returned the stares of the worm-like beings who called me to their corporate offices. Their mustaches were downcast. Their smoldering fibrous cigars hung limply from their lips. They stared at me mute. I imagine they thought I must be carefully considering their offer. Little did they know what they now beheld. I was no longer a man but areios, a grim reflection of myself in the dread god's aspect.

The vision confirmed that this offer was pregnant with the voice of the Fates. I accepted it with handshakes and tipped glasses. The witless creatures immediately set upon the plans to send me into space. Thereby I came to a land befitting gods. The third planet was given to man, but it is insufficient for me. The fourth planet is home to those who dwell in the heavens, there among the Tharsis volcanoes where lay the magnificent peak known as Nix Olympica. There I decreed my Pleasure Dome and there it rose from the barren soil where nothing had ever grown before.

Therein reveals why penning these letters is so vital. These words are nothing less than a new scripture of my divine inspiration. Once the shattered husk of this bright shining place is exhumed speculation must be cleansed of misconception. If those who now travel here have any intuition, they will by chance detect a creeping terror with every passing mile. Even the simplest of beasts know when death looms close.

So, reader, do these words fill you with a sense of prescience? If you find these pages tucked in the vest pocket of a frozen corpse do you think the disembodied spirit lurks nearby watching you read? Is it a man's ghost or perhaps the apotheosis of a demigod transcended now in the fullness of divinity?

If so pay it no mind. Take comfort in the paltry aspects of your everyday life. Eke out your meager existence. Fall in love and marry. Produce mewling brats and raise them. Kick your fledglings from the nest to make their way in a cruel and uncaring world. Live out your lives in silence for you never did anything worth doing or said anything worth hearing.

But know that you don't live lives of innocence. Man is indebted to gods and your debts will come due. When my wrath is unleashed your debts will be past recompense. Your damnation is as assured as the travelers who even now sail the windless oceans of emptiness toward glorious Mars. As your God, Jehovah, created a hell to punish you sinners use that as illustrative of your lives to come. Imagine being baptized in a vat of blazing hell-fires lapping at your skin to the gleeful tittering of diabolic horrors who eternally prod you with impossibly sharp pitchforks. It's a fitting image enough. Your reckoning will come quickly and come on a wimpling wing.

Your God stretched out his arms and died that your afterlife might be enraptured in the pleasures of paradise. He suffered the indignity of being nailed to a scrap of wood and hefted high over a garbage mound called Golgotha. He bled to death among common criminals as the authorities diced for his earthly belongings. And thus the Lamb of God was sacrificed for the sins of the world. You'll get no such sacrifice from me.

Chapter A (1): Ares Britannia and the Triumph of Mars

"Please, gentlemen, please!" Mr. Gavin Crossland shouted over the innumerable crowd that packed themselves into the upper room apartment. "I simply must check the weather. Give me a moment."

He rose up from his chair, winning himself free of the coiffures. The entire group hushed to dull murmurs and threw some quizzical looks, both his way and out toward the open window facing the street. Gavin's associate, Sir Thomas Listonn, also a prisoner of the coiffures chair, turned his head suddenly to take his own look. The squat man attending his hair cursed something vulgar in Portuguese. As Gavin rose he resisted the urge to smooth his hair knowing that it had been perfectly oiled in place. He winced a bit at the feeling of caked makeup on his skin, one of many new sensations he experienced for the very first time this day. Turning his back to the gathering he made for the daylight and placed both hands on the windowsill to thrust his head outside.

He looked out to his left and northward, sea breeze kissing his lips. His view was compressed by the buildings flanking Totara Street, but towering above them was the might of the sacred Mt. Maunganui, the indismissable landmark of Tauranga, Gate Pā, New Zealand. The young rays set the sky ablaze with a lustrous blue. The word azure was really more appropriate as blue seemed too pedestrian a descriptor for such an immaculate day. The morning was sizing up to be wholly ideal to launch the virgin space-liner It was a day the likes of which could only be crafted in destiny. It seemed universally pristine, like how mornings must have dawned upon the very creation of the world. The broad expanse above him was only interrupted by the speckled grays of great sea fowl that flew in lazy arcs. The deep bass of a ship's whistle blared, drowning out the lightly crying birds. The bass was deep enough to rumble the abdomen and deafen the ear. He knew that the dreadnought HMS Devastation had arrived while they slept. It was chief among the complement that would escort the launch.

The noise drew his gaze eastward out toward the Bay of Plenty and the unending South Pacific. The sky there hosted the bobbing forms of the four semi-rigid airships that would heft the virgin craft into that azure sky. Broad steamers flowed behind them like kite tails. The blues and reds of the Union Jack mingled wrestling with the emerald green of Tyneside Spaceyarde, Ltd. Though he couldn't see it for the intervening colonial structures, the metal cables that led down from those dirigibles funneled to the harbor and were stuck fast to the awaiting spacecraft. The very craft he and his team had designed which now would embark on its maiden voyage.

Gavin knew that he had no time to dote on the weather, but he relished the break from his slavering companions behind him. The petty obligations that kept him here were a waste of proper resources. He certainly shouldn't be held to the whims of this gaggle of Tyneside accountants, military officers, political envoys, privileged press and all the other ancillary personnel who insisted on carving up his time before the ceremony. He should be down on the docks with the liner making final preparations.

Sky gazing aside, he reached down to gather up a cluster of shining glass cylinders and wires that dangled from the window pane. Gavin raised them up to his eyes splaying a spectrum of colors into the room behind him. Squinting to read the measurements he mumbled to himself, "Barometric pressure and temperature up slightly, but still quite comfortable." He could hardly believe it. It was like he had given an order to God and the Almighty had accommodated to the last decimal.

Returning the instruments to their place, Gavin shouted over his shoulder, "Could a runner please rush off to Mr. William Henry Dines from the Imperial Meteorological Society? They have a bivouac setup alongside the liner. Ask him and the meteorological council for their measurements." In response, a young brown youth wearing a sharp red and gold trim uniform leapt to his bare feet and ran off into the hallway. As if in trade another boy, similarly clad rushed in, "Mr. Crossland! Mr. Crossland!" the boy shouted.

"Here," Gavin said, turning back to the room and waving to him.

"Warrant Officer Vecihi Hürkuş has a note for you, sir!" the boy said, waving a tightly folded leaf as high up as he could reach.

"Bring it here," Gavin commanded.

The boy ducked and weaved through the legs of those present, the flat of his free hand holding fast to his smart cap. The newspaper men all stretched their necks to gain a glimpse of the paper. The boy made it to Gavin and held the message out stiffly. Snatching it up, Gavin peeled it open and read over its contents. “Good news, gentlemen,” he said as the room hushed. Gavin looked up from the note to the throng of thirty or so onlookers. “Our fine Turkish submersives officer has completed his assessment. The life science systems are good for the launch.” A light round of applause rose at word that another milestone among countless checkpoints was scratched from the list.

“Messier Crossland,” Gavin’s gaunt and cross looking coiffure said, “please return to your chair and let us complete your greasepaint.” The man wore a puffy white apron now smudged with thumb-prints of pale fleshy colors. His thick, black eyebrows were drawn tight. With a gesture of feigned courtesy he motioned for Gavin to submit again to his chair.

“My dear coiffure,” Gavin said to the gaunt, peeved man.

“Messier,” the man replied, “I am not a coiffure, I am a tonsorial artist.”

“Quite,” Gavin said, “is more of this face paint really necessary? I must look more appropriate for a carnival than a christening.”

“All the world’s a stage, Mr. Crossland,” came a voice from the crowd, “and you find yourself the ringmaster with literally all the world’s awestruck attention.” Gavin searched for its source and found the face of Harry Blount, round and ruddy like a Lancashire gentleman. Blount stood half a head taller than the other journalists who’d been cordoned off packed up in one corner of the apartment.

“Harry really,” Gavin said, “and the world will see me playing the fool?” The thin tonsorial artist huffed offense at the slight.

“Look as you will to the gathering, my friend,” Blount continued, “but cameras have an ageless memory. Think of the generations who’ll see your image captured in flickering celluloid. It’s all for the cameras, my good man, a small price to pay for posterity.”

“He’s right you know,” said Sir Thomas Listonn who also sat at the mercy of the makeup artists. Sir Thom was a true gentlemen, his hair trimmed and styled perfectly just as it’d been trained. His neck was packed around with a towel to protect his starched collar. His sharp features had been dulled by the white grease that covered his naturally light completion. Gavin could only imagine how ridiculous he himself must look given what they’d done to poor Thom. With resignation, Gavin bowed a slight apology to his artist and went to submit himself to the chair once more.

Before being seated Gavin stole an instant to look at his family. They were seated in a tight row against the back of the room. A shaft of angular light from the nearby window framed them like a portrait. Gavin caught the eyes of his wife, Evelyn, looking right back at him. She gave him a slight smile though strained around the edges. The interplay obviously amused her, and good that it did, this day was hard enough on her. Gavin had to stop and admire her, she looked stunning. Her soft brown hair was all done up exposing her neck and shoulders. Her dress was brilliant green in honor of the ship yard. The sun caught the lithe silver necklace he bought her as a departing gift. His simple country wife presented herself like royalty in these stifling, uncomfortable surroundings. She held tight to their infant daughter Emily who thankfully slept peacefully. His two boys sat in chairs up close to their mother, Trevor six and August three. They kicked their feet incessantly, neither pair long enough to reach the floor. With a long exhale Gavin took his seat and looked sidelong at Thom who seemed similarly spent by the fuss.

A fresh round of shouts intelligibly blurted out from journalists.

"Lt. Hodson," Gavin raised his voice above them, "you hold authority over this room don't you?"

"Yessir," the Lieutenant replied.

"Could you recite the remainder of the itinerary for us? Loud enough so everyone can hear."

"Yes, sir," he said, eyes downcast to his pocket watch, "the non-exclusive press has another twenty minutes then ten more for those with exclusive access." The announcement was received with grumbling protests from the crowd. "Then five with the families before we bring you to your carriage, sir. We'll need to make time to meet with your Tyneside colleagues before we proceed."

"And there will be another carriage to take our families down to the platform?" Gavin asked.

"Of course, sir," the Lieutenant said as stiff as any man could muster.

"Half an hour, Thom," Gavin said, stealing a glance at his traveling companion, "have the stomach for it?" Sir Thom gave him a wily look in reply. Thom was much more accustomed to such attention. He was happy to share whatever portion of the spotlight he could.

"Alright then," Gavin said, "our representatives from the newspapers may proceed. Proceed my good men, proceed."

"Mr. Crossland!" shouted a journalist, "when can we expect to know the name of the new liner? We can't very well write the headline without it."

Gavin smiled much to the chagrin of his makeup artist. "You'll know when the champagne is broken against her prow. Next question."

"Mr. Crossland," called out another man, swinging his arm wildly to draw attention to himself, "tell us what makes this liner so different from its predecessors. And we've heard that she's not even all of British manufacture. Can she even rightly be called a British ship?"

Gavin looked a bit cross. He scanned the mirror before him to see if he could find who asked the question. Not finding the source, he answered, "Well, no single nation can take credit for enabling men to travel in space, yet likewise none can refute that the lion's share of the craft is the proud result of British ingenuity. The entire venture was funded under contract with Tyneside Spaceyardes, Ltd. of Newcastle upon Tyne. Yet, it's true, the engines were designed and assembled at the Watt's Worthinghouse in Edinburgh. The strahlendmach paddles are historically a German innovation, yet are now based on Scottish invention. These paddles were forged in the foundries of Northern Ireland. The hull was built section-by-section at the shipyards of Liverpool from Bessemer steel. The bio-submersives were, of course of Ottoman origins, commissioned from the Evliya Celebi Enstitü in Ankara. There isn't a liner or platform in space that doesn't use Turkish submersives.

"It's the nosecone of the craft that's the most notable advancement. It was meticulously constructed in the now legendary assembly yards of Port Canaveral, Florida. Unlike all crafts before her, this one can return us safely home. Most all the crew will live out their lives in space, but Sir. Thom and myself, along with the entire royal contingent are just taking a holiday. We will go and come back again. Mark my words. It will be an even more joyous occasion when we return. I hope to see you all again on that blessed day," Gavin concluded sharing a smile with his wife at the thought.

The journalists rustled about, jotting down notes on pads. Some had already fled the room to wire the latest revelations back to their awaiting editors. The next reporter broke the bustle with another question, "Why Mars?" he asked, "Wouldn't the Empire been better served if you'd established mineral rights on the moon like other nations?"

The question was interrupted by the stamp of bare feet on the wood floors of the upper room apartment. "Mister Crossland, Mister Crossland!" shouted the runner.

"Here, boy," Gavin said resisting the urge to turn his head. The gathered representatives from the press swung around, their pads in outstretched hands.

"Mr. Dines says to tell you," the boy said, "twenty-two degrees and clear skies. No sign of rain sighted."

"Someone tip that boy," Gavin shouted back with a smile. "My good men, we are going to Phobus!" The pressmen held their pads to the sides and gave a round of applause. Some ran off to telegraph stations with the breaking news. "Now what was that question again?" Gavin asked.

"Why Mars?" several shouted back in reply.

"Ah yes," Gavin answered. "Pay careful heed to this. Ares Britannia is a singular achievement in man's history. Not only does it possess innovations yet unknown to other nations, it's ideally poised to supply the raw materials for our industrial age. Now, I assume everyone in the room is versed in our current international status with other space-borne nations. The Empire has entered into treaties with the American and German establishments in much the same way the French did for a short time. The HMS Aspirant and the HMS Jewel of India have many times ported at Brighton Corporation's, Tranquility Base and even Russia's, Central'noj Buhty at Sinus Medii, while it was still in operation. But, that was all in preparation for this very endeavor. England will no longer be reliant on other nations, held captive to tariffs paid to America or to Germany's Goldene Zeitalter at Tycho Crater.

"It was by Lord Gascoyne-Cecil's order that the United Kingdom chose to blaze new paths rather than walk those beaten down before us. Claims upon the moon and other floating dwarf planets have been hotly disputed. The crown has also defended her mineral rights of these bodies, yet Martian territory has gone largely unchallenged. Without competition the Empire will freely mine, extract treasure and bring it back to earthly portage. Soon the stamp of Martian iron, gold, silver and platinum will be more plentiful than their lunar or earthly equivalents. Sir Thom and I won't be returning empty handed my good men. We'll be laden like no other liner before us."

"Dad, Dad, Dad!" Gavin's son Trevor broke in, pressed well beyond what his patience could contain. He broke from his mother's side and ducked between the legs of the pressing newspaper men. Trevor made it to Gavin's side, pulling demandingly at his arm. The lad brought his face close to his father and leaned in close.

Gavin held up a finger and quieted his son. "If you would excuse me," Gavin said over his shoulder, "my son would like to take the next question. Go ahead, Trevor,"

"Dad," Trevor asked, "you're going away."

"Yes son, I am," Gavin said, ignoring the frustrated expression of the makeup artist looming over him. "I'm going all the way up to Phobus just like I said."

"But how, Dad?" Trevor asked.

"Now Trevor, just like we talked about. I'm going up in that beautiful ship that's just now out in the harbor. That big ship your father's company built to take him safely to Mars."

Trevor didn't answer and couldn't meet his father's eyes. Trevor hung his head side-long and lopsided. His freshly trimmed hair fell in his eyes.

"Trevor," Gavin said, "you know all about flying in space don't you? Why don't you teach all these men about how liners fly in space. You know all about time boxes correct? Tell me," Gavin prompted, "and maybe you can help these fine men write their articles for the newspapers."

"It's all about old Lord Cavendish and the radiant energy," Trevor answered.

"That's right, the candidus agris," Gavin affirmed, "old Lord Cavendish. And what was the year he conducted that famous time box experiment?"

"Seventeen hundred and eighty-two," Trevor answered.

"Good lad, and what do those time boxes do?"

"They spin around at the ends of strahlendmach paddles and when they spin they change time and the paddle bends and snaps back and that pulls the liner and makes it fly."

"That's right, son. Many people have done this in the past. I'll be gone for a long time but I'll come home. Fret not, son. I'll bring you back a bright shining brick of gold mined on Phobus. Won't that be a treasure?" Trevor could only nod absently bothered by the eyes of so many strange men looking cross with him. "Now go back to your mother," Gavin said giving him a light push. Addressing the room he called out, "We'll take one more question then I think we'll be out of time."

Another man spoke up from the group, "And what will this cost the Empire?" There was a rustle about the gathering. "What do you say to your critics in Parliament who call you a chancer? They claim the returns are too far flung to serve the Commonwealth."

Sir Thomas broke in at this question, "All questions concerning the common interest can be directed to Lawrence Hargrave, he's the independent third party hired to guarantee the public trust." Protests and grumbling rose in the room. "No!" Sir Thomas contested, "Talk to the lawyers. You all knew this session was all about the launch."

Gavin leaned over for a hushed word with Sir Thom, "Thank you my friend. You always know when to be properly assertive."

"My pleasure," Sir Thom said.

"And that's time," barked Lt. Hodson, his watch firmly in-hand. "Everyone but Mr. Harry Blount must clear the room." Blount gave his colleagues a slight but confident smile as they were ushered out. The gathering complied reluctantly. Harry could feel his precious minutes trickling away as his competitors were ushered out but he expected it. He knew full well what he needed to say. As the others departed, the air in the room lifted and became breathable once again. As the noise from the journalists subsided the space became echoing and shades brighter with the dawning day.

The final touches were put on Gavin's face and the makeup men also bid their farewell, their expressions were no less sour. It was a relief to Gavin and Sir Thom both to have that task completed.

"Well, Harry," Gavin asked, "How do I look?"

"Like the hero of a grateful nation, inspiring really. How does this sound for a headline? Gavin Crossland ascends to Olympus later to dine at Zeus' supper table!"

"Sorry we're not going quite that far," Gavin responded, stretching his face against the tacky greasepaint about his mouth. "Olympos Mons is all the way up to Mars. We'll be some thousands of miles short."

Harry gave a nod to both men. "You know, you must be commended," he said addressing them both. "Keeping the name of the craft a secret till the very end is brilliant. It's lit a fire of speculation all around the globe. That pack of lapping dogs has been making guesses for weeks now."

"Oh?" Gavin asked, "what's the most popular name so far?"

"Let's see now," Harry said pondering, "The HMS Prosperity, The Empire, The Princess Royal."

"Princess Royal?" Gavin remarked, "but to which princess would they be referring?"

Smiling at Gavin's question, Harry added, "Of course the The HMS Victoria is a fetching guess."

Gavin shook his head. "Well, those certainly show some imagination. You'll learn the truth in a very short time I assure you. I promised you an exclusive Harry. Better ask your question now before Lt. Hodson escorts to the gangway. We've got a ship to catch."

"Actually," Harry said, "I don't have a question. I just wanted to shake your hand one last time before I see an old school mate off to Mars." The two men shared a smile and clapped each other around their shoulders. Harry turned and gave Sir Thom a sturdy handshake as well. "Right then," Harry added, "Godspeed to you both. And best luck with that pack of wolves they've thrown you into. I'm not sure what's worse. The extremes of space travel or the extremes of your royal contingent," Harry said shaking his head slowly.

"Now," Gavin assured, "just some first-class passengers who'll demand some extra accommodations is all."

"Is that what you think?" Harry asked. "Well, you'll find out soon enough."

Toward the back of the room, the dawn rose brighter through the windows, Gavin's wife Evelyn rose to her feet.

"Harry," Gavin said, "I've got another farewell to attend to. Thank you for staying behind."

"Oh, it was well worth it," Harry said. "I got my exclusive." With a nod all around the room, including to Lt. Hodson and the family that remained, Harry Blount said his goodbyes and bade his last farewell.

Lt. Hodson gestured for Sir Thom and his family to enter an adjoining room. Gavin noted that Mrs. Listonn didn't seem at all pleased. Her face was not what he'd expect. It almost gave him a concern for his companion.

The Lieutenant turned to Gavin with one final instruction, "I can only give you a few minutes sir, then I'll have your family brought down to their coach. They'll be there next to the ship before you embark, just as we rehearsed."

"With my thanks Hodson," Gavin said and the Lieutenant closed the door behind him.

Finally alone, the room fell to an unexpected silence. The sounds of the ocean and the noise of the milling crowd on the shore filled in. Gavin took the few steps from the makeup table to stand awkwardly with his wife and children. No one spoke at first. Trevor kicked aimlessly at the floor. His younger brother, August, had fallen fast asleep, curled up on his chair. Emily fussed a bit in Evelyn's bobbing arms.

Gavin gave Evelyn elusive glances. "You've caught me quite at a loss," Gavin said, "I can converse with journalists and engineers, meteorologists and politicians but now can't find a word to say."

"You handled the room masterfully," Evelyn choked back. "It reminded me how you convinced my father that you'd one day make something of yourself. If he was only here with us today."

They shared a smile. "An austere man, your father," Gavin said. He looked long on their infant daughter and cradled her head in his hand. "She'll be hobbling about when I get back."

"You'll miss her first steps," Evelyn said.

"Eve," Gavin started hunting for words, unable to look at her.

"Gavin, it's all different now. When this was all about blueprints and late nights and you traveling the world to visit a steel mill or spacialdrome, that was all difficult, yes. I didn't mind sharing you with all those people from Tyneside. All those dreadful launch ceremonies we've been to together in the past. I didn't mind when I had to share you with bankers or all those awful, intrusive people from the newspapers." Evelyn paused to look at Emily and Trevor both. "Gavin," she said, "before it was never you actually going up there. I've never had to see you fly off in one of your contraptions."

"Evelyn," Gavin put his arm around her shoulder. "We talked and talked about this."

Evelyn shook her head madly. "Don't take me wrong," she said with teardrops alighting on Gavin's cheek. She drew in some strong breaths. "Just assure me that you're coming back," she looked him straight in the eye.

Gavin spoke through his own emotions, "I have a great team, Eve. My design team is first rate, best in the world. Just think of the hundreds of men from all over who've worked on this. All those Americans we consulted with. All those who built the liner and are giving up their earthly lives to live on Ares Britannia. Consider all those people who've dedicated their lives getting us to this point. If you can't have faith in me think of all them. They can't all have failed."

"You have all my faith," Evelyn said pulling her husband close, their infant girl between them. She rested her face on his chest and Gavin held them both tight. Trevor stepped up and wrapped his arm around his parents' legs.

Gavin held his chin up. He didn't want to smear his makeup on Evelyn's hair. He struggled for something to say, something to leave with them before he left. Gavin felt her draw in a long breath.

"I'll let you go now," she said, "Just promise me you'll be back. That's all I want from Mars, my husband back to me and the children. Will you promise me that?" Evelyn pulled back to look her husband in the eyes. They shared an impassioned kiss Gavin smearing her face with greasepaint.

Chapter B (2): Bordering on Eternity

The clock wound down to the final hour. For Gavin and Sir Thom both, it was like being adrift in an ocean of people directing them this way and that. Their families were escorted off to their places at the christening. Gavin sent runner after runner to check the status of the liner. Everything continued to align perfectly. It was like Gate Pā, Tauranga was somehow directly beneath the moons of Mars. All they had to do was reach up as far as they could and catch them in the palms of their hands. The word was given and Gavin and Sir Thom were loaded into a carriage painted in Tyneside green.

Their coach rumbled along the sandy streets between the tall colonial houses until their driver came up behind the procession of carriages ahead of them. A short way off, Gavin and Sir Thom heard the band strike a chord and the final length of their triumphant ride took them to the shore.

The pomp of a grateful Empire had gathered to see them off. Out the small rectangular windows, Gavin saw more faces than he could number. They applauded vigorously as the coach rumbled by. Though Gavin had overseen the preparations to the minutest detail he was completely unprepared for what he saw.

Jerking to an abrupt stop, the carriage door swung open and they were blinded by the beaming light of day. Gavin and Sir Thom stepped out and looked around at all those who had come to see them off. The crowds consisted of many races and nations, representatives from all over the Empire. They milled about the beach with a tip of the hat and a gleam in the eye. Among them were some of the most erudite and well-to-do of all British society. Not to be denied, the locals of New Zealand were also in attendance. All walks of life wished to be present to see the nameless liner sent up on its maiden flight.

The public onlookers were cordoned off by scarlet ropes dangling along bronze poles. Whole families, dressed in their Sunday finest looked back at Gavin with awe and respect. The early spring day was becoming unmercifully hot, but the masses were shaded by the four enormous blimps that floated in the air above them.

The pathway to the docks was guarded by rows of soldiers in blazing dress uniform. Guarding the passage leading directly to the space-liner was an honor given to the key forces that wrested New Zealand from its native savages. Among them were members of the 42nd Regiment of Foot, the Highland unit that won honors under Lieutenant-General Duncan Cameron, their Scottish tartans adding another splash of color to the regalia.

The harbor had been cleared of all shipping with the exception of the complement of battleships and escorts both ported and away off shore. Their brooding dark forms swayed in the tropical waves. Among them was the immense dreadnought, the HMS Devastation, her outstretched deck guns already poised eastward to fire in salute.

Gavin and Sir Thom were led up to join the royal contingent who also shared the crowd's attention. Sir Thom stepped forward with familiar greetings for some of them, but they were all new to Gavin. He'd seen their pictures and could recall a few names. He knew their exact height, mass and weight in stones but nothing of who they were. He immediately recognized Lady Cecilia Underwood, First Duchess of Inverness. Her dress was royal blue with intricate black embroidery. It flowed with a satin flourish draped over her ample body. Her hair was packed tightly under a swirling brunette wig. She cooled herself with a Chinese hand-painted fan. Another passenger, impossible to miss, was a taller man with his hair down around his shoulders beneath a wide brimmed Spanish hat. His mustache was trimmed to a roguish edge but the browns of his topcoat and trousers made him look more provincial. He most surely was Lord John Cleland Cholmondeley, third in the line to become Baron Delamere. Gavin had contemplated how best to manage them but there was so little time to think given all the final preparations to ready the liner. He was sure that the long flight out would give him plenty of opportunities to cater to his investors.

The tight group of passengers took the final steps up to the gangway that fed into the beaming craft that bobbed in the sea foam. The vessel was easily double the tonnage of a modest frigate or tramp steamer. It was long and primarily cylindrical, crimping amidships down to about half the width of the fore-section. The largest of the strahlendmach paddle-wheels stood vertically at the furthest point aft, flanking the hull. Their total radius crested the narrow part of the tail on the opposite side of the dorsal stabilizer. As his gaze traced its lines forward, the two other strahlendmachs were offset when compared to the first. He marveled a bit at his own design though he thought it made for an awkward aesthetic. The secondary paddles were mounted at a forty-five degree angle from the ship's centre, leaning upwards on the starboard side. The tertiary paddles were mounted laterally, dead amidships, stretching out parallel to the horizon.

Between the engine fairings and the living quarters were a cluster of cylinders banded to the structure roundabout. With all the external stowage, this section was the widest overall. Encased there were the life-science and bio-submersive components, thick glass greenhouse cylinders reflected the rays of the sun. The largest were the tanks for the recycling water, algae blooms, compost stores, livestock and all the other living, breathing elements that imbued life in space.

Connected just behind the broad nosecone were two wedge shaped struts that extended laterally on either side, resembling the wings of aeroplanes but far too thick and weighty. Capping each wing were wide angular structures that each curved concavely around the liner's central cone. They resembled twin Tudor buildings that had been uprooted, bent to bow in the middle and then stoutly attached to each wing strut.

As they neared the ship, a special section of attendees was dedicated to the many Tyneside employees who had assisted with the final assembly of the liner. The attentive soldiers opened the crimson cords allowing Gavin and Sir Thom to shake hands with their Tyneside comrades. Gavin showered praise on them. Calling them by name and thanking them. Some were moved to tears. Sir Thom kept things far more English, a curt shake and a nod was all he'd offer. The band played the final measures a few more times than planned as the two Tyneside delegates neared the royal contingent. Finally standing a few feet off, they shared welcoming glances all around including the officers and navy men.

Beneath the giant portrait of Prince Albert, straining on its easel in the wind, the Right Honorable George Sumner, Suffragan Bishop of Guildford, emerged with his fellow prelates and accompanying attendants. Their flowing robes flapped in the Pacific breezes like sails almost carrying them away. Bent and struggling to take every step, the Bishop was led by his second, Reverend the Right Reverend John Granville Randolph, Dean of Salisbury. The bishop raised both of his hands, ancient and frail. The band ceased playing, the crowds hushed to a rustle, the soldiers of the 42nd Regiment of Foot snapped upright. Shaded under a purple fabric awning, Reverend. Randolph held out a small black book close to Sumner's face. The creaking country vicar of a bishop, stooped to whisper into the ear of his second.

Reverend Randolph shouted out to the gathering, "Pray with me from the book of Common Prayer to be used at sea! Confitemini Domino!" and so the men of God blessed the voyage. The prayer concluding, Reverend Randolph led the Lady Inverness up to where the green sparkling bottle awaited her. She bowed most ladylike and the Reverend kissed her lightly on both cheeks. Returning back to those gathered, he added. "The lady shall now christen the vessel. Before doing so, Bishop Sumner and I would like to express thanks for our fellow, the Right Honorable Francis Alabaster Beckett, Archdeacon of Bournemouth, who has gone before us. From this very place he took flight many months ago in Her Majesty's Ship, Aspirant and even now shepherds the flock on Ares Britannia. Shedding his earthly mantle, our friend now commands the title, First Ecclesiarch of Mars!" Those gathered clapped though only a small fraction could make out what was said. It hardly mattered. They followed along just as they were led.

With some difficulty, Lady Inverness took hold of her long dress and climbed the few steps up to the whitewashed platform. Of course her servant, ol' Gran followed behind bearing her parasol. Gran was normally not one to make a fuss but she constantly lagged behind. The Duchess, Lady Inverness had to hurry her along when the parasol slipped back and sun struck her face. It took some coaxing to get her oldest living servant to approach the ship. When she reached the top, she took up the ceremonially wrapped bottle, the cord choking its neck like a noose, the dangling lace appearing much like a burial shroud. The bottle was warm in her hand, heated by the Pacific sun. She stopped for a short reflective moment, back turned to the assembly to gaze at the ship. Duchess Inverness smiled through her round cheeks and turned to her audience. Her motions delicate, her eyes bowed, she produced some small pages from behind her Chinese fan. Looking brightly all about her she shouted out the christening speech.

"My dear countrymen," she said, "divine providence, has selected this ceremony to mark a new dawning age. It is an age that will extend our great civilization, our just and merciful laws, our devotion and our solemnity to other worlds. At this maiden voyage, we beseech the Judge of heaven to heed our contrite supplication. We pray for safe passage in the most frightful waters. We pray for strength and steadfastness to be imbued upon this vessel and we pray for the safety for all her passengers and cargo from now and forever after."

The warm bottle firmly in hand, Lady Inverness drew back in a most unladylike pose and prepared the pitch. "I christen thee," she called aloud, "the HMS Daedalus!" and she let fly. The doomed bottle swung across toward the metal hull. Slamming loudly it struck, spun wildly on its cord but failed to break. It merely resounded with an audible crack. Invisible lines striped the bottle but it remained stoutly intact in its wrapping of lace and aluminum.

Those who saw stiffened. Captain Napier cleared his throat. The Lady Inverness' shoulders fell. She glared at the champagne bottle as if the force of her will could shatter the glass. Defiantly it glared back. Breathlessly the crowd watched, as the well-crafted bottle hung at the cord's end.

Along one seam carbonated foam sprayed. Instants ticked slowly though the haze of anticipation. The pressure mounted and that foaming fizz steamed to a gush. With a burst, the cork soared skyward, the seam split the bottle lengthwise and the sparkling vintage dropped splashing into the bay. The Captain gave reassuring looks to his crew and the band struck up again, signaling the crowd to cheer. Captain Napier climbed up the platform to her side and shook her hand with words of assurance and appreciation. He handed her an olive branch, its leaves green and budding. She held it aloft for the crowd and then cast into the hatch of the ship.

"A safe return to us all!" she shouted above the cheers, the vast majority ignoring the slight inaccuracy of the statement.

Drums thundered and brass horns intoned the national anthem. Hats were thrown skyward and confetti was cast to the wind. Napier shared short words and handshakes with his superiors. He then gave the signal to make final boarding. The travelers broke away to say goodbye to their families. Princess Sandra was met by two of her sisters who shared tearful good-byes. Sir Thom shared hearty handshakes with his loved ones. Mrs. Listonn didn't crack a smile nor receive a kiss from her husband, she just stood stoically as Sir Thom turned and proceeded on board.

Gavin bowed to pick up his youngest son whose loud cries were audible over the cheering crowd. His toddling boy standing at his mother's side smeared tears and snot all over his cheeks with chubby hands. His wife, Emily in her arms, cried also, unable to contain herself.

Gavin's eyes were confident and reassuring. His face opened in a wide smile as he looked at his baby girl and bowed to give her a departing kiss. Evelyn threw an arm about her husband's shoulder and pulled him close. Unable to contain herself she bawled loudly.

"Now hush, my darling," Gavin said, speaking sweetly in her ear. "I'll be back home before you know I've left." Evelyn tried to find words but was too distraught. Releasing her husband she waved a kerchief to her face and blotted the tears from her eyes. She pressed those tears into Gavin's chest, reaching up he took it from her hand. "Thank you, my love," he said and gave her a long kiss goodbye.

The crew of the HMS Daedalus stepped politely up to their guests to interrupt their farewells and directed them toward the entryway. Lady Inverness mounted the steps again and Captain Napier extended his left hand, bidding the Lady to enter. With a quick curtsy she proceeded inside.

The other passengers entered in the order they arrived. Napier stood to personally greet each one. Princess Sandra, granddaughter of the Queen, stepped up lightly, clinging to her train. Napier tipped his hat to her as she entered. Lord Cleland, the one with the draping curls and Spanish hat, stepped up with sobriety. He halted before entering and spun to face the gathering. He held his cane aloft in a kind of salute, spun back on his heels and entered. He was accompanied by a short bald man, Dr. Boswell, who bowed his head slightly and only gave a curt nod to the Captain as he ducked inside. The next was a stout, elderly man, arrayed in the military splendor of a long career. Sir Archdale Wilson stepped toward the navy men, shaking each of their hands vigorously including Hürkuş, Elphinstone and finally Campbell. He was followed behind by his manservant, a dark skinned Nepali man named Argyle, luggage already in-hand. Thrusting his cane under his arm, Sir Wilson stopped before Napier. The two officers shared short words of well-wishing though none but them could hear for the fanfare. Sir Wilson had some difficulty surmounting the lip of the entry hatch, but Argyle offered a steady shoulder. Wilson gently refused his valet's aid and managed it on his own. They both vanished into the dark interior.

Sir Thom and Gavin weren't far behind. They too stopped to share a round of thanks to the Tyneside employees who were near the pier. The group posed for a photograph before sharing final goodbyes. Film crews flipped the cranks of their movie cameras to capture every fateful step. Sir Thom and Gavin maintained a professional candor but couldn't mask their excitement. Both smiled broadly. They gave one last look to their families and then passed into the ship.

In true military order, the crew members sheathed their sabers and marched into the HMS Daedalus. The officers were the last to board, stopping to line up, their ears overflowing with the cheers of those assembled. In unison they turned on their heels and filed in. The Captain nodded to each one in turn.

Now alone on the beaming white platform, Captain Napier turned to face the crowd. The band played louder. The bursting flashes of dozens of cameras snapped. Napier saluted the crowd, holding his right hand firmly below the brim of his cap. Snapping it back to his side, he stepped into his ship. As he passed, two of the lesser crewmen swung the stout metal door into place. The sound it made was louder than the loudest snare drum. They cranked the seal shut and the ship settled to an eerie quiet.

Inside the Daedalus, the crew escorted their passengers to the area housing their quarters. The passage inside resembled the interior of any large sailing ship, thick bulkheads and painted metal surfaces. A large tubular corridor called the Spinehall lead up through the middle of the vessel. Along the ceiling of that tube ran metal rungs like a ladder.

"How extraordinary," Lady Inverness said and a devilishly knowing smile crossed Cleland's lips. Even Argyle, the shortest of them had to stoop as they were led to their right to make their way up the spine. The crew turned them right again into the starboard strut.

From there the scene took a turn toward the surreal. The passage opened into a wider, almost trapezoidal chamber. Lady Inverness, Princess Sandra and their three attendants were the first to enter, able now to stand upright. Their eyes fell on the top of a small writing desk that jutted straight out from the wall opposite them, its legs bolted firmly in place, defying gravity. Looking right along the wall's surface, there were also protruding tables, chairs and furnishings that one would expect in a drawing room or den. There were couches and love-seats all finely upholstered consisting of hand-carved Indian Laurel. All of which had been affixed similarly, jutting uselessly out from the wall, perpendicular to the floor.

The two ladies stopped to gawk. The wall was not at all flat but curved obtusely away from them adding yet another level of absurdity. The furnishings had to be strategically placed to account for the curvature.

As each one entered they all stared into the room turned on its side as if they walked into a carnival attraction.

The other surfaces that made up the room's 'walls' were covered in dark wood paneling and the room was also equipped with what appeared to be something similar to a fireplace affixed a way above them. As they took a few more steps to look around, the near wall was equally unexpected as it resembled a ceiling. A chandelier was stuck fast about half way up, far above them hanging down side-wise, pulled naturally in this unnatural position.

"This is the commons," Gavin explained as if everything was perfectly normal. "We've set up some chairs for the launch but once we're underway, we'll swing her around so you can be more comfortable." No one bothered to ask what all that might mean.

The others all awkwardly ignored the room's elephantine presence other than Cleland. Cleland fluffed his hair back and his smile twisted another degree devilish. Boswell ducked oddly as he entered. Gavin took the opportunity to nonchalantly look over the expressions of the others savouring their stunned silence.

None dared ask. They merely listened to the crew's instructions and twisted their necks upward. Gesturing broadly, Gavin drew their attention to the wall on their left. "Once we get airborne, we'll pull this panel away and from here you'll be able to see out. There's another one on the other side though a bit smaller. This one on your left faces fore and that one faces aft. You'll want to look aft, but I don't need to tell you that," he ended with youthful excitement.

Delicately raising her hand, Lady Inverness said, "Mr. Crossland, where will the ladies be staying? Can you direct me to my room?"

"Certainly," Gavin said pointing straight up, "the ladies' rooms are right there." The entire party tilted their heads way back. Contorting to look past the chandelier they could make out the dark outline of a doorway lost in the rafters. "The men will be in the rooms here," he added, pointing at a matching door that was virtually right under their feet. Cleland took particular notice of the divided accommodations, which didn't escape the notice of Lady Inverness. The lady was pleased to consider that the staterooms were designed with propriety if not with any other discernible sense.

Outside, deep bass caught the guts of the assembly as the convoy of ships blew their whistles. Steam vented under down-turned valves that resembled frowning caricatures. Men scurried over the skin of the Daedalus to secure the mooring that led up to the bobbing blimps above them. Once that was secure they waved broadly up to the pilots who yelled back their acknowledgments. The Daedalus shook with a metallic moan, unsettling to the bone. Women gasped and fanned their faces. Men commended in sciolistic nods as if they had sure understanding of this engineering marvel.

A smell like ozone blew over the assembly from the water. A slight twinge of nausea struck a few onlookers. Ever so slowly, the mightiest of the strahlendmach paddles began to turn. The tip of each paddle spoke blurred, as if it had been merged perfectly into the background and yet it was in plain sight. It forced the gawkers to step back. This curious effect was most noticeable at the topmost edge as the spoke buzzed, shook violently and the rotated forward. As speed mounted they plunged into the bay, the reverberating noise pounding out an accelerating tempo.

Stepping far clear of the paddle-wheel, the Tyneside attendants waved red and white flags, signaling the air and seaborne ships to make way. Some men ran the length of the Daedalus and jumped straight into the water. The dirigibles angled their propellers and began pulling away. The metal cables went taught and hauled the Daedalus into the Pacific.

The band struck up again and the crowd responded with the most thunderous applause. The mighty battleships made off from the dock to the cheers heard round the world. The cheers were followed by the deafening fire of the Devastation's twin deck guns. Women covered their ears and children cowered at the legs of their parents. The Devastation shot salvo after salvo as the blimps gained altitude and the bright bronze Daedalus entered deeper waters. The four dirigibles finally hefted the craft up, streaming pillars of sea foam spilling down as she broke free.

Many onlookers pulled out long tubular spyglasses to witness the ascent of the launch. The dirigible cluster mounted up quickly. The big pounders continued their barrage of honor. The crowd watched as that fivefold formation mounted up to the clouds, growing smaller and smaller until they were lost in white streaks of nimbus. From that instant, the eyewitness reporters, the very eyes of the world, lost sight of the HMS Daedalus as it was embraced by the sky.

***

The passengers were still contemplating their new surroundings. The ship lurched as the blimps veered up and pulled the liner skyward. The ladies couldn't help but give a start as floor grew unstable beneath them.

"Please be assured," announced Gavin, "once we get past this part I'm sure you'll all be much more comfortable." Though in truth, this was all a wonder to Gavin as well.

Several crewmen were at the ready in the commons. They positioned themselves strategically about the civilians. The ladies clung to one another as the entire room, ever so slowly began to spin. The passengers felt their footing slip away and a sense of panic rose. There's nothing quite as unsettling as your entire world being moved right out from under your feet. The shards of the chandelier began to rattle. They all lined up at the wall's edge as gravity began to draw them closer.

"Quite a show, Crossland," Cleland called over. "If this is merely the first act then weightlessness must be a command performance."

Ever so gradually, the wall they faced dipped and the surface upon which they stood climbed up behind them. Try as they might, the angle increased until the floor was too steep for standing. The ladies gasped along with Dr. Boswell as they were forced to make the frightening step to the opposing wall which was rapidly becoming the floor. The faithful crew was there to hold their arms at the elbow to afford more stability. Boswell grabbed one of their shoulders almost dragging them all down. As the turn completed the oddly curved floor took its proper place, the chiming chandelier finally settling, its glass shards now facing the correct way. Sighs of relief swept over them as they adjusted their topcoats and padded their hair.

"There, you see?" Boswell interjected, "down was turned the wrong way round." Gavin thanked the crew and Sir Thom gave him a quick nod of approval.

"Now everyone please find a seat," Gavin said. "The crew has brought in several more chairs to accommodate us. I think some drinks are in order and if the men would like a smoke, this will be your last opportunity." This got Cleland's attention who gave a look of shock bordering on disgust. Gavin spoke again, "The curve in the floor may still seem unnavigable but you'll appreciate it once we get into space. Right now, I want everyone to witness a scene that so few have ever been able to truly appreciate. The HMS Daedalus is the first liner to give her passengers the gift you're about to see. You are not the first to see Earth from above but you are the very first to see it from front row seats." Gavin, swept up by the theatrics, ordered the crew to open the ports.

The accompaniment of blimps brought the craft to the very upper reaches of the atmosphere, until they couldn't lift them further. The Turkish Life Sciences Officer, Vecihi Hürkuş, confirmed that the oxygen and pressure was functioning properly. Officer George Elphinstone checked to confirm that the analytics engine was calculating their course correctly, quickly rattling controls with hands that appeared too small for a grown man. All the critical measurements were within tolerable limits. His lips broke a smile beneath the auburn hair of his mustache

Leaning over to his pilot, Elphinstone said, "Officer Campbell, our course is set."

"Course set and confirmed," Lt. Colin Campbell called out for his Captain to hear. "Our next stop, the port of Phobus."

The strahlendmachs came up to full effect and the Daedalus began tugging at her leash. She would wait no longer and they snapped the cables free. Under their own power, the virgin engines strained against the relentless pull of the earth. The ship rumbled and again the passengers' sense of anxiety rose. Gavin and Sir Thom both assured them as best they could though Sir Thom needed some reassuring of his own. Finally giving up her babes, the earth titan, Gaia, relinquished claim and the HMS Daedalus moved off toward orbit free of all earthly obligations.

Cheers from the crew echoed up the metal corridors. This more than anything began to allay their fears.

"Men," Gavin commanded, "open the port," and at his command the crewmen slid back the broad metal panels on both sides that concealed the impossibly thick glass windows behind them. Blinding light sprayed in. At least Boswell still had his shaded spectacles. As they blinked past the mild pain of revelation they saw before them the reigning majesty of creation. Silence was their only praise. The blue familiar sky-scape was already fading and beneath them and the curvature of the earth was visible. The deep jet of space overruled the sky, but couldn't dampen the bright blue glow of the brilliant orb behind them. Through the layers of clouds, the outlines of the continents were discernible. The shapes were just as maps depicted, but this was no illustration. The world was laid out before them in all its splendor. It was a very long time before any of them moved or spoke again.

Princess Sandra was the first to tear her eyes away and look at the equally splendid display ahead of them. She could see more stars than on the clearest night at her father's country home in the Swiss Alps.

"Is that the universe?" she asked blankly.

"That," Cleland said in reply, "is all eternity."

The Daedalus continued to climb and pitched east, chasing the earth's rotation. With the secondary and tertiary engines engaged, the craft's axial spin lent the illusion of gravity. The centrifugal effect was achieved gradually. Lady Inverness found the sensation nauseating and excused herself to her quarters. Her servants, led by the venerable ol' Gran, followed one of the crew through the far door and into the opposing section.

Argyle was also unnerved by the sensation and likewise sequestered himself in fearful prayers to his Nepali gods. Not so for the others, especially Gavin who stood riveted with Sir Thomas close by him. He had imagined spaceflight for so many years and now to be standing away from the earth was a moment that forced tears. His thoughts went to Evelyn, if only she could be here now. At their orbital speed they watched the entire breath of Africa sweep beneath them in a matter of hours.

Captain Napier came by to check on them. Finding them in good order he shared a few informative words. "We'll be looping around the Earth to pick up speed and then off to the moon before making the long trek to Mars. Keep a watchful eye out and you'll see the whole world before we make off."

Cleland couldn't help himself, "Around the world in eighty minutes," he said.

Princess Sandra later noted in her diary how wondrous Earth appeared from on high. She wrote of her surprise that they were so high up that no trace of man's presence could be seen. An otherworldly visitor passing by could see the natural beauty but have no knowledge that so many nations were busying themselves down there. All the toil, strife, loves and losses went along undetectable.

She felt the deep tug of the engines as Captain Napier gave the order to make the final break and shear away. The blue of the vibrant living Earth fell away behind them like an enormous marble and the Princess was enraptured. Within arm's reach, Cleland stood near her, likewise captivated. He glanced toward her, intent on reading her expression, but his eyes caught the glimmer of her necklace. As she leaned forward to peer through the glass, the key shaped charm had slipped out from between her breasts, drawn down by the artificial pull. Nearly expressionless, Sandra's blue eyes, bluer in the reflection of the beaming earth, looked down to see the dangling charm. Expressionless still, she tucked it back neatly into place without any regard for Cleland and cast her gaze back toward the spinning world before her.

Chapter G (3): Sighting Martian Shores

Life on the Daedalus proved more tedious than anybody had anticipated. Almost every mundane task was complicated beyond measure. The passengers were like children at times, relearning the basics of walking, eating, drinking, hygiene. The women found this particularly awkward as poise required the utmost concentration. The principles of grace and decorum never accounted for artificial gravity. The spinning motion of the craft at least created some semblance of normalcy. The oddly arching living quarters were at first a challenge to navigate but soon became familiar. The servants were the only ones forced out of the gravitational effect. Duty required that they master entering and exiting the ship's axis and thereby forced to contend with weightlessness. Cleland found free-floating a good romp at first, bounding up into Spinehall, but his childish antics were short lived. Before long he developed a muscle strain that he found an annoyance.

The liner's maiden voyage was far from flawless. Many of the defects were only known to the crew, but those in the waste disposal system caused considerable discomfort. Cleland spoke the most of it. Chamber pots were flushed out into sliding drawers in each room but the system that safely recycled the waste was faulty. Vecihi was the sole recipient of complaints and gruffly passed the blame to the anonymous Turkish builders behind the submersive systems. Complain as he would it inescapably fell to him to manually flush the pipes when things backed up and the smell became rancid.

Gavin did his best to help the crew keep everything orderly but it was no easy task from within the craft. He knew full well that the blocked septic offset the delicate balance of the finely tuned cycles that sustained prolonged spaceflight. The lack of waste lowered the effectiveness of the necessary reactions which ultimately lowered the availability of drinkable water.

With Vecihi's agreement Gavin advised the captain, "Bathing must be restricted and water rationed." The water ration likewise restricted their ability to reconstitute dehydrated food. Several of the livestock then needed to be slaughtered prematurely which seemed somewhat counterintuitive to Crossland. When questioned, Vecihi would dismissively reply, “dengelemek, dengelemek” which Crossland understood to be Turkish for something close to juggling. Thankfully the captain’s report indicated that the locomotive functions of the ship were in order. They were well on their way and navigational measurements were favorable.

Despite the long months the passengers didn’t mingle much, though some made a better effort than others. Lady Inverness was hardly seen at all. This went overlooked for the first several days but then Captain Napier, Crossland and Listonn started frequenting her door. Without permitting entrance she would merely bleat out assurances until they were assuaged. After a week of this, Sandra was finally permitted entrance and upon emerging she reported that her ladyship was unwell but had no need for Dr. Boswell’s services. Still, in partnership with Argyle’s cooking skills, the doctor prepared some wholesome soups and dosed them with ignatia amara to assist with the digestion.

Lady Inverness was not the only quiet one of the voyage. Boswell was never far from Cleland until Lord Cholmondeley finally locked himself in his room only opening the door when meals were served. Boswell would politely apologize for him, rubbing slightly at the off colored birthmark on his bald head. “He’s composing his great epic and cannot possibly be disturbed. To bother him would be like disturbing Coleridge when composing Kubla Khan.” It was an acceptable enough excuse and therefore he was left in peace. Lady Inverness had no sympathy but Cleland’s time in seclusion was all the less he spent with Sandra.

Sir Wilson was the one with much to say. “Are you familiar with how I gained the title, Sir Archdale Roland Knyvet Wilson, Second Baronet, Wilson Baronetcy of Delhi?” was a common question that he asked. And of course none had, which offered yet another opportunity for Wilson to expound. “Then you’ve not heard my arguments concerning my vehement debates at parliament with then Prime Minister William Ewart Gladstone. Where should I begin, you see, for months, a detachment of British troops were besieged in the Sudanese city of Khartoum…” He freely engaged everyone who would listen either to his politics, military exploits, or his many opportunities to mingle with international heads of state. Most often, Argyle would be the only faithful audience even though he had heard the stories ofttimes before.

Gavin Crossland proved himself to be magnanimous and took the responsibility to ensure everyone's pleasure. Listonn made similar attempts, but was frankly not all that good at it. He was pleased to let Gavin be the showman while he stood back and observed. Crossland knew the role well. Gavin wasn't at all imposing but was merely quick to avail himself. This was the same skill he employed to procure the larger and larger aerospace and architectural projects that had secured him passage to Mars.

When not focused on the travelers he would anxiously monitor progress. He carried a slide rule in his vest pocket and produced it to double check Campbell's figures. And he was right to do so because even the slightest miscalculation would doom a voyage like this one. The French had lost both the Audacieux and the Commandant Teste while trying to make a similar crossing. It was the creeping fear of all spacefarers to become lost in the featureless aether.

***

Gavin pondered the burden of space travel. Long years working with his design team to create liners and platforms and yet he had no appreciation for the dulling weight of these long months. After a hundred and sixty painstaking days the last weeks worsened to agonizing. His thoughts would often wander back to home, Evelyn, and the children. If it were possible, a single letter from them would have made all the difference. As if he could drop them in the post, he spent some hours writing letters home he was unable to send. Upon his return he would relive the voyage with his wife and children as he lived it. The thought of that warm night around the fire reading letters and telling stories was a blessing.

Gavin's role as the one with all the answers slowed but not to a halt. The occasional questions from the others made for some distraction. When the Captain informed them that they were close, Princess Sandra asked Gavin, "Why is it that we are nearing Mars and yet can't see it from the forward windows? Shouldn't it be always before us?"

"Your highness," he replied in a voice carefully instructive, "our course is set to meet Mars as it makes its way around the sun." He led her to the grand view in the sitting room where they first entered. The black wash of space lingered as it had for months and yet still seeped with grandeur. “The path of the Daedalus makes it difficult to see as Mars is away from view, off the edge of the windowsill until we get much closer.”

“Yes of course,” she replied, but actually didn’t quite grasp the implications of orbital paths and travel over such distances. But in due time the destination was sighted and the band of travelers emerged from their rooms to gather in the commons, to look out the constantly spinning view forward. The servants served tea, biscuits, sugared dates and cordials, ones that had been especially reserved for just this occasion. Crossland and Listonn didn’t join them, instead diving into the gravity free spine of the ship and pulling themselves up Spinehall along the Jacob’s Ladder. Gavin was beginning to get his “space legs” but Sir Listonn not so much. His hair billowed annoyingly and his head ached. They thrust their way to the command deck where Captain Napier floated behind Lt. Campbell, who was at the helm, and Warrant Officer Elphinstone at the Navigator’s station.

“Permission to come forward, Captain,” Crossland asked as he poked his head past the aperture. Turning listlessly, the captain nodded in greeting. The command deck was spherical and provided the only view that wasn’t nauseatingly churning. Before them was a grand circular window interlaced with a spider web of brass.

“Come in, lads,” Napier said, “but mind yourselves. It’s a bit cramped.” Railings along the walls of the orbicular deck splayed out in all directions dovetailing at the spinehall entrance. Gavin hurried to pull himself in. Listonn followed behind with difficulty, yanking himself through. Mopping a handful of his hair aside, his fingers returning, slick with sweat. And there it was, still a full forty degrees or so from centre, at about two o’clock. At this distance the red world was still a bit smaller than the moon appears on an autumn night back home. They were certainly close enough to make out its dominant features. The white frosted polar caps were easily discernible from the rest of its ruddy countenance. The deepest canal striped its full round face. The brilliant reflected red cast a slight rose beacon into the room washing crimson over every surface. The two were breath-taken even more than previously.

“Elphinstone,” Napier ordered calmly, “check our course.” The young engineer nodded and began rattling the ship’s analytic engine. It responded sharply with the chatter of its inner workings as it's gears and levers worked round. He had to make several adjustments to the position of the forward port, rotating it in it's frame and reading the tic marks of precise degrees at its edge.

"Steady as she goes, Captain," he reported, "we'll make Phobus in three days, eleven hours and forty-three minutes on my mark." Napier beamed with a captain's pride.

"Enter it into the log, son, and make your stroke bold!" They each turned about in the weightless compartment and shared vigorous handshakes with broad smiles stretching every face.

"Look!" Campbell blurted out. "You can see Phobus crossing, there at about ten o'clock." A black dot passed the equatorial line of the planet making its way around.

Listonn strained to look. "How do you know it's Phobus? Couldn't it be Deimus just as well?"

"No, sir," Elphinstone answered, "Deimus will be around the backside."

In the dead silence of the command sphere, Gavin started to sing, "Wider still and wider shall thy bounds be set;" followed chorally by the others,

"God who made thee mighty, make thee mightier yet, God who made thee mighty, make thee mightier yet." Call it trite or sentimental or emotional, those five men bonded in a shared moment that could never be reproduced. As if in a waking dream they had already reached Ares Britannia.

***

The final days of the flight were a flurry of activity. Crossland hardly slept and spent as much time in the command sphere as Captain Napier would allow. The Royal contingent and the crew found themselves staring outside whenever they could. Even the nauseating turn out the windows was tolerable. Napier would make his way there also, to take tea with lemon, offer assurances, and share tips on living without weight.

Growing all the more inquisitive, Princess Sandra asked, "Can they see us also? Those at Ares Britannia? What do we look like to them? Like another star in the sky?"

Napier gave her a father's smile. "We stayed true to course, mum. Those waiting for us weren't sure of the launch date, but they know we're close and will be watchful. And you're quite correct, be sure that they see a new star in the heavens, one that's not on their charts and one that's heading right for them. Those people living in darkness have seen a great light."

The final landmarks were sighted shortly after and the red planet grew enormous in the portholes. The cloud of asteroids beyond Mars became visible, like stars that crowded up together and winked in and out in a slow rolling tumble of glittering lights. It was like Mars was nestled in a dense field of lights. Actual stars failed to twinkle in space, but these did as tumbling facets of their surface reflected fleeting rays of sun.

Deimus came into view though they steered clear of it. It didn't resemble earth's moon in the slightest. It wasn't a perfect circle, but was coarse and oblong. In the churning view-port everything seemed to swirl as it passed. Nearing their destination brought Cleland out of his reclusive melancholy. He planted himself in the commons, penning notes and scratching sketches out of a dribbling inkwell.

The Daedalus made frequent course changes and it came inside Deimus' orbit. They were very close now. So close that missing a single moment seemed like an unimaginable loss.

Argyle prepared a special Nepali dish of wild rice and saffron, but other than Sir Wilson, most found it too spicy. Crossland and Listonn were permitted in the command deck though were instructed to stay quiet. Elphinstone's child-sized fingers rattled away at the analytics as he pulled himself over frequently to read the measurements on the forward port. There were multi-lensed magnifiers and sextant-like devices required for such exacting corrections. Listonn donned his suit coat, but Crossland wore a baggy white tunic, knowing how overly warm the command deck could get. Napier was stoic and obviously uncomfortable in his dress uniform.

Adjusting the spin of the strahlendmachs, Campbell swung the ship around to the foreordained approach. Phobus swept into view with the yellow glow and black lines of Ares Britannia just beneath them.

The other passengers were all pressed close in the sitting room, fixated on the forward view. Seeing the platform firsthand was a far cry from its illustrations. "They're like birdcages," Princess Sandra said aloud, clutching tightly a lace kerchief in her hands.

The platform was a bundle of intersecting domes of black steel struts housing paned glass like painted lampshades. Some struts were larger than others. They acted like supporting exoskeletons making distinct radial patterns as they fanned out and dropped down to the Phoban soil. Lights from within shed a yellow glow that stretched out in angular shafts from the central cluster. Halls emitted from the centre at irregular points leading to other rectangular buildings interlaced with pipe-works and enormous tanks of various sizes. One shaft was distinctly larger and longer than all others. It made its way across the barren landscape to the horizon, its final destination concealed from view.

Phobus seemed very small but Mars made for a commanding backdrop. Glints of red light reflected off every sweeping line on the Martian Platform.

Spotlights also blazed up at them, resembling burning lanterns. A light mist vented from a tall central tower that rose up, black and imposing from the main buildings. All but Gavin Crossland stood and admired the scene. Crossland pulled himself forward by grabbing Listonn and Napier by their shoulders.

"What's that?" Crossland said, his mouth gaping. He took a long look at that imposing central tower. It was thick at the base and oddly textured as if it had been hand beaten from bolted metal sheets. The peak was bulbous and seemed out of place with the flow of the structure beneath it. More yellow glowing windows went around its crest and flashing beacons adorned its crown. "Whenever did they build that?" he said giving voice to his thoughts.

Listonn gave Gavin a quizzical look and smoothed his mustache Captain Napier pulled his shoulder free of Gavin's grip and straightened his topcoat. As Crossland further studied the platform he began to notice other unexpected features. Two of the radial buildings were completely unknown to him. They certainly weren't on any of his blueprints. He couldn't guess their purpose and completely disagreed with their placement. There was an additional central dome that again eluded his understanding. The most disconcerting change was the absence of the mooring tower.

"Campbell," Gavin asked, "can you bring us around to the other side?" The youth's face looked like he'd taken a boot to the pills.

Napier spoke for him. "By no means, Mr. Crossland. We've rehearsed this in your simulations a thousand times. We can't break from that now."

"But the tower's not there," Crossland retorted. "We can't run the docking procedure, there's no mooring arm. Maybe they redesigned it – put it on a different side."

"Mind yourself, man," Napier returned in the strong voice of authority. "They'll get a cable up here shortly and get it sorted."

Listonn listened intently to them, not sure what to make of the development. The two junior officers attended to their flight controls, frozen stiff at the exchange. They still felt the intense pressure, especially now that their scripted process was null and void.

Napier directed his staff, "Lt. Campbell, once we reach the docking range hold her steady and let's wait for them to get a line up here. Officer Elphinstone, we may need a course adjustment to keep her in place. Just keep her within tolerable range and account for axial revolutions." Both men gave ayes in response.

***

Back in the commons shared by the royal contingent, those gathered spoke quiet words of first impressions. Dr. Bosswell leaned close and whispered in breathy heaves into Cleland's ear. "I've not seen a drawing of that have you?" he asked pointing out the brassy plated tower that jutted up higher than all others. "It's positively garish."

Cleland cracked a half smile. "Perhaps that's in homage to Crossland's John Thomas." They both shared hushed laughter. Others glanced over to catch the joke, but failed to hear it. In the silence of eternal night, two puffs of gray smoke plumed at the base of the largest dome. The small group was straining to make out the occurrence when two metallic bangs struck the ship. They could feel them straight up through their feet.

"What was that?" questioned the Lady Inverness, "Are we under fire?"

"Impossible, my lady," Sir Wilson said. He held up a miniature spyglass to assist his aging eyes. "Thank goodness there's no cannons in space."

"No cannons you say?" Cleland leaned back to catch Wilson's eyes. "Are you so sure?"

"Sure as anything," Sir Wilson replied. "International and now interplanetary treaties were forced upon the Germans just after the American's settled the Tranquility platform on the moon. Wisest move in man's history. Just imagine it, man. Out here with no drag or resistance a shell could travel for miles, straight and true. Wouldn't take more than a pea sized shot to pierce this hull. And think of a war back home with bombs raining down anywhere you like without warning. It's a ghastly thought, man. Damned be the fool who one day breaks that treaty." Wilson pursed his plump lips and brought the glass slowly back to his eyes. In all his flourish, even Cleland took the moment to consider.

"Then, dear Sir Wilson," the Lady Inverness said, "whatever was that sound?"

***

On the command deck, Elphinstone pushed himself away from his press-keys and drifted the short space to the rounded wall on his left. Floating as if in slow motion, he flipped open a leather pouch fastened to the wall and pulled out an awkward device. Between two paddles were a series of baffles like an accordion and two plugs were attached by snaking tubes. He stuffed those plugs firmly in his ears and drew out a third that ended in a cone like a stethoscope. Blue eyes wide and blinking, he pressed the cone to the wall and listened.

"Whatever is he doing?" Listonn whispered to Crossland.

"It's called a yack-mouth and that thing under his arm's the clapper."

Not finding that answer particularly helpful Listonn merely nodded and held himself steady in free-fall. Even without the listening device, all could make out a light rapping. Elphinstone retrieved the ship's log and began jotting letters with a crudely sharpened pencil. Catching Listonn's struggles, Crossland added, "It's Morse code. They've sent over some steel cables capped with electrical magnets. They're tapping on it down below to send up docking instructions."

"Give him quiet now," Napier snapped. Listonn nodded, an expression of understanding softening his features.

"Yep," Elphinstone said in a mild Cockney, "No gangway fer' us. Goin' to have to do this the old fashioned way." His broad nod was not echoed or appreciated by the others.

"What's the problem," Gavin asked, "What happened to the moorings? I expressly instructed-"

"That's all we know," Napier interrupted. "Settle back and let's doc the ship. Warrant Officer," he said, "what's our approach?"

"Course received, Captain," Elphinstone replied. "I'll punch in the numbers and relay them to the flight controls." Spinning upside down, the young officer neatly replaced the yack-mouth and clapper and pulled himself, one hand over the other, to return to the analytic machine.

"Right then," Napier said, "Lt. Campbell, take us in, you civilians clear the deck."

"But, Captain," Gavin protested.

"I'll not hear it." Napier stated, "Clear the deck, Mr. Crossland. You're the builder alright, Gavin, but it's my ship. Let us do our jobs."

Gavin didn't bother to hide his disquiet. He needed some of Listonn's assistance to get turned around and then they helped each other until they both could safely grab the array of pipes leading back into spinehall. Gavin stopped quickly to look back through the port at what should have been his Ares Britannia. The flight crew then went about the delicate operation to maneuver the Daedalus into position. The time altering drives were much better at forward motion than the precise changes that were now required. Campbell was already sweltering in the heat of the command sphere. His uniform clung to his metal seat as sweat poured down his back.

As Gavin and Sir Thomas pulled themselves along spinehall, Listonn was a stream of questions. "What's all this now?" and, "Who authorized this?" and, "How could this have happened?"

As they readied to turn into the starboard strut Gavin spun himself around to face Listonn. "See here, Tom, there are a great many variables when building in space. It's not like back at home. There are many things that speculation can't account for. It's all numbers on a slide rule until you can actually get here and start building. I have all the same questions, but first off we have our guests to consider."

Listonn took a deep breath, pulled his billowing hair away from his face and relaxed a bit. Gavin continued, "Now they aren't going to like being weightless any more than we do. They need to change into their metal laced clothing and prepare the walk over to the platform."

"Walk?" Listonn asked turning a lighter shade.

"Not walk outside mind you. There's a kind of gangplank that will be inflated, warmed and pressurized. But it will be a beast to traverse for the uninitiated. And we all count as that I'm afraid."

"Right," Listonn returned. "How can I help?"

"Help by keeping your upper lip stiff. Let's go in there, explain the situation and get them off to ready themselves. As a safety precaution, I'll go over first. I'll ensure that every provision has been made on the far end and then we'll get the others over."

"Yes," Listonn said emphatically, "Yes of course. That honor should be yours regardless."

"All that aside," Crossland replied taking a few breaths himself. "When the time comes, I will need you to assist Lady Cecilia. She's already feeling ill from the travel and I'm sure she's not going to take this well. Stay at her side the whole way and help keep her upright"

"Right, I'm your man."

"You're your own man. Now let's motivate the troops."

Crossland and Listonn, pulled along until they again reentered the gravitational effect in the ship's extremities. The two were welcomed cheerfully as they rejoined the passengers in the sitting room. Gavin led the talk on making their boarding preparations. He informed them all to don the metal threaded clothing that had been especially tailored for their time on Phobus. He made special note of their shoes with the modified soles. Princess Sandra had three pairs to choose from. He explained how the gangplank would be extended to the ship and once it had been properly filled with air and warmed to a tolerable level they would all be permitted over to the platform. There were questions of course, but not many. Crossland chose his words carefully and Listonn lent his air of confidence. This was no problem at all. A minor inconvenience at best. Just a small obstacle to surmount before seeing what they had traveled so far to see. The Royals made off as instructed, their sense of awe and wonder perfectly intact.

Campbell was sorely challenged to get the Daedalus into position. Once satisfied, Vecihi had to ensure that the docking seals were secure on their end. The external doors, the same ones used to embark back at Tauranga, all had pressure sealed chambers between the interior and the bitterness of space.

There, Vecihi put on a cumbersome vacuum suit that resembled a diving bell with stubby arm protrusions. Similar suits had been employed to build every livable establishment in space. The ones on the Daedalus were innovative in the sense that the occupant had a wider range of motion and the bell could sustain longer shifts before replenishing life support. Vecihi rolled the bell out of storage and allowed it to float aimlessly in the pressure chamber while he firmly secured it with thick metal cables. He unscrewed the circular entry hatch and crawled in.

A single forward facing port gave the hatch a cyclopean appearance. Now inside, he worked the valves that slowly allowed the atmosphere to drain from the chamber and brought the heat up in his diving bell. It was painstakingly slow, but once completed he spun the external hatch lock and took his first step out into space. None of the passengers could see him outside but they were thrilled with the news of the procedure.

Rising slowly from Ares Britannia came the worm-like tube that would allow the travelers entry. It rode up the two cables that were magnetically locked to the Daedalus. Using only his hands, Vecihi pulled himself along until he could reach the edge of the gangway and guide it into position. After making initial connections he pulled his suit inside to complete the coupling. This would take hours but nothing could be left to chance. The connection would need to be tested and retested to ensure that all the seams were sealed.

The passengers grew pensive, but were calmed by Crossland. It was an easy sell considering the consequences of error. Satisfied, Vecihi completed the seal and again entered the ship. His suit's stores were running low and he desperately needed to relieve himself. He removed his suit and manipulated it through weightless space back to its resting place. He reported status to the captain and then went to don his magnetically laced clothing. It took several more hours for the gangway to reach a livable temperature.

At this point Crossland's resolve was wearing. He spoke in engineering jargon under his breath, "I really need to devise a pre-warming sequence", "Damned if we can't do better than telegraphy," and so on. It wasn't long before he left the group and was again bothering the command crew. "I'm going over now," he informed the captain while spinning oddly to get his topcoat to fit straight.

"Gods man!" Napier replied, "you'll go when Officer Vecihi Hürkuş gives the word and not sooner."

"Vecihi," Gavin asked, "what's the reading in there?"

Vecihi wiped the sweat from his forehead thinking more on how badly he needed a smoke than Gavin's question. "I don't know," he said, his Turkish accent thicker than normal. "Maybe it's okay. Probably sixty, seventy percent by now. Procedure says we give it another forty minutes. Can you wait forty minutes?"

"No, sir, I cannot," Gavin said and pulled himself out of the spherical command space to the beleaguered protests of the crewmen. Back in spinehall he found Listonn trying to keep himself stable in the tubular hallway. The stiff clothes he wore made it harder, his pressed pants and dark vest already wrinkled.

"Alright Tom," Gavin said breathlessly, pulling himself along, "I'm going to head over."

"Right then," Listonn replied, "I'll hold the fort here."

"Good man, I'll tap up the lines when it's time for everyone to come down. It was hard enough to convince the crew that I should go first. Let no one down – no one – until I give the word. Are we straight there?"

"Right as ever was."

Now wearing magnetically augmented shoes, polished to a spit shine, Gavin affixed them firmly to the floor till he felt a solid contact. He'd meant to practice wearing them. They should be much more effective on the decks in Ares Britannia unless he was about to find more surprises down there. His mind raced with worst case presumptions.

Try as he might, he couldn't keep his feet planted while opening the external pressure door. He kept losing his grip and breaking into free-fall while spinning the wheel. It took a few tries, but he finally got it open. A blast of cold air rushed in blowing him back a space, thankfully not enough to send him into the opposing wall.

It was cold, deathly cold, far colder than he expected. His ears popped and his first breaths blew in the thin air. For a space he feared that his hasty actions may have lacked wisdom. He rubbed his arms briskly. He regained footing, letting the soles take grip as he steadied himself, properly oriented in three dimensions before the gangway.

There was no pull from the moon below. The angled pitch of the gangway held no significance. It was just a dark passage without so much as a light at the end of the tunnel. He was already familiar with its design, but had never been through a practice run himself. The interior was burlap-like canvas that had an unfolding metal framework that extended in four or five foot sections. It was roughly round and he couldn't help but find it similar to an intestine or birth canal, though he was quite sure that he didn't possess a prenatal memory of his own birthday. There were guiding poles along each side within easy reach and metal plates along the floor to accommodate his magnetic soles.

He began to make his way, one foot after the other. Movement was hampered by the instability of the gangway which pitched and buckled with every step. A few times, he tried to dislodge his shoes and merely pull himself along the railings. Even this proved difficult considering the buckling passageway. He steadied his breathing and had to pause more than once to recover. His breath froze in billows before him but he could sense the temperature rising with every step. He kept his head down to ensure the placement of every footfall. His thoughts were so focused he was quite unprepared when he heard someone call his name.

"Mr. Crossland? Mr. Crossland I presume!"

Gavin looked up to see a round face in the round opening below him. "Welcome to Ares Britannia, my good man! Welcome!" Another face joined the first and both men stared up at him. The first man was in his thirties with sandy hair showing signs of gray temples and growing recession. The newer face was younger with a military cropped haircut. The expression on that face wasn't at all welcoming, more stoic and stern.

"With whom am I speaking?" Gavin asked pushing the words out through short breath. The first man answered with a chortle,

"I'm Reverend Beckett and with me is your master builder, Mr. Culverton Havelock-Allen and we are very pleased to make your acquaintance!" Gavin blinked repeatedly, thinking through fog.

"And my pleasure as well," Gavin called back swallowing hard. "I'm sorry you have me at a disadvantage or I'd shake your hands."

"Not at all, not at all!" Beckett called back. "Come on over and we'll have a proper greeting." Gavin worked his way down the final twenty or so feet to cross the odd angle into Ares. His feet met the more stable metal deck and he brought himself upright, fixing his shirt and jacket. Still out of breath he took a minute to survey those around him. The entry was poorly lit, stuffy and frightfully hot as it pumped air up the gangway. Several men, floating neatly in midair, were staring at him quietly. They were casually dressed. Primarily overalls and grease stained shirts. Beckett wasn't dressed like a vicar, more like another worker. Havelock-Allen was a bit more done-up, again in a worker's uniform but more kept, more pressed and proper. Beckett reached out a warm hand and shook Gavin's energetically.

"Right then," Becket said, "Francis Alabaster Beckett at your service and very excited to meet you. How was your trip? Is everyone on board in a good way?"

"Quite, sir, quite," Gavin replied, "and who all do we have here?"

"Yes of course," Beckett started in, "Again, Mr. Havelock-Allen, your building chief," he said, drifting aside. The younger man's expression was hard to read. His eyes were penetrating and yet his face more like a fool's or simpleton's. As Allen and Crossland shared handshakes, a shorter man ducked and weaved his way forward, almost fluidly in the near absence of gravity. He had well-oiled hair, thin, just barely covering his head. His sleeves were lose and bound up at the bicep. He wore small silver rimmed glasses and a fine vest with watch chain flowing in the weightless air.

"Sir Thomas Royden," the little man broke in taking Gavin's hand. "A pleasure, sir, a pleasure."

"Sir Royden, yes of course," Gavin replied returning the shake. Crossland was still catching his breath but he began to size up these men. Their faces had a common feature, a puffiness known to those who'd been in space for some time. "Truly a pleasure."

"Truly, truly," Royden spat out. "Three cheers for Tyneside," he said raising his fist in the air.

"And," Beckett added, introducing the others in turn, "these men are members of the building crew, this is Mr. Piter Duncan-Smith, this is Mr. Curtis Warren whom the lads all call 'Miser,' and this is Mr. Jacob Jagendorf, whom we all call 'Bull. '" Gavin greeting them all said,

"It's very good to meet you, men, surely. But where is Mr. Christien Crohne? He's not indisposed I hope?"

"Not at all, the doctor was just here with the key box," Beckett explained along with quick head nods from Royden.

"Key box?" Gavin asked, looking blankly.

"Yessir, the key box," Beckett answered directing Gavin's attention to a rectangular hole in the floor just along the wall at Gavin's right foot. Crossland leaned over to peer down and see a number of interlocking gears and shafts. He couldn't even begin to fathom their purpose other than a key must fit a lock if he followed.

"I'll have to learn more about everything here in a bit," Gavin said looking back to the men about him. "I look forward to getting to know all of you, but first we have the matter of receiving the other passengers from the Daedalus. We were expecting the mooring tower to be in place to assist with the crossing."

"Yes that," Royden explained, "damned inconvenient that."

"Rather," Crossland agreed, "what's with that then? What happened to the moorings?"

"Concessions," Royden answered, "concessions."

Beckett paused for a bit to consider Royden's answer but then nodded in agreement.

"I'm sorry," Crossland replied.

"What Sir Royden means," Havelock-Allen explained, "is that we've had to make certain changes to maintain the effort."

"Changes," Crossland repeated.

"Yes," Havelock-Allen continued, "we've had to make a great number of changes."

"Like what?" Crossland asked. "Please, if you'd allow me, but without the tower loading the ore is going to take quite a bit longer. Not to mention the awkward passage of our guests back on the Daedalus." The group gave each other looks. Gavin made a best attempt to read them. It was obvious that no one was volunteering an answer. Changing the subject, he addressed the vicar, "Reverend Beckett, when I give the word, the ship's crew will begin leading over the contingent. I don't want to give that word just yet, but can I have your assistance giving them the same welcome you gave me?"

"Of course, sir," Beckett said with a smile.

"Now if you lads would allow me," Gavin said, "I've got words for Sir Royden and Mr. Havelock-Allen. It's just Tyneside business is all. You know, company rot and bother."

Piter, Miser and Bull looked at each other a bit cross. Havelock-Allen, glared at them and nodded back up the hallway. Bull, towering above the others, turned his wide frame, breaking his feet up from the floor and letting his motion spin him hovering. The others followed after, floating along behind him. Gavin looked over at Beckett who hadn't moved as yet. Beckett nodded looking over the remaining three before rushing off to join the others, just a few paces away. Royden burst out into a flurry of hushed whispers,

"Understand, Mr. Crossland, we've been under enormous pressure up here, insufficient supply, labor disputes, constant redesigns-"

"It's, it's alright," Gavin said, "First things first, I need to keep this to short answers. Allen," he said looking at Havelock-Allen.

"Call me Culverton, as you will, sir," he replied in a stark military tone.

"Culverton, thank you. Tell me straight. Is there anything of concern in either in the staterooms, the Arboretum or any points where we'll be holding the ceremony? Any concessions that I need to be aware of?"

"Sorry?" Culverton asked.

"Ah, are they too cold or too hot? Is the air the correct mixture are the bio's all in order?" Culverton looked over at Royden who shrugged. He looked off, notably at a loss.

"Uh, yes," Culverton said, "I'm sure we get used to things up here but that's all proper."

"Anything?" Gavin pressed. "Anything at all that might make them uncomfortable? Like walking up this gangway. Anything like that?"

"No," Culverton said emphatically. "No, sir, this will be the worst of it."

Gavin sighed, "Good, good to hear. Now," he said addressing them both. "What of the mine? I need the progress in ten words or less."

Royden drew in a sharp breath. Culverton shook his space-life puffy head.

"What?" Gavin asked. "What's wrong?"

"You see," Royden said, "It's all their damned fault. Damn insurrectionists, mutineers they are."

"It's not all that," Culverton broke in, "There's been disputes," he said.

"Disputes," Gavin acknowledged.

"Labour disputes with the miners," Culverton explained. "Typical really, compensation, living conditions, rations whatever they damn well think they can bleed from us. Beckett's been the one to keep things going. He's the only one they'll talk to."

"Yes," Royden blurted out, "It's all that union organizer, Barabbas."

Culverton rose up and stared him down.

"Barabbas?" Gavin asked, "Who the devil is that?"

"No one," Culverton answered, "that's just it, he's no one."

"I don't follow," Gavin said questioning.

"He's the name they call their union organizer," Culverton explained. "Just is no one's ever seen him. It's probably just Othello, but no one's saying."

"Othello?" Gavin asked.

"One of our foremen at the mine," Royden explained, "sort of their spokesman."

"Well," Gavin said thinking, "there can't be more than thirty or forty of them, but I'm learning a great many things for the first time here. Let me be clear. What is the level of production? How much ore do we have ready to ship?" Gavin looked at them both, they both obviously found it difficult to answer. "Do we have any? Any at all?" Gavin said.

"Yes, there's ore alright," Culverton answered, "just is we don't know how much. Iron, gold, platinum, it's all there. We know they're working around Limtoc and the secondary dig sites. We just don't know how much. Beckett's been trying to find out but they're not saying. Holding the ore hostage as they can."

"We don't go back there," Royden broke in again. "Beckett, he's the only one who'll go back there."

"Back where?" Gavin asked.

"To the mine site," Culverton answered. Royden gave Culverton a deflated look. "There's been some violence," he added.

"Violence?" Gavin asked gravely.

"Like I said," Culverton answered, "disputes."

"Right," Gavin said, wiping the sweat from his brow and taking a nervous look over his shoulder, back up that intestinal tube of a gangway. "Lads," he spoke with an even weightier gravity, "first off, I know it's never easy to share bad news. But really, it's all manageable. I appreciate you being upfront and it was imperative that we spoke of this first. Bloody fortunate really. Now I don't need to tell you what's all if any of the others learn of this, especially Sir Thomas Listonn. You all have shares riding on every shipment we draw from this place, but no one sees a penny if we lose the backers. Your men, can they be trusted?"

"Trusted?" Culverton asked, "Undoubtedly so."

"They need tight lips and we need to limit the number of those who assist the contingent. Very limited. Just a handful. The most trustworthy among them. Quite frankly our fate's in your hands, Mr. Havelock-Allen. Are you up for it?"

"I hear you loud and clear, sir," Culverton stated, nodding his head in dedication.

"Good man," Gavin assured. "And Royden we need to speak to Mr. Crohne right off."

"Doctor Crohne," Royden corrected.

"Yes," Gavin stuttered, "Yes of course. Where the devil is he?"

"He's," Royden said thinking, "He's uh, up in Babel Tower."

"Babel Tower," Gavin replied nodding, "Yes, I guess I do know what that is." Gavin looked back up the hall at the others who waited pensively. He caught Beckett's attention and waved him over. With a few gliding strides across the metal surface, Beckett closed the distance to join them. "Now here's what's next," Gavin instructed. "Mr. Allen, please inform Reverend Beckett and the others of everything I just told you." Culverton nodded firmly. "Sir Royden," Crossland continued, "take me quickly to the Arboretum, the quarters set aside for the contingency, and then up to Babel Tower."

"You're going to see Christien?" Beckett asked.

A bit shocked, Gavin spoke back, "Yes, yes of course." With a look of slight, awkwardness he said, "After I've given things a quick look I'll come back here and we can head up the line to the ship. Culverton, please assist Reverend Beckett with our guests, make sure they all get over. When that's done come join us with Dr. Crohne." Culverton considered this for a moment. Gavin almost expected push back but instead Culverton agreed.

"Right," Gavin concluded, "Great pleasure to meet you all again. Quite a momentous occasion and all. You've all done brilliantly as I'm sure I'll come to grasp here in a bit. Now, Sir Royden, if you wouldn't mind, and please forgive me if I need my time. I've not gotten used to getting around."

"Of course, of course I will," the little man took Gavin by the arm to steady his step.

The work crew waited in the dark hall sharing first impressions and commentary about those unaccustomed to space. A few removed their boots to float about freely, more comfortable without magnetic restrictions. Culverton Havelock-Allen spoke like a military officer and commanded his men to keep it buttoned. Beckett understood as well and lent his agreement to Gavin's directions. Gavin and Royden stepped off into the inner reaches of Ares Britannia. Royden kept one eye over his shoulder as they went up the shadowy corridor and into the antechamber beyond. He shared nervous glances with Crossland who quite frankly didn't know how to take the little man. Once Gavin was sure he was well out of earshot, he spoke more with Royden. "You're a good man, Sir Royden. I know it's never easy to be the bearer of bad news." The short man smiled and adjusted his glasses. "Tell me something," Gavin asked. "Why did Beckett find it odd that we're off to see Dr. Crohne?"

Royden cracked a brief smile, "Oh, nothing really. Just Beckett's way. You know, vicars are all odd sorts."

"No," Gavin said, "not really. He must have meant something."

"Just that, the doctor doesn't come down much. It's rare we see him at all. He sends his orders down the chute and we pick them up."

"Down the chute? Sir Royden, you're the general manager of Ares Britannia. Why are you taking Crohne's orders down the chute?"

Royden smiled again, broadly, "Just our way up here Mr. Crossland. We're a tight knit group you know. The builders. Tight knit."

"But what of the miners?"

"That's what it's all about see? The builders and the miners. They are like two tribes up here. Two nations separated by that long hall that stretches across Phobus." Royden became calmer. A bit freer to talk with Gavin in the quiet dark of that chamber. "We're like bands of black savages shaking their spears at each other from across the jungle."

"A house divided can't stand, my good man." Crossland shared.

"No," Royden agreed, "Not at all."

"Well we have some building of our own to do then, eh? You and I. We're both Tyneside men. We owe it to the company, the investors and the Empire. Are you with me?"

"Doubtless. Doubtless, Mr. Crossland."

"Call me Gavin. We've got a few short days to mend this and I can't do it alone. Be my eyes and ears up here, sir. This is your platform. You know all these men and those miners as well. Keep me in the know and I'll return the favor. Royden nodded again, checking the hall for occupants. That resolved, at least to Gavin's satisfaction, they proceeded in. It wasn't the tour that Gavin had dreamt of these many months.

It was dark in the larger halls. Gavin knew the need to conserve energy, but he didn't expect it to be so dark. The building crews were off in the outlying buildings. The central domes were hollow, vacant spaces that echoed; echoes that once started seemed to travel a long distance only to return in weaker and weaker waves. Like the husks of dead cathedrals after all the parishioners have fallen to the sin of doubt.

He didn't even have time to appreciate the forested meadow that had been reproduced on the Phoban surface. The staterooms seemed orderly as well. They carried the same dark wood theme as was built on the Daedalus. All this was to his design and specifications. His confidence rose somewhat. He began to see the creation that his architectural team had devised so many years ago. He started to regain that sense of pride. That wellspring of accomplishment. Determining that he had no concerns with the contingent coming over, they made their way back to where the gangway reached up to the Daedalus. Tapping the, "ok" signal up the cables, Gavin and Royden went again into the interior. Havelock-Allen watched them intently as they left, Piter, Miser and Bull watched along with him.

"Out-worlders," Beckett added with a smirk. The burly workers nodded in agreement and turned to wait for more outsiders to invade their quiet sanctum.

Chapter D (4): A Vulgar Reception

More Morse code leapt up the guide wires to the Daedalus. Elphinstone's use of the yack-mouth served him again and quickly conveyed their instructions to the others. Two of the primary crewmen were to escort each member of the Royal contingent in the same order they boarded the liner. The crew of lesser quality was to stay aboard with Captain Napier only joining them after the ship had been properly secured.

The Lady Inverness was dressed in a full gown that had required all three of her maidservants several hours to don. Two of them worked continually to keep the train of her ladyship's gown from billowing and ol' Gran worked to keep her upright as she made her way. She shared a dressing room with Princess Sandra who consequently barely had time enough to fix her hair. The Lady Inverness' gown was a forest green with yellow embroidery. She felt that a nod to Tyneside Spaceyarde Ltd. was warranted. She didn't care for the "metal shoes" as she called them as they really didn't complement the outfit to her liking.

The dress, especially the shoulders and sleeves, was invisibly wound with a crisscrossing pattern of inter-working metal threads. The stiff skeleton helped them maintain its proper shape. This was true of all the clothing tailored for the contingent to assist with their overall appearance and the gravitational simulation. Its effectiveness remained untested.

Even moored to the Phoban platform, the high berths on the Daedalus could still continue their rotation, maintaining the illusion of weight. Now it had come time for those who loathed the weightless sensation to contend with its challenge. There was no avoiding it. Spinehall beckoned and each one had to make way to the station despite the abject awkwardness in doing so.

Cleland found the look on the Lady Inverness' face nothing short of priceless. She went from feeling ill in her seclusion to facing the absurdity of balance without counterbalance. Try as they might, the servants themselves spun and whirled as they attempted to assist the Lady Inverness into the weightless core of the craft. Cleland's devilish ridicule soon subsided as he saw that she truly found the experience unsettling. At her age, she was not up to the task. She stood before the passage toward the spine, her sweeping hat perched high on her head.

Finally, two white uniformed sailors took hold of each arm and helped her ladyship take her first weightless steps. She was nothing short of mortified. Unable to keep her feet beneath her, with every step, her legs began to fly up in front of her, startled she began kicking and soon she got all twisted round, the sailors nearly groping her to keep her stable.

"Here, here!" Lord Cholmondeley intervened, dismissing the sailors with a wave.

"Lord Garrick," Lady Inverness warned with a sharp tongue.

"Garrick? Christ knows no one has called me that since Methuselah's funeral."

"Don't lay a hand on me, sir, I'm quite capable of seeing myself out," the Lady Inverness insisted.

"Of course you are, my lady, but then I wouldn't have the great pleasure of accompanying you." The Lady Inverness gave Cleland a probing look and then conceded to receive his aid. Cleland smiled his characteristic crooked smile. He took her by the right hand and placed the other at the small of her back as if dancing. "Now," he said, "as you've noticed I rather enjoy the absence of weight so follow my lead and I'll teach you to waltz on air." The Lady Inverness, no stranger to the charms of men, allowed Cleland his wit and his will.

"Lead on then," she permitted.

"Now, every step we take toward the spinehall, we will get lighter and lighter. When we lose it all I'm going to push lightly on your back and steady you with my arm. We'll be flying, you and I, and we'll fly all the way between here and Ares. Are you ready?"

"Proceed," the Lady Inverness commanded and so Cleland complied. With well controlled execution, Cleland led the way. Cleland held her fast and the Lady Inverness gripped tighter. At times her anxiety got the better of her, but Cleland lent just the appropriate portion of strength to their stride. This abundant wellspring of confidence imbued her with the will to pass through the spine, enter the gangway and begin her long trek down the canvas-lined tube to Ares Britannia.

The others followed suit. Sir Wilson watched Cleland with her ladyship intently. He first fought a need to intervene, but after seeing Cleland's tact the feeling abated. The young man had his refinements despite his roguish antics. Princess Sandra also observed but her expression was more droll and disinterested. When two of the crew extended their white gloved hands to escort the Princess, she excused them both and proceeded by herself. After observing Listonn's problems controlling his hair she'd taken precautions with her own. She wore it bound tight with many times the pins she would employ back on earth. The tactic served her. Boswell was rather stunned at her ability as he didn't recall ever seeing her enter the weightless sections before. And he was fairly certain as he often indulged his eyes with her form. Dr. Boswell wasn't about to take the trek alone and insisted that three crewmen be at hand to assist his passage.

When it came to Sir William's turn he halted to hand his walking cane over to Argyle.

"I shan't be needing this," he indicated. Argyle merely nodded briskly and accepted both the cane and gloves graciously. Wilson refused help but did need some assistance to slip free from the centrifugal effect into the true openness of the liner's core. He gave a look of satisfaction to Argyle before moving, and then went hand-over-hand along the wall.

A touch of concern turned him back as he recalled Argyle's discomfort on the voyage. Perhaps it was his to help his manservant. To his surprise, his valet had overcome his aversions. Argyle had donned his dress uniform, the bars of a Lance Naik showing proudly on his shoulders. Even so formally dressed, Argyle literally leapt into the spine and nearly bound up the way in feats of acrobatics that propelled him quickly along.

"Argyle, my good friend!" Wilson shouted out to him. "There are adventures left before us aren't there? There most certainly are!" Argyle broke his first smile of the voyage, for he was more a dour, sullen soul.

"Kaphar hunnu bhanda marnu ramro," he said.

"Better die than as a coward live," Wilson translated. "No cowards on Mars my friend! Only gods walk on Mars!" Argyle found the canvas-lined channel easy to traverse. In fact, he allowed his fellow travelers to gain some space and then bound up the way in long silent strides. The lead group grew close to the end of the gangway. Cleland and the Lady Inverness had almost reached the landing when Beckett called up to them.

"Ah, excuse me," Beckett shouted, "the ballrooms' closed for renovations but you'll find dancing on the terrace nothing short of marvelous!"

"Well met, Martian," Cleland called back, "you've neither the stature nor complexion that I was led to expect." The Lady Inverness was reminded of her prejudice toward Cleland's more juvenile traits. "At least I'm pleased to see that you've left your ray gun at home. I profess, we come in peace."

The Lady Inverness spoke up, interrupting him, "Ares Britannia," she called down in the voice of a statesman, "I am Lady Cecilia Underwood, First Duchess of Inverness, Lady Cecilia Letitia Gore, cousin and emissary of the Queen, appointee of the governors of the Empire and all her commonwealth. I come empowered by Her Majesty in her charge with all rights and privileges. With whom am I addressing?"

Cleland gave her a slight look and asked quietly, "Did Victoria make you memorize that?"

"Of course not, I made it up," she whispered back.

"Ah," Beckett faltered a space, "this is Right Honorable Francis Alabaster Beckett, Archdeacon of Bournemouth - purely an honorary title mind you as I'm a bit far from there at present. Representing Tyneside is Mr. Culverton Havelock-Allen, the head foreman."

"Reverend Beckett," Lady Cecilia said, "Sir Thomas Bland Royden was to greet us, is he in your company?"

"The man's name is Bland?" Cleland asked her under his breath.

"Yes," she whispered back turning to look at him, "whether by birth or tastes has yet to be ascertained." Cleland broke out into a boisterous laugh, leaning back some until he pulled her back with him. Lady Cecilia immediately regretted entertaining his discourtesies.

"No, ma'am," Beckett said. "Sir Thomas is currently at the disposal of Mr. Gavin Crossland who only just preceded you. Mr. Culverton Havelock-Allen here stands as Sir Royden's delegate." Culverton gave Beckett a disapproving look.

"Is he," she said, "very well, Mr. Havelock-Allen, do we have permission to enter?"

"Granted, m'lady!' Beckett said, "and you're most certainly welcome." The travelers funneled their way onto the landing and took their first steps into Ares Britannia. Piter, Miser and Bull were there with the other oil and grime stained builders who greeted the newcomers with less vigor than Beckett. The good vicar was no stranger to social graces. This served him well and helped quell the physical awkwardness. He was well versed in averting his eyes, when any of the Royals began struggling he merely looked the other way and allowed them to regain their composure. Culverton mostly stayed quiet, counting the moments until he could get away. A curt 'hullo' and firm handshake was all he offered.

He had almost completed the rounds when Sir Wilson caught his hand, "Havelock-Allen you say, sir?" He asked Culverton, Argyle coming up at Wilson's right shoulder.

"Yes," Culverton answered, "have we met, sir?" somewhat stunned by Wilson's expression of familiarity.

"I've not had the pleasure, but I met your father, Lt. General, Sir Henry Marshman Havelock-Allan. I have that right?"

Culverton took on a grave aspect and expression that was almost the antithesis of expressions. Wilson thought he might have somehow misspoken. "No? I'm most sure of it. If memory serves you have a brother too don't you?"

"Yes, sir," Culveron replied drawing to attention. "You're quite right. Just not about my brother, Theodore Henry, he passed when we were young."

"Oh," Wilson said, his face adding to the deep sincerity in his voice. "How so, son?"

"Ah, an accident I'm afraid. Shot dead from a firearm at my father's house when he was six."

"Dreadful, sorry to hear it."

"And you are?"

"Oh, of course, I'm Sir Archdale Wilson of Delhi and this is my companion, Lance Naik Thaman Gurung Thapa, formally of the 25th Punjab Infantry."

"You're a Gurkha." Culverton said to Argyle shaking his hand. Argyle nodded in confirmation.

"Bloody right he is," Wilson broke in, "right from the Hazara Goorkha Battalion. We met in the same bloody business where I met your father.

"May I be so bold, sirs? Do you have them with you?" Culverton asked Argyle. "I've heard stories of them in my youth but I've never seen any first-hand. Just drawings in books." Wilson paused to let his friend speak for himself. Again, Argyle held his tongue and nodded in confirmation. Wilson spoke up again,

"He keeps them slung behind him, a bit untraditional I know, just his way with them."

"May I see them?" Culverton asked. Holding out a weathered palm Argyle silently declined. Culverton caught himself, "Yes, my apologies I've forgotten. You're not supposed to draw them. They must draw blood right? Each time they're unsheathed? It's been a great many years since I've been home, home in India."

"Not at all, not at all! There's no offense in it man." Wilson answered. "Now, Argyle, spin around so he can at least see the grips." Gracefully complying, Argyle loosed his soles from the deck plates and drew himself around. As Wilson indicated, two long knives were sheathed neatly, bound to his coarse leather belt. The crossed handles were ivory colored with waves of dark brown like a bull's horn. They were fused flush with the metal tang and worn smooth with expert handling. The scabbards expanded widely toward the points, evidence of the traditionally broad tip at the end of an acutely angled blade.

Culverton marveled, "It's an unexpected honor, sirs," he said gratefully, "truly an honor."

"The honor's ours, son," Wilson exclaimed. "It was an honor to meet your father. Gods, that was back in the 1850's," he said, eyes distant in recollection. "I'd like to say I knew him well, but the General kept his distance. Wise that, it was a damn bloody affair. Didn't know who'd be at your bedroll one day till the next. Wasn't a time to fraternize. That was the first time I saw a real war. Saw it look back at me. You'd think I'd had my belly full of it but not the way it turned out." Wilson glanced around and noticed that Cleland was listening in, not that it bothered him.

Beckett clapped both his hands together catching the attention of those gathered. "Welcome again all," he said, "I understand that your personals are being unloaded. Please allow me to escort you to your quarters. As you recall, I was sent along ahead of you to help make preparations."

Culverton dismissed himself from Wilson and Argyle, "I need to get back with Sir Royden, Francis will see you to your rooms."

"Very good, sir," Wilson replied, "the three of us will need to speak more, of India, Delhi, Nepal, all the thoughts of home." Culverton nodded and, slipping free from the deck, propelled himself deftly along the wall at a hurried pace.

"Extraordinary man," Wilson provided as a footnote as he fell in with the group making their way deeper into the platform. Cleland again swiftly came to Lady Inverness' side. The group walked up the entry hall, through the antechamber and into the interior in much the same way as Crossland had experienced it. The group's progress was much more leisurely, like a tour group at a museum or place of historical importance. They spoke casually as they went. They mentioned the challenges of walking without the expectation of gravity's pull. Boswell complained and Beckett offered words of instruction and encouragement. When they entered into the first dome, their sense of awe was restored to them. The beams as viewed from the inside had a coppery sheen, like metal that had been bathed in fire. The short glass panes assembled like mosaics that stacked high up the sides and crested the vaulted roof above them.

At that time of day, Mars glowered on high, thousands of times larger than the moon appeared to those standing on earth. The sun, though seemingly smaller, contested the glowing presence of the red planet. The spectacle surpassed all preponderance. No artist's rendering had done it justice. No fanciful imagining was able to picture what it was like to look upon it. It was like the glass was merely a portal and one could step through with ease and out into a living dream-scape of celestial fires.

"Now that is what brought me here," Cleland said and many voiced their agreement. Beckett stopped, grinning as he re-imagined his own first impressions.

"Can we tell night from day here?" Princess Sandra asked.

"That takes getting used to," Beckett offered as they slowly continued on, heads all upturned as they went. "Phobus loops round Mars approximately twice a day and we lose daylight once we go behind it. Ares is located some ways north of Phobus' equator so we do enjoy the sun when she peeks around Mars. Still, it's much different than taking a long journey back home. You must train your mind when to sleep. You begin to appreciate resting in rooms without windows. I'm sure you'll find your staterooms accommodating for just that reason."

Sandra continued her observant stance, the words she'd later pen in her journal already forming in her mind. It was a while before the party realized that the place was largely empty. The echoes of their passage were a bit disquieting. The place just seemed larger than expected, yet surprisingly lifeless. That sense dissipated when they approached the solarium.

"Do I hear flowing water?" Princess Sandra asked.

"That you do, miss," Vecihi answered, "water must be pumped like a heart," he said beating his chest. "It must flow like blood through the veins of the platform."

Beckett grinning broadly said, "Just up ahead is the gate to Ares. Would you like to see it?" Sandra was at a bit of a loss how to respond.

Seeing that, Beckett called over to Piter, making his way up behind them. "Piter," Beckett said, "Royden's rules be damned, let's turn up the lights and show our guests the gates."

"What would be his objection?" asked Listonn with a questioning and marginally cross look.

"Um," Beckett answered, "can't say really. Sir Royden has a lot of rules. I'm not quite familiar with why they're so important but he's quick to hold us to them. I can attest it would take a sizable volume to write them all down." Piter, the gaunt, continental-looking builder, scratched the rough stubble at his throat and looked at Miser. "Come on, men," Beckett prodded, "just for a bit, I'll apologize to Tom."

Piter slipped off to their left. They were quite amazed that he could see in the low lighting. They heard a bit of fumbling and then a low, electric crackling like bacon on a hot pan. Lights came to life all around them shining on the gates to Ares Britannia.

On either side were two marble statues, illumed from the floor, that were worn down with age as if excavated from an ancient ruin. They were naked with the exception of armored greaves and helmets. Short capes were draped over their shoulders and each carried a spear and shield. The shields crawled with reliefs of crouching snakes with bulbous heads. The statue on the left cast its gaze left, its right eye sculpted shut. The one on the right had eyes cast skyward, the tip of its spear tilted in the direction it gazed. Across the top of the doorway was mounted a bronze plaque with a chiseled inscription.

The letters bit deep and black, shadowed by the floor lights.

Phobus and Deimus quickly drove Ares' smooth-wheeled, chariot to him and bore him up from the wide paths of earth into his richly wrought carriage and then straight lashed his team till coming to high Olympos. - Hesiod, Shield of Heracles

Above the plaque was the bright seal of the British Royal Astronomical Society. Beneath it, offset on either side, were two other sigils. These were the familiar symbols of the Extra Orbital Trade Authority and the Tranquility Association of the United States. It was a great mix of international flavors that were almost clashing in their officious appearance. Sandra continued scratching notes in her mind. She couldn't help but remark that the right-hand statue resembled Mr. Havelock-Allen. The face had his distinctive jawline and it wore the same cropped hairstyle. It was her recollection that Greek statues more often had thick curls. The resemblance had to be purely coincidental if they were in fact authentic. Cleland and Boswell weren't particularly impressed, communicated such to each other and didn't care to conceal it.

Beckett held both arms out wide and the flanking builders each took hold of the bars on either side and wretched the gates open. The doors scraped the floor with a metallic screech. It took the men several strong, two-handed pulls to wrest them open, heaving as they scratched and strained to pull them wide. Beckett gestured broadly, with each heave almost masking the awkwardness of the moment. Once the doors were open wide, Beckett strode in without looking back and the group shuffled in behind him.

As they entered the largest area in the central cluster they walked into the tales spun by Publius Ovidius Naso or Lewis Carroll. The first thing that caught them was the trees. Again their eyes were drawn skyward as they beheld a small wood. Very terrestrial trees were thriving in the heart of Ares Britannia. Some were exotic like abiu and masau while others were easily recognizable like citrus and apple. The shorter trees were nestled among stout pines and sugar maples that stretched to the heights. The deck was covered with soil, turf, fallen pine quills and dried leaves. About the slight trunks was every variation of shrubs, some flowering in full bloom. The rush of a brook could be heard all around. The smell was rustic and living. In Mars' red stare the flow of air carried white tufts of seed drifting slowly in its unseen hands.

"But where's the water?" Sandra asked. "How does water flow here?"

"It runs beneath the floor, ma'am," Officer Vecihi answered, enveloped in his surroundings. "It runs beneath the soil and the insulation even inside some of the supporting beams. All part of the submersives. The algae blooms and recycling vats use all this." Waving his hands out broadly he said, "This is what you can do when you've got something this big. There's nothing like this anywhere else. Nowhere else in the universe. Hiçbir şey, nothing." Sandra found the information a tad unsettling.

"Wait till you see the Aviary," Beckett.

"You keep birds on Phobus?" Sandra asked, doubting whether or not to take the term literally. "Surely birds can't fly here. Can they?"

"Ah yes!" Vecihi answered for him, "most cannot but some, quails, different kinds. Bok herif, very good." Sandra had no understanding of Turkish, but gathered that Vecihi's hand motion behind his backside translated the meaning. "And bees!" he added, "some bugs fly too. They need to relearn but when they do they fly." With courteous apologies Beckett informed them that a full tour would be provided once settled.

As the group began to make their way again Vecihi paused. He had a nose for the submersive balance. He drew in long breaths, looking for the musty organic smells that indicated a healthy, breathing system. He became perplexed by some acrid smell he didn't recognize. His first thought was that it must be some rot or uncontrolled fungus. Decomposition was all part of the equation so that didn't indicate misgivings if the progress was kept in check. This was something else. A smell he couldn't make out. That was disconcerting. You should never smell something unexpected be it on a liner, orbital or stationary platform. He made a mental note to investigate. It was due time for him to take up his duties as the life science officer. Most of that was spent in rubber trousers laying out flat under deck plating in the slime ridden underpinnings of any submersive substructure. Might as well get to it as that's how he'd spend the rest of his days.

Their quarters were originally intended of the platform's officers, though they were recently renovated for just this occasion. They were arranged in concentric circles within the scope of a secondary dome. At least the travelers were accustomed to living in arching staterooms though now laid out on their sides. The women's quarters were separate and a ways distance from the men's. They of course were lead there first and the remaining party then moved on. The rooms themselves were very small, much smaller than any ocean or space liner they'd ever seen. They were significantly smaller than the accommodations on the Daedalus.

Boswell couldn't hold his tongue, "We're trading gravity and elbow room for floating about in vaulted crypts? Nothing but the entire universe above us and we are relegated to living in mausoleums. These rooms make the ship's look palatial."

"Nonsense," Cleland spoke inappropriately loud so everyone could hear. "We've spent months on that vessel and will be back again in a few days. You're on Phobus, man! Come rest your head in the guest-house of the personification of Fear and Terror! I'm sure his vaporous minions will soon be round to induce nothing but the most frightful dreams!"

Boswell shied away, rubbing the birthmark on his head.

"Which reminds me," Cleland continued, "someone retrieve my periodicals. I've a prime selection for frights and night terrors. I'm very happy to share them if anyone else is looking for a bit of a jolt."

Beckett cordially showed each traveler the room that had been assigned to each one respectively and each one entered with curious expressions. The Daedalus crew assisted the servants with the bags, trunks and sundry cases. The circular hall looked just like an ocean liner before castoff. Dr. Boswell caught Beckett's attention and said, "Give me twenty minutes or so after the crew brings round the luggage and I'll head to the infirmary. Can you, ah, take me there or will someone here on Ares orient me?"

"The infirmary?" Beckett asked.

"Yes, of course," Boswell answered giving Listonn a blank look.

"Yes," Listonn broke in, "the infirmary. Dr. Boswell here is going to check on the condition of the personnel and we need him to start in the infirmary."

"Oh," Beckett replied, "I get you. Just that no one's infirm at the moment. Peruse the infirmary all you'd like, just there's a great lack of the infirm you see. Running a clean ship up here."

"Well," Boswell looked at the floor, "makes my work easier. I'll make a holiday of this yet. Still, let me stop off there to familiarize myself. We brought quite a few medical stores so I can certainly help get that sorted."

"Dr. Crohne keeps all that in order," Beckett countered, "we'll need him to unkey the lockup."

"Unkey?" Listonn asked.

"Yes," Beckett explained, "that bit of a gear box thing that does the locking and unlocking. Very well, I'll take you there as soon as you'd like." Just then a few of the crew came floating up with more bags. Nods all around, the three separated to attend to the practical demands of the moment. As Boswell turned up the hall he passed Cleland's open door. He was in his room rummaging about the far wall.

Not bothering to ask, Boswell allowed himself in, "Damn cramped no matter what you say," he said pulling himself through the doorway. "Damn well smaller than the Daedalus."

Cleland looked back briefly, "Well James, we just can't expect creature comforts in a land without creatures."

"I recall talk of creatures back in the solarium."

"Indigenous creatures, my man," Cleland corrected, still intent with the stained wood paneling of his stateroom wall.

"Of course. What are you doing?"

"I feel a draft."

"Drafty old place in a land without drafts, the place gets all the more contradictory."

"Man brought the creatures and man brought the draft. Wind blows artificially up here. All part of Officer Hürkuş' submersives. Not been keeping your ears perked, James. What were you on about in the hallway?" Cleland asked, his back still toward Boswell as he felt along the moldings and edge-work on the wall.

"Nothing really, just got to find the infirmary at some point. Though I hear they have a great lack of infirmity around here."

"Disappointed then? Perhaps you were expecting mining or building injuries to keep you occupied. Bloody stumps and broken ribs? Difficult to fall down a mine shaft in a land with no falling."

"No, not all that. You've got so many people living up here and no brickets. Every colony in space gets brickets. Studied through the veritable encyclopedia of its pathology before we left. The doctors back home were ghoulishly looking forward to my field notes. All on about progressive stages and relating one symptom to another. Which reminds me, I should confer with Vecihi on the status of the fauna. It affects them too."

"Oh, Boswell, you continually mistake me for someone who's listening."

"Oh, Cleland, you're listening. You're always listening. You've so much to hear even when no one's speaking. Now I'll have my fun when I take inventory of the elixirs. I hypothesize that all the bottles furthest back will be a few pours light."

"And why do you so hypothesize, dear doctor?"

"Oh I've mentioned my suspicions but now I'm almost sure Wilson's been lapping up the sauce."

"And how would he come by it?"

"Argyle, the little prig. He slips his little brown arse past the cooking stores and helps himself. Thick as thieves those two. And Argyle is a minion of many talents."

"Well," Cleland added, getting frustrated with his search. "Can you blame the man? Making up for Crossland's lack of foresight. Why not just tap the flask Wilson keeps at his vest and smell the vintage - hey, oh!" Cleland shouted.

"What is it?" Boswell pulled forward attempting to look over Cleland's shoulder.

"Get the door, man, shut it." Fumbling about like a marionette, Boswell turned and secured the door behind him. He gave a quick glance in the hall and saw others busying themselves, absorbed in their unpacking.

"Look what we have here," Cleland spread out his fingertips and pressed upon the panel that lay between his hammock and a small nightstand. With just the right push, it slipped back and giving it a slight tug, slid sidelong into the panel next to it.

"What do we have here?" Boswell asked. There on the end table was an electric torch lamp, called a brandish, resembling a wax candle without flame. He twisted it around in his hands finally coming upon how to turn it on. Grabbing hold of the door frame he pulled himself into the aperture he's discovered. Inside was a small crawl space, but it wasn't so small that he couldn't move about comfortably. The passage was lined with pipes, cables and wires. It ran lengthwise across the back wall. He could even make out the metal steps of a staircase of sorts to his right. Boswell came up behind him and poked his head inside. "So Crossland has all kinds of little secrets hidden about the place," Boswell said with an impish savor.

Cleland waxed sardonic, "Be less dense. It's probably a service shaft, disguised as paneling for cosmetic reasons. I'm sure the other rooms must be similarly equipped." Wide eyed and excited, Cleland turned to face Boswell, "Check your room when you return. Tell no one of this! Or I swear I'll have the tongue from your head!"

"Right," Boswell replied with a smiling chortle and an edge of insecurity. "Mums and all. What are you thinking, John? Look in on mousetraps and cobwebs on Mars?"

Cleland smiled reflectively, "I think I know where we can stash our opium but I also think I'm thinking a whole lot more." The two shared a childlike, devilish smile and Cleland drew himself back into the room and pulled the hidden panel back into place.

Chapter E (5):
The Land of Shinar

Crossland and Royden made their way to the base of Babel Tower. It was only a short distance from the staterooms and as before they didn't see another soul along the way. "Where is everyone?" Gavin asked, "don't we pay builders to build?"

"Building elsewhere," was Royden's only answer. When reaching the tower's base, Gavin could instantly see that it was clearly an afterthought in the design. Stylistically it was all out of place, thrust rudely down into the more elegant forms of the interlocking domes. It leveraged the load-bearing structures where three domes met, but was effectively bolted into place with crude patchworks of metal. The rounded wall sections did appear hand beaten as he was sure they must be. There were no shipments from earth that included plating fashioned for this purpose.

"So instead of a mooring tower you built Jacob's ladder? Mars wasn't already high enough?"

Royden offered no reply. The doorway wasn't readily apparent. There was a section of the brazen plates looked like they could be slid aside but there was not a latch or handle for doing so. The only feature of note was a copper yack-mouth thrust out of the wall on the right. "So we call for him then I take it?" Crossland asked. Royden nodded and slipped forward.

"Allow me," he said. Lifting off the mouthpiece, he tapped its cone shaped end with his index finger and called out, "Uh, Dr. Crohne? Tom here. Um, I have Gavin Crossland with me. He's just arrived and wanted a word. I know we have the gathering later but he insisted. Can we pop on up?" There was a long pause.

Crossland looked up to the gloomy spires in the ceiling where the tower met the roof. He began getting impatient, but Royden ignored him and waited. Something metallic clashed behind the skin of the tower. Like someone had dropped something heavy as impossible as that was. Royden got his feet planted and then effortlessly pulled aside an enormous portion of the tower wall. "As you please," he said, inviting Crossland to enter.

Gavin gave the inside a quick look before he passed in, seeing a wide array of pipes and tubes, some of which were leaking steam and spitting globules of water, making the air inside thick and malodorous. Some of the copper tubing had corroded into white and turquoise streaks. The interior was otherwise barren. Nothing but empty space.

Royden, following him in, pointed upwards, “There’s a railing just over there,” he said “but just takes a good jump to get up to the top.” Having no proper way of bounding up a tower, Sir Royden crouched a bit and then sprang up, quickly rising up into the shadows and then pulling himself up by the railing on the wall. Much more awkwardly, Gavin tested his footing to make a similar attempt. Quickly giving up, he took hold of the railing at its base and pulled himself up to the top hand-over-hand. In the lofty ceiling, there was a pressure door mounted in the centre that was thankfully illuminated by small electric lights. Royden drifted over to it and grabbing the wheel, spun it on its well-oiled screw until it popped upwards. He pulled himself in and looked back at Crossland who did his best to do the same.

Crossland’s eyes were strained as he entered having adjusted to the seeping dark of the tower’s interior. The room above was awash in the red glow of Mars. He squinted to allow his eyes to adjust. As his vision cleared, the bulbous interior of the tower’s masthead was difficult to comprehend. It was like examining the contents of a dream room confounded by half-conscious thoughts. At every angle the room seemed ephemeral, incorporeal. He couldn’t determine which way to look. A ring of windows surrounded the room’s widest point. They made a red glowing circle of rectangles that stared out into the aether. Mars’ full glory dominated the forward view, staining the interior blood-red. Aside from the windows there wasn’t any empty space. Every other surface, floors, walls and ceiling was covered with a complex assortment of instruments, glass, shifting machines, crackling electronics and pulsing hydraulics. It was like everything in the room stabbed oppressively inward at its occupants, pointing at its centre and invading the open space. Instruments like sharp scalpels, needles and bone saws gave the sense that a clutch of mad surgeons were about to descend upon every living organ.

“Mr. Crossland!” came a welcoming voice from somewhere slightly behind and above him on the right. Gavin turned around in the circular pressure hatch to look up that way and saw Dr. Christien Burill Crohne, a man he only knew from pen for these long years. Crohne floated up near the ceiling beneath a workbench affixed above him. He had spun around to face them, wearing a dark apron that covered him from chest to toe with lashes that tied around his thighs and calves. He also wore dark gloves that stretched up past his elbows. His apparel almost perfectly camouflaged him in the dark space. He had ample gray hair and was clean shaven, the rims of thin round glasses shined in the light.

"Ah, Dr. Crohne," Gavin said finally pulling up out of the hatch. Royden helped draw him up and then closed it neatly behind him.

"Doctor you say?" Crohne asked as he pushed off from the wall to glide down to him. "I'm afraid I've been out of practice too long to deserve that title." Crohne's face was deep lined and worn, furrowed with more than just age, despite the puffy, inflated features of a space-dweller.

"Yes," Gavin said trying to work his feet to take hold of the deck plating. "The others just called you 'doctor' so I thought it was customary." Coming up beside him, Crohne removed his gloves and offered his hand,

"Mr. Crossland," Crohne smiled with a firm shake, "after ten years of letters and now to finally meet. It must be well past a decade by now."

"Yes, finally," Crossland answered, still swaying to steady himself. "And it's been wonderful corresponding. As you instructed in your last letter, I did pass along that sealed envelope to my wife. Letters from Mars, she was the talk of her ladies' auxiliary. And per your instructions she didn't reveal its contents. So be assured your wishes were honored." Gavin paused, prompting Crohne to fill in the blanks.

"I'm sure," Crohne said, holding Gavin's hand and shoulder until he found his footing. "I take it that Mrs. Crossland and your children are all well. And to assure you, you look well for your first time in space, like you were born here."

"Ha," Gavin said nodding, "hardly. I thought I'd gained my legs on the trip out but not so much it seems. And yes, I left my family well, but understandably concerned."

"Well," Crohne replied, "Life on Phobus is hardly comparable to life on a liner. It's just different enough to make you start over again till you get the hang of it. Our bodies possess a design flaw that we just can't revise. Now I'm dreadfully sorry that you came all the way up here, I feel amiss. I had every intention of joining you once I made some last minute preparations."

"Not at all," Gavin answered, "no trouble at all. I was rather curious about this place. You failed to mention it in any of your letters or blueprints. Unless of course that you included them in that post to my wife."

"Yes," Crohne replied, "but Gavin you've only just arrived. We should get you settled and then have a proper time to update you on our status."

"Well you see," Gavin said, "that's just it. We need to confer before settling."

"Go on," prompted Crohne.

"So, first I have some questions, you see I'm quite at a loss and I'm sure our guests expected me to be in the know. If I'd known the mooring tower wasn't in place I could have readied them appropriately."

"Ah," Crohne interjected. "Sir Royden," he said turning. Royden sprung to attention. "I have some tea brewing in the press, right over there. Fill a few flasks for us."

"Um," Royden replied, pointing back toward the entry hatch. "Allen will be coming up too."

"I took the liberty to ask him to join us," Gavin spoke up.

"Alright," Crohne said, "I suppose we'll need four flasks then. I'll unlatch the tower door for him." Giving Gavin a courteous nod, Crohne effortlessly drifted over to a contraption of gears and protruding levers. Royden shoved off and floated up toward where a piping set of glass-work was being warmed by an electric element. Shifting this lever and that, Crohne called back, "Now to your questions."

"Well," Crossland stated, fumbling, "doesn't seem like there's time to properly address everything."

"I'm sure I can surmise your questions," Crohne said, "perhaps you'd allow me and that will allow you to be more specific?"

"Yes, please."

Crohne completed a complex set of adjustments at the lever-box. The metallic clank was heard echoing up the tower. Pushing off again from the levers Crohne drifted back, talking nonchalantly all the way.

"First off," Crohne said, "I'm sure you're concerned about the missing mooring tower and likewise you were startled to find this tower instead." Gavin nodded in agreement. Crohne continued, "I had the tower built so we could best manage the mining operations. The original intention was to ensure greater safety precautions, but then it became more necessary for previously unforeseen reasons. The initial concern was that we may be unaware of a disaster at the dig until any rescue opportunity was lost. The tower served to better oversee the building projects as well.

This surveillance then evolved to also assist with matters of accountability. Given limitations of supply, the mooring tower was forfeit. To be plain, we have a labor problem here on Phobus."

"Yes, yes," Gavin replied scratching the back of his head. "As Royden was appraising me. He told me about this Barabbas chap stirring up the miners."

"Oh," Crohne said turning, "What did you tell him, Tom?"

Royden sailed back with the tea. The flasks were globular and he needed both arms folded to hold them to his chest. Each glass globe had a bent flute-like pipette that stuck out of one end. Landing alongside them he passed one to each, retaining the extra for Havelock-Allen. Gavin had yet to use that style of receptacle. Crohne nodded his appreciation and receiving his glass he rolled it in his hands demonstratively, allowing the tea to fill the flute and warming his hands with its contents. He took a quick sip, a rubber gasket below the stem drawing in air.

"Ah, yes sir," Royden replied, "Allen and I both were telling him, really. Not in front of the others mind, Mr. Crossland came over alone." Crohne waited looking undividedly at Royden who continued, "Just that uh, we've had, disputes, between the camps and that they, the mining camp, have their demands and uh, we only have estimates as per their precise productivity."

"And you mentioned Barabbas," Crohne added.

"Yes," Royden said, "we, I mean I, mentioned Barabbas."

"So tell me," Gavin asked, "what about this mysterious union organizer?"

Crohne considered for a moment. Then he said, "The miners' believe that if they conceal the identity of this anonymous fellow then he can't be sacked. We can't very well replace the entire crew so it's a well-considered concealment though with almost all certainty it's Othello."

"They mentioned him also," Gavin said, "who's that now?"

"Othello," Crohne answered, "is what they call the chief mining official. Sans their alleged organizer he's their leader though, in fairness, he does also possess supervisory responsibilities. He was a great asset really he has a great deal of lunar experience prior to coming to Mars. His name's Didier but mostly the builders call him Othello. He's a dark skinned man you see and some thought him a Mohammadan and perhaps even Moorish, which led down the Shakespearian path and so on. But he claims that he's merely their spokesman, just Barabbas' yack-mouth or perhaps more aptly his clapper." Just then the pressure hatch spun open and Havelock-Allen's well cropped head came into view. Looking around quickly he caught Crohne's eye. "Allen," Crohne spoke up greeting him. "Come join us, Tom here has tea for you." Culverton drew himself up from the hole, closed and sealed the door behind him with more clashing metal. "We were just telling Gavin about our imaginary friend Barabbas."

"Oh?" Culverton asked.

"So," Gavin asked addressing Culverton, "the Royals getting settled? No, ah, incidents?"

Culverton just shook his head.

"Good to hear," Crohen continued. "Piter and Miser are with them?" Havelock-Allen nodded. "On their best behavior I trust."

"Yes," Culverton answered, "I spoke to them."

"Good," Crohen said, "let's finish this and attend to them personally. So then," he said returning back to Gavin, "Let's clear up this Barabbas rumor. Since the mining operation is such a discrete section of Ares they holed themselves up past the choker and erected their own little fiefdom. The life support out there further granted their autonomy. They then controlled all access to the excavations, exploratories, pre-production, they assumed full control - out of sight but never of mind - and invariably we hadn't accounted for this in the design. Tom here was literally beside himself. Simply a management nightmare. Once the miners began obfuscating their activities we countered with this place. Gave us God's own vantage."

Taking a moment to consider, Gavin asked, "So they increased productivity once they knew you were looking down on them?"

"Precisely," Crohen answered, "in effect we called their bluff. They'd have to move the operations to the other side of Phobus to act covertly. They'd need us to build that for them. Come see for yourself." In a near effortless motion, Crohen pushed up off his toes, spun thirty degrees clockwise and swept toward the windows. Culverton joined him though more energetically. Royden stopped to give Gavin a polite smile and offered to help him. With an equally polite declination, Gavin chose to keep mostly to the floor. Though this was more difficult with all the protrusions in his way. In the end, he did have to spring up to see out the window and the enormous orb of Mars was there to look back at him. Crohne inhaled deeply, "Nothing short of majesty. Nothing short of purest majesty," but his words went right past Gavin who was lost in the immersive moment.

Gavin looked down across the breadth of his design. No artistic rendering or architectural model had grasped it. The lonely sparse outcroppings of rock cast long shadows across the red-washed dusty plain. The natural intricacies of the ridges and intersecting craters created a landscape that wasn't oft found on earth - undisturbed natural beauty. And to now look down on Ares itself; Ares Britannia. Ares was nothing like the lunar establishments like Brighton's Tranquility or the German's Goldene Zeitalter. Ares had the stately air of a monument. Ares was a wonder. Ares orbited an alien sphere on an unsullied frontier. The greatest frontier. The greatest frontier ever pioneered in the history of man.

"So look around us!" Crohne announced breaking into Gavin's thoughts. "I needn't give you a topographical lesson. Is it as you imagined? The ridge there is Drunlo crater off to our left, and Clustril's the one behind that. To our right you see Reldrsal and you can easily make out Flimnap just south of that. And there is our primary refinery, perched on the near end of Stinkney's crater. The mist you see rising from the stacks shows that the furnace is burning hot just as we'd expect from a bustling operation. You can see some activity off to the left there too, right along Stickney's upper lip. They're rummaging around under the eastern excavation. They're extracting ore my friend and ore by the shiploads."

Still transfixed, Gavin asked, "Is there a scope on-hand?"

Smiling broadly, Crohne said, "Allen, you'll find one in the cupboard just over there."

Culverton rushed off and opened the doors of a roundish cupboard that poked out from the floor and returned with a telescoping glass. He passed it to Gavin. Gavin accepted it gratefully and quickly brought it to his eyes. He scanned all along the grand edge of Phobus' deepest crater. Stickney made Phobus look like a potato with a bite deeply dug out of one end. That enormous gouge faced Mars in its tidally locked position. It was still hard to make out through the glass but there were men on the ridge. At least three of them. Each one was tied to the other in a draping, floating tether. They probed the rocks and were tapping with serrated hammers. They were conducting a resource evaluation. It was a procedure that Gavin had a basic understanding. Ares was not only a spectacle, but it was fulfilling its purpose. Ares Britannia was alive.

"Where is it? Where is the famous Monolith of Phobus?" Gavin asked. "I know it's near Stickney but where? Can we see it from here?"

"You can see the monolith," Crohne assured. "It's right there," he said pointing. "We've measured it now. It's 284 feet and 5 inches straight up out of the Phoban soil. It's like the hand of a titan stabbed it into the ground with one resounding blow. You could almost believe that someone placed it there but it's all fancy. This place is as dead as the day it was formed." Crohne grew quiet. From his peripheral vision he watched Gavin adrift in the moment. His face betrayed a complex mixture of emotions not the least of which being a sudden release of tension, the ease of reassurance.

"Christien," Gavin said gravely, "it's nothing short of paramount that we keep word of the miners from the others. If Listonn discovers that his ten-year investment is in jeopardy of unionization Othello and his lot will suffer the consequences of their folly and take us with them. Listonn couldn't convince the board to shut down the platform, but he could put an end to us. He could take this all away from us."

"He will never suspect," Crohne replied. "This place won't be wrested from us, Gavin. We've labored too long, my friend. Given up too much."

"I don't think Listonn will require a tour of the mine, he hates the weightlessness, he'll keep to central where he'll be more comfortable or may even return to the Daedalus. I might just suggest that to him. He'll want a look at the books though. He's a damnable bean counter."

"Sir Royden is our man for that charge," Crohne said giving Royden a proud look. Royden himself nodded slowly with a hint of doubt in his expression.

"I can assist with that also," Gavin added, "we'll just need to keep him distracted. Put a sparkle in his eyes to mask the more unsettling numbers."

"And we shall," Crohne affirmed, "There are many marvelous distractions here on Phobus, distractions of the most absorbing nature."

Chapter F (6): Reconstituted Ambrosia

Adjusting to life on the Daedalus was difficult, but the first hours on Ares were already proving more so. The travelers were only to spend a few, tightly scheduled days but that required entirely new adaptations for the duration. The Daedalus had maintained a day and night schedule that mimicked the equivalent on earth. The ship's interior lights would slowly fade at dusk and rise again at dawn. Phobus had a much more complex array of light and shadow. Tidally locked, one face of the natural satellite always looked upon Mars, just as earth's moon did back home.

The location of Ares Britannia was set near its northern pole, but offset toward the side that faced Mars. A day on Mars was roughly equivalent to one on earth, but Phobus revolved around Mars in less than eight hours. In the time spent between the ship's arrival and the call to the reception, sunlight stretched from one side of the platform to the other and snuffed out completely when they passed over Mars' night side. When the Daedalus arrived it was in the dark of early morning. With the rest period cut short, the reception dinner effectively became lunch.

With the guests getting settled there was a great deal to accomplish ahead of the christening, at least for the servants, crew and residents of the platform. Members of the building crew crept out from Ares' shadowy reaches. They were coarse but amicable sorts. Each one possessed that puffy faced, gaunt legged appearance. They, of course, were on their best behavior among the dignitaries, the more abrasive of them were virtually quarantined. Royden made sure of that. Argyle, along with the other cooks on the Daedalus, was escorted to the kitchens and introduced to their counterparts on Ares. There were special stores set aside for the reception and the other meals planned around the christening.

As the travelers unpacked, Argyle and his fellows received final directions as per the makeup of the kitchens and dining halls. Almost intuitively, the guest discovered a short table holding an arrangement of curiosities just inside the door to their rooms. The objects included a set of small wooden cylinders that could be uncapped at one end. There was also an inkwell, plugged up with a rubber stopper, a kind of quill and a box containing thin strips of paper. They were placed strategically below a set of brass tubes that stretched up along the wall by the door and disappeared into the ceiling pipes on a cathedral organ. Somehow, without so much as a single instruction, each one eventually determined that they could scrawl short orders on those paper slips and place them in the wooden cylinders. That message capsule was then placed in a suction tube that would deliver it quickly to the kitchens. Warrant Officer Vecihi pointed out that even this was part of the platforms respiratory system. Other tubes were dedicated to deliver other sorts of messages but they weren't the call of the hour. Drink orders started jetting about Ares Britannia.

Argyle proved to be very adaptable and demonstrated that he also was learned in mixing cocktails. No-one had cause to complain that their request wasn't prepared to order despite the obvious constraints. Given such, the tasks of the cooking and wait staff had all been reinvented with the greatest ingenuity. All the glassware was basically globular but varied in shapes and sizes. Some were more ovular or elongated than others. Red wine glasses and snifters were of course wider but failed to allow the aroma to escape. Some obstacles couldn't be surmounted. Regardless, the spherical theme carried its own remarkable aspect. It lent a style to space-faring which had an appeal even to the most discerning tastes. It was modern, space-aged. It bore its own sense of privilege that carried the special notes that Tyneside wanted and meticulously designed. All the glassware had that distinctive fine sipping stem that also permitted contents to be injected into the receptacle via baffled pouches the servants carried under their arms. The server would insert a slender lance into the stem and with a squeeze of their arm, inject the wine, brandy, etc. just nicely.

Regular meals on Ares were quite frankly plain in the most painful sense of the word. Soups were a staple, the soup-globes functioning similarly to the glasses with appropriately larger stems. Argyle, used to cooking in all kinds of extremes including bivouacs and foxholes, had prepared for this challenge. The reception dinner would require a wide array of both fresh and reconstituted vegetables and the fresh slaughter of a pygmy steer. Argyle had been expertly trained by chefs back on earth as per the dishes to be served though his instructors had only a conceptual understanding of how they should be prepared while weightless.

Ice to chill the drinks was never an issue as the cold of Phobus made freezing a simple exercise. Heat for cooking was more difficult to muster and relied on pumps back to the platform's energy wells. The ovens were heated by generator exhausts, siphoned up into the kitchens in precise amounts as selected by the cooks. This was a highly integrated system where every unit of heat was precisely measured and incorporated into the balancing act of the bio-submersives. The charge of the Life Science officer included accounting for the need to prepare meals. Not so much as a single thermal unit was wasted as Vecihi would point out. The various pots and pans were all covered by precisely tooled lids that contained small valves to either contain or release pressure. The livestock carried aboard were also part of the submersive balance. After just a short time in space, their muscles would atrophy which made for very tender and succulent selections. Even the toughest portions took on a veal-like quality which won over the worst critics.

The dining hall was the pride of Ares as it thrust out across the dusty rocks on the platform's northwest side. The virgin, untouched lunar surface was dredged out to cradle the long hall across the face of Phobus and the tall windows were set to receive the kiss of far reaching rays from the sun. Similar to the domes, the darkened fire-blasted copper and brass metal struts made a cage like construction that jutted out offering a spectacular panorama.

As the crew and servants from the Daedalus entered they couldn't help but stop to stargaze. Yellow electric lights were affixed to the widest pillars along its length that sputtered like burning candles. Similar fixtures of cold flame were spaced along the centre line of the dining table. The long table was an engineering marvel in itself. Finely inset craftsmanship of wood, stone and steel made for an artful presentation and many compensatory functions. The flatware was sterling at its face but the underside was purified steel polished to a luster. Magnetic points at each place setting held the utensil perfectly. Likewise, the glassware also had metal bases, clips and fasteners that kept them from floating about the room. Each plate was covered by a metal dome and often the diner would raise the lid to find that a particular course stuck to the top as well as the saucer portion.

The dining utensils themselves needed some minor modifications. Knives and forks were largely the same aside from their fasteners but spoons more resembled tongs with small opposing bowls at each end. In this way they could be used in the traditional way but also to grasp small morsels and consumed without muss. Recipes intended for fine dining in weightless spaces most always included some highly viscous sauces that adhered the portions to either the plate or the perfectly fitting lid. By holding the lid firmly in one hand the diner had their other free to select their precut portion with either spoon or fork without anything floating around.

Meal preparations required the chefs to slice the larger portions to bite size as the diner could not be expected to hold both the lid in one hand and cut the morsel with the other. After hours of preparations the time neared to serve. The staff lined up in rows around the table. It was painfully obvious which ones traveled with the contingent as opposed to those inducted from the building crew. The natives of Ares were able to find their way perfectly upright at attention while the newcomers fumbled and swayed in vain attempts to stand in place.

Neatly printed seating arrangement and menu cards were affixed to each place setting. Below the diner's name the courses were finely hand lettered and included the following list of courses.

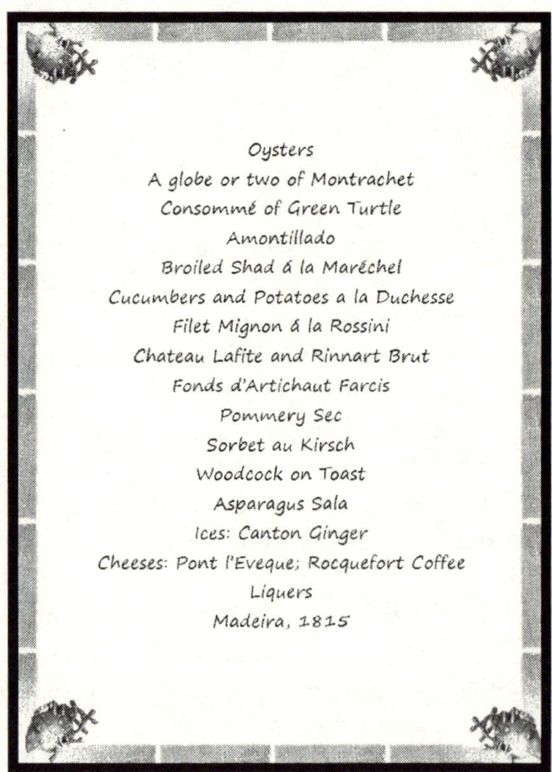

Oysters
A globe or two of Montrachet
Consommé of Green Turtle
Amontillado
Broiled Shad á la Maréchel
Cucumbers and Potatoes a la Duchesse
Filet Mignon á la Rossini
Chateau Lafite and Rinnart Brut
Fonds d'Artichaut Farcis
Pommery Sec
Sorbet au Kirsch
Woodcock on Toast
Asparagus Sala
Ices: Canton Ginger
Cheeses: Pont l'Eveque; Rocquefort Coffee
Liquers
Madeira, 1815

All these preparations nearing completion, the staff waited expectantly for their guests to arrive. They lined up along the walls behind the row of chairs on either side. Attached to magnetized channels in the floor, each chair had been pulled back awaiting their designated diner.

***

Crossland briskly made his way back to his quarters with Royden at his heels. He avoided contact with the others as he entered the rounded hallway to the staterooms. Proceeding into his room, he thankfully found that his personal belongings had all been delivered. They both stepped in and shut the door behind them. Stowing Royden in one corner, Gavin hurriedly rummaged for his vest and dinner jacket. They hardly had the chance to say a word when someone rapped at his door.

"Yes?" Gavin answered, arresting his progress.

"Crossland?" came a muffed voice, "where've you been?"

"Thomas," Gavin replied, "come in and meet another Thom." The pressure hatch spun and in wafted Listonn dressed to the nines but a bit flustered. His hair had been plastered to his head in a vain attempt to tame it which certainly wasn't a good look for him. His suit was black and he wore a Tyneside green sash in his lapel. Monocle clenched in his right eye, he turned to see Royden, somewhat cringing in the corner.

"Hello, sir," Listonn said, wobbling a bit before getting his footing.

"Very good to meet you," Royden said warmly. "My pleasure. I'm Sir Thomas Bland Royden, general manager of this establishment."

"A pleasure, truly a pleasure," Listonn replied shaking his hand vigorously. "My name's Tom Listonn as Gavin indicated. Now you are a Baronet correct, sir?"

"Yes," Royden replied almost bashfully, "the first such in my case, bit of dusty old history really," he said dismissively. Gavin, effectively abandoning Royden, went back into his luggage to find his dinner dress, a deep maroon jacket that was almost black. He picked off lint as he might, the garment billowing out in the weightless air.

"Uh, Listonn," Gavin asked, "wasn't Vecihi supposed to come around with flowers, for our lapels?"

"Um," Listonn said, "ah, yes, the little man's been on-and-on about it. Prize English roses he says, but who the hell knows where he's been growing them. Might just have to retrieve them in the hall."

"Just right," Gavin replied, "let me just put some water on my face and we can be off. Sir Royden here was just briefing me on the progress. I'm sure you'll be quite pleased to hear."

"Yes?" Listonn replied, "Why yes, good to hear. Tell me," he said turning to Royden.

"Well," Royden said, "it's very good progress. Building projects and mining excavations and heat management. Lots of heating problems really. Heat makes for quite a task up here. Difficult just to vault off on really."

"Tom, Listonn I mean," Gavin said, making his way over to the washroom connected to his suite. "There'll be time for a full briefing. Let's get to know one another and enjoy our first meal on Ares."

"Of course, I'm frightfully sorry," Listonn said with a short bow. "just a bit bothered after that trip up the, whatever it is you call it, to the station."

"Oh and I do apologize for all that," Royden replied over him, "there's so much in the way of explaining to be done, resource constraints, cost savings measures. I know it was very inconvenient, but I believe when you examine the general ledger you'll be very pleased with the many, ah, considerations accounted for." Royden gave a twitching smile to both men. "Now if you'll excuse me, I have some preparations myself before dinner. We have many special arrangements planned. Must see them through. And I've heard nothing but fine things about your chef, Argyle is it? I figured he'd be a Scotsman but no matter. We don't get much fine dining up here. This will be one to remember. Mr. Listonn, I'm again very pleased and looking forward to talking more over dinner." Royden extended his hand again and they shook, again. With that, Royden excused himself and nudged his way through the pressure door, sealing it behind him.

Listonn took a few short steps, dragging himself along to the washroom door, "He's a twitchy sort," he said.

Looking up from the elaborate faucet fixtures and washcloths, Gavin looked out toward the entry and said, "That he is. Like all these sorts out in space I think. It gets to them."

"Quite," Listonn agreed, "You could have told me you were going to disappear like that. The others all badgered me to no end. We're the Tyneside reps so it's expected that we're joined at the hip.

"I know, I know," Gavin said, "I just needed to look in on things before we brought over the contingent, you know, to make sure there were no more surprises."

"Right call there," Listonn said, "And? Are there any more surprises?"

"There's a lot of the unexpected here, Tom, but I'll give it to them, they're the ones here on Mars. They deal with this every day. Easy enough to sit back at home and stare up at them. The pragmatic has to take precedence. One disaster up here and we lose the whole lot. These people are heroes. Damn heroes for what they've accomplished up here."

"No need to sing that song. I bleed Tyneside same as you."

Gavin paused to give Listonn a concerned and questioning stare, "How are you feeling, Tom? You look a bit peaked."

"Me?" Tom said, leaning in to look at his face in the mirror. "No, I'm right as rain just not made for outer-spacefaring. I thought I was going to retch after that jaunt over," he said shaking his head.

"Well don't fight it, Tom, stay back on the Daedalus, the centrifuge will at least keep you upright. Might be better for the digestion."

"No," Listonn returned raising his voice a bit and steadying himself against the door frame "I didn't book the flight to sit on the aeroplane."

"Especially with no stewardesses providing distractions," Gavin said smiling. Listonn shared a smile back.

"Princess Sandra is enough of that," Listonn admitted, "if it weren't for that battle-axe at her side." They both laughed at that.

"And there is always Mrs. Listonn to consider wasting away with worry while her husband trips between planets. Right then," Gavin said seriously. "Let's you and I stay tight and quiet. We'll divide and conquer. Anything you learn you tell me and I'll do the same. We'll give this place a good looking over for good measure. Bit of an audit. We tell the others nothing, that's not why they're here. It's Tyneside business. They just don't understand this all like we do, Tom. We can't expect them to. Let's keep it in the family."

"Right," Listonn said emphatically. "I agree whole heartedly. "Best join forces and manage this, just like we discussed at length back on Earth. Rapper Dance for Tyneside."

Gavin, smiled brightly. "Tyne and Wear Yo-ho!" he sang back with a clenched fist and Listonn joined in, "Tyne and Wear Yo-ho!" Both clapped each other on the shoulders and made off toward the dining hall.

***

Gavin had originally wanted to bring a string quartet with them, but limitations weren't conducive. If he had found a way, at just this time, the four would be playing hymns including "Song d'Autome" and "Nearer my God to Thee." Instead, Royden had discovered that three of the builders had formed an amateur trio and sang to amuse themselves. One of the few pastimes they enjoyed aside from card games and arguments over the facing of weightless dice. So the three men had been promised extra shifts off if they performed a selection that wasn't bawdy or in any way offensive. He first asked them for something pious or patriotic but nothing qualified in their repertoire.

They at last arrived at a few folk tunes that Royden hoped would be appropriate for guests of their refinement. Perhaps the rustic tones would be somehow appropriate given their natural surroundings. So each of the three were given servant's uniforms, they were bathed and shaven - at least partially shaven - haircuts, fingernails cleaned and trimmed and shoes buffed. Even with all these attempts their baser nature was evident. Slouching, brushing hair out of their eyes to paste it over their balding scalps and wiping runny noses on their white servant's gloves. The three stood at the far end of the dining hall, just where it curved out with the scene of the brilliant star-field behind them. Royden listened intently as they warmed up. Their burly voices were rough but adequate. The first tenor led off with, "The Bay of Biscay" and the other two followed, deep and soulful.

The double doors at the far end swung open and a youthful Daedalus crewman announced the dinner. He called out their names with just the proper note of respect, "Sir Archdale Roland Knyvet Wilson, Second Baronet, Wilson, Baronetcy of Delhi, India and Right Honorable Francis Alabaster Beckett, Archdeacon of Bournemouth." The two walked in, largely ignoring their announcement, engrossed in conversation.

Beckett asked, "Really? But if the Americans take their war to the moon wouldn't that jeopardize trade with Ares?"

"Of course," Wilson said, "It's simply unprecedented. Defending orbital positions isn't at all similar to naval blockades like we know back home. The military implications will reinvent warfare. Our agreements with the Germans should suffice, but it's becoming another 'new world' up there." The two paused just past the doorway, Wilson looking stately in his tan uniform and brash display of military decorations. Beckett was in uniform as well but kept the religious regalia.

"Imagine it" Wilson continued, "there's no constables, magistrates or sheriffs on the moon. Multiple nations each staking their respective claims, holding fast to their sovereign rights. Prospectors combing the landscape looking for the richest deposit. The Yanks are a roguish lot. It's a wonder their lunar establishments haven't seceded from the union already." By that time Royden had made his way up along the rows of chairs to his right and joined the two conversationalists.

"Please allow me to interrupt," Beckett said, "but we must continue this as I have many other questions. Allow me to introduce you to Mr. Royden."

Leaning forward, Royden extended his hand. "A pleasure, sir," Royden said sincerely.

"The pleasure is mine," Wilson replied. "I must say, your accomplishment here is the pride of the Empire. And you should be the proudest among us." Royden swelled a bit, glancing back and forth up to the tall vicar and closer to eye level at Wilson.

"Oh, yes, thank you, um," Royden stammered. "Can I show you to your places?"

"Yes," Beckett said, "I made some requests per the arrangement."

"Of course," Royden replied. "You're here on the right next to the princess."

"No," Beckett said, "you must be mistaken I requested proximity to Sir Wilson. Can we make a quick switch?"

"Switch Wilson with the Princess?"

"No, sir," Beckett said, "Switch me with- no matter, not worth the fuss."

From behind them, the young crewman announced the next arrival and the youth snapping to a military salute, "Captain Charles Napier of the

HMS Daedalus." Smiling broadly at the boy, Napier clapped him on the shoulder.

"You look fine, lad," Napier said, "you do the ship proud." Beaming the youth stood at attention. Napier placed his cap under his arm and proceeded in regally.

"Ah, Charles," Wilson greeted, "first things first, meet Mr. Royden."

"Um, Sir Royden," he corrected, "Sir Thomas Bland Royden, uh, the first." Napier accepted Royden's handshake in his starched white glove, greeting him pleasantly.

"Beckett and I were just discussing the implications of an American civil war spreading to their lunar entrenchments," Wilson proceeded.

"Ever the armchair general, Archdale. You should have kept your commission," Napier replied.

"Balls," Wilson said, "old war horses and glue factories."

"You know Tranquility wouldn't receive us when we first passed," Napier said. That's why we needed to make for Goldene Zeitalter, at Tyco. Damn glad we found someone who spoke bloody English."

"I didn't realize," Wilson said, amazed.

"Clear violation of the Maunder Agreements. I intend to report it to the Extra Orbital Trade Authority upon our return. At least the Kaiser's men know how to play by the rules up here. How do I get a drink?" Napier asked looking to the servants.

"You mean you haven't used the letter tubes?" Wilson asked. "Of course you haven't, you're staying back at the ship." Turning to servants, Wilson echoed, "Get this fine man a brandy!" One of the servant girls pushed off from the wall and held out a drinking globe which Napier accepted with a nod.

"I'm not often one to drink before dinner but I'll have one myself," Wilson said. Beckett requested one also, but Royden refrained. As the drinks were dispensed into the glass spheres other guests arrived. Vecihi came in, Culverton with him. The young crewman announced them dutifully. "Ah, Culverton," Wilson welcomed with open arms. "Come over, we're just pouring drinks. Though I'll be damned if you can't get the brandy to warm in your palms. At least back on the ship a drink knows to stay in the glass."

"And piss knows to stay in the pot," Vecihi added. "The kitchen can warm the drinks. About the best we can do. Cold is easy, hot is difficult, very tricky to get right, very tricky." With a snap and a tick, Royden sent the servant to fetch warm drinks. Wilson made the introductions and doted on Culverton.

"Napier," Wilson said boldly, "I served with this man's father during the Indian Rebellion, Lieutenant General, Sir Henry Marshman Havelock-Allan, Order of the Bath. One of the best I served under. A great man. Man of the Empire."

"Pleasure, sir," Napier nodded.

"Now, Culverton," Wilson asked, "your father was with Brigadier-General John Nicholson during the storming of Delhi right?"

"Yes, sir," Culverton said in his straight but downcast way, "but um, we weren't traveling with him at the time."

"Of course not!" Wilson exclaimed, propelled by drink. "But no matter that. I'm sure you saw your father at many a triumphant moment.

"You see," Culverton said, "I left India when I was fairly young. In the summer of 18– I forget the year now. I had a nasty head injury and my father sent me to England for treatment. I was just a teenager. I was tended by the East India physicians, native as well. But when all failed they shipped me off. I was with my uncle when father was in Delhi. I heard stories though, from the letters he would send my uncle. He'd read parts of them to me. Thought that it was all part of my education."

"Sorry to hear that, son, what sort of injury?" Wilson asked.

"Nothing really," Culverton said dismissively, "just fell prey to some foolery."

"Come, son," Wilson said, "we all know how grim things got there."

"Um, there was a lot of unrest as you well know, especially in those days. The native boys would conceal themselves and throw rocks and broken glass at us, sometimes from rooftops. It was a bright hot steamy day just before the Kurbani holiday. My mates and I huddled to play ball along an abandoned street right near our estate. We played there numerous times. Nothing out of the ordinary. As far as I can reconstruct, there was a lad, Veejay, whose father was a rifleman in the brigade. He didn't like us white-skinned sorts and planned a bit of an ambush. He and his little mob took up positions in windows and along the roofs like battlements. When we were all in a nice tight circle picking sides they launched their assault. I think I was struck by a rail spike. I'm not sure. I lost my hearing in my right ear and also suffered loss of speech for a time.

They had a name for it but I've forgotten. Perhaps Dr. Boswell might know if I described it for him." Culverton took on a bewildered appearance like a wayward vagabond, like a malnourished orphan child slumped in a door frame He groped through dark patches of addled recollections.

"Well, good that you were properly seen to," Wilson said overlaying the awkwardness of Culverton's state, "bloody cowards those lads. Hope they got a thrashing back in kind. Your father was a good man to see you treated. If you'll indulge allow me to tell you a story,"

Wilson began, "This was also during the Mutiny and I was a young lion back then. Just commissioned with East India and eager to advance. The Sikhs still held parts of the Punjab and tales of the Retribution army were still all the talk. But the mutiny was an entirely other matter that none of us junior officers saw coming. When it broke, Nicholson took us all to Jullundur. Even in the saddle it was a back breaking passage. Brutal terrain in that country. Nothing but rocks and najas for miles. Wasn't the worst forced march but tedious I assure you. Arriving at the camp, we relieved the men and brought the officers to the mess. As custom dictates we had to wait for your father and Nicholson. They didn't show right away you see so we were all pensive after the ride out. And we could be a damn surly lot when hungry. Finally, Nicholson strides in along with your father and starts coughing loudly into his glove. So we all look over to them and he announces in a voice chill as the November Wyche, 'Sorry men, that I've kept you from your dinner,' he says plain as you like. And looking each of us in the eyes he says, 'but I've been hanging your cooks.'" Wilson took a pause, taking a long drink through the stem of his glass.

"Hanging the cooks?" Beckett asked.

"Yes!" and Wilson repeated, "'I've been hanging your cooks,' he says, just like that. Come to find that the native regimental chefs had poisoned the soup with aconite. That Nicholson was a wily sort. The Punjab did that to him. The Sikhs captured him you know. He suffered terribly while captive but he learned by damn, he learned. He ordered those brown bastards to taste their own meal and when they refused he fed it to a monkey. The little blighter died on the spot. Barely had a morsel and keeled right over. A tree right outside served as a gallows and he had them all strung up, no trial, no judge, executed them while we all sat waiting for our supper. Now Nicholson gave the order but you know, it was this man's father who strung them up personally," Wilson added pointing at Culverton with his hand that held the glass sphere. "That was the thing about Havelock-Allen and we all knew it. Chilling sort, your father. The Punjab made us all hard men but it was men like Sir Henry who brought it with them."

"Did you see the bodies?" Beckett asked.

"Of course we did," Wilson replied, "wasn't a toss from the mess but the sight of those hung bastards wasn't what stuck with me. It was the mettle of those men. Men whom without hesitation who threw up those ropes. Men like Henry who would wrap his hands around their throats, pull tight the knots and see them swing by his own hand. Nicholson, Havelock-Allen, all them in India during those days." Wilson gave a slow look over the small assembly. "They taught me well and good a lesson I'll never forget. To defeat guile you must understand guile. You must believe that people are capable of it. You must look it in the face and not allow it a flinch. Without indecision or second guesses it must be snuffed out. That's just the way of it. I understood on that day what it takes to defeat guile. I knew then that I'd follow those men to hell. Straight into the bloody maws of hell."

Beckett opened up again to ask another question, but he was stifled by more announcements at the door. Lady Cecilia Underwood and Princess Sandra proceeded in with her ladyship's attendants at each elbow. The men turned to greet them as appropriate when ladies enter. Lady Inverness had the more commanding presence, but Sandra made the grander entrance. Unassisted she had already learned to conduct herself with an air of elegance beyond what the others had mastered. She moved as if the weightless state was no longer a hindrance. Her dress was rigidly wired and magnetized, but the final length of her train was allowed to billow freely. It became a flare of color in her wake, alive with breath and fire. Her earrings were strings of diamonds, but nothing dangled, each fitting locked one stone to another in a serpentine curve. Her signature, key-shaped necklace was fastened with a spot of adhesive to her chest. Beckett noticed that it lay flat today raised up above the cleft of her breasts. As introductions went around, Sandra was hardly attentive. Her gaze was star-ward. After courtesies, she brushed passed the others to make way to the windows by the trio of singers at the end of the hall. The chorus must have found her unabashed, child-like fascination inspiring as their singing became all the more exuberant.

"I can certainly see why she made the trip into space," Beckett added in his jovial tone. The others nodded in agreement. Cleland and Boswell were the next to arrive. Boswell seemed to be in a better mood and his appearance was especially polished. Cleland seemed oblivious to the scenery, but passed a careful eye over the maidservants. They were all very dark skinned women, Asian, or perhaps from the West Indies. Like a buffet of assorted international delights. One in particular returned his gaze. She was young, had the sun washed look of an islander and her face had not fully puffed up, evidence of a relatively new arrival. Her proportions were almost cartoonish, like how a native girl might be made into a caricature in the sidebar of a newspaper. She raised a well-manicured eyebrow. A smile cracked Cleland's lips and it put a wider swagger to his gate as he entered.

"Lord Cholmondeley," Lady Inverness greeted attempting to draw him away from eying the help.

"Cecilia," he said returning her greeting but not her gaze, "why not just call me Lord Delamere since you are so enthralled by titles and ancestry."

"You've not earned that yet, young man," she said, billowing with dry ice. "So do tell us Cleland, how is your great celestial epic coming? Will you be entertaining us at dinner with verse?"

"Not yet, my lady, not yet," he replied, still refusing her gaze, but staring at the women in the lineup. "I've spent more of the trip reading than writing. An odd quality of space travel I'd not anticipated. The eternal void has a rather introspective aspect that inspires reflection over expression. I've found its unassailable expanses a catalyst for very inward journeys."

"Well," Lady Inverness said, "I'll not pretend to understand a word of it. So what do you find so compelling to read that couldn't have been read back on earth?"

"I read about us," Cleland replied. "I took the liberty of obtaining every swatch of pulp published about our journey before we left. Though certain contacts I have in the industry I acquired some that had yet to be published, ink still wet, as they say. Most all of it was about Crossland really and overstated the same points repeatedly. It took only a matter of weeks to lap up all the drivel, but what I wasn't expecting was other news that was alongside announcements of our departure. Grim dark stories of all kinds of villainous personages lurking about where one least expects."

"Failed to share with the rest of us then?" Lady Inverness retorted, "an oversight I'm sure."

"I was sequestered with my thoughts. Just as I wanted," Cleland replied. "You're welcome to any of it for our journey back."

"And you found grim darkness while exploring these pages."

"Of the darkest sort," Cleland replied, eyes widening.

"So the articles were fixated on Mr. Crossland? I'm sure he'll be pleased to hear that. Nothing about yourself? I remembered that there was some blurb about your female conquests before we left as I recall."

"Incorrect associations derived from attempts to decipher my poetry I'll wager."

"No, these were more of the eyewitness variety. Some viscount's daughter as I recall; a Madame de Laclos unless I'm mistaken."

"I'm sure you must be. Miss Emilie d'Laclos is merely an acquaintance. Someone who does secretarial work for me at times. All else is fabricated I'm sure."

"So what then, John," Lady Inverness asked, "What grim darkness did you find in those pages that surpassed the black of the sky?"

"Oh!" Cleland exclaimed, "murder most foul and the administration of just punishment." He turned his gaze, transfixing Lady Inverness. "On May the seventh," he explained, "that American scoundrel, Dr. H. H. Holmes, was hanged from the neck until dead."

"Never heard of him," she replied.

"I have," Beckett spoke up. "He ran that murder castle place in Chicago during the World's Fair. Lured young girls there and sold their bones to medical schools right? They hunted that man across the American continent before they found him. "

"Precisely!" Cleland exclaimed. "Though his name's Herman Mudgett it seems and perhaps he wasn't much of doctor to speak of."

"He knew enough to profit from it," Boswell offered, sounding with educated authority. "There's money to be made selling bleached skeletons to the right institutions. Most limit their criminal acts to grave robbing. Seems like this Mudgett chap was more enterprising."

"Ghastly dinner conversation," Lady Inverness scolded.

"Didn't you spend some time in Chicago?" Beckett asked turning to Culverton. "You lived there for a space before coming to Mars, didn't you?" but before Culverton could answer there was a new arrival at the door. Now dressed properly for dinner, Crohne strode in with long, well-practiced steps. The young navy man leaned toward him as he arrived.

"Christien!" Culverton greeted a bit too loudly.

Crohne excused the lad, "No need now son. My kind associate has announced me." Joining the group he completed his own introduction. "My friends, welcome to Phobus and Ares Britannia. I am Christien Burill Crohne, the on-site architectural specialist for this fine establishment. I see that you are in the good hands of Sir Royden and Mr. Havelock-Allen, drinks in your hands and smiles on your faces. I'm pleased to see that you're well seen after."

"Indeed!" Wilson said raising his glass, "a pleasure." Pleasantries were shared all around. Vecihi looked oddly cross as he sniffed something again he couldn't place.

"But I don't mean to interrupt," Crohne said, "sounds like I halted an engaging conversation."

"Not really," Lady Inverness stated.

"Dr. Crohne," Beckett said, "we were talking about Chicago and the punishment of the American murderer, H. H. Holmes."

"Punishment?" Crohne asked.

"Yes," Beckett answered, "Lord Cleland here was telling us of his reading on the voyage out." Crohne turned to Cleland, who reiterated.

"Yes," Cleland said, "the verdict was levied by their courts, hung the man just before our departure." Crohne appeared reflective, staring off and sighing briefly.

"If you'd pardon, hardly pre-dinner conversation is it now?" Crohne asked.

"Finally a gentlemanly assertion," Lady Inverness exhaled, "at last Mr. Crohne understands manners. Or is it Doctor Crohne?"

"Yes," Boswell interjected and extended a handshake, "I didn't realize you were a doctor till we arrived."

"Not a practicing one," Crohne corrected. "Call me as you'd like, but Christien is my Christian name."

"So Allen," Cleland began again, recalling where they'd left off, "you said you were in Chicago?"

"I hadn't," Culverton stammered.

"Hadn't stated or hadn't lived there?" Cleland pried.

"Of course he lived there," Crohne answered on Culverton's behalf. "That's where he and I met actually. Ares has American investors there. Many of us found their way to Mars through that city either physically or financially. And you knew that Dr. Holmes fellow didn't you, Allen?" All eyes turned to Culverton who seemed very uncomfortable as a result.

He crawled back in his shoes. "Yes, well no," he admitted, "I was never formally introduced. I worked for him indirectly. He hired a large number of builders, masons, carpenters to build his hotel, that murder castle, as it turns out. I had a number of clients about the World Fair. He was just another among many."

"Extraordinary!" Cleland said, "You had a hand building that place! That very place?"

"No!" Culverton protested, "I was a general contractor at one point is all. Only saw the man on one occasion, along with his lawyers to sign the notes and such. Not remarkable really. Typical American. Tall, awkwardly tall. He came in, said a few short words, signed the papers and left. For whatever that was worth. I never got paid for that job. None of my crew did. Along with a score others. He was a criminal on many counts. The world's better rid of him."

"But you saw the castle right?" Cleland pressed. "The papers described that it was a labyrinthine maze of inconceivable design. The entire second floor devoted to trap doors, unexpected stairways and escape routes. And the basement! Vats of acid and a kiln to dispose of his victims. Simply medieval in its torturous intent."

"No, sir," Culverton added, "Well yes, I saw the place, but it was just a commercial building by my take. I heard all that afterwards of course, but didn't know a thing at the time. The crew I hired renovated some storefronts and re-paneled some of the hotel rooms. All part of Holmes' plan it seems. He hired a number of crews to work the place so no one knew it all. He was the only one that knew the true lay of the place. He'd fail to pay us so the workers would walk off. Ingenious in a macabre way, how he built that place without anyone knowing, meticulous and ingenious."

Lady Inverness wouldn't be denied further. "I trust that Mr. Crossland won't keep us waiting longer or I'll soon be put off my appetite."

"Cecilia!" Cleland said, "finally a topic keen enough to castrate boredom and you're dwelling on gastronomy?"

"Mind a lady," Wilson dared. "The men can speak freely after dinner I'm sure."

"Pah!" Cleland released a plosive sigh of disgust. "Well if we must wait, I'm taking to smoke before dinner. Boswell, do you have the sachet?"

"I do," Boswell answered, producing a squat pipe and reaching for his vest pocket, "and I'll have some myself."

"By no means!" Royden spoke up from his hidden corner of the conversation a look of abject horror on his face. "Who allowed you to bring a lighter to the platform? We can have no such thing on Ares, no such thing." He made a move to take the offending paraphernalia, but Boswell pulled them away.

"What are you on about, man?" Cleland asked. "No smoking on Ares?"

"Is true," Vecihi spoke up. "Very bad. Air here is very rich. Flame will burn very hot, very, very hot."

"So no smoking after dinner?" Cleland asked. "We could smoke back on the liner."

"Actually," Gavin Crossland spoke up from the doorway Listonn right by his side, "it's far more dangerous to light that on the Daedalus."

Boswell looked to Cleland to lead an objection, but found none. Cleland returned the items to his pockets, including Boswell's stash of tobacco and kept a stiff upper lip. None doubted that these rules would be broken when objecting eyes were no longer upon them.

"Finally, Mr. Crossland," Lady Inverness said with a stabbing glare. "You've certainly taken your liberties."

"My sincere apologies, my lady," Crossland said with a short bow.

"Yes, Lady Inverness," Listonn added, "please accept our apologies." As Listonn continued his contrition, a young servant caught Gavin's attention.

"Excuse me, sir," she said barely audible. Gavin turned abruptly, caught off-guard. Something about her soft brown eyes disarmed him, the way her plain hair dashed across her face. Those eyes were respectful and pleading.

"Yes?" he answered, "What? What's this now?" She placed a drinking globe into his hands. He fumbled to accept it as it wafted in space. She inserted the lance from her wine baffle but took over long to fill his glass.

"You're from Earth, right, sir? One of the men from Tyneside? Did you bring the post with you sir?" she said.

Bowing low he turned an ear to listen, "I'm sorry, the post?" he asked.

"Yes, sir, from Maryanne Kingsley, my mother, she should have gotten the papers."

"Papers you say?" but Gavin was unable to finish.

"Mr. Crossland," came Lady Inverness' unyielding voice. "You've kept us waiting long enough." The girl slipped back into line. Gavin nodded briefly to excuse himself.

"Apologies all accepted Mr. Listonn," Lady Inverness concluded. "Now to dinner." Royden quickly clapped in response and the servants went into action, showing the guests to their designated place settings and assisting them to their seats. It took some doing but the magnetic strips in their gowns and trousers were affixed with these very chairs in mind. Most all the newcomers began circling the table to get to the opposite side but not Crossland. He sprung off awkwardly but was able to squirm in space until he could grasp the back of his chair and pull himself down. The servants offered their assistance but he shooed them away. Lady Inverness' maidservants held her gown in check and saw her stately to the table. Sandra tore herself away from the view and lightly landed at table. The trail of her gown billowed with the mists of heaven in its wake.

"Sir Royden," Gavin said in greeting, "very good to see you again. And you also, Christien," he said nodding Crohne's way. Nods of greeting came back as they also took their seats.

"Nice to see we've all been acquainted," Boswell said impishly.

"Actually," Gavin added, "Christien and I have been corresponding for years. It's like we're brothers after working so closely in spirit despite the great rift of space." Crohne nodded again in agreement with an observant expression. Lady Inverness squinted down her nose at the menu cards. She produced reading spectacles attached to a long sliver handle. Commandingly she stated,

"You may serve the first course. Are the oysters fresh? I'll fore-go if they're not impeccably fresh."

"Fresh yes!" Vecihi answers pointing resolutely at the ceiling. "Oyster farms very good in space. They are friendly with the blue-green algae. Very amicable. Like welcome neighbors."

"Mr. Crossland," Lady Inverness said getting his attention from across the table. "I will look to you to start the dinner conversation as we've quite exhausted our current intercourse. At least you have some boring formalities upon which to attend, correct?" The moment was well anticipated and Gavin rose to the occasion.

"Very good," he replied as the servants began floating about the room, setting covered trays of delicate morsels. "I see that everyone has met and I again extend my apologies to you all. While you're being served let me take this opportunity to commend our hosts. Sir Royden," Gavin said, directing their attention. "Without your astute management none of this would be possible. You've sacrificed your life for country, but you shan't go unrewarded. As the leader of this platform I commend you. Your name will be remembered forever as the first governor of Mars. Here, here!" In agreement, the group applauded in their seats. Royden's sweaty face shined in the yellow sconce light. He smiled modestly. "And to the building crew," Gavin continued. "My deep appreciation to Christien Burill Crohne and Culverton Havelock-Allen, two finer men I shall never meet. You have done the impossible my good men. You have built all this where no man broke soil before. You are gods among men I say. Nothing short of gods. Hear, hear!" And again the group applauded. Cleland rapped his fashionable walking stick against the floor but that's as far as his interest would allow.

"Yes, yes," Lady Inverness broke in, "know that your accomplishments are the wonder of a grateful nation and the pride of Her Majesty the Queen. But this fails miserably for conversation. I assure you that everyone will be recognized deservingly at the ceremony tomorrow. I should know, I wrote every word to be spoken. But aren't we under represented at this table? Isn't Ares Britannia a mining colony? Shouldn't the mining chief, or head, or master of blocks, or whatever he's called be present?" Culverton and Beckett looked up at Crohne but Royden answered,

"Uh, quite, yes very astute of you. Per Tyneside's hierarchy the miners are considered subordinates and this dinner was set aside for the executives." Listonn shot a slight look over at Gavin who clearly caught it but refrained from giving any evidence to that effect. "So you see," Royden continued, "they needn't be present. I assure you they are well aware of their vital role in our accomplishment." Lady Inverness flit her hair back into place as she grew more accustomed to eating with a set of spoons that functioned more like tongs. To her pleasure, the oysters were impeccably fresh as Vecihi attested and wonderfully prepared." Surprisingly delighted she asked,

"And should we also applaud Warrant Officer Hürkuş for the quality of the oysters. They are as you promised."

"Thank you Lady Underwood," Vecihi replied, "as I'm sure you'll find the consommé of Green Turtle as well prepared. I'm sure that's Naik's work I suppose?"

"Correct you are," Wilson confirmed smiling with pride at his servant's culinary prowess. "I had the good pleasure of sampling these courses before we left. It's nice that my dear companion was so versed a chef as well as his other contributions to our company. He is a man of many talents I assure you."

"And what other contributions are those?" Cleland asked.

"Well as my valet of course," Wilson answered though his thick cheeks. "Though I hate to call him that; oversimplification. You know, I don't see it on the card but I understood that he'd also graced us with his chocolate covered cherries. He's a fine way with them, just tart without being too sour."

"He's a confectionist too?" Cleland asked.

"I look forward to that," the princess said, "they are simply my favorite."

"Really" Wilson noted, "I wonder if he learned of that somehow."

"When we were young, our mother would get all us sisters Sittingbourne cherries drenched in dark chocolate" she said with an almost dreaming recollection, "They were so decadent. I always thought they were what sin must taste like. Mr. Crossland," she asked in her light, unassuming voice, "we passed by those two majestic statues at the gate to Ares, are they in fact likenesses of Phobus and Deimus, the sons of Mars?"

"Of course they are," Culverton answered loud with a scoff. The interruption was abrupt enough to draw every eye. Culverton scratched his cropped dark hair and looked away. "I mean obviously, standing at the gates of Mars."

"Not so obvious really," Crohne said. "What my colleague means to say is that here, in the realm of their father, one would only expect to find them about."

"I might find that surprising," Wilson lent his opinion. "As I recall from my schooling the Greek gods had much to fear from their sons. The god Zeus slew his own father shortly after birth as memory serves. A reflection of their culture built around the younger usurping their elders.

Like a divine justification of supplanting the old with the new. Yet another example of where religion is politics and politics religion. You learn that in the Punjab I'll tell you; Sikhs and Muslims and Hindus. If man can't draw a line around their territory, they'll draw it around their beliefs. Wherever two or more men can draw a line between them they'll draw it and the rest is politics."

"Not so, sir," Culverton said, somehow both softly spoken and yet assertive. "For Ares and many of the Olympians, the story is very different. There are disloyalties of course but not so between Ares and his sons. Even in the passage on the plaque. There's very little preserved about Phobus and Deimus, but what we do have speaks of their devotion to their father, unfailing devotion. Not at all what we would expect from the personification of war, dread, and terror but that's just the way they are; unfailingly loyal. Perhaps the Greeks knew well of the deep ties between men who fight in wars. Men who've warred together. Courageous men who faced fear and beheld dread, and achieved a mastery over them."

Sandra broke a wide smile, "Why Mr. Havelock-Allen," she said, "you seem to be quite the scholar and philosopher, perhaps even the hint of a poet."

Cleland waved an empty drink globe expecting it to be filled, "Didn't the Greeks learn all they needed of divinity after they bent the knee to Bacchus?"

"Spoken like a true libertine," Wilson said, tipping his globe toward Cleland.

"Libertine you call me?" His Cheshire expression expanded. "Libertine!" he shouted uncomfortably. "Libertine! Libertine! Didn't the American's fight a war to become a nation of libertines? Make me a libertine or give me death! Too bad they're too crass to reap the rewards. Show me a man who isn't a libertine and I'll show you a fool every time. But, all your compliments aside, we were hearing from Mr. Havelock-Allen." Turning towards him Cleland bowed slightly with a wave of the frills at his sleeve. "I bow to you, mister. You've made an astute observation. I must add that thought to my epic about this place. How fear and dread bear a heartfelt devotion to war."

Lady Inverness huffed, "We go from hanged murderers to hanged cooks to war, fear, and dread," she said. "Mr. Crossland, I look to you again to give us something better to discuss. They call this place the first wonder of Mars. Can't someone tell me more about the wonder of it all?

We have a tour scheduled tomorrow correct? Immediately after the ceremony to see the place we've thus christened. Elaborate for us please. What all shall we be seeing?"

"When we were approaching the gates," Princess Sandra said, "Reverend Beckett mentioned that you have an aviary. I can't wait to see it. The birds must fly like in dreams. It's a wonder they can fly at all. I can hardly believe it's possible."

"A wonder it is," Beckett assured all.

"And so we'll all see it," Gavin said. "We'll be holding the christening there."

"Well planned that," Boswell scoffed. "Sounds like a fine place to be shat upon."

Cleland leaned over to his friend, "You've a mental block, my man," he said, "shit trickles up in space."

"And now we talk of excrement," Lady Inverness said. "Please continue, Mr. Crossland. Where shall we go after the room of soaring excrement?"

"Thereafter," Gavin began again as the servants cleared the table for the next course, "we shall go to the observatory and survey the new territory that extends our nation's borders."

"Wonderful," Sandra approved.

"Yes, Princess," Beckett said. "If you like this view, you'll be astounded by the observatory. It's difficult to tell which is more breathtaking."

"I must find my way there." Princess Sandra stated almost under her breath. She turned slightly, almost catching Cleland looking at her from the corner of his eye.

"Wonderful, wonderful," Lady Inverness affirmed, "tell us more."

Gavin sent a questioning look over at Royden who was notably uncomfortable.

"Wouldn't want to ruin the surprise," Royden said. "It will be quite the spectacle. Everything has been properly accounted."

"Nonsense, Sir Royden," Lady Inverness broke in, "never cared for surprises and never will. Relay the schedule."

"The algae vats!" Vecihi announced proudly. "When will we see those? My great master at home Koca Mi'mâr Sinân designed it beautifully. There is a glass walkway that runs through the vats, a great tube that allows us to watch the blooms at close quarters. You are surrounded on all sides by bubbling algae, flooded with electric light. Now that is wondrous!"

"What interests are there in algae vats?" Lady Inverness asked.

"I'm sorry," Royden stammered, "Whereas there we intended to take you all along the glass walkway that encircles the vats, it isn't really fit for a tour."

"Why not?" Vecihi asked. Royden swayed in thought, seeking the right words.

"There are…" he said, "incompletion's that need your expert attention Officer Hürkuş."

"Incompletion's?" Vecihi replied, "sorry, as in not-complete?"

"Yes," Royden stammered, "as in, they are not complete."

"Is there any danger?" Listonn spoke up, clutching the monocle in his eye a bit tighter.

"No, no, no, no," Royden blurted in rapid succession, "not any such thing."

"Mr. Listonn," Crohne said briskly, "there are a good many of us here in good health, as I'm sure Dr. Boswell has discovered."

"Ha," Boswell spat, "I'll say. You must be quite a physician, Dr. Crohne. So many people in these harsh environs and none infirm."

"I take it we shall not be touring the infirmary will we, Dr. Boswell?" Lady Inverness said, "we'll entrust that to you. I can't say I'm wholly displeased to fore-go the algae. Officer Hürkuş, we leave that to you. As for the rest of us, what else will we be seeing? Again, isn't this a mining colony? Shouldn't we be seeing gold or silver or at least rocks with glimmering deposits?"

"Actually, my lady," Gavin said. He drew in a breath, looking to Royden to prompt him but nothing came. "Next we are to visit the dry dock." Gavin's suspicions were unfortunately confirmed by the grimace from Royden's reaction.

"Dry dock?" Lady Inverness asked dripping with contempt.

"Come, Cecilia," Cleland said, "Tyneside's a company of shipwrights. We must make our way round to the dock workers, sweaty backs all straining at the rigging, etcetera, etcetera."

"Dock workers," Lady Inverness repeated.

"Um," Royden said, "the dock is another wonder to be assured. You see, Ares is quite unique in that it's intended to provide a very comprehensive set of services. A section of the builder crew is skilled in servicing space-liners One of the things they've built is a rocket propelled lifeboat per your architectural designs, Mr. Crossland."

"Yes, of course," Gavin said.

"Rocket you say," Captain Napier spoke up for the first time at the meal, "very innovative that."

"Yes, well," Royden explained, "you see that was to be the place where the Daedalus would have docked and you would have all disembarked accordingly. But, uh, as you are all so aware, the gangway, along with other aspects of the dock, is also incomplete."

"What other aspects?" Listonn asked, his brow turning white with the intensified clenching.

"Uh, there are air leaks."

"What?" Listonn exclaimed.

"Mr. Listonn," Crohne said, "You've no need for concern. What my colleague is relaying is that there are many challenges building on a lunar surface and these are merely some of them. Captain Napier," Crohne said looking his way, "How does a space-faring vessel contend with leaks?"

"Well," Napier said, fingering the pommel of his saber "Every liner leaks, it's just the way of it. It's something you attend to, not something you can stop." Gavin noted a slight chill, but made nothing of it, far too engrossed by the conversation.

"Still," Listonn said, "there are other implications. I'm convinced that we're safe of course, but we have a shipping schedule to meet. This christening is a great milestone. The HMS Commonwealth will be making her next voyage out and this time, without extra supply, she's to be refitted here at Ares. These orchestrations must be very precisely managed, down to the very grain of rice and drop of water. Are we operational, men? Napier, what do you say? You're the senior officer at this table."

Napier breathed a heavy breath before he answered, "I've learned at my age to keep a still tongue and a watchful eye. My duty's to the ship." He gave everyone a quick look over. "I'll leave you all to get this sorted."

Princess Sandra leaned over to Lady Inverness' ear, "Cici," she whispered so none other could here, "is it getting cold in here?" but Lady Inverness dismissed her, focusing on the conversation.

"Well, at least we'll be seeing the observatory," Cleland said.

"I'm sorry, Lord Cholmondeley," Crohne asked looking at Cleland, "were you speaking to Princess Sandra?"

"What was that?" Cleland asked his eyes looking to Sandra, catching the glint off the silver key at her breasts.

"Oh, John, really?" Lady Inverness said wiping her mouth on a napkin she let float in the air.

"What's on now?" Cleland said not covering his offense. "I was referring to all of us surely."

"I'm sure," Lady Inverness said with a tone that belayed her true thoughts.

"Come now, son," Wilson asked, "I thought you were a man of different persuasions."

"Different persuasions?" Cleland asked astonished.

"Yes of course," Wilson said. "You speak the language of Sodom and Gomorrah and all. Last I heard you were gallivanting with that Irish playwright fellow whose name eludes me. You know the one, Portrait of Dorian Grey was one of his."

"Mr. Oscar Wilde isn't it?" Lady Inverness asked.

"Yes, yes," Wilson said, "that's the man."

"Yes," Cleland answered with a roll of his eyes, "Oscar Fingal O'Flahertie Wills Wilde." Boswell smiled slightly to himself and shrunk back an inch. "He's one of my many literary associates," Cleland said, "what of him?"

"That's the one!" Wilson assured. "Wasn't he convicted as a sodomite?"

Cleland's face went rock hard, hard and steely, "What do you mean to infer, sir?" Cleland asked, stiffening.

"Please, man," Wilson said, his breath visible as a light haze as he spoke. "I've traveled all the world. As Vecihi and I will both tell you, there are men of many persuasions." Wilson and Vecihi shared knowing looks and a short chortle. The servants began to get uneasy and started slipping their way back toward the opposing walls. They looked to each other in concerned silence. Cleland pushed himself up, breaking the invisible seal to his chair and hovered a few feet off the table. He worked a bit to get there but being suspended did make him more imposing.

"I demand an apology, sir!" he spat, pointing at Wilson, his breath a jet of white. "I will not stand such accusations. I will not be publicly branded a homosexual no matter what planet-" but his eyes crossed as he was surprised by the puffing visibility of his words. "What the devil?" he said. The others began noticing their own breath as well, and the chill that had fallen so subtly about them. Princess Sandra crossed her arms over her breasts for warmth. Though it had crept up very slowly, all of them now felt it like a frost over morning lawns.

The dark, young girl among the servants gasped loudly. All heads turned to her and she exclaimed loudly, "Barabbas!"

Listonn loosed his monocle which floated free in the chilling air and said, "Who the bloody hell is Barabbas?"

Chapter I (7): Christenings and Accolades

Royden buckled under the pressure and confessed to the likely cause of the cold air. Unable to look anyone in the eye, he reported that it was certainly the doing of the mining colony. The miners had been known to express their displeasure by drastically reducing the temperature throughout the platform. The building crew controlled the atmospheric regulators, but the miners held the larger bank of generators and thereby controlled the heat. Going well beyond the ravages of discomfort the real threat came across unequivocally. After Royden provided these explanations, no drinks were served after the meal. Listonn was far too put off and Royden could do little to reassure him. It was ultimately up to Gavin to ease his nerves. Thankfully, the terms "union" or "union organizer" never came up. Despite that, there was other damage that begged action. Given the state of affairs, Lady Inverness canceled the formal tour. Seeing that this was clearly outside of her purview, she left it for the men to address. She excused herself and the Princess from the table. Lady Inverness' attendants, led by the watchful eye of ol' Gran, helped the Lady from her chair and likewise out of the dining room.

Gavin leapt after them with a gentlemanly composure. "Lady Inverness, may I have a word," he asked.

"You may," she answered, but maintained her steady progress. Gavin had to work hard to pull himself along the wall and yet compose his words and his demeanor.

"Lady, I want to season what you've just heard with some exposition on the enormity of-"

"Mr. Crossland," she interrupted, "I make no claims to comprehend any of the more inventive wisdom required to bring people into space nor to build habitations herein, but I do have my own mind. I have every intention of stating my mind to the Queen and the Prime Minister, upon our return. And I'll warn you not to underestimate me. I'm just as comfortable in front of parliament as I am in Her Majesty's drawing room. I would suggest that before we leave you make a proper reassessment of our readiness. Upon the flight back I will allow you to sway my opinion, but as of now my view is less than favorable." She gave him a tall-browed look of finality. "Good night, Mr. Crossland," and she turned her head up the hall in a way that made it clear that she wouldn't turn it back. Gavin stopped and watched the group make their way. At least the Princess gave him one sympathetic glance before gathering up the train of her dress and gracefully proceeding with them.

Upon returning to the dining hall, Gavin dodged Boswell and Cleland as they huffed past him. Within, Gavin found Royden holding his own against Listonn, but Royden was in dire need of a rescuer. The others had broken out into small groups. Sir Wilson and Napier chatted. Crohne and Culverton were nowhere to be seen. The servants and singers had all exited. To reach them, Gavin had to pull himself directly over the top of the dining table, ruffling the tablecloth at every pull. Joining Listonn and Royden he chose to lend confidence.

"Alright," Gavin said so only the two could hear, "the Duchess is understandably concerned, but that is more than reasonable. I believe she'll look to us for assurances."

"Assurances?" Listonn said, much more audibly, "I seem to be short on those myself."

"Now, Tom," Gavin said to Listonn, "we accounted for this, all of this. We need to pool our resources and clean up the bits and bobs. No need over-inflating anything before a proper look-see." Catching the trail of his monocle, Listonn consented. Listonn had no interest in seeing Ares tainted. "Good," Gavin continued, "Now let's start with the miners. Sir Tom, they've sent us a message. If we call them from a yack-mouth will they be willing to talk?"

"Uh, yes, yes," Royden answered with a contradictory shake of his head.

"And we can do that from your office?" Gavin asked.

"Yes, yes," Rodyen answered blinking rapidly.

"So," Listonn said, "Will Barabbas answer himself or shall we get his secretary?"

Gavin dismissed the question and said, "Let's meet at Royden's office in the morning. We'll call over to the camp and I'll talk to them. I'm sure they'll want a Tyneside representative from Earth. It'll also give us a chance to look over the books, labour logs and accounting." Royden nodded a slow agreement. "Good then," Gavin said, "We'll meet there at 8:00 deck time. That will get us a good lead ahead of the ceremony." Listonn nodded his agreement as well. "Now as per the plan," Gavin continued, "afterwards I'll meet with Christien and Allen to inventory the building projects. I believe we can get Napier to survey the dock. The Lady Inverness will respect his judgment. Officer Hürkuş will attend to the algae vats and Dr. Boswell will continue his examining of the crew. Sounds like we have some good news there." Listonn seemed calmed by the definitive course of action as Gavin had hoped. Polite goodbyes were shared and the three made their way out. Behind Listonn's back, Gavin took Royden by the arm. Royden looked to him and Gavin mouthed the words, "be there at six," and Royden nodded his understanding.

Though safely back to their rooms, the travelers were restless. Boswell sneaked into Cleland's state room and both stayed up late into the simulated night. Their stash was opened and strong drink flushed into globes. Royden be damned, they struck matches, lit their pipes and brooded long by the fleeting glow of an electric torch. Cleland was bereft and he wrung his fingers incessantly, picking at black ink from under his fingernails. "Damn well let that bastard get the best of me," he said over and over.

"Who? Wilson?" Boswell asked astonished.

"No, damn you," Cleland said, "Crohne. That bastard bathes in oil. Keep a watch on him. I know his sort too well. Too damned much like me."

As everyone was settling, Sandra made no move to undress. She merely dismissed her servant and bided her time. When she could no longer hear any noises from outside in the hall, she very slowly undid the latches on her squat stateroom door, squirming at every scratch of metal. Once freed, she opened the door just enough to pass. She lightly pulled herself from her room only to find Lady Inverness wafting slowly in the dark waiting for her. "Oh," Sandra said startled, "Sorry, ma'am, I was just —"

"I know what you were just, girl," the Lady Inverness replied. "You were going to wander the platform. Don't worry. I know you weren't going to meet with Cleland. The gossip all be damned, you're not his sort after all." Sandra looked at the Lady Inverness' dark outline, fleetingly in the darkness. Sandra cast her head downward. Her mind flooded with recollections of boarding school, smoking American cigarettes and getting into trouble with her sisters. "But," Lady Inverness continued, "I figured I should wait up and seems with good reason. It's not safe to wander alone girl. Not with what we've heard tonight. I owe it to your aunt. Don't give me reason to worry."

"Yes, ma'am," Sandra said.

"I had ol' Gran read the leaves before we came here. I should have known better. Go to bed, child," the Lady Inverness said. With a weightless curtsy, Sandra resigned herself and pulled her light form sidelong, back into her room. Lady Inverness waited to hear the latches seal before returning to her own.

***

Morning was at first indiscernible as the orbital position of Phobus was behind Mars' night side. The fast moving body soon sped past the Martian horizon to be bathed in beaming sunlight, sailing past the crack of the Martian dawn. Sandra cursed that she'd been unable to witness her first Phoban dawn. Long before that whistle blew Gavin was up, washed with a damp towel, formally dressed and on his way. A grateful Royden was waiting in the hall when he emerged.

"Good morning, Sir Tom," Gavin greeted.

"Morning, but Tom is fine really," Royden said and they were off, Royden leading the way. The office of the manager was not as Gavin envisioned, though he'd imagined the room a thousand times architecturally. Somewhat similar to the finer rooms in the Daedalus, the walls were paneled in dark woods. The finish was peeling a bit, perhaps due to over-dryness. Royden's desk was fixed to the floor, as one would normally expect, but every corner of every wall was stacked with tied bundles. There were enormous metal file cabinets, each drawer bearing a pencil scratched manila card bound in a metal frame. Gavin was notably struck with the sheer volume of material amassed in the crowded little space.

Royden struck into his explanation. "Ah, the stacks do settle over time, but we can't make any sudden moves. Things will start flying about and then I'll really start losing track of things. I've, ah, attempted to keep it ordered by subject matter. I, uh, I guess it all depends on where we should start."

Scanning the task before them, Gavin replied, "I'd say we should start at the beginning but I'm not sure where that's to be found." Gavin stretched a stiff neck and chose a fresh approach. "Let's just talk, you and me, Tom, before Mr. Listonn gets here."

"Alright," Royden agreed.

Thinking this way through this, Gavin put words to his thoughts, "Tom is, not you Tom, Tom Listonn is a man of numbers. He's a bean counter. He's all about metrics and measures. The chief number of all being at the bottom-right of the balance sheet. If we don't show him some numbers he'll dig till he finds some. And I don't suppose we want that to happen do we?" he said with a knowing look into Royden's eyes.

"No, we most certainly do not," Royden replied.

"Right. So Tom, you I mean, you are charged to find the very best numbers you can for when Listonn gets here. When you find some, pass them to me and I'll familiarize myself as I can to help guide the conversation. Right then? Does that work?"

"Yes," Royden said, looking about the piles. "We can make that work." Royden shrugged a bit and then carefully went to a stack and lightly began parting bundles to scan their content. Gavin could do nothing but stare, which didn't make Royden anymore at ease. Unfortunately, only moments had passed before Listonn showed up himself, the grim figure of Miser at the door behind him.

"This be the place," Miser snorted in his garbled tone.

"Thank you," Listonn replied with a touch on condescension. "Here you both are," he said as he entered, "didn't think to gather me up before you came?"

"Tom!" Gavin replied smiling, "and a good morning to you. Sir Thomas and I were up early and thought we'd come around to gather you closer to eight. And how are you? Did you take breakfast? I'm sure we can have Miser or Piter or someone to bring some around."

Keeping his head down, Royden stuck to his search.

"No, no," Listonn replied, "and I slept horribly if I slept at all. I should have gone back to the Daedalus. Those floating hammocks are frightful. So you've started looking into things have you?"

"We have, we have," Gavin replied looking over at Royden. "Just started though."

"Well let's get to it," Listonn said and began grabbing for stacks himself. "Sir Royden, I'd like to start with shipping manifests and materials management."

Royden scrambled, picked through piles and started passing stacks to both of them. Without asking permission, Listonn took a seat at Royden's desk, donned a pair of reading glasses and began to pour over the documents. Being a much more orderly sort, Listonn unbound each bundle in turn, organized the contents, dog-eared the pertinent pages and bound them up again perfectly squared off. He asked for ink and paper after a while, cursing mutely about writing without gravity, and began jotting down his own figures. Questions began to flow out from him. "Where's the manifest that corresponds with this order? Why doesn't this spreadsheet balance? Why are all these figures mixed in with hazard drill results?" Royden weathered the scrutiny better than Gavin anticipated. Perhaps they had chosen a good man to be the first governor of Mars. At least he was good for weathering scrutiny.

"I don't understand," Listonn exclaimed holding out pages removed from separate bundles. "We have this log of labour and this log from the same day obviously written in someone else's' hand. If you wrote this one," he said holding out the page in his left hand, "who wrote this one?" he asked of the one on his right. Royden stammered, failing to offer an explanation. "Well," Listonn concluded, "one of them contradicts the other so one or both must be inaccurate."

"And what of that?" Gavin asked.

Listonn replied emphatically, "It means that it's very difficult to determine who's working here at Ares Britannia presently, who's once worked here but since left and who we have on their way."

"How's that?" Gavin said.

"This record," Listonn explained, "shows the arrival of eight new workers, six men and two women. Three of the men are penal recruits, two are debtors and the other is a skilled mine fitter. The women are both penal. They arrived on the HMS Jewel of India, fifth November, 1895. This other log shows the departure of seven laborers bound for the moon on the Jewel's return voyage. The two women's names are mentioned plus others, all women, leaving the platform on twenty-eight, October of the same year. So did they come or did they leave? And when did the Jewel arrive and when did it depart?" Listonn and Gavin both looked up from the page at the sheet white face of Sir Royden.

"I, uh, don't have an answer," Royden replied abashed.

"I have an answer," Listonn blurted, "bloody shoddy work is what it is. We'd need to corroborate with the India's log to figure out which one's right."

"I, ah, only receive those forms from Mr. Havelock-Allen," Royden stammered. "He tracks all the various crews and staffing needs, for the miners, builders, support staff, all of them. He also logs the shipments, coming and going."

"But you handle the bloody accounting," Listonn pressed. "How do you account for the labour costs, the life support costs? Food supply, living arrangements? Do you even know how many people currently reside on Ares Britannia? Did they get up for work today or are in bed sleeping? Are they-"

"Sir Royden," Gavin said, "Doesn't Christien help you with this? From my correspondence with him it seemed like he had quite a detailed understanding of labour, management, submersive costs, etc., etc." Royden looked oddly up at the ceiling. Gavin and Listonn almost couldn't help looking up as well.

"Dr. Crohne doesn't come down from his tower much," Royden choked out. "He focuses on his blueprints and design plans and such. It's most pressing you know. One miscalculation on a design or set of building instructions and-"

"Maybe that says it all right there," Listonn said snide and cutting. "Well, this is just one case," he said grasping other bundles that floated before him. He quickly thumbed to some pages with turned down corners. "Dispensing with the slipshod records, it's clear that we're rotating through labourers much faster than I thought. The builders and miners both. Some leave for the moon due to infirmities, yes, but there's far too many for all of them to have brickets or runny noses."

"Maybe that's why Boswell hasn't found any," Gavin noted.

"Maybe," Listonn replied, unbelieving. "It's going to take a long time to get this all sorted," Listonn said with a long, drawn out shake of his head.

"Now," Gavin said, "let's take a step back. We've found some poor records, but that's book-keeping. Ares is all about production. Let's give our call over to the miners and settle that. You can hardly expect that they can keep good books when half the platform's not on speaking terms."

"Right, right," Listonn agreed, "Good point. Rapper Dance for Tyneside."

"Tyne and Wear Yo-ho!" Gavin shot back. "Well now, Sir Royden, can we call over to the mining camp?"

Royden stopped his searching through pages and spun to address them. "Oh," he said, a bit shocked. "Ah, ok then, right over here." Royden pulled past his desk to the wall nearest the doorway. He took hold of some stacks of bundles and pushed them away with both hand. The bundles drifted, one apart from the other, and almost made a cloud of tumbling rectangular formations of paper. Listonn swatted one away as it came near him. It looked like Royden was doing a swimmers freestyle through an ocean of a surreal paperwork limbo. Behind the stacks was a pipe organ set of brass tubes, all aligned and flowing up to the ceiling and directly into the walls like clutching fingers or thick vines.

"Right then," Gavin said, "Here's the plan. Let's convince one or two of them to attend the christening."

"Oh no," Royden said, "they won't come."

"But we should invite them, yes?" Gavin argued. "If they agree I can talk to them beforehand. Maybe craft a show of solidarity. I mean it's only in their good interests to come into agreement, resolve their difference and get on with it."

"Well if that's the play you should use, Beckett," Royden said, "they like him. If anyone can convince them to come over, it's him."

"Can I call from Beckett's room?" Gavin asked.

"Why yes," Royden answered, "all rooms in the administrative dome have yack-mouths."

"Brilliant, you'd think I designed the place that way. You two stay here and keep digging. I'll get with the reverend and call the miners. Wish us luck."

"Gavin," Listonn protested, "I want to come with you and listen in, hear for myself."

"No, no, Tom," Gavin insisted, "we need to spend our time wisely. I need you here to continue your review. There's just not time."

"Alright," Listonn said reluctantly and Gavin rushed out. Royden fiddled with his hands, while Listonn looked sternly through his readers, licking his thumb and flipping aggravated pages.

Hurried and distracted, Gavin made it out into the hall and closed the door behind him. He dealt with the latches with frustrated painful motions. Now secured, he used the frame to turn about and bound up the hall. In only a few steps, he quickly found Piter and Miser loitering about. Gavin couldn't help but note often they seemed to be loitering. After quick but polite greetings, he asked for their assistance and they led him to Beckett's door. After only a single knock, Beckett answered, pushing out the door from within. They found him in a partial state of undress, his holy raiments partially buttoned, fastened or tied. He was adorned in brilliant purple vestments. The colors on his cuffs and collar resembled the interlocking shards of a stained glass window. The red sash about his shoulders had intricate embroidery that almost appeared to be a topographical representation of the Martian surface complete with canals swiping across in obtuse arches.

"Why, Mr. Crossland," Beckett welcomed, "Good morning to you! Sir Tom gave me a shout up the yack, said to expect you." Beckett led Gavin into the room and shut the door behind them, giving a kind regard to Piter and Miser's grim stares. Beckett, well acclimated to his surroundings, had placed different articles of furniture, strategically locked in place, to make moving about easy. Starting with a left hand to the back of a desk chair, it led naturally to a pipe fitted securely to the wall, which led to an ornately carved post on the bureau. Gavin only had a brief instant to glance around. Bundles of wrinkled laundry were pushed into the corners. The hammock had been loosed from its fastener and bunched up like a fishing net against the wall. An open traveling wardrobe had been leather-strapped to the writing desk and held fast with tarnished buckles.

"Very good yes," Gavin said, "Sir Tom informs me that you've a way with Othello and the miners."

"As much as anyone does I suppose," Beckett said. "You really want them at the ceremony?" he asked with the questioning look of mirthful unbelief.

"I'm afraid it's only suitable, right? And from last night's display it seems like some reconciliation's in order."

"Ah then," Beckett said, "Good to have the vicar on-hand. That's our sort of business."

"How did you come into their favour exactly?" Gavin asked.

"Hard to say. I think I just hit it off with Didier, you know, the man they call Othello. Seems like he had some trouble concerning his wife a ways back and I've been looking into it for him."

"Trouble you say?"

"Yes, uh, she's gone missing it seems. Only plausible event is that she stowed away on one of the liners and made off. It happens sometimes."

"Really? Just made off?"

Beckett offered a slow nod in reply. "It's a hard life out here," Beckett said with the voice of a pastor, "especially for women. Men are lonely and prone to their desires. More of them and we get some rough ones up here. It's better for the married women as long as their men can protect them. Marriages can dissolve up here as fast as they're formed. The work is hard, the days are long. The sheep of this flock don't have much in the realm of distractions. Before I came there were no regular church services and here I am preparing to head back with all you. I've been debating that decision lately."

"Oh? They're like sheep without a shepherd are they?"

"Well, hardly an unbiased answer coming from me. I'm supposed to look at everyone like that. Sinners are good for business, eh?" He said with a grin on his long face. "Well then, I sent a tube over to the mining camp, told them that we'd like to talk about last night's antics. I just got the note back when you came knocking. Didier's waiting for us."

"Alright, what's his exact name again?"

"Didier Marouani, though he doesn't mind being called Othello. Takes it as a compliment I think."

"And tell me if I can ask one more thing?"

Beckett motioned for Gavin to proceed.

"What's your take? Is this Barabbas a fabrication or a breathing soul?" Beckett looked off and shrugged glancing off to the corners.

"Who's to say?" Beckett answered. "There's no likely candidate from that lot. Othello's the brains over there. But it's not like they ask if you're a rabble rouser before signing you up to come here. Given the criminals and miscreants, who knows? If he's real, Barabbas is most likely Didier, but what's it matter?"

Beckett took the clapper under his arm like a bagpipe and put the yack-mouth fixture to his ear. He puffed at its mouth and called out, "Didier? Didier? It's Beckett, are you there?" Gavin could hear a rich deep voice speaking at the other end respond, muffled tones from a muffled source. "No, no," Beckett spoke on the line, "it's a Mr. Gavin Crossland. He's a Tyneside Spaceyarde's man from Earth, only just arrived." The muffled voice carried on and Beckett stared at the ceiling as they spoke. "Well I've only just met him myself. He's led the architectural team that built the platform and had a hand in that new liner they arrived on. What more do you expect? You can ask him yourself, he's standing here waiting." The voice came to an emphatic breathy resolution and Beckett concluded, "Well, I suggest you play your hand well, friend. Here's the opportunity you've waited for. He can only help." Removing the yack-mouth from his ear he passed it over. "Good luck, Gavin," Beckett said dryly as he handed it gently over. Gavin brought it to his ear and pulled the outstretched cone to his mouth.

"Uh, yes, this is Gavin Crossland, do I address Mr. Didier Marouani?"

The man on the other side didn't answer at first but then a hard, concatenated form of English spoke back to him, "Aye, dis is Didier," which sounded more like Did-de-yea, to Gavin's ear. "How you feelin' over der, Mr. Crossland? You nice an wam?"

"Uh, yes," Gavin spoke up assertively, "We're feeling very comfortable. Thank you for turning up the heat. Thank you very much."

"So," Didier said, "Wat'chu got to say?"

"I want to formally invite you to come to the christening, you know about the christening don't you?" Beckett nodded to affirm that the miners were aware. "Yes, you see it wouldn't be proper if you weren't represented. We owe you a great debt and I'd very much like to meet you, your team and Barabbas."

"Ha!" Didier shot back, "You ain't goin'ta see no Barabbas and I ain't comin' to your do."

"Look," Gavin said starting to sweat and fumbling for the next word. "I want you to appreciate the importance of your actions and what it means for all of us. I'm traveling with some very important people who have grave power over us, you, me, over all Ares Britannia. This is a very important occasion, historic in fact. I need to talk to you and I need to talk to Barabbas. You must have demands and I'm the one who can get them for you."

"You say you're so important but o'ters more important dan you. Maybe I talk to dem."

"That, my friend, would be a calamitous mistake." Gavin stared Beckett in the eyes, reading him while they talked. "You'll just have to take my word for it. If you have any hope of getting what you want bring your demands to me." There was a long pause. Gavin continued staring at Beckett who glanced down at the mouth piece and gave a slight shrug.

Didier's voice came back on the line. "How can you gif me wat I want? You don't know wat I want."

"Then come over here, meet with me before the christening and tell me."

"No," Didier said unyielding, "I'll not come dere. No way."

"Didier," Gavin said, "Othello, please. It would mean more than you can imagine."

"It's like dis. We won't be chillin' your do. You do your do. We make it nice and wam. Have a nice do wit all you important people. When you're done wit da do, we meet at da choka'. Just you and Beckett. No one else and we talk."

"The choker?" Gavin asked.

"Beckett know da place," Didier added. "Do your do, den we talk."

"And Barabbas will be there with you?" Gavin blurted.

"Ah, ha, ha!" Didier said mirthlessly. "No way. As for Barabbas, I speak for him. You worry about ch'you. See you den meesta Crossland and we'll see what ch'you can do far us," and Gavin heard the line disengage with a pop. He passed the yack-mouth back to Beckett deep in thought.

"So?" Beckett asked without asking, "Didier wants to meet at the choker? You did very well, Gavin! I didn't think Didier would want to talk in-person. You impressed him. He wants to size you up. Look you in the eye."

"And that's a good thing?" Gavin asked.

"A very good thing! He could have turned the platform into an icebox and shouted demands over the yack-mouth. You did brilliantly."

"Reverend Beckett," Gavin asked still a bit dazed, "may I ask a favour of you? During the christening, I'm going to tell the others about this conversation, but I'm going to paint it with brighter colors, get me? I won't mislead them, obviously, just going to add a little colour right? Uh, make it optimistic. We have every reason to be optimistic don't we?"

"Of course, Gavin," Beckett beamed looking down from his lofty stature. "I'll be right there to back you up." Gavin nodded his thanks and left Beckett's chambers in slow, dream-like motions. Gavin found his way back to his room to finish dressing for the christening leaving Beckett to complete his own preparations.

***

The aviary was yet another glory of glories of all the glories of Ares Britannia. One of the tallest domes, it stood almost equal in height to the cone of the escape rocket that stood proudly nearby, just up a short external passage that stretched its way over the rough Phoban terrain. Just inside the widest archway into the aviary dome, a raised path struck forward to its centre flanked by swatches of black soil, sprouting with emerald grasses. Closest the path the grounds resembled an English garden, so lush and bright it bore a green that defied nature. Thicker grasses rose up quickly the farther away from the path, in golden brown like waving wheat, resembling a grassland or prairie, thicker stalked plants that reached up for the light. Electric floodlights were attached to the black burnished beams that rose high above, illuminating the tall pines and alders that spread majestically up toward outer space. In the embrace of those trees resided the avians of Ares Britannia. Very few birds were able to fly without gravity. There were other complications as well, behavioural as well as biological. Some species could exist in space but failed to enter regular reproductive cycles. The Coturnix Quail was one of the few that fit the tight criteria. Not only could they adjust to foreign environs but, if properly handled, could flourish. There were several varieties present in that grand space. The English variety had primarily white plumage with brown speckles while the Rosetta displayed deep earth and ashen stripes. They were dizzying to observe. These birds that would dart from one branch to the next, twittering their pleasant song, another integral component contributing to the cycles within cycles that supported the sustaining balance of transplanted life in space.

The tallest trees were at the centre and en-wreathed a patch of ground that made for a small grotto. The male servants and some of the Daedalus crew were already there, making preparations. Lt. Colin Campbell was among them directing the others. He was wearing his dress uniform which suited him very well. He looked the part of his command. Elphinstone was nearby, his mop of hair pulled to the side in an attempt to look fashionable for the day. He couldn't get past the fact that they weren't setting up folding chairs. Wouldn't there be a need for folding chairs? Instead, they set up brass poles that held cords to section off the attendees by rank. One row was set straight up the path to the centre so the procession could use it to maneuver into place. Other solitary poles had been planted all around that came up to four feet in height. They held brass handles so those attending had an anchor by which to steady themselves.

Warrant Officer Vecihi Hürkuş was there of course working with a small group to clean up the area. He had already become familiar with the members of the resident submersive crew he inherited upon arrival. All good men who had done well to ensure that life on Phobus was sustainable. He was impressed really. They had all performed admirably. But still, he noticed smells that he'd not expected and at times noticed that the lichens covered stones and trees too broadly or not broadly enough. Some patches of earth seemed too dry while others showed signs of being dug up and replaced where it was imperative that they be left undisturbed to form compost. Perhaps things were not yet to his tastes is all, perfectly functional obviously, just not to his tastes.

Argyle was there, though the men addressed him as Lance Naik Thapa. Some delicate savory finger pastries had been prepared and light morning drinks served. He ensured all was ready in his speechless, unassuming way.

By far the most captivating groups were the photographers and those that operated the moving picture apparatus. Elphinstone pretended to understand the devices, being an engineering expert, but these were well outside the scope of his understanding. Bending time to propel space-liners and the inner workings of strahlendmachs was a far from bending light through a lens to imprint a chemical coated series of celluloid plates in rapid succession. But it only seemed proper for him to know, being the ship's engineer. There were to be four crews set up to film the occasion from four different vantage points, but one of the cameras was missing. They brought two along in the Daedalus and were to use two that had been shipped to Ares previously. Only one was found and the building crew professed to only ever knowing of the one. No matter, three would do. Just another last minute adjustment that required some attention.

As luck would have it, they had arrived on the eve of St. Crispin's Day, adding an additional air of fate, providence, destiny to moment. The Daedalus had a proud crew and prouder still that they had arrived on this auspicious date. A dead-on shot as it were across the black gulf of the silent sea. The film crews setup the cameras on fasteners on the large beams. The event would be recorded in many dimensions, one at eye level, one at the left flank roughly eighteen feet above the assembly, and the other completely overhead, looking down upon the ceremony. Still cameras were also present, where the floodlights gave them the best illumination. The spirit was nothing short of electric. They were as proud as those Englishmen on the fields of Agincourt, hearing for themselves old Harry's fearsome rhetoric. It was a great day to be British and a marvel to be on the feast of Crispin's.

Gavin arrived well ahead of the others to ensure everything was perfectly arranged. Campbell came over to him, granting assurances. Gavin wore white gloves and a fine suit interlaced with the wiring that kept it in precise shape, though a bit starchy by earthly standards. His checklist memorized, he went team-by-team asking all sorts of questions. "Is that the best place for that camera?" "Would it capture more from over there?" "Is that goat cheese on the pastry?" "Isn't there something a bit richer?" "Will the Duchess require additional assistance? She must look regal. What would be the best camera shot to enhance her regal appearance?"

In the midst of his supervision, Vecihi pulled him aside, a concerned look on his Turkish features. "Gavin," he said, "come," and the two made their way, well away from the others, into a thicket of brush out of eyesight.

"What is it?" Gavin asked. Vecihi looked back, to ensure no one was looking their way.

"Look here," Vecihi said, pulling himself to the ground and digging in the mat of pine quills and moist soil. His hands and fingernails becoming coated, he furrowed out a small patch of black earth that floated up a bit in a small cloud. "Here," he said.

"Here what?" Gavin asked.

"Here," Vecihi said emphatically pounding the earth, "take off your glove."

Gavin did so. Vecihi grabbed hold of his wrist and pulled his hand into the patch of earth he'd uncovered. The earth was damp and cold, clammy. Gavin's eye's searched Vecihi's look of concern. Looking up at Gavin, past his thick eastern brow, Vecihi said, "feel that? Too cold. The worms aren't moving. And smell. What do you smell?" Gavin drew in a thick nose of air.

"I," he said, "I don't know. What should I smell?"

"You don't smell that? Bad smell," Vecihi said, wrinkling his nose. "Like lye maybe," he said sniffing again. "And, what you don't smell. Should have a good smell. Like a farm field after tilling. No good, just bad. Very bad, Gavin, very, very bad." Gavin really didn't need more bad news, but in this area he was at a total loss.

"How bad, Vecihi? What do we need?"

"Not sure," he replied.

"You need to get sure. I need to know, maybe send something back to your people on earth? Something they can analyze? Send you back what you need on the next shipment?"

"Maybe," Vecihi said.

"Got to do better than maybe."

"You're right. Before you leave, I'll draft up orders," he said nodding in thought. "Meantime, I'll keep sniffing."

"Vecihi," Gavin said, "Keep this between us. I take it that there's no immediate danger?"

"No," Vecihi replied shaking his head.

"Good," Gavin continued, "just keep it between us right? And when you write your orders, write them in Turkish."

"Say again?"

"In Turkish man, write them in Turkish, no need to lose anything in translation. Tell them like they need to hear." Vecihi's look was beyond quizzical, more like disbelief.

"Alright," he said.

"Now let's be back before we're missed," and the two rejoined the gathering.

The hour had come and the steam whistles blew a tone for the special assembly. The entire building staff, aside from the essential maintenance crew, was to attend. They came to the aviary in their dark and ruffled clothes, unshaven faces, and the women with their hair tied back or stuffed under bonnets. Lt. Campbell acted like a church greeter, standing just inside the archway and assigning his men to escort the new comers to their assigned sections. They were a motley lot he noticed, all ages and sizes. Puffy heads and spindly legs like everyone who's been in space too long. Not a friendly sort either. He started with an expression glowing with pride, but found few to return his sincere hand of friendship. It wore on him quickly as the few dozen arrived and took their place, bobbing in the air a foot or two off the ground and slowly settling in a dull rustle. Argyle's breakfast treats seemed to perk them up a bit. They appeared delighted anyway, some feeling very privileged to sip a fine beverage and sample such tasty morsels. Argyle had made plenty so there was more than enough to give to all who wanted seconds and thirds. Havelock-Allen arrived with Piter and Miser in tow. The building crew paid them heed as they took their place in the section just behind the one set aside for the dignitaries. Campbell kept waiting for Crohne but none knew where he was or when he'd arrive.

Campbell kept an eye on his pocket watch and at just the top of the hour, he and two of the lads stood up at attention. He looked to the camera crews to begin filming. He and his accompaniment snapped their sabers and drew themselves up along the cords with military discipline making their way from the archway, up the path left clear from the procession at the centre. Once in place, they turned to face the group and

Campbell sounded his shrill ship's whistle marking the start of the christening.

Reverend Beckett was the first to enter, leading two of the builders who had been dubbed his altar assistants. Each one pulled behind them a burning brazier that puffed out sickly sweet incense, burning with an electric element so as not to violate Royden's chief prohibitions. They pulled themselves along the central chord, hand-over-hand, till they arrived at the front and pulled themselves to a proper upright position. The air was oddly silent. The quails sang. The ventilation fans whirred. The assembly ruffled about and some dared whisper to each other. It added a weighty solemnity to the ceremony.

The next to arrive was Sir Royden, dressed in a black poplin waistcoat and a jacket lined with black glace silk that had been brought to him on the Daedalus. His dashing appearance was foreign to the locals who responded with a rush of hushed commentary. He followed up the cord and joined Beckett and his incense bearing assistants. The royal contingent then began to enter, in the same order they did on the day of their departure under the blazing New Zealand skies, beneath the backdrop of Mt. Maunganui's majesty. The Lady Inverness was first of course, followed by the princess. Ol' Gran was with the servant girls faithfully keeping her ladyship's train in place. Cleland and Boswell followed and arrived as expected, tragically fashionable, Cleland with a flourish made all the more so in contrast to Boswell's staunchly appearance. Sir Wilson was close behind and he insisted that Argyle make the procession with him up to the front. Just one more in many acts of honorable admiration the old soldier lavished on another loyal soldier's behalf. The visiting Tyneside staff followed, Sir Listonn first and Crossland just behind. The two men were dressed in their business formals, the green sash of their brand stuffed neatly in their breast pockets. Captain Napier was the final attendant, joined by his senior officers. He was more stoic now than back at the ship's launch, or more reserved would be a better description. The gathering complete, Beckett held out his arms projecting the bold purple of his religious robes, draped with gold chains, glinting rings shining from his fingers. Chatter was heard over the crowd with the rattle of the cameras. A beam of light was repositioned to shine on Beckett directly.

"My friends," Beckett called out, "citizens of Ares Britannia, representatives from Tyneside Spaceyardes, royal guests, Her Majesty's subjects all, welcome to the celebration of the feast of St. Crispinus and Crispianus, and the christening of this bold platform. Before we proceed, we bow our heads and honor a moment of silence for our honoured dead. Those who have lost their lives in space. The many who sacrificed themselves in the building of this platform. The void is the most hollow of graves. We bow our heads and pray." The builders and Daedalus crew bowed low in a dreadful silence much to the surprise of the Royals who'd not known of this sentiment. Many of the builders and liner crew mouthed quiet prayers and some shed tears. Beckett took a long moment, a long mournful moment. The Royals could but only find their own thoughts and prayers to honor as they could. Finally, Beckett raised his eyes, flecking a tear with his finger and then folding his hands before him.

"People of Ares," Beckett declared loudly, "I've only been with you these short months, but I've developed a deep kinship with you. And before I turn the ceremony over to her esteemed ladyship, Cecilia Underwood, first Duchess of Inverness, I wish to steal a moment. I know, theft is not befitting my station, but as you've heard in my sermons I'm not one to dote on standard conventions of morality," he said with a knowing smile. A low rustle spread through the group. "In fact, you've all taught me a thing or two about the sacred and the profane. But now, I wish to set all rumors aside," he continued. "We know that Captain Napier and his fine crew have allocated space on the HMS Daedalus to permit my return home, but I'll not be leaving. When all of you signed papers and became the permanent residents of this most unique address you all sacrificed loved ones, dear homes and dear friends and said goodbye to cherished memories that you hold dear but will never again relive. I too have a life back on Earth. I've an adoring wife and three beautiful children all of whom wait expectantly for my return. But I cannot merely live among you and then slight your sacrifice by leaving you behind. It's isn't Christian. It's not what our beloved savior would do. And as such, I have decided to remain."

"Captain Napier," Beckett said turning to the Captain, "I thank you for your kind offer, but I must decline. I do hope my ticket is eligible for a refund. I mean it as no slight to your fine ship and seasoned crew." Napier broke a smile and held up a dismissing hand, there was no need for apologies. "So you're not rid of me," Beckett said turning back to those gathered, "You've got a lot more churching left ahead and I'm here to scare the sinner out of you or be damned in the attempt. The small crowd rustled again, the visitors followed along though a bit awkwardly. They couldn't but suppose that things were just different for those who lived in space. Turning to her ladyship, Beckett directed their attention over to her, ol' Gran led her toward the centre and stood by her side. Lady Inverness held several small note cards from which she read her speech.

"Loyal subjects," she projected, "I, the Duchess Inverness, Lady Cecilia Underwood, greet you on behalf of our reigning majesty, Queen Alexandrina Victoria, monarch of the United Kingdom of Great Britain and Ireland, Empress of India and as of today, Ruler of Mars. Here, at Ares Britannia with this ceremony, now, by royal edict, I officially pronounce to become a province in the grandest of empires to stand among the ages of man. Rome, bow your head in shame, the Pan-Hellenic dynasties, Alexandrian and Ptolemaic, look away. Persia with your hanging gardens, be lessened in the light of this grandest of wonders in which we stand. For in His divine providence, God has blessed the expansion of our British people. We who bring truth to the heathen, who bring agriculture to barren lands, who bring industry to the naked and unnourished, who bring civilization to the savage. The tree that flourishes behind me, rooted in English soil, is now a living monument. It is the largest living thing ever to reside away from the cradle of our earthly mother. It is a symbol of a migratory destiny that our great empire this day advances. We are the first people to claim a home far from the lap of any ocean wave or prevailing wind. It is upon this tree that we shall strike the glass and properly christen this platform, not only marking the hour but also launching into the next, for Ares has been erected for the future of our great people. I hereby charge all of you to perform your duties with pride knowing that a grateful nation looks to the heavens knowing that their comrades are here, labouring tirelessly to assure the generations to come a prosperous place among the great powers of the Earth and the emerging solar colonies."

Lady Inverness paused, inserting her notes lightly into the sleeve of her dress. She looked about for Royden, who slipped forward and passed her the bottle, nodding politely. Lady Inverness accepted politely in return and turned to face the broad trunk behind her. In a similar, unladylike fashion as she did back in Tauranga, she flung her hand back, the green bottle held firm and pitched forward. Her weightless state didn't serve her, the swing went wild, the bottle shot off, lost in the branches and she flung backwards, the train of her dress wrapping between her legs as she tumbled.

"Stop! Stop, stop the cameras," Campbell shouted out. The camera crews ceased their clattering. The crews slumped as they relaxed and took the time to reload. The crowd rumbled among themselves, murmuring and rustling. Some sailors hurried off into the branches for the missing bottle while Sir Wilson, Sandra and ol' Gran attended to the Lady Inverness. Her wig had been dislodged, but Sandra immediately helped put it back in place. Gavin shared an assuring word to Listonn and glanced over the group looking for Crohne, but wasn't quite sure if he was over by Culverton or not. Royden pulled himself forward and addressed the group.

"That's alright now," Royden said somewhat more commanding than they were used to hearing. "Everyone back in place. Come to order," and they complied. Composures regained, the cameras rolled again. Sir Wilson moved over to the Lady Inverness and grasped the lady's left arm in his to steady her while holding fast to the brass pole nearby. Bottle again in-hand, she pulled back and pitched again and again, missed the trunk entirely, the bottle speeding through the branches to set tufts of foliage floating about in the air. In the end, the cameramen took a shot of her at the ready and then a separate shot of the bottle, hurling through space until it struck squarely, a bright sparkling cloud of foaming champagne bursting out into the air in every direction. History would fail to record that it was Piter who did the throwing. The group was quieted again as the ceremony wasn't over yet. Another rush of whispered tones raced through the group. Listonn looked over at Gavin with a sly, knowing smile. Again taking her place, the Lady Inverness had one final official act to perform. Snuffing and clearing her throat, she began anew.

"By royal order of Her Majesty, in the right of due proceeding with the endorsement of Prime Minister Robert Cecil, Third Marquess of Salisbury and his parliament, has founded the Royal Victorian order of knighthood and related titles. And on this day, true accolades are in order. Mr. Crossland," she commanded looking over to him. Almost robotically, Gavin took a stiff move to come before her trying as he could to remain upright in mimicry of life held fast to the ground. "Mr. Gavin Henry Crossland, as a duly appointed representative of the Queen, I command you to kneel before me." Gavin gave an odd look about him and drew his legs up, trying as he could to lower himself to the floor. Listonn came to his side and assisted, nodding curtly to the Lady Inverness until Gavin was appropriately lowered. The Lady Inverness continued, "In the days of old, a man was knighted by the placement of a sword upon each shoulder but we are no longer living the days of such knights. Today is modern age and you, Mr. Crossland are one of that age's great designers. In honor of your achievements, leading the vast team of talented and learned men, we hereby knight thee in a way more befitting." Turning to her side, she looked to Captain Napier, "Captain," she said, "may I have the box I asked you bring. Complying, he shifted over, holding the box out so that the Lady Inverness could work the lock and open in. Curious himself, Napier looked down, not slightly aghast at what he saw. Napier looked over to his chief's and internal debate raging across his expression.

Reaching in, Lady Inverness lightly loosed its contents from the blue velvet lining that held it fast in a perfect form fit setting. Holding it up so all could see, she revealed a four-barreled revolving flintlock, exquisitely crafted with a long ivory handle and interlaced leafy vines carved up each barrel. It was an object of impeccable craftsmanship and it dazzled with the beauty and power befitting a symbol of the expanding empire. She held the weapon in a firing position and Gavin lowered his head. "Mr. Crossland," she said, "I hereby knight thee, Sir Gavin Henry, to be known hereby as the First Marshal of Mars, special grantee of the Royal Victorian order of knighthood," she said gently touching the business end of the weapon neatly upon each of his shoulders. "Also accept this firearm as your badge of office and a gift from Her Majesty who considers you the pride of her lost Prince Albert and the love of a grateful nation. Rise, Sir Crossland, and accept your badge of office." Struggling a bit to get his feet back under him, Gavin came more or less to a standing position and held his hands out to receive the flintlock. "And be careful," Lady Inverness said at a level only Gavin could hear, "the damn thing's loaded." Nodding his thanks, he took the gun in his right hand and held it sidelong to his chest. He spun lightly in the air to face the gathering who sounded in a moderate round of cheers and applause. Listonn clapped loudest with cheers for Tyneside and shouts of, "Hear, hear!" and "Yo-ho!" The ceremony concluded, the group was dismissed and ushered out the various exits back to the workday world and the ever pressing needs of life on Ares.

As the group dispersed, Gavin address those closest to him. "I thank you all for this," he said, gesturing slightly with the gun.

"Watch it with that, son," Napier said a bit crossly, "perhaps best to put it away." With an embarrassed rush, Gavin returned it to its case, Lady Inverness handing him the key. Now stowed, Gavin tucked it under his arm quite unwilling to give it up.

"Now then," he said, "the matter of the miners." As Gavin began afresh, he noticed that Burill Crohne had joined them. "Um, Beckett and I talked to Othello," he said with a nod of agreement from the reverend, "and as you noticed they weren't in attendance as we hoped. But, the good news is that they are very amicable and ah, Beckett and I will be meeting with them directly to discuss their grievances in detail. Sorry, Tom," he said to Listonn, "they were very specific, just Beckett and I are to meet them."

"And what of this Barabbas fellow," Lady Inverness asked, "will he also make an appearance?"

"I'm afraid not," Gavin answered, "they seem set on concealing his identity."

"All so needlessly mysterious," she commented.

Royden clapped twice loudly and builders dressed as servants brought fresh drinks. "A toast then," he said and all nodded in agreement as they took up their globes. Gleefully he pledged, "to Ares Britannia!"

"To Ares Britannia," they all resounded sipping from the glass stem.

"And to the knighting of Sir Crossland," Royden added to an equally resounding, "Hear, hear," and more drinking all around.

"Well done," Cleland added, playing absently with his earring and giving Gavin a sidelong look. "You'll be even more the talk back in England when we return. You're quite the up-and-comer, Sir Crossland."

"Yes, Sir Crossland," the Princess contributed, "a wonderful and most deserved title." Gavin offered bashfully humble thanks to each in-turn.

"Now ah, about the firearm," Royden ventured. "You'll of course turn that over to Captain Napier and remove it from the platform, yes?"

"Ah, no," Gavin countered, "I'll put it in my stateroom, I'll keep it quite safe I assure."

"Making history indeed!' Sir Wilson announced loudly. He took a long exaggerated drink from his globe followed by a waving gesture that he needed it refilled. "The day was sure to come, but never thought I'd be one to see it." he said in a mock toast, "may the bloody fool who fires the first shot be damned to hell for it."

The Lady Inverness cut in, "Ladies, gentlemen, and respected others, I make one final announcement. I say our journey here is a success and I'm now ready to return home. Captain Napier, ready the ship for launch, I'd like to be packed up and shipped out tomorrow."

"Aye, my lady," the Captain responded. "She'll be space worthy by the morrow."

"Now," she said, "I'm going to retire. Have my meal sent to the room I'll be dining alone. Oh," she gasped looking over at Sandra. The others looked over as well to find the princess in a swoon, drifting somewhat limply, her globe floating into space. "Dear, child," Lady Inverness said taking hold of her shoulders. "What is it?"

Princess Sandra's eyes rolled a bit but she came around. "Oh," she said, "dreadfully sorry, it's nothing. Feeling a bit faint."

"Are you alright?" Lady Inverness asked.

"Yes," Sandra said perplexed. "I've a tooth bothering me but fine otherwise, I have no idea why I slipped off."

"Sir Wilson," Inverness said, "please see the princess to her room."

"No, no," Sandra replied. "I'm fine. I can see myself back. I think I just need some rest." With a bobbing curtsy, the Princess excused herself and made her way back to her quarters. The Lady Inverness gathered up ol' Gran and bid farewell also. Ensuring that he was beyond notice, Cleland took the opportunity to silently slip away. Boswell, who was almost always clingy, didn't even notice when his companion left in a puff of secrecy. The others remained to chat and drink while the mixed group started removing the brass poles and dismantling the cameras. Crohne moved up beside Gavin and congratulated him lightly.

"I appreciate it, Christien," Gavin said, "but we've got to talk. There's things we've got to make right."

"Oh?" Crohne pressed.

"Of course," Gavin said perhaps emboldened by his accolades. Not one to miss out on good eavesdropping, Boswell caught on and slid a bit closer. Gavin continued, "There's a great many troubling things. Just now I've got Officer Hürkuş expressing concerns about the temperature of the soil, there's still the matter of the unexpected building projects and what about this Barabbas subversive?"

"I don't follow you, Gavin," Crohne said.

Gavin toyed with his ear, "I believe I'm a 'sir' now."

"Sir," Crohne said in a deadpan.

"I've trusted you up here, Christien," Gavin said, "it can't be all on Sir Royden to keep the ship right. I must hold you accountable." Crohne had no reaction. Gavin looked at him and away several times, unsure how to read him. "I don't know, Christien. I'll hear what Othello has to say and get to the bottom of this Barabbas affair. You and I can talk at length thereafter, but there are going to be some changes to come as a result. And if I win their trust, I need to get Boswell over to examine the miners."

Hearing his name, Boswell came closer. "Yes," Boswell said dripping with innocence. "Oh, talking about the absence of brickets are we?"

"Yes," Gavin said, focusing on the immediate topic, "anything new there, Doctor?"

"Well," Boswell said confidently, "I've been continuing my rounds and I do find expected things of course; head lice and some rashes that required a spot of ointment. Doesn't appear that any of the women are pregnant, though they could be concealing the expecting mothers as I can't account for everyone."

"No?" Gavin asked.

"Ah no," Boswell answered, "strangest thing. Can't seem to find them all. Not entirely sure, mind you. There are some misspelled names, men as well as women, but there are definitely some missing. Just don't know what to make of it," he said shaking his head.

"Christien?" Gavin asked.

"That would be a matter for the general manager, Sir Crossland," he replied.

Boswell looked for Cleland, but didn't see him. "Did either of you see what happened to Lord Cholmondeley?"

"I believe he left shortly after the Princess," Crohne said in his dry observant tone.

"Would you excuse me," Boswell said a bit bewildered. Gavin could only give Crohne a stern last look and they both silently agreed to leave the discussion for the time being.

***

When certain he was away from prying eyes, Cleland embarked on a mission. Knowing the presence of the service passages, he'd been able to formulate a mental map of the hidden maze of Ares Britannia. After some short wanderings about the central domes, he began to notice a pattern in the wall sections and decorations that revealed where the service ports entered and exited the tunnels. As he suspected, you needn't possess an advanced background in structural engineering to understand the basic needs of ventilation, electric wiring and hydro-pressure to catch the purpose of such tunnels. You can't very well rip out an entire wall section in the case of an emergency. Access to these features was an abject necessity. But, for one such as him, it was a playground of opportunity. Stealing back to his room, he locked his door and opened the concealed panel at the back. If his analysis was correct, a turn up those metal steps and a slip around to the right should take him to the vicinity of the observatory. After a short jaunt through the stagnant, dry passage he proved his theory right, but as he made his way he was certainly confused by the complexity. There were dozens of offshoots and ancillary passages. The observatory was a good destination for the novice as he merely had to keep always taking right turns until he arrived. With a bit more forethought, he was quite sure he could get almost anywhere on the platform.

He had to open a few panels to get his bearing but he finally found the one he wanted. He knew instantly after drawing it aside. It was very low, near the floor, but as it moved aside he looked down the metal deck plating that lay beneath a narrow hall ending in a glass wall overlooking the rugged landscape of Phobus. And there, silhouetted against the backdrop of a dazzling star field, was the figure of Princess Sandra. Her back was to him, her dress bare at the shoulders. She had done her hair up, a bit old-ladyish for his tastes but was appropriate and fashionable enough. Her slippers floating nearby, she hovered a few inches off the floor but held by a hand rail that ran along the glass. Cleland slid free of the opening and was able to quietly close it behind him. He drew himself up and lightly proceeded up the hall as hushed as he could.

Getting close behind her, he drew his gaze to the great outdoors and said, “Feeling better I hope princess.”

“Oh!” she spun clutching her hand to the key at her breast. “John!” she exclaimed, “how did you get in here? I’m quite sure I latched the door.”

“Did you?” he asked with the raise of an eyebrow, his golden earing catching the reddish light. “I hadn’t noticed. You’re feeling better then,” he said emphatically. “You’ve found quite a breathtaking room haven’t you? You can clearly see this crater and that crag and that, tall monolithic formation over there.”

“Well,” said Sandra. “I see you’ve an advanced knowledge of Phoban topography.”

“But of course. One can’t travel abroad without some knowledge of what sights to see and which to avoid.”

“And what sorts do you find best, John?” she asked.

"Oh, I'm still aligning what I've heard with what I see, to see if everything is as they say."

"As they say," Sandra said vainly attempting to follow.

"Oh you know, people talk and say all kinds of things. Then you see for yourself to determine the truth of it. The most delightful appearing packages don't always contain the greatest gifts. That's a child's Christmas folly. We both are too advanced to be deceived by brightly wrapped packages."

"And what is the cure for this folly, John?" she said turning toward him.

"Well!" he scoffed, "you unwrap the package don't you? Tear it all off. Rip it to shreds. No folly in that. No one outgrows the fun of tearing off the wrapping."

"Oh, Sir John," Sandra said, "you've a mind for metaphors, don't you?"

"All part of a writers' palate aren't they?"

"Indeed, but by the calendar it's St. Crispin's isn't it? Not a traditional day for unwrapping."

"Can't we make our own St. Crispin's traditions? Someone has to make them up sometime?"

"Oh they do but I rather like St. Crispin's just as it is. Always reminds me of Shakespeare's Henry V, you know?"

"Once more into the breach?" Cleland quoted with a look as sly as he ever mustered.

"Ah yes, I see you are, 'God for Harry, England, and Saint George.' Isn't Harry Mr. Crossland's middle name? Oh, Sir Crossland I should say. Extraordinary man, don't you think?"

Cleland gave a long exhale. "Yes, of course."

"Of course," she echoed. "I wonder if he's about? I think I'll go find him and thank him for this indescribable view. As well deserving a man as he should hear it don't you think?" Taking a few glances out the window he had to nod in agreement. "What," she asked, "Have your metaphors run out on you?"

"Princess, I am never at a loss."

"Never? Sometimes we all find ourselves at a loss don't we? Well then, shall we take our leave out the surely latched door, or do you have some other means of escape?"

"No, Sandra, I believe the door will suit me fine. After you." he said with an overly deep bow.

***

Boswell couldn't help but be a tad frantic. No amount of title, education or good breeding saved him from being susceptible to frantic moments. He couldn't find a single soul as he worked his way from dome to dome until he got to Cleland's door. He found it locked. He knocked loudly but no one answered. Boswell has a strong suspicion that Cleland was further exploring the service tunnels. Just what his friend would do to see what other opportunities they offered. Thankfully the doctor had found a similar panel in his own room through which he could make pursuit. Entering his stateroom, he locked his door, struck up the electrified candlestick and made off into the cramped tunnels.

The passages were deathly cold and more so as he continued. He came to an intersection and debated which way to turn. "Cleland," he whispered up each side. Hearing nothing, nothing at all, he chose at random and continued. At first he tried to count left vs. right turns in their proper order but there were soon too many to remember. The fear of being lost touched him. He turned both ways debating to continue on or to turn back. "Cleland!" he called out again. "Shit!" he called out, "Bloody fucking shit!"

He doubled back but was hopelessly lost. There were too many passages. Did he come from the second on the left or was it the middle hall? Should have been bloody well dropping breadcrumbs had he been thinking. He took a breath to collect himself. Trace thoughts wandered across his mind. Thoughts of his family and associates back on earth. He shook his head in a bit of deprecation, if they could only see him now.

As chances were, he found a dull glow up one passage. He'd not seen one before in this maze, so he went that way thinking that it could very well lead back to the commons. Instead it was a small room with a low ceiling and some oddities spread about. His eyes first fell on a stack of equipment that was strapped to the wall. There was also a table bolted there that had miniature reels and spindles and tools for knifing and adjoining lengths of film. 'Curious,' he thought. All of these were items of which he had a rudimentary understanding. Bolted firmly to the centre of the room was a projector, the companion device that he knew would play back a recording. Full spools of film were held at the end of metal arms. Stacks film canisters were bound up with twine and stowed under the table. He'd no idea how it worked, but understood the ocular "anatomy" of it. The optical illusion made by flicking a progression of images before the eye to simulate movement on a two-dimensional space. There was a dial on the wall that raised the electric lights up and down. For the moment he forgot all about being lost and reveled a spell at his interesting discovery. There was a reel of film loaded in the projector and he figured there must be a simple way to activate it. He fuddled around a bit. Turned a knob here and flipped a switch there. Finally, he found the right one. A light burned bright in its inner working that was directed through a set of expanding lenses. Gears began to turn with a frightful noise and the adjoining reels spun at a quick pace. Distracted at first by the machinations, he didn't quite connect the projection but the lit movement in his peripheral vision drew him to look upon the bare patch of wall to his left.

Blurry, patchy monochrome images in the color of burnt sepia were splashed on the wall. Truly extraordinary he thought, seeing a motion picture for the first time. He had to step back to make it out, back toward the passage where he'd come in. He finally had to wipe off his glasses on his shirt to ensure he could make out what he was seeing.

In the flittering light, there was the form of a woman, naked, in a reclining position, floating a couple feet off the ground. The wall behind her was featureless. It could have very well been filmed here on Ares, but who knew? Her white, bare legs were toward the viewer, the hair on her genitals, a dark patch on her white skin. Her hair was long and dark and surrounded her head in a cloud. He couldn't tell if she was breathing. He'd seen some medical still photography to document patients, conditions and procedures. This image had a clinical tone like that. Another figure moved on from the right wearing a white robe, as white as the woman's skin. The new figure turned to face the camera to show that he was wearing some kind of garish devil mask. It was vulgar, made of paper-mâché or some other crude substance and painted some brash colors that appeared as various gradients on the flicking film. The man seemed to snicker in an overly dramatic set of gestures, like comic fiendishness. Again turning his back to the camera he hiked up his robe to reveal his bare backside. "What is this now?" Boswell said aloud. The masked figure reached back under his anus and proceeded to pass excrement into his hand. Repulsively, he kneaded it with his fingers, coating them with it.

He turned back toward the viewer, working it in both hands, presenting it to the camera. He then proceeded to smear it on the body of the woman. Dear God I hope she's a cadaver, Boswell thought. He was disappointed to see her begin to move in response to the man's touch writhing a bit as he coated her with dark smudges. The devil-man reached out with his left hand, wads of the stuff still clinging to his fingers and went to touch her face. Whoever was filming pushed the camera forward for a closer shot. The stained fingers touched her forehead and the devil-man dragged them down, over her eyes and onto her lips. Suddenly the film cut-off, draping Boswell in gloom, the projector rattling a bit and the end of the film flapping free. Boswell was thankful that the display ended. Looking back at the projector, he saw that it continued to grind and turn. In a further surprise, an armature automatically loaded another full reel into place.

A fresh scene was spread across the facing wall and feeling an infernal grip he felt compelled to watch again. The same woman was there in a similar position and again naked but now obviously deceased. Splotches of decay were evident about her extremities. Even given the crudeness of the image it was easy for Boswell to tell. He'd seen enough necrotic flesh on the living and the dead. The woman's face was notably beaten and swollen. He believed he could also make out lacerations and contusions that could have very well been given before death. He couldn't be sure. She was still caked with excrement, now dry and flaking off. He felt a pang of guilt. The borders of his tolerance were surpassed by the macabre. On countless occasions he'd seen cadavers and even horrifyingly mutilated patients. At school, theatrical demonstrations on live subjects were common. But this was something else. He knew deeply that he shouldn't be watching this. The devil that made it was damned but such images also stain the onlookers' soul. He saw shadows move in the flickering images so there was certainly someone else in that room, maybe more than one person. The man with the devil mask came on again, sliding in from the right hand to press his paper face in the camera. Woefully out of focus you could hardly make him out. He backed up and again hiked up his robe to reveal himself. He was aroused and he turned sideways to present himself. He then wrested that poor girl's body away from the wall and took hold of it, pulling to towards him. Having seen far more than enough, Boswell looked away. He tried to turn off the projector reversing the way he activated it but that somehow didn't work, it kept right on playing. He glanced back at the image and saw that it had become violent. He flipped the switches and spun the knobs finally slapping senselessly at its case trying to deactivate it. The guilt pounded in his head like pressure mounting in his veins. Like his neck was too taut, so taut the muscles attempted to choke the flow of blood to his brain. There was damnation in that film, an unwritten mortal sin that surpassed all forgiveness. To view that thing must seal shut the gates of heaven. No saviour's blood could wash that horrid stain from your soul. "How do you turn this fucking thing off!" he yelled and as if by vocal command it ceased.

His hands were red and raw from striking its case. They smarted in the air before him. The projector wound down slowly, the clack of its rotation coming in shorter and shorter pulses. He had no idea what stopped it. Nothing he had done. In the half-light of the room he jumped as his electric candlestick rose from the floor where he left it. There was a man there. He suddenly became aware of another behind him who must have drifted silently up the hall. Bereft and gasping he circled to see another, cast over in darkness. The man behind him held up a cable that ran to a metal tube bolted to the wall. He had severed some kind of electrical connection to the projector. Without speaking the three pressed toward him. Boswell could only breathe in shallow, quavering gasps. Boswell stared at the man behind him, clutching the stand holding the camera. Staring into the dark space where the man's head should be, he asked,

"Are you Barabbas?"

The man swung his right hand in a broad arc and struck Boswell in the temple with a metal pipe. The force of the blow smashed Boswell sidelong into the projector, many of its protruding parts piercing his hands and arms. The blow dazed him to near senselessness. He felt a long metal shaft thrust into his midsection. He felt it hit below his ribs and then pass out the other side. He could almost picture that flat plane of metal cutting through the core of his abdomen. Another blow stuck him again. Then another, and another, and Dr. Boswell spent the last agonizing moments of his life being beaten until his body could take no more and expired.

Course hands pulled his body along a passage illumed only by the very candlestick Boswell had brought with him. His body was thrust into a long rectangular container, a metal box about the same size and shape as a coffin. Levers were pulled that pressed his form into lye slacked with water that directly started about the process of dissolving his body.

Chapter H (8): Pantheons

Not taking any time to change, Beckett and Crossland made up the interconnecting passage that led to the 'Choker', a wider point about midway between the central domes and mining camp. There were no finishing touches in this part of the platform. Arched steel supports ran like a ribcage and the floor below them was Phoban soil, warmed by broad buried pipes that pumped heat toward the domes. The walls were jumbled lengths of pipes and cables. There were no windows here but every few steps there was a massive pressure door to be sealed in case of emergency. At the foot of each door was a box-like socket set by the door frame, a matching one on either side.

"Beckett," Gavin asked, "that gear and lever key that Christien has, is that the only one that works those locking contraptions?"

"You mean you don't know?" Beckett asked. "I figured you must have designed it that way. No clue how it works, but Dr. Crohne can work almost any door from anywhere he can plug into one of those sockets. And once he locks them he's the only one who can unlock it. Figured it was a strong arm management policy."

"Yes," Gavin answered thinking. "So it would seem." The two were then arrested by a metal bang that came up the passage before them. "What's that?" Gavin said with a fright.

"That," Beckett said, "is a show of force. They're striking the walls with lead pipes."

"What the hell for?" Gavin shouted and the banging continued.

"To show that they're ready for a fight," Beckett answered. "I believe you know there's been tussles."

"Bloody hell," Gavin cursed and thankfully the banging stopped.

"Didier!" Beckett called up the hall. "It's just me and Mr. Crossland, just like we said!" Gavin couldn't help but think, "Sir" Crossland but it was no time for formality. "We're not armed, Didier, you can come up and throttle us all you like!" The two waited quietly in the dark hall. Lights then rose up ahead and they could see a makeshift barricade. Welded plates and enormous rocks made for a formidable looking strong point. Five large men stood up behind the barricade. They were dirty, like they hadn't bathed in their lives. They were dressed in heavy suits that were designed to withstand a vacuum for a short time. Brass collars adorned their necks where a metal helmet could be bolted down. Their bare arms were sweaty and bulged with strength. They brandished an assortment of weapons, metal pipes and jagged shafts of steel that had been sharpened like a shiv or broad knife. "Didier," Beckett greeted, "a fine welcome."

"You know, Beckett, got to be saf," Didier called back. He was a startlingly small man, who was nearly bald, but sported a finely shaved beard and mustache He was dressed just like the others, nothing outstanding distinguished him. He had an imposing wrench in one hand and his forearms were wrapped in thick chains. The ends of those chains floated free as if he could use them as weapons as well. "So dis is da man. Knight now I hear. So nice for you."

"Yes, Didier," Beckett answered, 'This is Sir Gavin Crossland here just to talk, just like we said."

"Yes," Gavin called up, "a pleasure."

"So," Beckett said, "are we going to shout at each other or can we come over? You see we are unarmed, just like we agreed."

"Ya," Didier answered, "you come up, but you stay on dat side right? You stay on your side, we stay on ours." Beckett gave a frustrated eye roll and shook his head. He then drew himself along the two-score feet that separated them, Gavin right behind. As they passed the obtrusive rocks, Didier hefted his wrench. "Far enough," he said. Gavin gave a quick look up at Beckett, stretched his neck and shoulders and addressed Didier directly.

"Good, sir," Gavin said, "where do we begin?"

"Do we begin by you talkin' or you listenin'?" Didier asked.

"You're right," Gavin answered, "You're very right. I came here to listen, Mr. Marouani, do I say that right? Marouani?"

"You say it fine," Didier replied, "See if you hear fine. See if we be trustin'. You folks. You ask us to be trustin' all de time." Didier gave a slow look to his companions who nodded grim agreements. They scratched their unshaved faces and kept their arms in plain view. "So you see for yourself, Sir Crossland. We got de nice show of force but we know. We got nutting. Da bruisers come down here wantin' a fight we got one but who we kidding? You own us. We like babes."

"What do you mean?" Gavin asked.

"I mean da air," Didier said drawing in a large breath. We got our own plants down here, makin' our air but not enuf. You shut de doors and we ded. All of us, but you die too, cuz we own da heat."

"Yes," Gavin said, "we are all very aware of that."

"Your fault," Didier said, pointing his wrench at Gavin. "Didn't know how fast we'd grow. How the mine would be so hot. Had to compensate. Put da big generatahs down by us. On dis side of da choka. You turn off da airh and we turn off da heat. We all die. Stalemate, Sir Crossland. Stalemate."

"Now, Didier," Gavin said, "why ever would we do that? We are all vested in this place. We can't operate without you."

"Oh no? Why not? Flush us all inta space. Start overah. What are we to you? Just workahs who could be replaced, that easy."

Gavin spoke looking at Beckett for support, "I think you've misjudged us. No one wants to do any harm to you. I can speak for everyone you've got nothing to fear."

"Oh no? Where do we start? Let me ask you dis. You got any mail for us?"

"Mail?" Gavin asked.

"I didn't tink so. Not one of us has gotten any mail for years." Didier's grim companions all nodded in agreement.

"None of you?" Gavin asked.

"Not a one. Back when we got mail we got it opened. You read it before we got dem. Read the ones we sent too I'll bet if they sent em."

"Preposterous," Gavin said. "Your right to the post is guaranteed by law."

"Der is no law up here, Sir Crossland. Ders no lawyers ant no judges. Ders' just Piter and Miser, comin' round to crack skulls. Dats the law here. Builder's law."

"Well that ends here." Gavin said with the voice of a gentleman. "I was made marshal when I was dubbed a knight just now. So I'm Her Majesty's law now. Give me your post and I'll hand deliver them on my return. Each and every one of them."

"Oh yeah," Didier asked. "My wife got a sistah on da moon. You gonna take dat too?"

"Yes. I'll walk from Tranquility to Tycho and back again to hand it to her no matter what platform she's at."

"Ha," Didier said. "Maybe alright for you, but maybe not. I almost went to da moon before I came here. Hear it may be worse there, I don't know."

"Worse on the moon?" Gavin asked.

"I hear dea're slavahs on da moon. What you say? Bettah to be a slave on da moon or a prisonah on Mars? Which one?"

"No, Didier, you can't consider yourself prisoners. People are coming and going from Ares all the time. I've seen the records."

"Yeah now," Didier said. "Comin' and goin' are dey?

"Yes," Gavin assured, "We've got three liners now that can make the voyage. They can't necessarily bring you back to Earth, but you can go to the moon or one of the orbital platforms freely. Once your contractual obligations are fulfilled you're free men."

"How about my wife?" Didier asked.

"Your wife, yes, Beckett mentioned."

"He did huh? Did he tell you dat she's gone? Gone with da brickets?"

"Brickets," Gavin asked looking puzzled at Beckett.

"De brickets, de brickets, de brickets, everyone gets the brickets," Didier said. "Back a ways, de come down here sayin' dis one got da brickets or dat one. Odd ting though. Seems like the fair ladies get the brickets more den da men. Fair skinned ladies. My wife had fair skin. She got sick ya, said it was brickets. I've not seen her since. Dat was a long time ago."

"I'm sorry, Mr. Marouani," Gavin said, "you have me at a loss. You see, I was informed that there are no brickets on Ares Britannia."

"Ha!" Didier laughed along with those on his side of the defenses. "You got ya head up ya arse. Everyone in space get the brickets. Everyone. Just when and what kind. Some lose da hair, some bleed from der teeth but everybody gets the brickets out here. Da strong, da weak, da young, da old. Everyone."

"So I don't understand," Gavin said.

"So back when Piter and Miser, de come down here. De say, dis one is sick. Got to come wit us, so de go. Neverah see dem again. Must be lot of people in de infamary."

"Ah, no," Gavin said slowly, "quite the contrary."

"And den der's the policies you know da Tyneside papahs."

"No, I don't know," Gavin said, his spirits falling.

"Jink, jink, jink, dat how it is up heah. All about da jink."

"I'm sorry," Gavin said, "I'm just not following."

"You da big man and here I is teachin' you."

"Yes," Gavin said, "inevitably you are. Teaching me a great many things."

"So when you get herah, de say, hey man, you need da policy. So if you die dey send good money back to ya family. People die up here a lot. You sign dis. You sign, de take your wage."

"All of it?" Gavin asked.

"No, but a lot. Den you say, hey boss I want good hammock. Da one I gut full of bugs. And de say, 'ok but you gotta pay da jink.'"

"And what does a bug free hammock cost you?"

"Hard to say, de market seems to change a lot. You got da jink, seems like dats what it cost. You got more jink, cost a bit more. It's like that. You got ta hide your jink just like Barabbas hides his face. You got to hide up here, Sir Crossland. You say hid is good. But now, no jink. No one knows about no policies and you don't get da ore. You get nothing from da mine. Not a damn dusty rock. Not till we make it right. All of it. Everyting."

"What else do you need to make it right?" Gavin asked swelling with resolve.

"Betteah food," Didier stated

"Done," Gavin said with strength. "What else?"

"Honest work dey, hard work for hard pay, no hard work for nutting."

"Done. And I'll find out what happened to your wife and everyone else who is missing. And I'll make good my promise about the post. If I have to do it by hand myself or I'll be damned." Didier gave Gavin a long looking over. He turned to his companions. It was difficult to find the hope in their eyes. Gavin could judge character. He'd made his life judging character.

"Just like that?" Didier asked softening.

"Just like that. My word as an officer of Tyneside Spaceyarde, Ltd. You will be satisfied."

"I don't know, Sir Crossland," Didier said. "Sounds too easy. You know, sure. And Beckett know. But you're going ta leave soon."

"I'm not leaving," Beckett spoke up.

"Sure," Didier continued, "you stay but everyone else leaves. Then what? Piter and Miser come back around. And where is da marshal? Oh, he's back in space playin' postman."

"No," Gavin said, "It's not like that. If there have been crimes committed and I don't doubt there has, there will be justice. I've got a liner full of armed sailors who'll apprehend anyone I need to make sure things are set right." Didier took unsure glances at his friends. They respected him too much to speak, but their faces spoke volumes.

"Ok," Didier said, "I'll take dis to Barabbas. We'll talk. He says yes, we'll make you a deal for da ore. Everyting on papah. And you be sure, we got da ore, Sir Crossland. We got gold and silvah like you nevah seen. Like no one's eveah seen. We know how to mine in Phobus. We tapping deep and I tell you, we tappin' good."

"Othello," Gavin said, "you have a deal. It would be my good pleasure to shake on it."

"Not yet," Didier said, well behind the barricade. "You keep your hand and keep your head. I talk to Barabbas. We get everyting down on papah. Then there'll be time for shakin'."

"Watch my head you say?" Gavin asked.

"Ares is a deep place and Phobus be an old moon. De dak places here, Sir Crossland. Very, very dak. De got a kiln back dere, Sir Crossland. De burnin' somethin'."

"A kiln? What are they doing with a kiln?"

"We don't nethier. Don't know what to tink. But de burnin' and who knows what? And de got passages. All kinds a little passages all over de place. Who knows what de hidin' back der."

"Didier, I'm sorry, but that's a lot for me all at once."

"Just know dis, you don't know. Remebah dat. You don't know. Keep dat and keep you saf."

"I will remember." Gavin agreed without much understanding as to what he was agreeing to.

"Da talk over, Sir Crossland. I hope I see you again. If I don't I won't blame you."

"Oh you'll see me again, Mr. Marouani. You'll all see me again." The miners pulled their weapons and made two rapid bangs against the metal, bang-bang! And with that the "negotiation" was over.

***

The crew of HMS Daedalus came alive with preparations. Gavin had pled with Captain Napier to give him ample time, but the Duchess

Inverness had commanded their departure and she was the Queen's delegate. They'd only wait as long as she'd allow. Most of the sparse crew was deep in the bowls of the liner refitting for departure. The strahlendmachs wore hard on the engines and anomalies could crop up. Little bits of misplaced time and space that could foul up the works. A nasty business if they weren't corrected. Every gear and every junction needed to be stripped, checked for fractures, oiled and returned before they could depart. It was a very vulnerable time for long-haul liners. In many ways she was bared to the very bones and lamed in the water. Just so much stellar flotsam until the engines could be fired up again. It made for long tedious work but the crew was able to meet the demand. They knew well the cost of failure and left nothing to chance. They made Napier proud. He took the time to walk among them. He was a leader who knew how to shed gratitude for work well done.

Once the men had all their orders, Elphinstone and Campbell beseeched the Captain to allow them to return to the platform. They wanted to say farewell to their good mate, Warrant Officer Hürkuş to tip one last pint, as it were, before they left.

"Go on, lads," Napier said, "I'll go below and get soiled with the men. But if you come back drunk you'll spend the ride back in irons," he said in all seriousness, "I'll fly her home myself."

"Right, sir, never dream of it, sir," they both said, soberly to say the least.

"Tip a pint for me and give Vecihi my best. He's a credit to his people." Napier sent them off and went below decks to supervise the refitting personally.

For the royal contingent it had been a tediously ceaseless "afternoon" posing for commemorative photographs. An eternally ponderous process, the photographers took takes, retakes and further retakes requiring additional time to reload the cameras.

Cleland found it all painfully boring. He did as he could to escape them and head back to his room. He at least had enough opium to make the process tolerable. Every time he passed by Boswell's room he pounded on his door but he didn't answer. Cleland had begged his father, the third Baron Delamere to let Boswell join the contingent. Paid for his inclusion with old Delamere money, and not a small amount of it. As much of a boor Boswell could be, they were like minded and literary, though Boswell's own writing wasn't fit for a penny dreadful. Boswell's absence wouldn't be missed by the historians but it was felt deeply by

Cleland. He most likely found more doctoral duties or some other malfunctioning part of this Martian monstrosity.

They had one more, semi-formal meal which Boswell skipped as well. The Lady Inverness did also. The others were there, Sir Royden and Havelock-Allen from Ares, Listonn, Princess Sandra and Sir Wilson going on about his war stories. This time Argyle joined them at the table. He still remained speechless but nodded affirmations after every word Wilson spilled out on the table. Wilson was already insufferable to listen to and more so with that little brown man nodding the whole time.

Miser appeared at the entrance, but remained in the doorway. Catching Culverton's eye he waved him over. Culverton was notably irritated. He dotted off the corners of his mouth and excused himself.

Cleland could just overhear him as Culverton neared the door. "What?" Culverton asked.

"It's just like back in Chicago," Miser explained as they drifted out of the entry and made their way. Wilson could no longer hear what they were saying.

Cleland couldn't help but notice that the Princess was melancholy. She feigned interest as all ladies were trained but it was a mockery of interest to be sure. Her eyes revealed the truth. With no announcement, she rose from the table and the men of course rose out of courtesy.

"Feeling alright, Princess?" Wilson asked.

"Yes of course, you are kind, Sir Wilson," Sandra replied, "but I'm very well. I don't know what that spell was that came over me but it's passed. Maybe ol' Gran's been practicing her charms."

"Very good," Wilson said, giving her a peck on the cheek as she left.

Cleland's pride still stung from their encounter at the observatory. He sat again, affixing his pants to the chair and fiddled with his curls. Wilson started off praising the exploits of the Indian martial races during the rebellion.

"You should have seen them fight back in '58," Wilson resounded, "the 25th Punjab infantry was called the Hazara Goorkha Battalion. Fearful soldiers like none others. They shoot like marksmen but they're even more fearful in close quarters. Those kukri blades are murderous." Argyle accepted the praise with humility.

"So tell me," Listonn asked, "what is it about them? What makes Argyle's people so fearsome?"

"It's their bloody sectarian branch of their religion," Wilson blurted, not slightly drunk. "In their sense of earthly balances there are great creators and great destroyers and they worship the destructive forces. As followers they are agents of the same. Oh, they may appear to be farmers and shepherds but they harbour beasts in their chests. Picture if you will, going to Sunday service every week and instead of hearing love they neighbor from the pulpit you heard 'slit his bloody throat.'" The others all looked at Argyle, perhaps in a different light than before. Here he was, a little man who feels a religious obligation toward destruction, preparing their meals and always about as Wilson's valet. Argyle's own pair of kukri knives ever bound up neatly in the small of his back. "I forgot who said it," Wilson spoke overly loud, quaffing another long draw from his globe. "Show me a man who claims to fear not death and he is either a liar or a Gurkha."

Having heard beyond his fill, Cleland pushed back and loosed himself from his chair.

"Good evening, Lord Cleland," Sir Royden called after him but Cleland ignored him.

Princess Sandra had gotten to him. He was prone to it he knew. He was a man of satisfaction and he could not stand its denial. He slammed the door to his room shut and attempted to pace. He couldn't pace of course which was more maddening still. He debated returning to the Daedalus where at least the gravity would allow him to pace but no. He stared at that panel. That hidden door at the back of his chamber. One click and he could steal into her room. Not very gentlemanly at all. How would she react? Would she scream like the young girl she is, a shrill scream that would send every hand running? That would be difficult to manage. The Lady Inverness would be outraged. She'd have that oaf Napier slap him in cuffs and shackled in the brig. That could make for a long ride home. He thought about that H. H. Holmes monster back on earth in America. Hung from the neck until dead for all the unearthly things he did to so many women. But that was murder for profit, not sport if there's anything sporting about it. Maddening as women could be he could almost see it. Nothing so sinister could be voiced but they did drive him mad. The Princess drove him mad. Madness be damned. He had charmed women both older and younger than Princess Sandra. He was no monster. He was learned, courtly and silver tongued. He would play his hand at this. Pressing in at the hidden panel he drew it aside and ducked in, faithful to return it into place in the passage behind him. His nose was assaulted by a foul smell, like burning lye or some other acrid substance. So much for the stink, that was Vecihi's lot. John's lot was conquest and there was new territory to conquer.

His navigational skills were now honed to perfection. He knew that the steps up brought him above the hall of the men's portion of the rooms. Following it along to the end naturally brought him to the lady's. Dropping down the steps on the other side he only had to count the panels till he hit the third door. Like a true gentlemen, he rapped before he entered but immediately after rapping he allowed himself in.

"Now Sandra," he said, "do not cry out," but his words were drawn from him. She hovered at the far side of the room, facing him. She's let her hair down and it fell in curls on her bare shoulders. That flirting tempting key was at her breast, lying flat. She was still dressed … mostly. Her gown had been removed and the metal laced hoop of her train drifted in the corner nearby. Her eyes were a stunning blue in the light of the electric candle.

"Why, Lord John," she said in her light feminine voice, "not what one would call an appropriate entrance."

"No," Cleland's words sounded almost dull and lifeless compared to hers.

"Perhaps you should explain your rude intrusion to a lady's private room."

"Ah, you see I, I've come to seduce you."

Princess Sandra burst out laughing. It was a full-on laugh, from the diaphragm. Full bellied and sincere. "Oh dear, John, I am one of the most chaste women in the whole of Britain. My sisters and I are commodities. The Queen is our aunt for God' sake. We are worth our weight in gold and each of us will be married off to secure the wealth and welfare of our nation. And here you think you've come to seduce me."

Cleland stood fast. He stood strong. He stood as a man and he looked at her with a look to penetrate though he found himself impotent to do so.

Lady Sandra played with the key at her breast, fingering it as she looked at him. She clutched it hard in her fist and with a sharp tug, broke the wraith thin silver chain that held it. She brought it to her lips and kissed it. Her lips were still a blood red from her lavish lipstick which rubbed off a bit on the key. She held it in her open palm and with a blow from her wet lips, sent it adrift toward Cleland. It billowed a bit, but flew true wafting within his reach. He snatched it from the air, the two ends of the chain still snaking about like living things. Sandra gave a look down to a trunk strapped to the wall, near the floor to Cleland's left. He worked himself down and opened it to find a box nestled in her clothing. It was twenty inches or so long and perhaps eight deep. There was a small silver lock on its facing edge. He stopped and looked back at her, but she stared on, not a muscle moving on her face to tell what she was thinking. He breathed deep, cleared his throat and fit the key in the lock. It entered perfectly and he turned the key on well-oiled tumblers. Lifting its lid, he peered inside. And frankly he was almost shocked to the point of blushing. He blinked a few times and then looked up at Sandra with a smile like few others he'd ever smiled.

"Oh, Lord John," she said and she reached back and started unfastening. "You see it was I who seduced you." She let her corset fall down a bit from her shoulders. "But heed a simple warning. When you leave this room I will be the same chaste and unsullied woman as when you entered."

"Unsullied," Cleland smiled. "I'm not your first seduction."

"Of course not, and all the lovers I've taken have kept my simple rule. If there is any word of this in the tabloids I won't be the one to suffer for it. I am loved by many and that love is of a persona, a person I play for my audience and it serves me well. Keep that appearance intact and I may seduce you again."

"May seduce me again?" Cleland asked with an eyebrow raised.

"If you please me. Consider this a test. I do hope you don't get anxious when tested. Some men feel so very pressured. But I assure, if I don't like the main course I shan't come back for seconds." Cleland drew the box from its concealed place. Sandra pushed off the wall and floated toward him.

"Oh, you'll find I'm very proficient with these," Cleland said, "Your pleasure is assured."

"Then cease using your mouth to talk," she said now close enough to place a slender finger on his lips. "I so wanted to wait to be weightless for this," she said in a tone that slipped through Cleland's very being and resounded within him.

Their embrace was deep and greedy. They relinquished themselves to each other and their heads swelled in the drunken heat of the moment. In their throes, neither of them considered that someone else may be present in the lattice work of tunnels behind her room. Nor were they aware that some panels contained tiny spy glasses. Nor did they realize that every room in Ares Britannia was designed to be air tight as to allow for precise atmospheric control. These functions had to be very, intricately exact, just as Vecihi Hürkuş so liked to remind them. A hidden slot on the service panel leading to the princesses' room slid open and their proclivities were observed by prying eyes.

The lovers wrestled, floating in space, enraptured with the dizzying height of their affections. That pair of invading eyes looked long on them. They looked as long as they liked until they no longer liked. The stranger's hand took hold of a metal valve. The valve was fastened to a pipe that led into Sandra's room. At each turn, the vale opened and a hiss became louder as a vapour held within was allowed to seep into the sealed space of Sandra's room.

Cleland lavished himself on Sandra. They were so betaken they became lost, hopelessly lost, in each other's arms. There came a point when Cleland was sure she swooned. He continued his vigourous thrusts, but he grew alarmed as she began to grow limp in his hands. He thought she lied about her spell earlier so she could make off to the observatory, all part of the seduction in retrospect. John noticed that the air seemed richer. He thought it was just his breathing, of course one gets winded. He was winded but there was something else, something somehow depleting. Could it be the weightlessness? His thrusts slowed. His arousal left him. He took Sandra lightly by the back of her head and tried to catch her eyes.

"Sandra," he said but she couldn't respond. Her breath was stilted. Her eyes rolled back in her skull. He found his own breath hindered. There was a steely taste in his mouth. An ache crept into his joints as if he was fevered. He let Sandra go to float freely and he turned to make for the panel in the back of her room. As he neared he could hear a hissing like a motorcar's tire had sprung a leak. Like a venomous serpent or agitated cat was permanently voicing fear and aggression. As he neared the panel his vision blurred. There were wavy lines warping everything like he was looking through a fun-house mirror. His breath seized and he gasped. He clutched at his throat to clear his airways, but they shut tight.

The man at the other side of the panel was overwhelmed to see Cleland die so close to him, so very close to his very hiding spot. It was like a gift. Another valve deftly reversed the flow of gas. The room that was just then a deathtrap became a life sustaining environment once again.

The man pulled the panel open and gathered up their remains. He pulled them both lightly into the dark hall within, leaving the rest of the room completely as the lovers left it.

Chapter Q (9): Adrift in the Rocks

Gavin Crossland and the Reverend Beckett barely spoke as they made their way back. The lights in the passages remained dim and the hall resonated with echoes. The reverend did his best to pry Gavin's thoughts from him but to no avail. Once back up the hall on the dome side, Gavin made it a point to curtly thank Beckett for accompanying him. Beckett accepted with sincerity and said, "It was my great pleasure and perhaps some real good will come of it." Beckett made a final attempt to detain him with anecdotes. He started in about certain members of the building team, parishioners who also expressed grievances. Gavin had no expertise in the ills of the soul and left them in Beckett's good charge. So resigned, Beckett mentioned that there were some people he needed to visit in particular and would let Gavin know if their issues were of Tyneside concern. "Where are you off to next, Gavin?" Beckett asked. Gavin excused himself in response, politely refraining to answer.

Gavin made off alone through the intersecting domes, thick with thoughts. It was almost impossible to consider the stories he'd just heard with complete objectivity. But the solution he sought was far more complex and thereby daunting. Listonn knew that there were complaints among the labour force that could impact production, but had not yet heard the term, "union" used just yet. The Lady Inverness could be easily swayed with technical jargon as long as the tangible results affirmed his statements. He had to thread this needle with a fishing line so thin it was invisible in the water. He made several frustratingly wrong turns. Try as he might to picture the blueprints in his mind being here was quite another matter. Perhaps his recollections were flawed or too many changes had been since his design. Again he found domes unoccupied, the builders now off to their duties in the structures adjoining the central platform.

He finally found the proper landmarks that oriented him toward Royden's office. Approaching up the arching hall he found the office door wide open and unattended. More frustrating still, Royden wasn't there. Thankfully Listonn wasn't there either. Gavin let himself in and closed the door behind him. He took up the Yack-mouth and attempted to determine how to make a person-to-person call.

He rattled the call button to see if he could get any response, “Yes,” a male voice like a grinding millstone replied. Gavin didn’t recognize the voice.

“Hello? Yes, hello?” Gavin asked, “are you at the switch box? Sorry to bother, but can you connect me to Sir Royden’s personal room? The man who answered didn’t reply. With only silence to consider, Gavin debated asking again.

Without another word from the operator, he heard Royden’s meek voice come along the wire, “Ah, yes, this is Royden. Who is this?”

“Sir Tom? This is Sir Gavin. I’m in your office. Come round and meet me would you? It’s urgent.” Royden agreed and clicked down the receiver without another word. Gavin hadn’t paid much attention to detail during their last time in the office, but he could certainly tell which bundles had been reviewed by Listonn. He rifled through bound up papers of irregular sizes, glancing quickly at the ones Listonn had earmarked. After a short time Royden appeared at the door in a rush.

“Shut the door fast and lock it,” Gavin directed. Royden complied and then turned his short, guilt ridden face toward him. Gavin paused, reacting somewhat to Royden’s spineless timidity, so unseemly coming from the first Mayor of Mars. “Sir Tom,” he said, “I’ve just returned from our meeting with Othello and have learned a great many things. Now we need a plan of action and you and I are going to carry it out.”

“Yes, of course,” Royden replied. Gavin sniffed loudly, as he looked off and gathered his thoughts. He lifted the deep green sash from his jacket pocket and blotted his forehead.

“So then,” he stated, “Othello does leave an impression. You can see why he speaks for them, the miners and this mystery man, Barabbas. But, his demands are not unreasonable. In fact, like many of his sort you can pacify him easily with a few token gestures. It’s just like labour suppression back on earth in every respect.”

“Excuse me?” Royden replied with a look of abject horror on his face.

“Really,” Gavin replied, “it’s perfectly obvious to me what you’re about you’ve just overplayed a bit here and there.”

“Overplayed,” Royden mimicked, the grimace still contorting his features.

“First off,” Gavin said, “we must restart the post.”

“The post?” Royden asked, “you’re talking about the post?” the look of horror softening.

"Of course," Crossland said, "cut off someone's communications to family and they feel needlessly isolated. It's difficult enough that they give up so much to come to space. For those with family they need that precious lifeline to all that was once familiar to them. Let's create some kind of standard envelope and force them all to use it. We'll need a stencil or a typesetter to print the addresses. Nothing hand written can be placed on the outside so they can be opened and resealed in an identical wrapper to allay any suspicions of tampering. We can tell them that this is a new regulatory policy from Earth. Blaming legislative policy is best to transfer the onus away from the company. Everything sent to space or from space must be so prepared. And we need to mock-up some kind of sealed drop box so they think that no one can access the mail until it leaves Ares and so cannot be tampered with when being delivered here."

"You endorse the practice of reading their mail?" Royden asked, still as shocked.

"Of course I do, man!" Gavin nearly shouted. "These bastards are unionizing we can't have them garnering support from Earth. They could send something to the wrong people or much worse, a major news publication. The damage could be irrevocable. It was good what you did, but it was the way you went about it. Just needed to take a slightly different tact to keep up appearances."

Royden was dumbfounded and looked away in stark astonishment. "I see your point Gavin," he replied, "brilliant really. Brilliant."

"Now let's address this whole notion of paying for amenities. Were you aware that your three ruffians were extracting wages from the staff for niceties? Better hammocks, nicer foodstuffs, longer rest times, that sort of thing."

"Yes," Royden replied, unable to look Gavin in the eye. "They send a good deal of their gain back to Earth. Bit of a gray market. Someone on Earth supplies them with the finer accoutrement's and the building chiefs send the money back home. And then there's the insurance contracts."

"You know of them then?"

"Yes," Royden said slowly, "I know of them." Gavin issued a breath of exasperation.

"I'm sure it's all a scam right?"

"Yes, right, at least as far as I know."

"Bloody short-sighted bastards," Gavin spat. "Well, that's all muddled in Tyneside business now. They might have gotten away with it, but now it's a bad reflection on us. Bad for business. I'll need to deal with their partners back on Earth when I return, but that won't alleviate our present problem. Let's promise that upon our departure you will launch a campaign to make an exact account of everyone who claims to have purchased this life insurance. Even if the miners can't produce papers to confirm the purchase. I suspect that the builders were sold them too?"

"Yes, quite."

"Blast," Gavin said getting angrier, "The bleeding bastards should have known better. Marching Bull around like he's some bare-knuckled James Figg. The miners are looking for satisfaction and we must give them some semblance of justice. They've painted Piter, Miser, and Bull to be the villains in all this so we can pin a nice bit of blame on them. Detain them to quarters on bread and water or whatever else is done up here. The disciplinary action must appear harsh. Say that they've been denied all commissions and shares. The commissions part will speak to the miners especially as they will believe that the trio won't benefit from the miner's hard work. Yes, I think they'll like that." Gavin, caught Royden's gaze no longer allowing him to look away. "But you know, Tom," he said, "we have a much graver matter to address."

"What is it?" Royden asked.

"We need to give Othello an explanation of what happened to his wife." Royden swallowed. He then took his own Tyneside sash and blotted his forehead. "Do you know what happened to her?" Gavin asked. Royden cleared his throat and begged Gavin's forgiveness. "Regain yourself, man," Gavin said.

"No," Royden said coughing into his kerchief.

"Well," Gavin said, "here's where your slipshod records will serve us. We can't say that she abandoned him for the moon. He knows that the Americans still make slaves of Negroes there, even those who are fair skinned. I'm sure they make slaves of anyone really. We must fabricate something absolutely plausible. We've already fed him the line about the brickets. No need to come up with something else, just need to add a more believable spin to the yarn. We have protocols in place that in cases of severe injury or illness a labourer may be transferred to a liner for care given at superior facilities. We've got to get the timing right, but let's tell him that there was an accident. Let's tell him that Crohne gave her a medicine that caused a reaction, uh, an inadvertent poisoning. We had to get her on the HMS Commonwealth or the India and she's never returned.

Presumably she's still on-board waiting for the next trip back. That's perfect really."

"No offense, Sir Gavin, but how so?"

"To buy time, Tom. That would give us more than enough time. He'll pine away waiting for the next arrival, but when that liner docks we'll spring our trap and set this all aright."

"And what trap will that be?" Royden asked, his words faltering. Gavin smiled broadly for the first time. The muscles in his face had almost forgotten what it felt like to smile.

"Oh, a trap I know well. Not a new trap mind you. Quite frankly an old one. But not old in the stale sense, old in the tried and true sense." Royden couldn't help but find Gavin's shift in demeanor assuring, even calming. "I need to talk to some people back home in whom I trust," Gavin continued, "union breakers, people with military affiliations who can send up some marines to keep the peace. Oh mark me, Tom. Othello has raised my ire. I'll not have the dream of the empire held hostage because of some meager extortion and insurance fraud. Othello has crossed me and he'll rue the day."

"You know I'm more than somewhat startled, Sir Crossland," Royden said. "I imagined that you would feel more sympathy for Othello and his crew."

"Well of course there's been misconduct but that's a secondary affair. You gave those three too much leeway. But I don't blame you, Royden. They got away with it because Christien spends too much time up in his Babel Tower, you can't be expected to deal with all this on your own."

"No I can't, can I?"

"Of course not, especially given the damnable problem with the generators and the temperature imbalance. The miners couldn't have gotten away with this if not for that. No, I'll deal with that problem as well. And as for you, Sir Royden, a man of your stature must be given the necessary platform from which to lead."

"Platform you say?"

"We'll hire you an assistant, someone who's got a knack for all this paperwork and number tracking. It's not your job, Tom. You're to take command, not keep books. That's part of the problem, not enough hands for the job. Not enough of the right hands. Once you're unburdened from these mundane chores you can keep to what's important. Keep to the main thing. Don't let anything draw away your focus. We'll give you some strong arms to put down the rabble and some strong minds to keep everything orderly." This seemed to please Royden very much. He broke into his own smile and softened his contorted face. Gavin gave him a pause to bask and then asked, "So did Listonn say he found anything else during your time together?" Concern swept back over Royden's face.

"I suspect as much but he didn't let on."

"No problem," Gavin said, continuing to lend confidence. "I can settle him. It's really all about the ore. And if we execute our next interactions with the miners flawlessly we'll get the ore. The ore changes everything. Now to pull this off we can't have any interactions between Othello's people and the contingent. They cannot be allowed to talk to Listonn, the Duchess, Napier, anyone. We'll have them ship the ore in containers up the hall and take it from them at the choker. It's flawless really. It'll make them feel safer. To ensure that there's no violence the builders must be unarmed and not show any signs of aggression. This is essential, Tom, there can be no violence. We'll have the miners deliver the containers and then they can back off. Only once they're a good distance we'll have our people collect it. Right? No chance of a fight breaking out."

"I'll see to it personally."

"Very good and keep Beckett at the choker too, at all times. That will be the clincher. The only thing I can't figure is this Barabbas chap. He's just a bloody wild card in all this. I hate to think that there's someone with half a mind over there who might raise some kind of objection." Gavin paused and looked about absently. "Is he even real? And what if he is? Maybe we just let them keep their perceived ace up their sleeve. Oh, I'll make a good show of it, demand to deal with him directly and all, but concede in the end. It won't matter once we get some marines up here to put them in their place. Sir Royden," Gavin said, taking him by the shoulders. "I believe we have it. We're ironclad, man. Rapper dance for Tyneside."

"Rapper dance for Tyneside," Royden replied with less than proper enthusiasm.

Gavin finally achieved a moment of indulgent peace. There was work left, but his breath came easier. He wasn't sweating as profusely as before. It was almost a Zen-like moment of clarity, an inward achievement that rivaled the outward that was unfolding before him. He had no intention of finding Royden administrative help. He did intend to find a replacement and have Royden sacked. He could easily find another

Tyneside junior executive who'd be willing to give up their life on Earth for the enticement of Martian titles and status. A few of them leapt to mind. Young upstarts looking to make a name for themselves. He looked back at Royden with feigned respect. He'd clean up this whole mess just as he had many times before.

A steam whistle blared which shook them both to the bone. After the first harsh sound, it blew again with two short blasts, and again with two more, and another pair blew again. The alarm repeated that same pattern ceaselessly and the two went to cover their ears from the noise.

"What the hell is that?" Royden asked at a yell, to be heard over the jetting steam.

"That's the dock's general alarm," Gavin said, looking as if he could see through the bulkhead toward the source of the blare. "Something's wrong with the Daedalus."

***

The rough metal corridor that led to the gangway was sealed off. The antechamber just inside was stuffed with those who had already responded. A number of the building crew were present, their drab garb creating a patchwork of earth tone clothing. Listonn was there, his monocle floating free and Wilson was right by him. Argyle was also close at hand with a look of bent concern on his angular foreign features. The Lady Inverness was present with ol' Gran and her other attendants. Her face showed concern but she remained her unshakable self. The group was huddled together forming loose concentric circles, floating in a contentious knot beneath the one circular window at the top of the chamber. Their legs fanned out like blades on a ceiling fan. Each one there strained to look out above them. Once Gavin & Royden pressed their way in, they took a look for themselves.

Against the brilliance of the star-scape they could see the Daedalus at a dizzying angle, her broad underbelly lit up by the sun. The fore section wasn't turning. The gravitationally-imbued living sections were cocked sidelong at about ten o'clock-to-stern. All her interior lights were turned off making her look like a ghost ship adrift in a wave-less sea. The only sign of life came from a single flashing light at the rear of the vessel. It looked as if someone had a small light or torch pressed up against an aft view port, flashing at irregular pulses. If it weren't for that electric light flashing in its bowels one couldn't tell if anyone was aboard. She was moving away from Phobus just fast enough that she seemed to be shrinking away from view at a trajectory that still kept with Phobus' orbital path but slowly drifted further away with each passing second.

Listonn had both hands clenched on the sill of the round window edge with his mouth wide as if someone had given him a shot to the pills.

Gavin pulled up next to him and asked, "Who sounded the alarm? What happened?"

"I don't know. One of the builders," Listonn snapped back. "She's just off her hinges. No one knows why." Gavin scanned the eyes of those around him. He saw that Bull was there, but he was the only native he recognized.

"Is that Morse code they're flashing?"

"Yes," one of them said, "it's a mayday." Gavin stretched out to look the opposite way, back toward Ares. There he could see the spire of Babel Tower rising above the other structures. The lights around its edge were lit. He thought he could almost make out the vague silhouette of Crohne looking out across the domed rooftops at the floundering liner.

"Where is Princess Sandra?" the Lady Inverness asked of ol' Gran and Lanny both, repeating the question over and over. She was steadfast but held to a sense of urgency a woman of her stature was allowed. "Lanny," she said to her younger attendant, "go to her room to see if she's alright." The youthful girl nodded and began inching her way back in compliance.

At a full, scattered rush, pulling themselves along hand-over-hand, a small group came tearing up the vaulted passage toward the gathering. In the lead was Campbell followed closely by Elphinstone, Vecihi, and a few others of builders' crew right behind.

"Make way, make way!" Campbell said, ruffling past the others. "Get them unpacked, lads," he shouted at the others with them. Campbell and Elphinstone both started stripping off their uniforms as fast as they could. The builders pulled up metal folding doors with a deafening clatter. They rolled up toward the ceiling like shutters. Behind each door was a bay that housed a rotund contraption that looked like a squatting bronze idol in the guise of a semi-mechanical human mockery. The builders began to unfasten these things from their stowage, pull off their heads and disassemble their chest sections to reveal a hollow within.

Gavin pushed over to grab Campbell by the arm, "What are you doing?" Campbell gave Gavin a stern but respectful look.

"We're going up there, sir. Look," he said pointing at the Daedalus and that flashing light. "They say the mains are still down for the refit. Got to go up and fetch them back."

"But how will you-" Gavin didn't finish this thought as the realization of their gambit sunk in. "God be with you both. So they can't just finish the refit and fly her back?"

"Not sure, sir. Galashiels or Benny might manage, but there's no one up there to fly her," Campbell explained while he continued to snap off his suspenders and drop his trousers. "Georgie here's my navigator, but he might make co-pilot yet," he slapped Elphinstone on the shoulder. "How many pints you put back, George?" Campbell asked him.

"You call those billiard balls pints?" Elphinstone scoffed. "Pah, only makes my hands steadier." Listonn shouldered his way through the gathering to come to Gavin's side. His monocle still trailed lazily in the air beside him.

"But what's the plan?" Gavin asked Campbell at a loss.

"We'll go up there, latch on a cable to pull them back. Once secure, we'll reattach the gangway and be top notch. Dock again with the platform and get her fit for travel."

Listonn cut in, "But, why do you both have to go? If you're our only two pilots?"

Campbell and Elphinstone gave each other a moment's look.

"If one of us doesn't make it, Campbell said gravely, "maybe the other will," Elphinstone looked up at Gavin and Listonn in silent agreement. "She's pulling away too fast. We're not going to have another chance."

"Is Dr. Boswell here?" Gavin asked looking around. "Will someone fetch him? There may be people hurt up there," but no one made any immediate moves to fetch him.

Vecihi and the builders had almost completely dismantled the pressure suits, a freakishly large gloved hand spun in a meandering circle next to him. A bronze metal submersive helmet was on a slow drift toward the ceiling. Vecihi was cursing and going on in Turkish.

"No time, no time," he repeated busying his hands with the task. "You're not going to have long," he said looking to Campbell and Elphinstone. The two Daedalus crewmen backed into their respective suits backside first. They had to pull their legs up tight to the chests before extending them down into the leg structures.

"How much time can you give us?" Elphinstone asked Vecihi.

"Twenty minutes tops," Vecihi said, "maybe twenty-five before the CO2 comes back on you." Elphinstone tried to look up through the dangling arms and legs of those gathered above them.

"What you say, Colin? Ten minutes there with the decompress?"

"No!" Campbell assured, "seven maybe. We'll set the hook and then pop in at hatch three, wait for the internals to come up, and then head on in. Plenty of time." Gavin looked back up at the Daedalus and did some quick estimating of his own. He had always been able to work formulas in his head. The time didn't add up to him. He hoped that it was just his poor assumptions. Campbell and Elphinstone were both able spacefarers. They would know better.

Vecihi and the builders assisted them with reassembling the pressure suits. They quickly gathered each missing limb in turn and fastened them back in place with a complicated array of latches, screws and levers. The suits were akin to those worn by deep sea divers, but far larger and bulkier. Their range of motion was limited. As the bronze helms were fitted in place the circular glass port fogged with their panting breath. They were both breathing heavy, steady but heavy. Their field of vision was narrow.

"No time to do rechecks, just give it the once-over," Campbell instructed Vecihi, his words coming muffled. "Seal up the helmet and let's fire up the engine." The builders by them spun each suit around and fastened the shafts of a large metal wheel into the fittings on the suits' generators. Each wheel bore a handle which protruded laterally aligned with one of its four spokes. The handles rode on bearing so they could spin freely.

"Hold steady now," the builder said bracing himself. Campbell and Elphinstone took a firm grip on handles welded to the wall, their feet dug into the locks fastened to the deck. The builders spun the wheels wildly. Campbell and Elphinstone held on as well as they could, pulling opposite the spin of the wheel. Something in the suits' pack caught and steam bled into the air. The whole suit began to chug and sputter. The generators sprang to life with a sound that forced everyone in the enclosed space to wince in discomfort. The builders stopped the turning and waited observantly. Assured that the generators would run on their own, they drew out metal cables from spools along the wall. Their final task was to hook those cables to the backs of each suit.

Vecihi slapped Elphinstone's helmet hard and the engineer turned his whole body to look out through the viewing port. Vecihi peered in at him expectantly. Elphinstone drew in some long breaths and gave a thumbs-up with the ridiculously large thumb of his gloved hand. Vecihi nodded that he understood, but continued to pore over the suit checking its seals.

Yelling to be heard through the suit Vecihi said, "The suit looks sealed, but we'll take our time with the air lock. If you've got a leak we're pulling you right back." Elphinstone wouldn't have it. He shook his head along with his whole upper body in a stiff necked gesture. Campbell shook also within the confines of his helm.

"Clear the deck!" Bull shouted out with a voice none dared oppose. The dozen or so in the room were quickly pulled from the chamber into the adjoining hall. Wilson assisted the Lady Inverness along with ol' Gran.

"Where the devil is Lanny?" Lady Inverness asked. "Sandra can't be over there, can she?"

Members of the group bobbed like buoys as they were shoved into the hall. Vecihi was the last one in with Campbell and Elphinstone, still checking and rechecking the seals on their suits.

"Not enough damn time!" Vecihi shouted. Campbell took him by the arm with the mailed hand of his pressure glove. He looked at Vecihi intently. It was already getting feverishly hot in the suit and sweat was beading up all over Campbell's face. Vecihi looked out through the view port above him, to the Daedalus which was getting smaller and smaller by the second.

"Allahaismarladik!" Vecihi shouted at him so Campbell could hear him through the helmet. Vecihi pulled over to look in at Elphinstone and repeated it again, "Allahaismarladik!" Campbell released him and Vecihi hung his head low and ducked out of the room. Campbell and Elphinstone watched him leave as he flicked droplets of tears into the air. Vecihi passed through the hatch leading into the hall and they saw Bull slam it shut. The big man pumped the hatch and then waved a sign through the small window fixed at eye level on the door.

Hindered by the awkward bulk of their suits, the two made some palsied motions to centre themselves under the circular window atop the chamber. Once settled, they looked over at Bull, still in the window slot and nodded their readiness.

In the dark hallway, Bull turned his broad frame away from the door and over to the wall. The others closest the door pushed past to get a look at the window, Vecihi right with them. Bull took hold of the yack-mouth mounted to the wall next to him amidst the draping array of conduits and wires.

"Crohne?" he called in booming and resonant. "They's ready," and he returned it to the wall, turning his expressionless, stubbled jaw back toward them. Gavin didn't know quite what to expect. He hovered just a few inches off the deck. In the barely lit hall he could hear movement in the wall by him. Right by his feet he saw that curious rectangular socket he noticed when he first reached the platform. That odd elaborate complicated electro-mechanical apparatus that never appeared on any of his blueprints. There was almost a pang of jealousy really, of the invention of such an infrastructure. Such an integral function to manage a platform in space that had totally eluded him. In the glint of the meager light he could see the gears within turn. Metal shafts pivoted and pushed forward. Locks tripped and springs broke free.

Back in the sealed antechamber, Campbell and Elphinstone's heart rate hadn't slowed any. They both looked up through that circular window directly under the drifting form of the HMS Daedalus. They both knew to control their breathing. They both knew that the unbearable heat from the suit's generator would be lifesaving once they hit the void. Campbell took a nervous glance over at the window on the door. He just caught Vecihi's eye peering in at the lower right corner.

A metallic clash struck the entire room. The window above them split on its hinges and parted like unfurling flower petals.

The air about them popped like a cork from champagne, grabbing them violently around the arms and legs. They were spat out, blown free in a rush of white noise and venting gas. As he flew, Campbell felt the tug of the thick metal cable that was affixed to his back. He involuntarily reached out with both arms and kicked with both legs. He tried as he could to keep the Daedalus in his forward view, but his path was imprecise. He needed to adjust around thirty-two degrees or he'd shoot past. He tucked his right arm in close to his body. With a very light touch he turned a miniature valve just inside his glove. Steam belched hard from his suit which nudged his tumbling flight slightly to correct his path. He overcompensated and had to do the same on the opposite side. He only could make a few corrections. He already feared he had overused them. But steadily he saw the Daedalus draw closer. There were plenty of outcroppings that he could use to take hold. He began scanning up and down her skin to find where he could make contact. He thought that slamming into her might be best, bring a halt to his momentum and make for a hatch. But he might bounce off. He might ricochet at an angle and get disoriented. He tried to look around for Elphinstone but didn't see him. He had to concentrate on his own landing.

The metal hull of the Daedalus was getting closer, less than a few chains away. Campbell extended his arms and looked for a latch, strut, or faring to use as a hand hold. There just wasn't a ready grip, nothing obvious to aim towards. He worked in his glove to make another course correction. The hull just behind the American made nose cone came at him like an iron wall. He was speeding headlong into a literal wall of metal. It was too late to veer off. Campbell cried out the last few yards before he collided head first into her unyielding exterior.

Campbell's forehead struck the inside of his helmet. Still speeding with the force of his ascent his suit skidded and scraped around the tubular arch of the Daedalus' bow. His vision was a blur of welded, riveted plates. He reached out on both sides. He grasped hard for anything, clamping his hands closed over and again to blindly catch something. Still moving at a dizzying speed the metal sped out of view and again he saw the jet black of space. He had skipped off and flown past. He grabbed down in futile denial. He was out past the ship. He was heading out into space. He continued to scream. He yelled in the soundless void with no one to hear him.

A sudden jerk took the wind out of him and bled his speed into a twirling spin. The thick stranded cable at his back wrapped around him and he caught it with both arms. He worked it down with his gauntleted hands until he could use it to steady himself. He needed a minute to ward off the dizziness, but the cable was solid. Using it to pull himself around he looked back at the ship. He could see her shadowed side below him and all the way back to Phobus and the lights of Ares Britannia, far, far below. That cable had bent around the hull of the ship and then made a slow broad curve all the way back to that tiny dark circle of the antechamber leading back into the platform. He had run out of line. He now dangled at the end like a watch dropped from its fob.

The mass of the Daedalus pushed up toward him still continuing its ascent. The cable stretched as the great bulk of the ship approached. Campbell went hand over hand and inched his way up the cable to meet the ship. He was on the wrong side so he looked for a way in. Exterior hatch number five was closest. It was identical to hatch three on the opposite end. Either one would allow him entrance. He shook sweat from his eyes and tried to shake off the pain in his arms. Using the cable for leverage he made it back to the skin of the craft. A smile stretched across his face and tears welled at the corners of his eyes. He was only a few feet from the door latch. There were a number of rings that encircled it where the gangway attached to the hull.

A thick metal hook on his chest was the perfect size to catch those rings. He crawled on his belly to reach it. He clamped the hook into place and the stubby fingers on his mailed glove were just long enough to screw it down. He turned that screw with everything he could. Once in place he waited. In a few moments the same cable that held him fast would still the Daedalus as well.

He rolled around so his back was pressed against the ship. Stretching his head way back he could just look down to Phobus. The Daedalus' flight rapidly took up the slack on the line. As the strain hit that ring he felt a groan wrench though the hull. It was a silent straining vibration but it was profound it its depth. It pulled deeply like a barbed fishhook caught in Campbell's bowels. The ship lurched as its full mass pulled against the cable. The drag of the line spun the ship. Its broad expanse turned. Campbell was awestruck. All that tonnage spinning around at the very point his small form lay holding desperately to that line for dear life. The ship swung to its widest point and the cable went taut and into a spinning vibration, like catgut on a cello that struck a note too bass to be heard, even if space allowed. It cast out pools of tonal reverberations that rippled through the cold iron around him, straight into his pressure suit. The pull held the ship fast and it bounced back lightly on the line. The tight vibration slowed to a flopping pulse as the Daedalus reversed its path and inched back toward Phobus below.

Campbell could barely move. Catholic prayers blew out of his dry, parched lips. He hailed the blessed mother for holding him safe. He hailed Saint Christopher for coming to his aid. He lay there until he regained his senses. There was blood in his eyes along with the sting of sweat. He didn't remember how he'd split his brow. He drew his right arm out of the suit's sleeve to wipe his face clear. He balled up his fist and rubbed the condensation from inside his helm's cyclopean view-port.

"Georgie," he said at last. "Got to get inside, Georgie. Not much time left, mate. Not much O2 left." He began looking around out there in space, everywhere his field of vision permitted. His fellow officer was nowhere to be seen. "Georgie!" he called out despite the futility. Getting his hand back into the suit's sleeves he was just able to push off from the ship. Still latched to the cable he had enough lead to come upright and look around. Drawing up the steel line, the powerful magnetic soles of his shoes sealed to the hull. With firm ground beneath him he steadied himself. He stood straight up off the ship his hand on the cable as thick as a flagpole back to Ares. "Georgie?" he asked the silent void around him.

In the glint of the sun he saw a shape like a bottle opener, like the corkscrew a waiter would use to pierce the top of a wine bottle to serve his guests. It was a broad spiral line that glowed with repeating circles shining in the sun. It was spinning as well. It turned with that engaging corkscrew pattern. It looked like snapped fishing line as the catch fled into deep water. At the leading tip of the spiral was a beaming white ball, like a partially deflated balloon that had burst and was jetting off into the sky. Encased in the collapsing shape of that deflating balloon was a struggling, frantic, desperate Warrant Officer George Elphinstone. His line had broken from the platform. His path was far from the ship. There was nothing out ahead of him except eternity.

"Oh, Georgie boy," Campbell said as he pulled his hand free and made the sign of the cross. He could see air spraying from Elphinstone's suit from multiple points all around. His seals hadn't held. A few chilling seconds later the spray stopped altogether. George flailed his arms and legs in all directions in a hopeless final spin towards his end.

"Just let it come, George," Campbell said as he watched, "just let it take you." Tears came thick to his eyes. The knot in his throat blocked his words. "Don't fight it, man. Just let it come. Just let it come, mate." Campbell prayed for his soul in the words of a prayer prayed for men who died in space. Time was fleeting but Campbell kept on watching. George's arms slowed to a wave and then stopped. His legs stiffened and his body stilled. His course continued off into the truncated infinity of a near measureless ellipse around the red planet until years later when it would finally end in planet fall.

Campbell chose not to speak his last goodbye but dropped to his knees to work the latch that was part of the port access door and prepared to head inside.

Chapter 1 (10): The Tears of the Thousand Eyes

From within Ares Britannia, the onlookers couldn't tell which officer had made it successfully to the Daedalus. Try as they might, between the bulky suits and the frightful display it made it impossible to tell one from the other. They only knew of sure that one hadn't made it.

While those gathered were struck gawking, Piter and Miser showed up and began barking orders. They looked as unkempt and surly as ever and Gavin wondered if they ever bathed. With Bull's assistance a few of them set to ensuring that the line to the Daedalus was secure.

"Wot ya think, Bull?" Miser asked, "Can we yank 'em back form in 'ere or we need to take a walk?"

"We can stay 'ere," Bull replied, racking his nails over the stubble at his neck. "They're already walkin'. No need to risk another. When they get back we'll be waitin' for em."

Gavin looked over the three but chose to keep his thoughts to himself. Listonn breathed a huge sigh of relief, putting both hands on his knees and thanking all the saints whose names he could remember. The air in the tight space had grown moist and warm and the pressing of the throng made it seem all the more oppressive. Gavin took his chance to bolt, sifting his way through with impolitely stated, excuse me's. Listonn caught that he was leaving and called after him, but Gavin gave him no heed. At a hurried pace, he began the long weightless drag from the dock to Crohne's tower. He reached into his vest pocket for his watch, but was startled to find that it had been lifted. He cursed at the damnable unnamed builder who right now must be admiring his prize.

He arrived again at the dimly lit junction where three domes intersected and the very phallic tower. He was shocked to find the wall section pulled aside and the blank abysmal aperture beckoning entry. The yack-mouth had been removed from its receiver and floated limply in the stale air.

A crackle like a recoding tube broke from the mouth and an electronically concatenated voice broke loose, "Come on up Gavin," came Crohne's words from the free floating yack.

"How the bloody hell did he know I was coming?" Gavin asked the stagnant air with hopes that the yack-mouth wasn't sensitive enough to send it up the tower. Out of compulsion he returned the voice piece to its rightful place and proceeded into the doorway. He was now almost accustomed to moving about in all directions so it was less of a strain to rise himself up to the tower's bulbous height. The trapdoor in the ceiling was open as well so Gavin poked his head through. Crohne was just inside, hovering a few feet from the floor. The room burned with the bright arch of a waxing Mars resplendent in blazing colors. There was someone else there also, another man-shaped silhouette against the burning red, hovering near the hatch.

"Now Allen, these are our guests," Gavin heard Crohne say, now recognizing that Culverton was with him. "Please see to it personally that the final linkage is completed just as I asked. Pull Faraz and Standish off the East-end project and use them at the stem on our side of the choker. And it will be most efficient if you send them outside. We need the best for this, Allen. Nothing can be left to chance. I want everything to work the first time. With their help you'll be done within the hour. Now go."

Turning toward the hatch, Culverton was washed blood red in the reign of Mars. Given the light's particular angle, the mesh along the far window made a black lacey pattern of shadows across Culverton's face. He looked cross to say the least, almost enraged, wrathful, devilish. Culverton didn't offer any sort of greeting and pushed his way past Gavin like only a veteran of space-faring could. Crohne called after him, "Don't be a little cunt, Allen, you knew that this would happen. That's why we have the word inevitable in the King's English." Upon hearing the slur, Culverton's neck stiffened but he kept right on going.

"What's all that about now?" Gavin asked Crohne as Culverton descended out of earshot.

Crohne brushed a handful of gray hair out of his face, his brow furrowing into parallel layers, "That is the inexorable outcome when foremen fail to recognize that architects are those charged with seeing the end from the beginning."

Gavin's face was a mask of frustration, "If we didn't already have too many concerns I'd attempt to delve your meaning. But time is against us and you and I must confer."

"I couldn't agree more, Gavin," Crohne said while distractedly looking about the contents of his study.

"Christien," Gavin said, trying desperately to hold Crohne's attention, "I assume you observed what just happened outside.?" Crohne nodded mutely that he had in fact observed the event. "So?" Gavin asked, "I don't expect that you'd like to offer an explanation?"

"I've none to offer. Not until I learn more if it," Crohne replied, "most likely an issue with the mooring."

"Of course," Gavin replied rubbing his temple and covering his expression. "I imagine we should get someone to examine said issue forthrightly. I gather Napier and his crew might insist upon a lengthy explanation upon their return without so much as a modicum of patience. But I have another pressing matter we must settle. Napier's anger will subside I'm sure but only if we retrieve the prize we were sent to retrieve. Our most pressing need is to secure the Daedalus' intended cargo. You see, I think we can get Barabbas and/or Othello or whoever people say they are to relinquish the ore as anticipated."

"Oh?" Crohne replied. "That's certainly good to hear."

"Yes, I think we've made some good inroads in the last few hours, but there are a number of crucial moves left to make on the chessboard. And I need your help with this, Christien. I've given my direction to Sir Royden, but we both know he's not up to it without your assistance. The need is twofold and entails a short term and a long term goal. First we have the most pertinent need to get some fat, overflowing drums up past the choker and into the belly of the Daedalus. Once that's accomplished we then have a long term plan to consider. That's where I must rely on you."

"Go on, I'm listening," Crohne said as he pushed off and up toward the ceiling. Though fumbling, Gavin worked himself around so he could get a footing and a short leap up to Crohne's position.

"So," Gavin said, "Othello told me a number of things and in short, we need to address his concerns. Like any disgruntled laborer, he needs placation. Note, I'm not suggesting we meet his demands. That's just poor all around, but to get this sorted we need to show the miners that we mean to offer some relief, respectfully and pragmatically, just enough so that they agree to bring the ore up from their camp. I don't think they'll agree to come farther than the choker but that's perfect. That's really all we need."

"Agreed," Crohne said as he pulled a key-lever box from among the apparatus that littered his workspace. Gavin paused to look at it. It was different from the one he'd seen before. The levers were longer and there were more of them. The box in which they were attached had the same width and length but was taller, so it would stand up higher after being depressed into one of the floor sockets. The dull metal shafts were rough, but well fashioned. It stunk of fresh grease.

Distracted Gavin couldn't help but comment, "How ever did you come up with the design for that?" he asked.

"For what?" Crohne asked simply.

"Those lever keys. I understand them in principle. You're penetrating the circuit ducts and hydro lines, the access that accounts for water pressure as well as some of the machine works."

"You're only missing the fact that I'm also leveraging the bio-submersive systems by overriding their master scheduler. This whole place is really about bios," Crohne said waiving his hand in a half circle about him. "He who commands the bios commands the platform. But you know that, Sir Crossland. You're the master architect of all this."

"Seriously?" Gavin gasped, "Isn't that dangerous? The analytic engine is very sensitive. I wouldn't even dare to touch that. Not even with Vecihi guiding my hand. I mean, get one of those little metal tumblers out of place and algae could back up into the septic or the septic backup into the laundry or drinking water and then the whole of the recycle backs up. I know enough to leave that to the Turks."

Crohne smiled lithely, "Again, evidence to the contrary seems overwhelming." Crohne turned to look down at Gavin. He drew in a nose full of air. "I've been using these keys to run the platform for years now and we both seem to be breathing. Can't say that I've found any excrement in the drinking water either. No imminent danger here."

"Alright," Gavin said looking away from Crohne's blue eyed gaze.

"The beauty of it's the key part of the equation which drove the development of the system," Crohne explained. "All the infrastructure was already there just as we designed it. The key-box is just a means of regulating control and restricting access. We can thank you for that, Sir Crossland, the author of the master design. All I did was pull a few connections together that were unapparent to you merely because you were denied the up-close vantage we enjoy here on Phobus."

"Right, brilliant," Gavin stammered, "a brilliant connection, most literally. Now help me with a few more, and I must insist upon your undivided attention." Crohne's face waxed expressionless and he gave a short mid-air spin to look down on Gavin who continued. "So Othello told me a few things and I must get your take. Make sure I'm seeing things right." Crohne remained focused but expressionless. "Now of course," Gavin went on, "it might not be Othello speaking though he does impress me as the solitary front man, really a free thinker. But we can't dismiss the possibility that there is a Barabbas out there as well. As such we can't assume that winning over Othello is the only goal." Speaking to a reaction-less audience was not one of Gavin's fortes. "But let's address his grievances shall we?"

Crohne blinked but offered no response. So Gavin continued, "Right then, Othello mentioned something about the economics around here. That they've been forced to sacrifice for living arrangements, softer hammocks, better meals but it was more than that. He mentioned the sale of insurance policies. Do you know anything about that?"

"Of course I do," Crohne answered.

"You knew that Piter and the builders were soliciting payment for these policies among the staff?"

"And Culverton also, though the other three worked both the direct sales and the collection services. I understand it's a little scheme he learned during his time spent in Chicago among the Americans. They are an enterprising lot."

"So help me here, of course these people earn wages, most of whom have those wages forwarded to their families on Earth or directly to their debtors or whomever. The remainder becomes somewhat disposable up here. They can gamble or purchase the few things at the Tyneside stores or save to purchase passage back to the moon if that's their want. But it seems like Miser, Piter and Bull are running a junior grade extortion ring of sorts."

"Extortion ring," Crohne echoed.

"Well, yes, that's not the phrase Othello used but I'm using it. Not that I'm making accusations. But the more I think about it, the three of them traipse about the place like a band of ruffians and the weak fall prey to their little scheme. Regardless they must be working with someone back on Earth. It's all about where the money goes right? So they collect from these workers and where do they send the proceeds? And what do they get in recompense?" Crohne offered no additional insight. "Well anyway," Gavin said, "that'll be mine to figure upon my return. In the meantime, I will have Royden manage things better up here."

"You will," Crohne said emphatically as to ensure it wasn't misconceived as a question.

"I'd like you to assist him with that of course."

"Of course, I'll give Tom all the help he needs."

"But really, Christien, you can't assist from a distance. Royden's going to need you to come down and help him directly. He needs you to prop him up really."

"Help him directly, prop him up, of course," Crohne replied dry as gin.

"Good," Gavin said searching his thoughts for his next point. "So we'll inform the miners that we'll track down everyone's policy. We'll get it all sorted, beneficiaries, legal guarantees and I'll try to get Tyneside to bankroll any grievances. They won't like it but there's too much at stake. Then, when we come back here with a garrison we'll ensure none of these shenanigans continue. But this alone will not allay the miners. No, they need some theatre. They need something apparently decisive to demonstrate our resolve as an acknowledgment of their grievances. Miser, Piter and Bull need to be confined to quarters and I need you and perhaps Allen to make that happen. I've already discussed this with Royden but you know full well he doesn't have the spine for it. He just doesn't have their respect. Now if it comes from you and Allen then they'll comply. It doesn't have to be for long. Just long enough for us to secure the ore, plump up the Daedalus, and we're on our way. Once we're past that then you can let them loose again. I'll send the next liner to Mars with some Tyneside militia to keep the peace and we'll be forever done with it."

Crohne's lack of expression became unnerving. It was unnatural, like something outside the limits of human capability. Gavin couldn't help but note that Crohne neither agreed nor disagreed. He just floated there suspended by the lack of gravitational draw. Gavin couldn't help but fill the speechless vacuum. "Othello mentioned to me that he's lost track of the whereabouts of his wife. Given his status I can't see how we can overlook that entirely, all sense of special treatment aside. And I've been thinking about just that and I've come up with something, an excuse of sorts."

"And what's that?" Crohne asked interrupting. Gavin chewed his lower lip.

"We're going to tell him that she was put on the HMS Jewel of India for medical assistance and has been residing there ever since."

"And why would he believe that?" Crohne asked.

"Well for all we know that could very well be spot on. Damned if I know based on how Royden's been running things. They all refer to you as the platform's doctor. You could vouch for validity of our claim."

"And why haven't I informed him of this prior? And what was the ailment in question? And when did this supposedly occur?"

"Uh, we'll tell him that she insisted. We chose not to inform him to honour her wishes. Perhaps she found it a bit of an embarrassment. She couldn't face him if the issue was compromising. That seems the most plausible excuse and I'll even check in on that on our return."

"Seems needlessly complicated, why not just tell him that she was unfaithful and made off with some sailor to reside on the moon?"

"We can't tell him that. Othello mentioned something about slavers on the moon. Might as well tell him his wife descended into hell."

"Didier believes that there are slavers on the moon? I find it interesting that he'd be so astute."

"So you think there's truth to that?"

"So I hear."

"Well, leave it to the Yanks to carry on even after they killed each other in droves to work that all out. Well, that works contrary to our ruse, but we'll gin up some documentation, something that looks official, a passenger manifest or similar. It will sow enough doubt to be passable. But there's still one last matter to address."

Crohne looked bored like he deigned to continue the conversation.

"Othello also mentioned about the passages that interconnect various places on the platform and that you're operating some kind of kiln over here."

"A kiln? Are we potters now? Purveyors of insurance policies and decorative earthenware."

"No," Gavin said exploring the room with his eyes, "he made it sound more sinister than that."

"Sinister?"

"Yes, I didn't really follow what he was getting at." Crohne's expression broke into a cross scowl. For the first time he appeared frightening and imposing, almost imperial. Gavin paused giving him the moment. As Crohne began again there was a new tone of authority in his voice,

"Didier should have better considered how we would respond to his games with the heat. We can't be expected to feel secure unless we took back the reigns of our own security. Every time he tampered with the temperature he adversely offset atmospheric pressure and density. Not to mention its composition. He blew seams all over the platform. It takes us days to repair. You who are so keenly aware of the dangers of muddling the bios should place the blame squarely on him. If he made so much as the slightest mistake it would mean all our lives. His little threatening pranks could cost us everything."

"So you do have a furnace over here? Where is it? What do you use for fuel?"

"Gavin," Crohne said, "Isn't it enough to know that we have a proper understanding of things up here and know best just how to govern ourselves? Your new revelations should only confer a greater confidence. We really have no need for Tyneside militia to come up here and waste our life support on saber-toting tin soldiers. If you felt that Piter and Miser were playing the role of the hooligan, how much more will uniformed marines?" Crohne's eyes were half closed, but still stunning blue in contrast to the bleeding red of reflected Martian light. "It all rings with the echoes of the East India company and we know ultimately that failed as a social experiment; trying to create some kind of quasi-governmental body that parades around both military and commercial. The motives don't mesh. One ultimately will choke the other to expiration. Phobus would become a land of petty tyrants and dwarfish emperors. Phobus is not a land for the weak willed or small minded. Let's not invite that lot to disrupt the balance of human capital that so outweighs the sensitivity required to ensure proper life support. Phobus was always meant to rule itself. Man's laws are not Martian laws my good, sir. So many familiar rules find no application up here."

Gavin stared back at him dull and dimwitted.

"And," Crohne continued, "it appears our wayward space-liner has recoupled with Ares." Looking past Gavin, Crohne motioned past him. Gavin spun around to look out the ports that faced the administrative domes and down to where the incomplete coupling attached to the platform. All three strahlendmach spindles were at a lazy spin moving the ship around in three dimensions simultaneously. The edged prow was cutting up to their left to swing the starboard hatches in alignment to that most umbilical hallway that extended up from the platform. Light danced along the hull like a brush fire. The flickering red of Mars glistened off the peaks of the strahlendmach paddles as they made their time-altering path through multiple realities.

"No time left to talk then," Gavin concluded with his mind overflowing with more things to say yet finding no voice for them.

***

The harried contingent of dignitaries moved like a bucking colt through the arterial halls leading back to their staterooms. Their faces were grave. They spoke little. The Lady Inverness was her commanding self, making her way up the passage with paltry assistance from ol' Gran. Sir Wilson was close by, Argyle only a pace behind him. Listonn still found it a task to move quickly and quite frankly it still disturbed his stomach, but he managed. Beckett had the lightest heart but he kept quiet. Vecihi had opted to stay back and assist with the recovery of the Daedalus. Like everyone, but perhaps more so, he wished to know which of his companions was lost to the graveless cemetery of space.

As the group rounded the arching hall through the men's section, Lady Inverness made no move to stop. She hurried past toward the women's wing right by Boswell's and Cleland's doors. Wilson and Argyle kept up with her, but Beckett and Listonn halted at the bulkhead to Boswell's chambers. Listonn gave the access wheel a pull but it was locked. He banged on the door and began calling out. "Dr. Boswell? Dr. Boswell? We've need of you at the dock. Doctor?"

Beckett watched the others hurry along waiting expectantly for a response.

As the Lady Inverness' party rounded up to the short space into the women's' rooms, they found Lanny in the hall, still gently rapping on the Princess' door.

"Hello, my lady," Lanny said with a weightless curtsy as she made eye contact with the Lady Inverness and the others with her. Not saying a word, Lady Inverness reached the door. She began pounding, rapping both fists hard against the metal bulk.

She called out, "Sandra! Sandra are you in there? It's Cecilia. Open up this instant!"

"Let me try the door," Wilson said with the voice of veteran authority. He gave the wheel a pull and found it locked. Argyle took the other side and they both went white knuckled as they attempted to force it open.

"Not budging," Wilson resigned, "could she be elsewhere? Have we checked the Observatory or the Aviary?"

"Yes sir," Lanny said, eyes to the floor. "I've looked in all the common areas, even the mess sir, thinking her peckish. Not to be found sir."

"Perhaps she is aboard the liner then," Wilson concluded with a huff.

"Oh, how do we open these infernal doors?" the Lady Inverness shouted. Argyle touched Wilson on the shoulder. His attention grasped, Argyle directed him to look at the ventilation panel not more than a few feet or so from the room. Wilson gave Argyle an odd look.

"You are a little man, my friend, but that's a small place." Argyle nodded with a broad smile that showed his small square, yellow stained teeth contrasting his dark lips. "Alright then, man, more than one way to traverse an obstacle. You might at least get a look inside anyway."

The Lady Inverness kept at the door, but the three maids were curious as to the men's actions. Wilson pulled his rotund mass to the floor, having to adjust his sword sidelong to make way. The brass frame of the vent was held to the wall with large protruding screws. From his vest Wilson produced a collapsible knife and unfolded it in both hands. With the flat edge he set about loosening those screws from the frame. The metal voiced its protest loudly as the screws gave way and began floating off in slow spirals.

Nearby, Argyle began stripping off his clothes. Each of his magnetic soled shoes came off with a pull. He attached them neatly in place on the floor. His stockings came next tucking each one neatly into each shoe. He then went about to unfastening the buttons down the front of his uniform. The servants were mildly shocked to see the little brown foreign man slip off his trousers in midair. Each article of clothing came off in turn, down to the cloth wraps that bound his waist. He was careful never to let his kukri blades touch the ground. He first let them float freely and then cradled them in his arms like infants. He tucked the twin scabbards into the ties of his wraps and stopped to limber up. Now disrobed he looked thinner, almost sickly gaunt. His arms and legs were wispy, as if breakable like twigs. But he was also tawny, his taut muscles tucked in tight against his ribs. As he stretched, his range of motion with every limb defied imagining. He could wind one arm clear around his back and then curl it up over his head in a single motion. His legs were equally limber, able to fold easily into a lotus even without gravity's assistance.

Listonn found his way to them. "Gods, man, what are you doing?"

Without looking up, Wilson addressed him, “A little bit of burglary. Boswell’s not about then?”

“Not at all,” Listonn said with a long stare down his nose at the disrobed man.

“And Beckett? Where’s he now?” Wilson asked, fiddling with his knife in the head of a screw.

“He excused himself without excuse,” Listonn said, now as fascinated with Wilson’s hovering attempts to gain entry into Sandra’s room. Achieving success, Wilson worked off the vent cover and looked into the dusty tunnel within. He glanced back at Argyle. “Don’t know, my friend. It is a small space,” he said. Argyle merely smiled in self-assurance and pulled himself down to the shaft. It was understandably dark and more than a bit cold despite the warm gust that came with the breath of the platform’s respiration. At this point even the Lady Inverness stopped her rapping and watched the Nepalese man do his work. Argyle extended a long arm into the shaft and leaned his head in tight. It took some work to get his shoulders at the right angle. He worked himself deeper, hands and arms pressed hard against the metal walls. He inched his way until he had to navigate his hips the same way he did his shoulders. It took him some jiggering, but like a contortionist he crawled in, his toes finally disappearing into the shaft. All they could hear was the shuffling of his flesh against the metal casing that pressed in all around him.

Wilson looked up with a muffled laugh. “Extraordinary,” he said looking over the others. The Lady Inverness and the servants could only nod absently. “Did you make it, man?” Wilson called up into the dark. “Can you get in?” Turning back to the others he said, “Perhaps we should have sent him with a torch,” which was answered by more absent nods. Some uncomfortable moments passed without a sound. The Lady Inverness was obviously growing more agitated. Wilson moved to the door and waited. Growing uncomfortable himself he knocked, “Come now, Thaman, did you get in? Are you alright?”

“Thaman?” Lanny asked.

“That’s my servant’s given name,” Wilson replied, “Lance Naik Thaman Gurung Thapa.” Finally, as if in reply, the latches from within were loosed one after the other and the pressure wheel began a slow staggered turn. “Ha ha!” Wilson exclaimed helping to turn the wheel on their end, “he’s succeeded.” Argyle opened the door, but only a crack, just enough so he could look out with a single white eye. “What now, man? Open up!” Wilson bellowed but Argyle shook his head in protest.

"Timi ra yo Duchess hru chaa," he said from within. Wilson's face became grave, weighted. He turned to the ladies and stated frankly.

"My apologies but only the Duchess and I may enter. I must ask the rest of you to remain here." The Lady Inverness went sheet white.

"Sir Wilson, what is it?" she asked.

"Come now," Listonn protested.

"Please," Wilson said, "the rest of you please wait here." Lady Innverness' servants, ol' Gran, Gael and Lanny, complied backing off to the opposite side of the hall. Listonn awkwardly planted his hands on his hips and remained where he was. Argyle opened the door to see that they had moved away and then allowed both Wilson and the Lady to enter. Once they came in Argyle closed the door and sealed it shut behind them. Listonn immediately drifted up to press his ear to the door, but couldn't hear a thing. Slowly the three maidservants gave each other questioning looks and then came quietly up behind him.

Now within, Argyle struck up the electric lamp revealing the vacant room. The first oddity they noticed were the sets of clothing that had been pushed off toward the walls. Easily discernible were the outfits worn by both Cleland and Sandra when they were last seen. The second thing they noticed was the concealed door which had been slid away at the back of the stateroom.

"I see now how you got in," Wilson said, "you think the Princess left the same way?" Argyle merely shook his head in disagreement. He pointed one hand to the open chest that lay strapped to the wall near the back. The Lady Inverness pulled herself over to it and gasped at its contents. Wilson pulled himself up over her shoulder and took a look for himself. He drew in a deep breath and pursed his lips. The Lady Inverness leaned down to the lock and pulled out the key that had been left there. As she suspected it was the charm that Sandra kept so often about her neck. Some of the paraphernalia had been removed. She scurried about to gather the articles and slam them into the box. Neither Wilson nor Argyle made a move while she went about that task. She searched the folds of the crumpled hammock that was unhooked on one side and billowed like a dead albatross against the wall. She searched Sandra's drawers to ensure there was nothing else to be found. Among the articles of obvious carnal application she discovered the opium sashay, pipe and lighter. She could only roll her eyes at the prospect of the two of them, under the influence of opiates. When she was finally satisfied she closed up the box and locked it with Sandra's key. She then turned to both Wilson and Argyle and indicated for them to come close.

"I'm no fool that I can't see Cleland's hand behind this. I'm sure they are both back there in that service tunnel in some state of undress. This is a very delicate matter and I need you both to exercise the greatest measure of discretion."

"We know, Cecilia. Argyle was right to keep this quiet."

"Yes," she said looking at Argyle intently, "and you have my deep personal gratitude. Will you now help me in this matter? Will you go back there and find them? They can't be far."

"Why would they have left at all?" Wilson asked. Turning to Argyle he asked, "was that shut up when you got here?" Argyle nodded. "Cecilia," Wilson said turning back, "we'll look certainly but there's something else here."

"Something else?" she asked in a cross but hushed voice.

"Why yes," Wilson said as he moved over to the beckoning passage behind the stateroom. The air was a bit more stagnant back there. There was a hint of an acrid smell as well, nothing that he could place. It smelled of an old sailing vessel back there.

"Archdale," Lady Inverness said, "we must retrieve them before they're missed."

Wilson padded the hilt of his sword. He drew in a deep breath and pushed off the door frame back to the main entrance to the stateroom. Without opening the door, he shouted so those outside could hear.

"We'll just need a moment. Thanks for your assistance but we're all well here. Listonn, are you there?"

"Yes!" Listonn called back at a needless shout. "Are they in there? Are they all right?"

"No concern, Tom. Can you see if they've found Boswell? They'll need him back at the liner. Can you see about it?"

"Boswell!" Listonn shouted back. "Does the princess need a doctor?"

"No, Tom, just see to it please. With my thanks," and Wilson withdrew. He stopped to straighten his uniform jacket and girding up his sword. "Fetch the lamp," he directed Argyle and moved back to the passage. He stopped to give Lady Inverness an assuring stare. "We'll go fetch them."

"Thank you, Archdale, do hurry," she replied. Argyle picked up the torch and bound off each wall to slip easily into the dark tunnel, suddenly becoming lost in the maze of draping cables and hissing pipes. Wilson had to pull himself in with less elegance, but did so purposefully.

Lady Inverness wished she could recline. Her shoulders were tense and she noticed that her hair piece had become unkempt. In the gloom of the partially lit room she found her way to the mirror and attempted to put herself back together. Seeing herself, she hadn't realized that she'd been perspiring through her makeup. The flawless white application had curdled in the heat to frightful blotches. She freely took liberties with Sandra's makeup and went to repairing the damage. Angry and agitated, she spoke to herself in the inadequate light.

"Fool girl," she said, her mind afire with the thought of the two of them together, "fool child." After a time she found the room lights and raised them. She cursed that she couldn't rely on the servants. Servants talk the worst of all sorts. "Blasted fool girl," she cursed. After she busied herself with regaining what she could of her appearance, she turned to face the blank space at the back of the room. She wondered if all the rooms were similar. Did Cleland know of them? Did he steal into her room and force himself like the arrogant brute he is? It certainly would appeal to his sense of mischief. Sandra still could have resisted, refused him. The key and the chest of carnal playthings were too telling. The very thought of the two siring an illegitimate child was unbearable. If the little fool did get pregnant there were ways of correcting that. Her mother, the Grand Duchess Alexandrovna, must never know. She couldn't help but wonder about her sisters, all of them were a bit wild. Marie was the only one with any sense and she will one day be the Queen of Romania. Beatrice was the wild one, over-governed by her passions. Victoria Melita was the quiet one but still sly in a mischievous way. Sandra was the one gem among them all. She was the one to come up here, to visit space and drag the train of her dress among the stars. Why waste that as one of Cleland's thoughtless conquests? "Foolish, wasteful girl," she cursed and cursed aloud.

Time plodded as she waited. At different times she caught the sound of movement back in the main hall. She may have heard muffled voices but no one knocked. No one dared. After almost an hour she finally heard movement in the dark passage behind Sandra's room. The light of a fading electric torch rose up and both Wilson and Argyle returned. Wilson's face told a grim tale, like the mask from a Greek tragedy. Argyle's head was downcast but stern as well.

"God save the Queen, Sir Archdale," she said, "what's wrong? Did you find them?"

"Christ I hope not," Wilson said, his voice a deep water.

"What is it," she said, her hand coming to her mouth.

"Cecilia," Wilson said, "it's nothing for a lady. Argyle is going to fetch Napier. We'll need to enlist his aid and a few of his good men."

"Dear God, Archdale, what is it!" she insisted. Wilson's face was ashen and withdrawn. He could only shake his head in protest but couldn't shed another word. "Tell me, Wilson, or I'll march back there myself. By damn you know I will."

"And you'd regret it till the grave, Cecilia. Dante Alighieri couldn't have envisioned such a hell." He gave her a look that was stern but also somehow pleading. "You'd regret it till the day you died."

Enraged and huffing she pushed past and made for the aperture. Argyle went to intervene but Wilson stopped him. Argyle lent the lady a bewildered look as she pulled the wide cage of her dress through the hole. Wilson gave an assuring nod to his lifelong friend.

"Go get Napier. Tell him only a few men, no more than three. Only those he can truly trust and who've seen a few things, you understand?" Argyle nodded his understanding. "I'll see to the lady." Wilson rubbed the tension from the back of his neck. "But she'll wish to all that's sacred that she'd listened. She'll wish to God that she'd turned back."

Chapter 1A (11): The Crypts of Mars

Campbell remained clinging to the outside the liner until his life-giving stores neared depletion. A quivering gauge set just to the right of his viewing port demanded his attention. The arrow that resembled the minute hand on a stopwatch quaked down into the red field painted on its scratched dial. He had secured the Daedalus as much as he could manage on his own. He checked, and checked and double checked, until he caught himself getting a tad light-headed. He had to concede to the limits of his fragile humanity. Demand prompted him to get into the airlock with enough time to adjust the pressure and draw in the breathable atmosphere. Working himself over to the hatch, he loosened the seals and the metal door blew wide with a rush of escaping air. He pulled himself in with the suit's squat, stubby arms. Reaching the panel within, he worked the machine until the hatch closed and he was sure of proper containment. The door now locked, he waited for the air to come back and the pressure to equalize with his suit. He held his thoughts in check while his breathing calmed and the sweat dried on his face. When the artificial environment in the transference chamber reached the proper levels the inner hatch opened and the outstretched arms of his comrades pulled him inside.

The men of the Daedalus fell on Campbell with a measure of praise and gratitude he could never have anticipated. At first his view port was blocked with the rush of figures that blurred past. He caught only glimpses of faces both jubilant and relieved. They cheered and shouted as some of them began dismantling his suit. His helmet was pulled off from behind and he finally could get a clear look at his fellows. The crew pushed in around him, eyes tearing and arms outstretched. They kissed crosses and saint's medals that dangled from chains around their necks. Some wept openly. One was slumped in the corner completely overtaken by his brush with mortality. Captain Napier was there, but held back to allow his crewman some space. None felt the weight of the moment more but he was never short on proper decorum, even in the most adverse circumstances.

Campbell reluctantly accepted the fuss. He was well beyond spent and fatigued. The shouting and smiling faces almost seemed directed at someone else. He was reduced to an observer in his own head, unable to discern if it was really happening. Captain Napier finally ordered the men aside and came up closer. Campbell was still being freed from the suit. The helmet spun like a top in midair above him. Arm attachments hovered close by. He was still set back in the cavity of the bulbous chest.

"Colin," Napier said, cool and authoritative looking at him intently, "are you alright?" The crew went quiet, almost awkwardly so. Campbell blinked back at him and took an instant to assess.

"Aye, Captain," he said, "I'm alright."

Napier looked him straight in the eye and then nodded in satisfaction. "You're a worthy spaceman, Colin, an asset to the crew. You've saved the ship and all aboard. We owe you our lives. Let's hear it for him, men, hear, hear!"

And the crew shouted in unison, "hear, hear!" accompanied by laughter, tears and further sighs of relief.

"And to Warrant Officer George Elphinstone," Napier's voice called out across his men, cutting against the cheering. Napier said, "A finer man I'll never know." The crew was instantly sobered. No voice spoke. No one stirred. Most all cast their faces to the deck no matter what angle or position they held. Their caps were clutched to their chests. Napier drew in a long breath. "Men, I've not lost someone under my command in an age. George has two little ones back home, now at the breasts of his widow. I'll not lose another one of you, not today, tomorrow or any hereafter. Ares Britannia is a death trap. The commission be damned. Rot all if we don't comeback with a single damn rock or a pinch of gold dust. We're gathering up our passengers and setting sail. We'll make for Goldene Zeitalter and get drunk on black German beer in a few months' time. We'll pour a stein for George and each take a long drink." Napier adjusted his uniform and pulled his cap down firmer on his head. He looked his men in the eyes and issued orders, "Turner and Morris, suit up and secure the gangway. Southway and Martin, I don't want any mistakes. You make sure they're properly fitted. Damn you if there's anything left to chance." Napier gave a serious look down at Campbell in his metal cradle. "Lt. Campbell, are you fit for duty? And I don't mind you saying otherwise."

Campbell took no time to consider. "Yes sir, fit and ready."

"Good man, I'll see you decorated. If you would then, get below for the fitting. Sooner that's done the sooner we're off. Crew, you have your orders, dismissed."

The floating group of men made their way back to their stations with final slaps to Campbell's arm and scattered thanks. Pulling himself out of the spacesuit, Campbell followed along with those who went below. The crew designated to step outside prepared for the spacewalk to ensure that the gangway was properly affixed to the hull. Once outside, they curiously looked for where the cabling broke free, but there was no evidence to be found at that end. The hooks and screws all seemed normal, nothing worn, sheared or snapped off. It was a bloody mystery.

Messages were shot back in rapid tapping telegraphic type. Sir Royden dictated through the operator. "State of the ship and crew? Stop. Which man was lost? Stop." Listonn was right there by Royden's side, shouting out questions concerning the ship's space-worthiness and when they could make for Earth. Warrant Officer George Elphinstone had always been the telegraph and yack-mouth operator. It seemed somehow off that someone else had taken the position. The Daedalus' crew gave short answers but had little time. "Elphinstone lost. Stop. Refit continues. Stop. End transmission. Full stop." Listonn's more detailed queries had to wait for their return.

In under an hour the ship was again fully secured to the gangway that allowed passage to the surface. Vecihi and Argyle were there with a few of the builders. Bull and Piter were among them, but Miser had left, summoned by Culverton to perform some other duties. Vecihi insisted on seeing Campbell. He scrambled up the passage and came aboard the liner, asking all along the way as per Colin's whereabouts. After being directed below, he found his friend tending the fit and grabbed him by the shoulders. Vecihi wept loudly like only a foreigner can. Campbell had spent his tears but took that moment with Vecihi to honor their companion.

Argyle was led to Napier and in his shattered English, requested the Captain's presence along with a few of his most experienced men, just as Wilson had directed. Napier asked why but Argyle shared nothing. Napier drew his uniform tighter across his chest, slapped the belt of his saber around his waist and complied. He needed Campbell to stay on the refit but he handpicked three others to come along. Before disembarking, Napier's took a mental inventory of the moment. Though shorthanded from the start he ordered another man to keep watch over the gangway. No one from the platform was allowed aboard until he returned. No-one was allowed under any circumstances. Napier also noted the need to have words with Crossland and Crohne both. This was a sorry state of affairs and he'd see them both answer for it.

***

Napier, Argyle and the three stout crewmen came down the gangway. A small group of builders was there who attempted to express their sentiments, pleased to see that the ship had been rescued. Napier and his men refused to respond. Grim faced and eyes fixed forward they ushered their way past. The builders stared after them somewhat bewildered. They looked blankly to Miser and Piter to read their expressions. The two leaders merely watched stoically as the group of outsiders went off onto the platform.

The small band from the Daedalus pulled themselves along the blackened halls of Ares, back through the officers' staterooms, ultimately arriving at the women's section. Listonn was doting in the hallway outside of Sandra's door. He was very much alone and aggravated beyond measure. He gave Argyle a distasteful look and then nodded a greeting to Napier as they approached.

"Sir Thom," Napier said in greeting with a hand to the bill of his cap. "What's all this about?"

"Hell if I know," Listonn shot back, "but I mean to find out." Argyle rapped on the door and Sir Wilson answered by popping it open a crack.

"Napier!" Wilson said, "come on in." Not to be denied, Listonn thrust himself between them.

"Now listen here, Archdale," Listonn said, "you will not leave me stranded in the hallway. I must insist that you and the Duchess-"

Wilson shut him up by opening the door wide to silently admit them all. Wilson extended his thick neck out into the hall and looked both ways, the corners of his mouth turned low. His large eyes were bulbous and frog-like. He kept one hand close to the pommel of his sword. Satisfied that they weren't observed he closed the door behind them and locked it tight.

Once inside, Listonn's eyes went everywhere to see what he'd been forbidden to see. The Lady Inverness was there, perhaps more disheveled than he'd ever seen her before. She cooled herself with that beautifully painted Chinese fan. Wilson and Lady Inverness had since cleaned the stateroom from top to bottom. All the scattered clothes were tucked away in the traveling trunks and bound tight. The lady had personally gathered up the opium and that dreadful box that could only be unlocked by Sandra's necklace. Napier immediately noticed the panel in the back of the room and the passages that widened out behind.

"What's this all about, Sir Archdale?" he asked.

Wilson stretched out the tension in his neck and shoulders. "First off what's the status of the ship? Are all hands well?"

"No," Napier said flatly. "The ship and crew are safe due to the decisive action of Lt. Campbell and Officer Elphinstone but it cost George his life. We'd all be lost to space if they hadn't come out to fetch us."

"Bloody hell. He was a damn good man," Wilson added nodding, "a damn good man."

"Was Sandra aboard?" Lady Inverness asked no longer able to show restraint. Napier looked at her questioningly. Wilson, his lips pursed, looked back at the Lady and then back to Napier.

"Princess Sandra," Wilson explained, "Lord Cholmondeley, and Dr. Boswell have all gone missing. Are they aboard the Daedalus? We hope to God they are." Listonn when slack jawed. Inverness' looked so hard at Napier the Captain felt her gaze.

Napier looked back at them both puzzled and cross simultaneously, "They were not nor are they aboard."

Listonn was flummoxed. "Well if not on the Daedalus then where are they? Surely someone can account for their whereabouts."

"We need to show you something," Wilson stated and looked down the blank passage beyond the hidden panel, "back there. Make your way quietly. So far it seems like no one's been by to check on us. We need one of you lads to stay here in the room in case anyone comes round." Napier agreed backing up Wilson's request with an order to the youngest of the three who came with them. Everyone else shuffled their way into the aperture and into the understructure of the platform. "Keep close," Wilson added, "the man who designed this place must have been mad."

The maze-like arrangement of Ares' service tunnels were impossible to fathom. After a few short turns it was clear that it would be difficult to find their way back. Wilson led with Argyle politely alongside Lady Inverness to help her along. Listonn, still not one for weightlessness, fumbled as best he could. The two remaining crewmen kept near their captain, a sense of military wariness about them. Wilson finally came to an open doorway with rounded corners, common to the bulkhead throughways about the platform. There was a deep chill in the air as they drew closer. There was also a silence that hung in that cold, an unyielding silence that could not be broken. Wilson stopped, blocking the way, and turned to face the others.

He gave a wandering look over them, "I'd tell you to steel yourselves but it'd do no good." With that, he pulled himself through and swung around to the side. The group then each crept, one by one, into the open area beyond.

The purpose of the room was difficult to comprehend at first. The floor wasn't solid, but consisted of a chain link mesh that stretched from corner to corner. It was too dark to see what was below the crisscrossed, interlaced metal lattice. The ceiling was low, almost too low to allow a man to enter. And it was certainly chilly in there. It was cold, like it was purposely sealed away from the heat. Their pulsing electric torches could barely illuminate the space.

"What are we supposed to see?" Listonn asked.

"Back there," Wilson indicated. Turning that they the group could see the silver glint of bent metal at the edge of their torchlight. In the back left corner there was a section of the chain links that had been pulled up and bent aside. "You've got to get down below, through there," Wilson added. Lady Inverness backed herself into a corner, opposite the bent metal flooring. She showed no fear but had no desire to go nearer. She had already seen for herself and that was more than enough. Argyle took up next to Wilson and hung silently vigilant. Napier held his lamp forward and ventured toward the opening, his men right behind him. Listonn basically crawled up after, soiling the knees of his pants against the floor, pulling himself along with his fingers thrust into the mesh-work. Wilson came up last.

The torn out section looked like it had been cut free with a welder's flame and then bent aside in bowing triangular sections. The hole was a few feet across, making for a makeshift trapdoor to the area beneath the floor. On the walls in the corner on either side there was writing, a scrawl that was applied with a sloppy brush stroke or shaft of charcoal. The black letters weren't English or any Romance language. The characters were sweeping with disconnected dots, slashes and swirls.

"What does that say? Is that Greek?" Listonn asked but none answered. Napier hauled himself over the hole and let his torch float in the air as he pushed himself down. Once below he reached up to grab the light and brought it down with him. They could see its white-orange glow flicker against his face. He took a good look around and stopped dead. They could just see his expression beneath the brim of his cap. He went blank and then slipped off to the side to let another descend. His two crewmen were next but they were hesitant at best. Listonn maintained that same slack-jawed expression, but rushed to pull himself down, frustrated beyond measure to have been kept waiting. Once in the space below, Listonn looked as the beams of the lamps played off each other stretching out fanning shadows. It was even colder down there than above the floor. It was a chill like creeping frostbite or bare skin against a block of ice. Listonn tried to look past the three men who blocked his way. He could just make out some circular objects past them, thick circular clusters larger and wider than a wagon wheel. Their movements disturbed the still air and made the circular bundles knock into each other hauntingly like billiard balls. The three sailors hovered immobile in the room looking at the scene.

"Bloody hell," Listonn said, "What are they?" and pushed the two crewmen aside so he could get a clearer look. He thrust out his torch at arm's length, as far as he could, toward the nearest bundled thing. He couldn't place what he was looking at. It was like a bound up package of rubbish but it had what appeared to be hair at one end. The thing had strands of long thin, frozen hair that fanned out like a halo. "What the hell?" he asked again aloud, looking hard through his monocle to focus. He then realized the circle was formed by the bent legs of a human body turned back upon itself. Empty black eye sockets and a silent screaming mouth pointed back at him. It was the body of a naked woman, turned round in an unnatural position. Her belly was laid open, her ankles stretched all the way around alarmingly to either side of her head, her arms dangling lifelessly to either side. The pinwheel corpse spun slowly in the air to show the gore of her chest and abdomen, blown out as if she had exploded from within.

The crewman at his left side gagged. Thrusting his head left and away he heaved, blowing the contents of his stomach into the freezing air in unsightly globs. Listonn had to swallow against the stench and the swell of saliva in his mouth. He felt his own constitution challenged. Looking at the nightmare about him, he saw that all the spiral bundles were all women all blown open and similarly postured. He couldn't even attempt to count the bodies lurking there in the half-light. There were two here and then three more further back and on his left maybe as many as six more. Each one was naked, ripped open, curled around with frozen faces crying out in abject horror. Unable to maintain himself, he vomited also. He let the lamp go, turned back into the dark corner behind him and tried to hold it back with his hands. The warm flow hit his fingers and gushed past, billowing out in the air. He couldn't concentrate for the constant retching until his stomach had nothing left to expel.

Napier removed his cap and held it to his chest. 'We need to take the platform,' he thought to himself, 'arm the lads and declare martial law.' The condition of the bodies defied reason. Each was a tableau depicting the broken, twisted wrenching instance of their death. Their inner cavities had been cut open suddenly, escaping pressure burst outward. The out rush caused the trunks of their torsos to expand and expose their now frozen innards. The tattered edges of the ferocious wounds literally clutched the air like gnarled fingers. As their bellies stretched their spine bowed backwards, snapping in multiple places. Some had twisted full around with the backs of their heads pressed up toward their backsides. Their faces were more ghastly still. Eyes had been gouged out. Their faces stared lifeless with eyeless sockets draining tears. Their mouths gaped open with no breath and no voice. The bodies bobbed weightlessly as the group disturbed their noiseless crypt.

"Madness," Napier spoke out though those remaining above couldn't hear him. "Poor wretched souls," he said just to himself. The rote words of funeral prayers welled up in his thoughts. "You always descend into hell," he said. "Poor wretches, you always descend into hell."

"Captain Napier," the Lady Inverness' voice called down from above. "Please tell us, the princess is not down there is she? She's not one of those poor girls is she?" Napier couldn't pull his eyes away from the bodies before him. He slapped his vomiting crewman hard with the back of his hand.

"Pull together, man," he commanded in a condescending tone. "Look over there," he directed. That sailor had to spit the foul taste from his mouth before he could comply but did as ordered. The three of them began looking over the corpses but Listonn kept his distance.

There were just so many. They fanned out and searched, peering around each body until the face could be found, to see if it was recognizable, what was left of it anyway. They looked into every gnarled face but their sheer number made it all the harder. At times the men had to touch them. They had to spin the body about to get a proper look. There wasn't much common among them. They found women of different ages and ethnicities but all were Caucasian Europeans. They couldn't identify any of them.

Listonn found himself unable to look back into the room. He faced the corner like a scolded schoolboy. He worked his fingers, trying in vain to strip the mess from them, but they were hopelessly coated. He pulled the sash from his breast pocket and wiped at them over and over, the Tyneside green blackening. Still they wouldn't come clean. In a panic, he pulled himself madly up the torn open flooring in the room above, tearing his topcoat on some twisted metal. Wilson helped him up back into the room.

"There, there," Wilson said reaching out a sympathetic hand.

"Don't touch me!" Listonn shouted at him pulling away. "Shut your damn face," he said as he pulled himself across the Greek letters that marred the wall on his right and made away from the opening to the mass grave beneath him.

"Captain Napier," the Lady Inverness called back again. "Please tell me she's not down there." The three men completed their ghastly search. All the bodies were in fact women. All were naked. All seemed to be in similar states but it was difficult to tell. Napier thought that some might have also been beaten. Their skin was obscured by frost and blood. It was so hard to tell what befell them. He made his way back to his two men. Conferring quickly he called back. "She's not here. No telling who they are. Don't know a single one of them." The Lady Inverness and Wilson both heaved a heavy sigh. They shared a concerned, but relieved look.

The walls of the chamber beneath the floor that served as a horrid resting place were covered in more Greek writing and pictograms that resembled crude, primitive cave drawings. They included images that could be human figures, some of unnaturally larger stature than others. The images were assembled into scenes that could be wars, where sticks that may represent spears were hurled at enemies. Some figures looked wounded or run through by these weapons. The stick men gathered around rectangular shapes that may be altars where animals were sacrificed on or about triangles that could represent bonfires. It was very coarse, pagan, savage and unbridled. It made the room all the more sinister, speaking whispers of willful purpose. Their search concluded, the three men thankfully drew themselves back up through the hole in the mesh-work floor, voiceless and depleted of soul. Wilson helped them up as to not catch their clothes on the jagged opening.

They took a moment. No one spoke. It was awkward. There was no point of reference to dictate what to do next. Finally, Wilson broke the silence. "We need to call Beckett down here,"

"No!" Lady Inverness said loudly, then immediately hushed her voice to a whisper, "we cannot entrust this to anyone who didn't travel on the Daedalus."

"Cecilia," Wilson plead, "these people need a burial. They need a man of God now. Of all the indecency at least their remains may be treated with dignity."

"No," Lady Inverness said in a plosive hush, "Sandra, John and Dr. Boswell are still missing and we have every reason to believe that they are somewhere in these foul passages."

"Why do we think that?" Listonn asked.

"Don't be daft, man," Napier said, "I assume that's how we found these tunnels? We suspect that our missing company found them first?" Wilson and Argyle nodded with understanding. Napier continued, "Then we need to find them and right soon. I want to get everyone to the Daedalus and make for home." Napier looked at Wilson with a face of chiseled marble and the fire of a burning forge. "Wilson, you've seen more dead than the lot of us. I couldn't tell. I looked long over them and I couldn't tell if they were alive before they," he paused searching for the words, "before they were made like that. What do you say? Were they alive before they were forced into a vacuum?" Wilson took a long space to consider.

"I don't know. I really can't say."

"I can't tell what this nonsense is all about," Napier stated. "I just can't make sense of it."

"Gentlemen," Lady Inverness insisted, "we have more pressing concerns, more pressing matters to attend. I want everyone to listen carefully to what I'm about to say. You've all now been brought into a circle of trust and not one of my choosing. So saying I mean no offense but I must call on each of you to swear an oath to me. You must swear on your good names that you will not discuss this with anyone. Not for the rest of your natural lives." She looked over each one in turn. She looked each one in the eyes. She looked long at Listonn who became uncomfortable and forced to look away. "I charge you," she continued, "with finding these three missing people and when you find them you may very well discover them in a compromising position. I say this now to ensure that there will be no misunderstanding. There are reputations at stake. Reputations I won't have sullied by loose lips and malicious appearances. Do I make myself clear?" Listonn's eyes dropped to the floor. The two crewmen looked at each other. Napier spoke up for all of them.

"I understand you, my lady. Your trust is not misplaced. I give you my word as the captain of this voyage and I speak for my men. When we find them we'll bring them to you directly. We'll put them directly into your good care."

"Very good, captain," Lady Inverness said, "I'm glad we have an understanding. You are a credit to your station." Napier bowed in response.

Listonn looked back at them all the more shocked and dumbfounded. He asked, "Shouldn't we ask Gavin to assist us? Surely he must have a blueprint of all these blasted halls."

Wilson and Napier both looked at him disapprovingly. "Listen to the Lady," Wilson spoke coldly, "no one else will know. Besides, I believe Mr. Crossland has some things to answer for. He's not indemnified of some responsibility here."

"You mean Sir Crossland," Listonn corrected. "You can't mean to suggest that he knew about any of this? Yes, things are in a sorry state but that's negligence at worst."

Lady Inverness joined in the chill look that grew colder than the freezing grave beneath them. "Mr. Listonn," Lady Inverness stated in a tone that could overrule the eldest statesmen of the Parliament and the Prime Minister besides. "Ares Britannia has been reduced to a cesspool and all responsible will be met with the furthest extent of the throne's most terrible judgments. There are crimes here committed both overtly and of the grossest negligence. As for whoever had a hand in the atrocity below, God almighty did not make hell's fire searing enough to adequately punish the eternal souls who've participated. And if Mr. Crossland had any foreknowledge then may God damn him in the same utterance." Argyle and the two crewmen stung with the deep founded sincerity of those words. Lady Inverness then addressed Wilson, "Archdale, please assist me back to my room. There are those with whom I would consult." Not actually catching her meaning, Sir Wilson of course graciously agreed.

***

Gavin met with a mild objection from Reverend Beckett upon again requesting his assistance. Gavin wouldn't take no for an answer. Beckett's reputation with the miners had proven helpful and Gavin wouldn't do without all available advantages. The two huddled behind the closed door of Beckett's room. Beckett had been eating prior to Gavin's arrival. The remnants of a small bread loaf, a wedge of cheese and brown wrapper of sliced pork were pushed off into a corner for later consumption. Beckett was dressed plainly, indistinguishable from one of the builders in his everyday clothes. Gavin suddenly became more aware of his own state of attire. He slapped off the onset of dust and grime he had acquired while moving about the platform in his formals.

Beckett unfastened the yack-mouth from the wall and called the switch operator who connected him with the mining camp. The call was instantly answered and Beckett, without so much as a breath, passed the mouth over to Gavin.

"Hello? Didier?" Gavin asked furrowing his brow.

"Meester Crossland, we talk again so soon," Othello's now familiar voice came deep over the line. Gavin didn't bother to remind him to use his proper title. "So?" Didier continued, "you important enough to get things done?"

"It's not like that, Didier. I believe you've failed to realize that others here are more than sympathetic to your position."

"We saw what happened to your nice shiny new lina. Are dere problems witch your ride home, Crossland?"

"Yes we did have some problems, Didier, and a man lost his life correcting them. That's the kind of men these are, Didier. Men who are willing to sacrifice. That's whom I've brought here from Earth. It's the kind of men we are. Now are you ready to hear our offer?"

"I picked up da yak and I'm listenin'. What can you do for me?"

Gavin kept his eyes on Beckett as he spoke, reading his face for feedback as he made his pitch. "As per the matter of the life insurance policies," Gavin said, "I'm having Sir Royden draft up papers. Everyone who's purchased one of these will be heard, their claim recorded and the promise will be backed by the full faith of Tyneside Spaceyarde, Ltd. Every claim will be heard and everyone will either have their investment returned or the policy replaced with one that's legitimized by Tyneside's own equity. Is this acceptable, Didier?"

"Go on, Crossland," he replied.

"As per the issue of the selling of goods outside the parameters of the Tyneside company store, all such will cease. I'll offer new bedding and a portion increase of daily food rations to all the miners upon the next arrival of a Tyneside liner. This will only be offered to those in the mining camp. It's not extended to the builders or any new arrivals that might enlist after the signing of this agreement. A key to the company stores will be provided to one of the mining crew who shall be designated as quartermaster. The appointee will have one of only two keys, the other of which will be held by Sir Royden. No one will ever be able to deny you sustenance again. Is this acceptable to you, Didier?"

"Go on," was Didier's only response.

"This will also include the strict enforcement of the working hours as dictated by your commission and corresponding shares. All forced work outside of that agreement will cease."

"Idle promises if there's no muscle. Who's going to keep da peace when you're gone?"

"In order to ensure satisfaction, I am willing to give you Piter, Miser and Bull as your captives until the next Tyneside liner arrives and relieves them. But I'll only give them over on one condition."

"And what's that?"

"You may incarcerate them at your camp but you cannot harm them, mistreat them, starve them or in any way mete out any form of vindictive retribution for their offenses." Beckett shook his head at the improbability of that offer. Gavin quieted him with an outstretched hand. "I'll not compromise on that, Didier," Gavin continued. "I must insist. We'll not be coarse about this. You can take them hostage as surety of this agreement but no more. An appointee of the builders must have ready access to check up on them at any time. If they so much as detect any form of misgivings this agreement is voided. We'll not repay wrong doing with more of the same. Are we of one mind, Didier?"

There was a pause on the yack-mouth. Didier broke in, "And will there be a trial for dem? Will we's be able to write down what they's done?"

"Yes," Gavin said, "it'll be done in the good order of Her Majesty's courts. They'll not escape justice up here."

"We agree to all dis so far," Didier stated, "what else?" Gavin took a breath and a fresh look at Beckett who seemed more unsettled with every word.

"Now most importantly," Gavin said, "about the missing women and specifically the matter of your wife.

"Our Dr. Boswell, the physician we brought along with us from earth, has discovered some medical anomalies here on Ares. As you've stated, Didier, everyone in space gets the brickets, but there's little to be found up here. As a precaution, Royden has been committing sick individuals to the good care to be found on the Tyneside liners as they came out here. Now there's been some negligence as Royden has failed to keep proper accounts. I know there's no excuse for it. He should have made you aware, but I believe he directed that your wife and several others to be transferred from the infirmary in order to seek superior medical attention. Now, I won't lie to you, Didier. This doesn't always result in transference to the moon but it can. I believe your wife was incapacitated and taken on the HMS Jewel of India for proper looking after."

"So she could be on the moon," Didier replied a bit colder. "Where on the moon? Did you send her to da Yanks? Yeah, day got good doctors there, the Yanks."

"No, Didier," Gavin answered improvising. "You see there's still dissension among the Americans and they're certainly not friendly to the Empire. We couldn't even stop at Tranquility coming out here. We've been working with the Germans, avoiding American platforms altogether."

"You sure about dat, Crossland? My wife did not go to da Yanks?"

"I am most assured of this, Didier," Gavin said with as much weight of confidence he could muster. "What's more we are heading back that way upon our return. I'll look for your wife myself. And I'll have them contact every outpost and orbital installation hosting a Tyneside office. I'll have them draft telegraphs to be wired to every liner captain who chances by. I will find her whereabouts, Didier. And I also want to hear from anyone else who's missing a loved one. Anyone of unknown whereabouts. I don't need an agreement for this, Didier. That's my personal promise. Spit on our contract and I'll still track these people down. It's just proper."

Didier did not answer, but the steady flow of his breathing could be heard along with the white static on the connection.

"Now, Didier, now this is what I want," Gavin said all business. "In return for all this, I will expect that you will deliver all the ore that's been earmarked for our return voyage to Earth. Along with it will be an accurate accounting of all its contents. This will include all your assessments of the ore's makeup and purity. It will be loaded in the proper canisters and opened for inspection before being turned over. Now are you going to send us back with a full shipment or have you and Barabbas been wasting my time?"

Didier huffed loud in the yack. "Your liner will overflow," Didier said without any measure of emotion. "We have gold, silver, iron and platinum. Some veins were seventy to eighty percent pure. Some were more, almost ninety percent pure. We have more tons collected than a dozen liner shipments could haul."

Gavin lit up like a blaze. "Then we have a deal?"

"We have a deal," Didier said and Beckett's shoulders dropped. It was not a gesture of relief more a gesture of greater tension and greater unbelief.

"But there is one more thing," Gavin said to Beckett's notable surprise. "I must insist, Didier, and I don't mean to offend you with this, but we must deal directly with Barabbas." Beckett's eyes widened at this. "You see," Gavin continued, "you've presented us with a bit of a problem. You say that you're the spokesman for your group but not the decision maker. That's not good enough for me. That's not good enough for legal proceedings. I'll not take a spokesman's signature for this. I will deal with your leader directly. You as his delegate may sign as well and whoever else you see fit. But his signature will be required or there's no contract. No more hiding behind anonymity. We'll resolve this like men, in person, face-to-face and eye-to-eye. Will you agree to this?"

Beckett's eyes dropped to the mouth of the yak in anticipation. The static on the line crackled and there was a low screeching sound like tinnitus but otherwise only silence. Gavin looked questioningly at Beckett who could only shrug in response.

"Alright," Didier's voice came back to them. Beckett was noticeably shocked. "I will have Barabbas there. We shall sign your papers and be ready with your ore. You pass us Piter, Miser and Bull and we'll drag the canisters up the hall to da choka."

"Very good, Didier," Gavin said nodding in satisfaction. "You'll not regret this. I'll have Royden finish the agreement and meet you shortly."

"Gavin," Didier said soberly, "we are entrusting you with our lives here. Do this deal and protect us. We are trusting you."

"You have my word, Didier. This marks the end of all mistrust. One unified Ares."

"As you say, Crossland. All our dead souls will come back and haunt you if you're wrong."

"Well I have nothing to fear then, Didier. We'll be along to the choker presently. The crew of the Daedalus is anxious to get underway. We'll have the teams ready to begin collecting the canisters." And without any further discussion, Othello disconnected the line. Nothing but dead air came over the ear-piece of the clapper. Passing the apparatus back to Beckett Gavin said, "Ever a peculiar fellow. To think that he was some part of dreaming up this whole Barabbas scheme. I'll give him props for dramatic flair I suppose. I'll be glad when this is finally behind us."

"You continue to impress me, Gavin," Beckett said. "Sir Gavin the Green Knight. After all this time to finally know which one of them was this Barabbas character. I still think that it's Didier after all. Who else could it be? Won't make for much of an unmasking at his drama's final act."

"Well, very good then, Reverend," Gavin said with an uncompromising air of finality. "I'm off to find Royden and get those papers for signing. If you would gather up Allen and meet us. We'll need to discuss the matter of our three offenders and about turning them over."

Beckett nodded in agreement. "Right then, see you shortly," and Gavin showed himself to the door. Beckett remained in place and watched Gavin leave. Beckett hovered as most of the natives did a few feet above the deck as if they were floating among clouds. He smiled a slight farewell smile as Gavin worked the latches and made his way out, shutting the door firmly behind him. Beckett waited a short time, long enough to ensure that Gavin was well away in his haste. The clapper and yack-mouth was still in his hands.

He raised the ear piece into place and spoke plainly into the mouth. "Yes, well, Othello agreed to Gavin's proposal. And once more he's upped the ante. Seems like Barabbas will reveal himself to sign the legal agreements personally." A voice on the other end of the line spoke and Beckett replied, "I can't rightly say how I feel about that. I was quite unprepared for it really. But no time for that, Gavin's off to make final preparations then up to the choker to seal the deal. I hope he'll have blood in the inkwell. Isn't that the only proper way to be the signatory of the devil?"

***

Gavin went along the now familiar passage to the Administrative domes. He was far more than spent, he was fatigued. His emotions were torn and raw. His mind wandered. He thought of his dear wife Evelyn back at home and his children. He could picture little Emily's smiling face, like in the mornings illuminated by a candle burning brightly on the bough of a Christmas tree. He thought about the intimacy of his bedchamber when he'd draw Evelyn into their bed and rightly ravage her. Odysseus would return from his misadventures to beat down any would be suitors and thrust deeply into the prize that was his alone. Perhaps it was time they had more children. It was calming and edifying and motivating all at once as he reflected on all his achievements. Enough raw ore for a dozen laden space liners. Everything was about to pay off. Gavin would mount the highest rungs of society and carve out a niche from which none could pry him. When rounding up the curving hallway he found Royden's office door open. Without any announcement he allowed himself entrance.

Royden was behind his desk, magnetic trousers holding him fast to his chair and a pen tipped with a pressurized ink bubble hard at work on the legal documents.

"Thomas, we're all set!" Gavin said in a rush, startling the little man.

"Good to hear," Royden said looking up at Gavin through his tiny spectacles. Sweat beaded on the bald dome of his head. The gray strip of remaining hair seemed somehow grayer in this light. Some of the pages on the desk had been cast aside, now beginning to float into the room.

"And what's more," Gavin said, "Barabbas himself will sign the contract."

"What?" Royden said aghast, shooting spit into the air.

"Yes," Gavin said victoriously. "I didn't force Didier to finger him on the yack. I thought this Barabbas fellow would much rather make some kind of entrance. As I was just saying to Beckett, obviously he must have some flair for theater, that one. But that will end it all Thom. No more mysteries to account for. It will all be in the light and we can deal with it plainly. This is precisely where we needed to be and we're there. It's all come round in our favor. How are the documents coming along?"

"Just proofing them now," Royden said staring off. "We finally get to meet Barabbas, the insurrectionist. The man the Jews freed so they could crucify Jesus Christ instead. All so very Biblical isn't it?"

"So the man frequented the playhouse and Sunday School in his day," Gavin said. "What of it? His signature won't mean a thing after I bring up charges and have him clapped in irons. Threaten to kill everyone on this platform will they? Freeze us all like some fishing boat's catch packed in ice? Preposterous. Bastards didn't know who they were dealing with. So Beckett and Culverton will be by shortly and we'll discuss the handling of our three building chiefs. That's the only bit left to tidy up."

"I hope you have another trick saved up for that one. They won't come quietly," Royden said with a nervous twitch.

"Well, we can resort to brute force. I'd rather keep Napier and his crew out of it but I'll enlist them if it comes to that."

Royden looked more than skeptical, "I don't know, Gavin, sounds risky. You'd better have quite the trick left to pull that off."

"Ha!" Gavin expounded, "I've got a very deep bag of them I assure you-" and his words were cut short by another shrill blast from the platforms alarms. Three short blasts followed by three long ones.

"Gods no!" Royden said, "Not the ship again?"

"That's not a dockyard signal," Gavin corrected, "that's a hull integrity alarm pertaining to somewhere on the platform." Gavin pushed off and back out the door into the hallway. Royden pried his pants from off his desk chair and made after him.

Gavin pulled himself along the walls with his body stretched out lengthwise behind him. He looked like a house lizard crawling flat-armed along lateral surfaces. Gavin entered the tallest of the Administrative domes and made for the ceiling. He drew himself upside down as he scaled the inward arching surface of the top of the dome. Outside Ares he saw the edge of night approaching on his left. It was the looming shadow of Mars overtaking the Phoban surface. Most of Ares was still brightly washed in the sun's rays on his right. The gracefully arching supports shining in tall triangular strips of reflected sun. The rubble and pockmarked terrain stretched out to the horizon. His view was somewhat blocked by the offensive bulge of Babel Tower, but he could see his way on to the mountainous rim of Stickney's Crater and where the long hall to the choker stretched off to the mining camp.

An expanding white plume spurted into space. It slowly rose, shaped like an inverted teardrop from just inside the widest spot along the hall. The spot that formed the meeting chamber they all called the choker. Gavin's eyes caught sight of motion near the plume. Outside Ares there were the bobbing forms of two men in bronze colored spacesuits, one of whom had been blown back toward the domes. The other was making his way quickly towards his fellow to check on his safety. They looked cartoonish out there, bulbous parodies of human shapes. Gavin then noticed another plume on the horizon as well, this one much larger, coming from the coning tower of one of the miner's buildings. It was a squat, gray trapezoidal structure, bound all around by massive pipes that drove into the ground. This expulsion of gas appeared black against the bright backdrop of the sun.

As Gavin watched amazed, Royden came up next to him. "My God, what's happened?" he asked.

"There's been a rapid depressurization," Gavin said somewhat absently, "but I can't see why." As the two men gripped the arching beams leading up to the dome's apogee, a section of the hallway past the choker blew completely away. The large metal sections flew aside and spun tumbling out into the heavens.

"Gods, man!" Royden called out. Another section of metal hall came loose and began its tumble into space. A blast of white gas formed a mushroom cloud that quickly dissipated into a haze. Another shorter, squat building on the miner's side blew open, a silent spectacle that seemed all the more unreal given the violence of its appearance. This time Gavin could make out figures that were blown free in the blast. Objects were spewed out, two or more of which could be people. It was difficult to tell at this distance. But most certainly something catastrophic had happened and human loss would weigh in the balances.

"Christ almighty, Royden," Gavin said, "the heat. All that heat is flushing out into space. We are solely dependent on the mining camp to provide the necessary heat. We must get everyone remaining to the Daedalus or we're all going to die. And most assuredly I'm going to be haunted by restless spirits for the rest of my life."

Chapter 1B (12):
Her Ladyship's Reprisal

Even in the deep back passages of Ares, Napier, his three men and Wilson all heard the alarm.

"Bloody hell!" Captain Napier called out at the top of his lungs.

"Is it the ship?" Wilson asked.

"No," Napier said, "Something else on this rotting platform's amiss."

"Are we in danger?" the youngest crewman asked.

"If we are what can be done about it?" Napier added. "Let's be finished here and get back."

"If we can find our way back," Wilson said, thinking aloud. "I hope Argyle, Listonn and the Duchess are safe back at the staterooms. Where can our people be? We've got to find them and be away from here."

They had discovered another room that added to the mounting nightmares of the dark places on Ares Britannia. The first thing that caught them was a stench. They smelled an acrid odor that was almost corrosive to their nostrils. Then as they approached they discovered that the heat was rising, almost sweltering. The men loosed the buttons on their coats and some abandoned them altogether. This led them to a room that had several curious features.

Occupying the floor to the lofty ceiling was a kiln, broad and round, which was currently lit and burning hot obviously the source of the heat. It glowed red in the shadows with glass windows on various sides that cast rectangular shafts of orange, flickering light to the opposing walls. The stink came from cylindrical tubes or pipes at the opposite end. The largest pipes were larger than oil drums and stunk of lye. Crusty white verdigris formed along the bolted metal panels that bound them all around. Other barrels were tucked in among them filled with nastier stuff of who knows what. Tanks of all shapes and sizes were capped with valves and hoses that ran off into the walls. Whether they were filled with acids or bases it didn't matter, none of the group dared approach too closely, much less touch them.

The three crewmen were anxious to leave and were not ashamed to show it. Their nerves were frazzled. They were oppressed by their dank surroundings. More unexpected and unsavoury discoveries weren't helping and now hearing the alarm pushed them past the edge. Napier gave the place one look over and then turned to leave.

Wilson pushed off toward the kiln to look into one of the windows nearest him.

"Where are you going, Archdale?" Napier asked. Wilson didn't turn but got up close to the glass. It was steaming hot so Wilson kept his distance, just close enough to look inside.

"What are they curing down here?" Wilson asked. As one would expect in a kiln, inside there was a broad slat that extended the length of the interior much further back than it first appeared. The kiln was actually set deeply into the back wall. The slat inside was marred black and piles of ash billowed about in the churning air as one would also expect. They were incinerating garbage of some kind, but why burn it? Waste could as easily be flushed into space. Unless the ash was some needed byproduct for the submersives. There were black, burned half objects strewn about in the ash. The heated gases made flows within the kiln that looked like milk poured into a cup of hot tea. "By damn!" Wilson called out.

"What is it?" Napier called back.

"It's an earring," Wilson said, catching sight of the white hot metal band that he'd seen stuck into Cleland's ear. Napier and the three men came rushing over. They all peered into the windows like they were penny moving picture boxes one would find at a carnival fair. They cupped their hands on either side of their faces to block the glare.

They watched the cascade of billowing white-black clouds of ash looking for what Wilson had reported. Suddenly the remnant of a jawbone came into view, with rows of blackened teeth clearly discernible. The young crewman jumped back. Some burnt vertebrae were close behind, swelling up and then swirling back into the ceaseless tumultuous parade. A portion of skull was next, the vacuous eyes looked back at Wilson for an instant as it spun and was sucked back into the cloud.

"Men," Wilson said, "I believe we've found our missing compatriots."

"Are you sure?" Napier asked.

"That was Cleland's earring I just saw. I'm sure of it," Wilson answered.

"I've seen enough," Napier said, looking into the kiln but speaking to Wilson. "Enough for a lifetime. We've dallied too long. I'm taking my men back to the ship and leaving. Gather up Listonn, the Lady Inverness, her maids and Argyle. You've got until the ship's ready, but not a minute more. Don't make us wait, damn you. I've got no patience left to shed."

"What about Crossland?" Wilson asked, "I assume your omission wasn't an oversight." Napier snuffed hot breath through his nose.

"He can damn well rot up here with the rest of his lot. I'll not take him on my ship. The devil take them all for all I care." Napier said now pointing at Wilson as he spoke, "But I won't leave you and the Duchess. Just don't keep us waiting. Gather them up. Leave their things and let's be going."

"Alright," Wilson agreed. The five men found it difficult to recall their way but they began the trek back to the domicile domes.

***

The Lady Inverness, ol' Gran, Lanny and Gael found their way back into their room. Listonn had become insufferably panicked and made a staggered but strenuous pace back into the men's section. Argyle was close at hand to calm him as he might. Needless to say, the small Nepali man failed to be of much help. Lady Inverness cast a farewell glance as Listonn went flailing up the hall.

Imminently composed, the Lady Inverness asked Lanny to close the door behind them and lock it up tight. She ordered Gael to bind up the panel that must be along their back wall as the one found in Sandra's room. Gael was able to find it easily and attempted to use the straps that secured their luggage to create a kind of barricade for what it was worth. The Lady Inverness then asked ol' Gran to prepare to entice the spirits. Gran gathered up all the electric candles she could find and set them bobbing about the room all around, forming a rough circle of suspended lights.

"We must quiet ourselves, girls," the Lady Inverness said, "There are forces at work here of which Gran is most attuned. Her lineage can be traced back to the Indus River from which flows the anointing essences that we need at this present hour." As her servants busied themselves as directed, the Lady Inverness packed Cleland's opium pipe and producing his glass lighter struck a flame. She breathed in several long drags and then passed it to Lanny. The Lady Inverness closed her eyes and waited for the narcotics to take effect. Soon, all had shared a few puffs ol' Gran being the last who drew in long drags until all the opium was consumed.

Lady Inverness began a low chanting, Gregorian like in timbre and quality. The three women joined with her in turn, improvising haunting harmonies and some dissonant counterpoints. The Lady Inverness opened her eyes to see her three servants starting to lose themselves in the meditation. She looked at ol' Gran's hands, wrapped around those of the woman to either side of her. Her hands were like parchment that had been scrunched into a wad and then unfurled and put back into place. Veins protruded on those skeletal hands that must have carried oceans of blood into those fingers since the day of her birth. All of the natural flow of womanhood emitted from them and penetrated them.

"Beseech the spirits for us, Gran," the Lady Inverness said in a cant. "Call out to those wretched women in the bowels of this horrid place. Their spirits must be offended and seeking justice from the living. They must know the whereabouts of our missing company. They must as sisters feel the lonely fear of our precious Sandra, lost somewhere in those dark tunnels. Clearly the spirits must feel her yearning soul, calling out for rescue. Call to them, Gran! Call out so we may find her!"

The four of them swayed with the chanting, the vibration of their songs swaying in the breasts and up their throats. Gran didn't start at first, instead using her native language, she spoke in the rustic tones her mother had taught her around campfires in the mountains of Romania. Like winters in the cold evening air, when the elders of her people would call out for guidance and the voices of the dead would show them the paths of their migration. They would show them the roads to take and the byways to tread but also warn them away from the passages that would lead to peril. Gran let her tongue slip into English and she said, "Oh, the gods of the Greeks," her voice was the sounds of old timber in the wind. The sound of an old neglected house that's fallen to ruin. "Oh they sacrificed dogs to you. Fighting dogs split open on brazen altars. Their mouths muzzled, their collars drawn tight. Oh, you bloody Greeks, you bloody, bloody Greeks."

"No Gran," the Lady Inverness intoned, "not the Greeks we must ask of Sandra. Where is Sandra?"

Ol' Gran paid no heed. She merely chanted on. "You cultic progenitor of Sparta, your issue pulses into the loins of Gaia. The drowning river Styx forces its way into her loins. Oh I wail for you Gaia! You're raped and ravaged and none stoops to save you! And within the caverns of your womb a child is conceived. A demigod among men. He walks taller than they. He walks with a swagger. His eyes are offset. He cannot see the world the way a man does. He cannot stay upon the Earth. The Earth will not have him. His mother Gaia is the Earth and she shuns the product of her rape. The child does not think to weep at his mother's disdain. He cares not for his weeping mother. She cries and wails within the earth and hates her offspring like no mother before her."

"Gran!" the Lady Inverness spat, "The Princess! Where is the Princess? Ask about the Prince-" and a metal clank rang about the square room on all sides. Lanny gasped. Gael let out a short scream. All were broken from the mounting trance and looked about nervously. The Lady Inverness' face went stern. "Lanny," she said, "check the door."

Ol' Gran was still in the swoon of her séance. "No!" she said, "No, this is not the demigod! This is merely his lackey, his foot soldier. His underling has arrived." With a weightless curtsy, Lanny turned to check the door that led back out to the hall. She found it still fastened.

"Still locked, ma'am," Lanny reported.

"Try to open it," the Lady Inverness commanded. Lanny faithfully undid the locks but the door wouldn't open. She tried with her meager strength to turn the wheel but it wouldn't budge.

"I can't open it, my lady," she said. A noise came from the panel at the back of the room. The women yelping fled to the side by the door, huddling behind their Lady. Lady Inverness would have none of it. She turned in space to face the panel as it opened. The room was heavy with darkness, the hanging torches the only way they could see. The metal panel slid aside and the leather straps were cleanly cut away by the silvery blade of a long knife. Gael started to bawl.

"That's alright, girl," Lady Inverness assured. "Don't give them the satisfaction."

Piter's lanky frame came into the room and he pulled himself to the side. He brandished his long knife openly as he looked back at them. Bull was right behind him, the massive ruffian crammed his extended frame through the small door and then stretching to his full height as he entered. He drew himself to the other side and glared down at them. The Lady Inverness stared right back, bold and unyielding. Someone still remained in the passage behind them. In muffled tones he called in at them.

"This room has been rendered sound proof. Cry out all you want and even someone right outside the door wouldn't hear a thing. Makes for nice sleeping doesn't it? These men are going to beat you to death and your bodies are going to join those lovelies you found in my little hiding place. No one will ever see or hear from you again besides us. We're going to be with you for a long time to come."

"Who is that back there?" the Lady Inverness said, stooping a bit to try to get a better look. "Too much of a coward to show yourself? Going to let these ruffians do your dirty work?"

"Oh my, Duchess," the shadowy voice spoke, "I would love to join them as I do so like to watch. Maybe we won't just do you quite yet. I may very well lay down next to you and hold you as you die, but that will come after. Oh, I do so like to watch..." The hiss of that last word trailed off. "But not just yet. I got someone else I need to visit. "Well, boys, have your way. If the lady is still breathing I'll come join you later but if not, it's just as well. Good night, my pretties. Fare thee well," and the man within the passage slid the panel back into place.

Piter and Bull descended on them. The four women fought as they could, frenzied with panic, terror and ferocity until the sheer brawn of the men overcame them. The hammer blows of clenched fists beat them down. The keen edge of Piter's knife kissed deeply. After a few short moments there were only the desperate flickers of clinging life left in them. Their bodies were like sacks of vegetables or sides of slaughtered meat as they were drawn away.

Chapter 1G (13): Non-Euclidian Geometry

Gavin and Royden sped down to the access point to the long central hall that led to the choker. Not surprisingly, Beckett was there with a number of the building crew who had been working on some project at this end. They were in the last moments of welding shut a massive pressure door to the hall, completely sealing off access to the miner's camp and the far end of the platform.

"Gods, man what are you doing!" Gavin shouted as they approached. Some of the builders looked back at him disconcerted behind their welding helmets.

Beckett's tall bearded face spun to see them as they approached. Without hesitation he responded. "Please, Gavin, there been some kind of catastrophe. We have to protect everyone on this side of the station."

"But there are people over there. We need to mount some kind of rescue."

"Gavin," Beckett said, putting both hands on his shoulders. "There were two men outside when it happened."

"Yes, I saw them," Gavin said.

"Good. They need to come back in and resupply. Then they can proceed back safely with a few of the others and look for survivors."

"But," Gavin said looking past Beckett's shoulder at the massive door still being welded into place. The blazing sparks from the welders' torches flashed with the intensity of a star, filling his eyes with sunspots. Royden had brought along with him the self-welling ink pen and contracts. He held them limply in his hands.

"It's over, Gavin," Beckett said slow and steadily. "They'll be no ore for you this trip." Gavin looked back at Beckett like a lost child. Gavin's graying hair fell in locks over his eyes.

"May-, may-, maybe if I were to suit up," Gavin stammered. "I could look for Didier and whoever else and we could still get to the ore. They said they had plenty and more to spare. Maybe they even had already stored it all up for us. Just need to get the canisters. Oh! Yes! We may not even need Didier. We can just get the ore and move it overland yes? Men in suits can haul it over. Maybe even straight to the Daedalus right?

See?" Gavin said smiling, "It's not over. Just another kind of a problem is all."

The builders working on the door couldn't help but overhear. They looked at each other with irate glances.

"Gavin," Beckett said trying to block his view to the door. "Let these men mount a search. I'm sure the crew of the Daedalus may also be of assistance. Once we determine if there's anyone still over there we can think about the ore. This is a serious matter. Let's treat it as such."

Gavin breathed heavy and began to relent. He relaxed. He noticed that his hands were shaking. "Thank you, Francis," Gavin said. "Of course you're right. We should head back to the others to see what's all with the ship."

"No I-" Beckett said looking back at the door, absently wiping his hands on his topcoat.

"What is it?" Gavin asked.

"It's ah," Beckett hunted, "It's nothing. I believe you're right. Let's the three of us go find the others. Good plan."

Still staring back at the door, Gavin had to tear himself away as the builders completed their work to seal it with unrelenting permanence. Royden sighed with resignation and released the pages of the contract to float off into the air, the ink and zero-grav fountain pen lazily drifted about with them.

***

Listonn broke away from the others at first opportunity and made for his stateroom. He blotted the stinging sweat from his brow with his vomit-stained kerchief. Once he had finally escaped the lurid oppression of those service passages he didn't say a word to the Lady Inverness or her maids when they parted. Argyle wasn't far behind him, making his own way to the men's quarters. Listonn didn't say a thing to him either, that little Indian foreigner who doted continually on Sir Wilson. He knew the little man was right alongside him the whole way back to his room, but he could bugger off. Where the fuck did the name Argyle come from anyway? The little shit was from the opposite side of the world. Fuck Wilson and Napier and all the rest of them while they're at it!

He rued the day he was told that he was going Mars, going to the fabled Ares Britannia. Rued the moment he set foot in that ridiculous pivoting room on the Daedalus when they first came on board. Rued the day he let Gavin convince him that this was the adventure of a lifetime. It would be greater than the conquering of Rhodesia! If Africa was the black continent, how much blacker are the plains of Phobus! Fucking madman, that Gavin Henry Crossland leading them all to this red hell in space.

Listonn burst into his stateroom and all was silent except for the sounds Argyle made heading into Wilson's room across the way. Listonn left his door wide open. He went to the wall and undid the straps around his trunk. He swung it wide and began rushing about to gather his things. As much as he now hated that liner, he should have taken Gavin's advice and stayed there. All his belongings would be tidied up, put into place, and ready for travel. He could close himself up in his private chamber and wait to be away from this infernal death trap.

Clothing floated in the air as they were flung around. For every item he thrust into his case another would be dislodged and float back out. With his back to the door, he didn't notice as someone entered behind him. In his addled state he was too focused, too intent on leaving, too intent on whatever it was that could get him off this platform. Everything was about leaving this place. The man turned and shut the door behind him. It fit into place with a knock.

Listonn spun around. "Ah!" he said in a voice that couldn't penetrate the sound proof seal on his door. "Allen!" he cried out, "what the hell, man? Why the hell are you in my room!" Culverton deftly spun on the very tips of his toes. He stretched his legs to the floor, but kept himself neatly aloft. He was dressed in something akin to a costume. His shirt had been cut into a kind of a tunic. His bare arms and abdomen showed that he had the physique of a Greek god. His arms were wound around with tight leather cords, so tight it was like they bit into his skin. His feet were bound up in sandals that came up to his knees and crude metal bracers were on his shins. His waist was wrapped around in a makeshift skirt. He bore the long length of a steel sword. It was a long straight blade most unlike the service sabers, which were curved and light as a rapier. "What are you made up to be?" Listonn asked.

"They sacrificed dogs to Ares, did you know that?" Culverton asked. "Dogs. Fighting dogs," Listonn ruffled his mustache. "That's what you sacrifice to the god of war you know? Not some sheepish herd animal like a goat or ram. At least a ram has some spirit eh? Not like some steer or oxen. Can you even gather why that Old Testament Christian God wanted some heifer cut open on an altar? What kind of god is he to lust for the blood of a cow?" Listonn looked intently at the polished weapon in Culverton's hand.

"Allen," Listonn said, "what are you doing here?"

"It's a legitimate question," Culverton admitted. "You're a Christian right?"

"Yes of course."

"Then explain it to me? Why does that Hebrew God lust for the blood of lambs and cattle? I mean, doesn't that say something about his nature? What kind of god does that make him?" Listonn feared the failure of adequately answering that question.

"Um," he fumbled, "Uh, you see, ah, it must be symbolic, yes? They were a symbol of some kind."

"A symbol. Of some kind."

"Yes, symbolic. They were a kind of symbolic prediction that one day God would sacrifice his only begotten Son, the Son of God you see, nailed to the cross and all."

"So, they are comparisons to himself, right? It's because your god is like an ox, or a cow, or a lamb. Because they are like him."

Sweat dripped down into Listonn's eyes. He looked about the room. He didn't know why. Maybe for a ready means to defend himself. Maybe out of creeping fear. "I ah, I suppose. That's really a better question for Beckett isn't it?"

"You know he's unclear on this also. The worship of the Greeks was never unclear. They had it all sorted. They didn't distinguish between the religious and the mundane. All life was religious to them. Piety was a way of living. Every breath they took was a divine act. But when it came to sacrifice, gods like Ares demanded fighting dogs." Culverton nodded in self-agreement as he stared intensely at Listonn. "You seem to be a bit of a dog, Listonn, but hardly a fighting dog. You're Crossland's little lapdog." Listonn was startled by the sound of the panel in the back of his room being drawn aside. Piter stuck his head in and looked up at them both. Listonn slipped back toward the wall. He could just make out more movement in the concealed passage behind Piter.

"Got the four locked up, boss. Goin' to be makin' some film?" Piter asked.

"If they're all still breathing," Culverton said. Piter merely shook his head and shrugged in an uncouth gesture.

"The Duchess?" Listonn asked, "you mean the Duchess? What do you mean to do with her?" Culverton raised his opposite hand, the one not carrying the hefty weapon, and affixed a mask to his face. It was a crude rendering of a devil face, or was it? Maybe it was supposed to be something else, some red-faced angry man. Through the snarling mouth of the mask, Listonn could see that Culverton's own mouth was drawn into a smile.

With a motion that started with the swivel of his hips, Culverton wound up like a serpent. His left elbow moved a bit forward, inching toward Listonn. His right hand dipped back behind his right hip. His brow dropped so he almost was no longer looking forward.

When he sprung, the thrust caught Listonn under lowest rib on his left side. The blade shred up through the soft tissue of his gut and the force drove it up through his ribs rending them asunder. The point came out Listonn's back. Listonn gasped loudly and grabbed Culverton by the wrist, the one that held fast to the weapon that was now firmly lodged in his chest.

"Fuck!" Listonn heard Piter say and could just make out that another man had come in to look up at him. Culverton smiled at Listonn now looking at him right in the eyes. Listonn mouth gaped. Spit was floating out into the air. Culverton tightened his muscles again and jerked the blade up higher. In weightless space Listonn was propelled to the ceiling. His head hit hard and the remaining force drove the sword up higher into his chest. Listonn squeezed tears from his eyes. The men behind the wall laughed a bit. Bull and Miser were both there, reveling.

Culverton shook his head in disapproval. "You wouldn't have made for much of a sacrifice, dog-like as you are. No, you wouldn't make for a very good dog." Culverton curled up so he could press his knees against Listonn's body. Pushing off he drew the sword from Listonn's chest. Listonn tried to hold fast to Culverton's arm but the man easily had strength enough to pull free. Pulling the sword straight back, the sharp edge dragged out through Listonn's grasp cutting his hands to the bone. A jet of blood came pumping into the air and welled up in undulating pools. Listonn tried to fan out his fingers on both hands to quell the flow of blood from his chest but the gash was too long. He tried to speak, but his voice was nothing but spit and arrested attempts at breathing.

They sealed up Listonn to bleed out in his stateroom. Culverton looked to his three companions and said,

"I hope Crossland at least puts up a fight, or maybe at least that little brown man has some life in him." Listonn's limp fleeting moments were spent in the agony of searing pain. Death did not come quickly.

***

In the stateroom across the hall, Argyle dutifully set about packing up Wilson's things. Sir Wilson's magnetized shoes were already polished and placed back in their tidy cupboards for storage in the wardrobe. The pants and shirts had all been folded. The magnets actually could be deftly stuck one to the other to make folding them away all the easier.

He had closed the door behind him when he entered Wilson's room. Even if he hadn't, he still wouldn't have heard what transpired in Listonn's room across the hall. But something did tip another of Argyle's senses. He didn't place it at first. Can's say when exactly he first noticed it. One magnetized garment was being very neatly fastened to another when he had to pause. There was a smell in the air, a metallic smell like iron, copper or steel. It wasn't the quality of the smell that caught him at first, but the strength of the smell. He was very familiar with that smell. He'd known it since his childhood. His father first introduced him to that smell in the way all Gurkha lads are trained up by their fathers. Someone nearby was bleeding and in large quantities. Argyle turned and looked at the closed door to his room. It remained still and silent. There was no indication that there was anyone outside.

Quietly and purposefully, he removed his uniform just as he did in the hallway not too long ago. He formed up his apparel in neat little bundles and stored them appropriately. He was left wearing only the wrappings that were drawn about his loins and the two kukri knives that clung to his belt. Reaching to the small of his back he removed them both, knowing full well that they were only to be drawn when there was blood to shed. That they shouldn't be returned until they had drawn blood. He grasped their handles until they were firm in his grip.

He went to the back of the room and found that hidden panel that was now so easy to find about the staterooms of Ares Britannia. Without taking a light source, he slipped into the hallway and started his way around the passages. It was easy to determine how to circumnavigate the rooms. He swung around over the top of the hallway slip over the ceiling to where Listonn's room must be. It was easily the source of the smell of blood. The panel to his room was open and silently, Argyle slid forward and peered in.

Listonn wasn't quite dead but he was in shock and convulsing. His blood was still pumping into the air from the cuts both front and back. Argyle considered ending it for him but there was hardly anything to end. It was already over. Droplets of blood were floating in the air up the passage some of which had struck splotches on the walls and floor. It was easy enough to follow and it was so easy to move silently in the land without footfalls.

The blood trail led up a passage that Argyle hadn't seen before. He crept along the floor and then slipped up the wall, keeping his body flattened out and close to the surface. It was easy given the exposed struts, pipe works and wiring. The hall finally came to a head and he could see the tall form of Bull standing with his back to him. The hall must end in a room just past him. Bull was a big man. His form completely filled the doorway to whatever lay beyond. Argyle couldn't tell how many were up there but he could hear whispering. There were two maybe even three more. Silently he said to himself,

"जय महाकाली, आयो गोर्खाली or "Jaya Mahakali, Ayo Gorkhali ; Glory to great Kali, Gurkhas approach."

***

Culverton hovered lightly in the projector room very much placid and intoxicated. He cast off his mask which was then lost to the shadows in the room. He drew in sharp breaths. This wasn't how he liked it normally but it filled him all the same. He basked in it, a euphoric state that was as much intellectual as emotional. The blasted contingent from Earth had ruined everything. The beautiful haven of Ares Britannia was tumbling down around him. They could only just hold on to its last fleeting chapter of history while it lasted. Miser fiddled with the damn machine, seemed like Boswell might have broken it during his death throws. Piter was just over his shoulder, "supervising" since he knew nothing of machines, much less moving picture machines. Bull kept a wise distance, at least he realized that there was no help he could offer.

"It's this spool thing right here," Piter said in the poorly lit room. "Not spinnin' like it should."

"I see that," Miser replied holding up his hands, "'wot good's that? Got to get it spinnin'"

"So make it spin," Piter said plainly.

"So make it spin," Miser said in mockery. "Twirl it with my little fingers should I?"

"Argh!" Bull shouted out, his face wracked with pain. He contorted up on his left side his right hand wrapping around his heart.

"What is it, Bull?" Culverton called out.

"Don't know," the big man said, "Somthin's bit me." Bull turned around to look for the source of the pain but there was nothing in the dark hallway. His hand came back wet. His shirt was soaking. "I'm bleedin'" he announced to the others. Piter came up from behind the projector and moved over to his large friend.

"Come on, you big wanka', nothin' goin' to bite you in 'ere. Let me see it." But Bull didn't keep still. He moved like a man possessed. Suddenly his big form forked over and his body was thrust aside. It was like an invisible pull of gravity had welled up.

Argyle slipped down from above the top of the door frame. Piter was focused on Bull's puppet like motions and didn't see Argyle coming. The short Gurkha spied the points on Piter's chest just where he had been taught to strike. His thrusts were quick and precise. His arms were a blur. The kukris were so sharp Piter's body didn't slip back with the blows. The blades passed through his face and into his skull. They cut through his ribs and into his lungs. After several quick downward passes, the final blows sliced deep into his chest and extinguished his heart. Piter didn't have time to react. He didn't have time to feel it. His body was cut to ribbons and there wasn't time to scream out. Bull gave his friend a sidelong glance, perplexed by what was happening. Argyle planted his bare foot and pulled back both blades from Piter's chest and pushed him backwards into the room. His right hand swung out and caught Bull in the neck. The weight of the kukris' crooked tip nearly took his head clean off. Bull cried out again in a low guttural utterance and his hands came to his throat to hold in his escaping fluids. It was no use, blood pulsed through his fingers and billowed into the stale air.

Miser popped up from behind the projector, aghast. At least the protection of the hulking device was between him and the bloody little devil.

"Wait, wait, wait!" Culverton yelled over to Miser, winding up snakelike again. "Come back over by me." Miser gave a nervous glance back at Culverton. Piter's body began to drift ghostlike until his back hit lightly into the projector. He balled up into a floating fetal position holding his face and chest. His whole body was quivering as it started a lazy spin to the right. Bull was sobbing now, unable to keep the blood in his neck. His face turned around to the wall beside him. The flickering from the projector lamp played speckles of light on his back. Argyle stood openly now looking in at the others. He held the two blades outright, red now smeared along their length. The blood was already sealing his hands to the blades. His face was threatening but controlled and precise. His black hair was swept out and wild. The muscles of this gaunt body were strapped tight, like cords of rope that had been bound into knots.

"Where you going to go now, you little shit?" Culverton asked him, pointing his own bloodied weapon. "You can stab a man in the back but quite another thing to face him eh?"

Argyle smiled broadly, the rows of teeth glinting in the dark. With an effortless swing he pulled himself back into the hallway. He was instantly lost to the darkness. They could only just hear him shuffling up the passage. Surprised by the unexpected move, Culverton thrust off the wall after him. He bounded to the projector table and pulled himself over the top of it, literally flying into the hallway. Miser started hyperventilating, horrified to be left alone in the room with his dying friends. He bid a hasty retreat up the hallway behind him in the opposite direction, happy to flee from the evasive Nepalese man.

Culverton burst into the hall brandishing his sword. He was amazed that a newcomer could move so quickly having only just come into space. There was no light in the hall. He couldn't see a damn thing. There was the faint glow from behind him, but the little man was out of sight. He tensed and moved up cautiously. He had to kill Argyle before he could get back and alert the others. If he made it to Napier and the Daedalus crew came back armed, he couldn't take them all. He wouldn't be clapped in irons by those fool sailors. Never. It wouldn't end that way. He slipped up the hallway, pulling himself along with his free hand. He made it back to the point where the service passage went along behind the staterooms. A few of them were open and light poured in from the room past the opening. It was apparent that Argyle could have made it to the commons. Blast all he could have made it and already be heading for the Daedalus.

A clean slice of pain hit him in the meat just over his right kidney. The cut was hard and deep and his head swam with it. He cried out long and gasping, contorting away from the pain. Argyle was pressed into the corner of the hall between two supporting beams. His blow striking true, he slipped out of hiding and doubled around into the light of the stateroom beyond. Culverton swung wildly after him, a wild swing that shot pain up the muscles of his arm and down across his thigh. Something from within Culverton surpassed its tolerance, like a bit of overstretched elastic. It was like the bright hot day at their father's estate when a gunshot rang out and his younger brother was caught in the temple by a speeding bullet. The contents of the boy's brain pan being spilled out on the dry brown grasses of that arid land. Unknowingly he had picked up his brother's head in his hands, the meaty bits of his mind coating his fingers. "Teddy?" he asked the silent air.

Culverton yelled from the depths of his diaphragm and it echoed up the halls of Ares louder than the alarm whistle. Pain no longer could control him. Culverton lunged into the room after the cause of his rage. Argyle had already gotten the main door of the stateroom open and turned to face Culverton as he burst from the hidden panel. Culverton took up his blade up in both hands and came at him with a wide downward swing. Argyle recoiled out the doorway and into the hall beyond but couldn't escape. Culverton's sword hit his collarbone on the right side and snapped it in half. He tried a weak riposte but the kukri failed to meet flesh. Both flying in midair, Culverton pressed his attack, spitting and swinging. His mind was lost in blind rage that only knew one purpose. Argyle deflected as he could but his defenses were failing. His counters were failing. Both arms swung both blades, but he was failing.

***

Wilson, Napier and the three crewmen arrived back in the commons, tired and spent from their journey. They were all sickened in body and mind. As they entered Sandra's room and then the hall, Wilson went over to the Lady Inverness' door. He rapped loudly, but there was no answer.

"Cecilia?" he called out. Napier told his men to wait. Wilson pounded on the door louder still. He tried the wheel but it wouldn't turn. "Cecilia?" he called again without answer. Napier turned to the youngest among them.

"Son," Napier said, "run back to the ship. Tell all hands to arm themselves and come back here. Lock the ship up behind you, Lt. Campbell will have the key. I want every man, no exception. I don't care if one's on the crapper. Get his arse off, put a saber in his hand, and get him down here." The lad was frazzled, but the stern words of his captain propelled him. He rushed up the hall and out of sight.

Wilson kept pounding on the door.

"Archdale," Napier said, "let's go check on Listonn and Argyle." Reluctantly Wilson stopped and joined the others as they made their way up the rounded hall.

***

Beckett, Royden, and Crossland were just then making it back themselves coming from the other side. Gavin was still a bit dazed, attempting as he could to find another solution to their latest predicament. There must be some way to come home in triumph, Ares properly christened, the Daedalus overflowing with riches. Return home to the sounds of those cheering crowds that showed them off into space. The more he thought about enlisting Napier's aid to search the miners' camp the better it sounded. It's their sworn duty really, to search for survivors. If Didier was telling the truth, they'd find the stores neatly assembled and ready for shipment. Just need to get them moving out over the rocky surface. It will be awkward, yes, but quite possible. Napier has his own interests in this. He has shares to earn as well. After they've done their duty, it'll be only natural. Make the best of the worst circumstances.

As the three made it back to their rooms they were surprised to see Napier, Wilson and two of the crew coming from the other way. They were so used to the dead halls of Ares it was a surprise to see anyone.

"Napier! Wilson," Beckett called out in greeting. "How good it is to see you!" The group was then arrested, to see Argyle's bare back appear in a gaping door frame. He was only wearing white wrappings about his waist.

"Argyle?" Wilson asked, and a shout like one from the very maws of hell came screaming from within that room. Argyle vaulted himself backwards, up at an extreme angle toward the ceiling followed by the howling form of Havelock-Allen, swinging murderous arcs with a flat bladed sword and crying out like a rabid dog gone mad.

Chapter 1D (14): Save Your Vespers for the Least of Souls

Culverton and Argyle tangled in a whirling spiral of death up near the ceiling. Napier, Wilson and the two crewmen went for their sabers. Royden, Gavin and Beckett pulled back carefully shocked at the savage dance above them. The movements of the two combatants were impossible to follow. Culverton was beyond reason and wailing like a banshee. His sword less effective now fighting a wrestling match instead of a duel. Their quarters were also too close for Argyle who couldn't land a solid stroke. They were both getting nicked and cut with blood spilling into the air as they fought.

Culverton caught Argyle's neck in an iron grip. He thrust him back into the corner of the hall just far enough to bring his blade to bear. The tip got into the top of Argyle's thigh, just below the hip. Feeling the blade pierce flesh, Culverton drove it as deep as he could, wrenching violently to dig it deep in the wound. Argyle wailed with his Nepali vocal chords. He bit down on his tongue hard enough to bite through it. He lurched with his back in a vain struggle to pull off the invading steel but it only widened the wound. His right forearm beat on Culverton's back. His left hand tried to break Culverton's grip on his steel.

Culverton ripped his blade back, casting a spray of blood and bits of flesh across the hall. Blood spat into the face of the crewman farthest right. Argyle was weakened but still struggling. Culverton pulled the sword high and smashed downward. It stuck Argyle in the head and opened his skull. Still grunting like an animal Culverton kept up the attack, smashing down on Argyle's head again and again.

Wilson leapt up toward them to join the fray.

"Archdale!" Napier called up to him but Sir Wilson was beyond words. He took a broad lateral stroke with his ceremonial saber. Not to be dismissed as an ornament, Wilson kept it oiled and honed to a deadly edge. The blow caught Culverton across his right leg on the side where Argyle had already cut him. Spinning away, Culverton pushed off the wall to fly to the opposite side. Wilson's enormous mass hung like a blimp tied to a mast. Culverton's sweat poured out from his hair like mist, his saliva frothed from his mouth. He remained a blur of motion seemingly energized by all the devils in hell. He planted both sandaled feet against the wall and launched himself like a projectile, lunging and slicing. Wilson was no fool, though new to weightless fighting. He parried with the skill of a seasoned veteran, but the clash of steel sent him off balance.

Gavin made a quick move and ducked below them, pushing headlong into his stateroom. Napier barked orders to his men. "Get around them!" he cried. And the three sailors tried to flank the two fighting above them.

Wilson came around and got some height above Culverton. He bumped up against the dying form of his lifelong friend. Argyle had dropped his blades and they were floating off away from the blur of the fighting. Culverton pressed his attack harder and harder still. Wilson held his saber in both hands and warded off the blows until his back was pressed tight against the wall by his friend. Napier got behind Culverton and barked up at him.

"Back off, man, you can't take all of us!" Culverton, distracted, sent a wild swing back around towards Napier. Seeing his opening Wilson thrust, stabbing Culverton firmly in his shoulder, enough to make him wince in pain. Culverton smashed Wilson's blade aside with his free hand and exposed Wilson's abdomen. With a snap thrust, Culverton opened up Wilson's belly. The bloody weapon slit through Wilson's uniform and his entrails were pulled out at the end of the blade. Wilson's eyes went wide. His loose jowls flapped open and his voice rasped like a death rattle. Still coherent, he looked down at his killer and beat his saber madly at his head. Culverton threw up his free arm and Wilson's blows hacked into the flesh of his forearm, cutting them to the bone. Wilson scooped the air with his left arm in a vain attempt to put his intestines back into place.

Lt. Campbell and Vecihi arrived, and all the remaining Daedalus crew with them. They'd heard the scuffle and held out their arms at the ready. Immediately their eyes were drawn up to the body of Argyle knotted up into a bleeding mass and the scene of Wilson and Culverton locked in their struggle of death.

Gavin Crossland emerged back from his stateroom. Clutched firmly in both hands was the four barreled firearm that had christened him a knight just a short time ago. He strained his way back into the hall, the buttons on his coat popping off. From the doorway to the next room over, Miser thrust his head out, a look of amazement on his wide eyes. Gavin saw him, his unshaven face dumbstruck. He looked like a circus clown with his face painted in a comic exaggeration of buffoonery. Without a second thought, Gavin leveled the gun at Miser's face, not more than a few feet away. Miser looked over his left shoulder just in time to see the flash from the muzzle as the lead bolt was loosed. The crack of the gunshot deafened them all, even Culverton in his unbridled rage.

The bullet hit Miser in the right eye and left a searing hot hole straight through the back of his head. His skull exploded in an expelling trail. Miser's body was blown back to hit the opposite side of the door frame and hung limply in thin air.

But the bullet had not finished its path. It sped like a rocket to the far end of the hall. It struck between two metal struts that held the outer glass skin of Ares Britannia in place. The glass shattered into a spider web of cracks that raced along its surface. The cracks reached out in every direction, widening and multiplying. The pressure within Ares found its chance to free itself into the void beyond. Nature abhorred the vacuum and heaved hard against those widening cracks to flush into the night beyond.

Beckett dove into the open stateroom next to him and sealed the door behind him. Napier turned toward Gavin mortified. His face was paler than his white beard. Napier yelled like his very life depended on it. "Dear God, Crossland no!" he shouted, but Gavin was already leveling for the next shot. Culverton was near the ceiling just a short upward angle from where the first bullet relieved Miser of his life. The quad barrels of the gun turned with the mechanical gears of the firing mechanism that pulled the next shot behind the hammer. Culverton stopped his murderous assault to look Gavin in the eye. His body began a short descent toward the floor. His face was matted red and bruised. Blood formed an aura around him from dozens of cuts. Both hands were reddened and sealed shut with caked ichor. Culverton yelled a final defiant cry with the rage of an angry war god. Braced firmly in his door frame, Gavin triggered his second shot. It hit Culverton squarely in the breastbone shattering it as the round entered his chest cavity. His body blew backwards. Shattered ribs poked into his lungs and heart. He released the grip on his sword, but it stuck firmly to his hand. His limbs collapsed inwardly and his body was pushed by the force of the shot straight back up the hallway.

Culverton hit the shattered glass at the end of the hall instants after the ball of lead that killed him. The weight of the dying flesh was well beyond the load that the glass could bear. The weakened section broke free between those supporting beams and in a continuous motion

Culverton was flung into space. His body shot off over the landscape of Phobus, his body convulsing slightly and then stiffing. His tongue caught in his throat just before losing consciousness. The last sight before his eyes was the tumbling blur of Ares Britannia interspersed between the star-streaked black of space.

The hallway became the barrel of a shotgun. It was a tunnel of speeding wind that sucked the air from every lung. Campbell and Vecihi were pulled over with a fright. Like white clad dominoes, the dozen men of the Daedalus went right along with them. They tried to take hold of anything, including each other. They let go of their weapons and grasped for dear life. They poked and thrust out for anything but they flowed like sand from an hourglass through the tight neck of that shattered hole. Their loosed blades became the merciful strokes of death for some but also slashed open limbs and faces. Few made it up the hall easily to merely die in the clutches of space. Their bodies bounced mercilessly off the walls and each other. The hall was a wind tunnel of broken bones and bodies.

Wilson and Argyle flew right out with the sailors, their dying forms still alive enough to feel the rushing fear of those fateful moments. Sir Royden was pulled back and spun headlong in pinwheels as his body fell in with the dying sailors. Miser's body shot out the door frame and up the hall at least leniently dead. Napier's cap was ripped from his head as he made for anything to anchor himself. He and his two last crewmen let go of their weapons and reached for the walls to brace themselves. Their hands were scraped bloody and their fingernails peeled off as they were torn up the passage. The flood of bodies formed a logjam of half-living men that blocked the opening for an instant before the oppressive suction broke limb from limb like splintering twigs to be flung blindly into space.

Gavin was caught in the door frame of his room. He could feel objects striking his back, hitting him in the back of his head. The contents of his room flew past him. He was blinded by the hair in his eyes. His shoulders and knees held him in place, but the pain was excruciating. The roar of wind deafened him. He clutched hard despite the pain. Instinctually he knew that letting go of that frame was letting go of his life. The wind pulled the breath from his lungs. He felt his grip slipping. His body started to go the way of everything else in that hallway.

Just as he started to cry out, the rip of air around him started to subside. The howl of the rushing air was drowned out by his cries. He gulped in air as it was becoming possible to breathe again. With a sucking sound the rushing air ceased altogether. Objects of all sorts floated around him, clothing, paper, the ear-piece to a yack-mouth, splinters of wood and bits of metal and glass. The air around him was still agitated, but it became instantly quiet, impossibly so after what just transpired.

His right hand went to his shoulder. There was a sore impression where he had been lodged in the door frame He had kept hold of the hand cannon, only due to the loop of the trigger guard caught on his finger. Gasping he turned to look up the hall. A massive steel pressure door had dropped down into place. There was a rectangular square view port set at head level but Gavin couldn't see through it from his angle. Breathing heavily, he could only stare at it. Stare at the life preserving precaution that he must have designed for just this occurrence though he never imagined it could be invoked by his own hand.

The wheel on the door to the stateroom further down and on the opposite side spun and it swung open. Beckett's bearded face poked out, wide eyed but unharmed.

"Ha, ha!" Beckett cried down at Gavin in a loud voice, his face oddly stretched into a toothy grin. Looking to the pressure door he bounded over to look out the window. He scrambled with his tall lanky frame so that he could get a solid look through. "Oh! You can still see them! They're not all dead yet!" he called out with the voice of child at play. Gavin stayed where he was unmoving, recovering. He was sore from every angle. He was still dazed and looked at Beckett through strained eyes. He hadn't caught his breath yet. He couldn't get a grasp on Beckett. Couldn't figure what he was doing.

Beckett loosed his belt and put his hand down his trousers. He worked his hand vigorously. He stared out the view port doing nothing less than abusing himself. After a few breathless moments a warm stain filled his crotch and his eyes slid back in his head at the misplaced climax. As pulses subsided, Beckett turned to see Gavin staring up at him. Beckett rolled his eyes and smiled, laughing like a kid.

"Oh, you don't understand," Beckett said down to him. He continued to steal glances out through the glass window. "When they showed me. When they showed me everything, after I got here. I mean, I've never been part of such a thing before. It was like, it was like, well it was the closest thing to divinity I've ever felt. You have no idea what it does to you. How it makes you feel.":

"How what makes you feel?" Gavin asked, his mouth pasty and dry, "What did they show you?"

"You don't know?" Beckett said, his expression enraptured. "The murders, my man! The serial murders that have been going on up here for all these years!"

"The, the what?" Gavin asked.

"Oh that Culverton was a nasty man. He just hated women he did, but only fair skinned ones. Imagine that? You know, maybe because he was raised around all those brown people. Maybe it's when he got back to Britain when he developed his ghoulish tastes for whites! He's just like that Jack the Ripper chap, but he didn't keep himself to whores, hardly! Up here he could have anyone he wanted. And, oh, he wanted all of them."

"And you knew? You knew about all this?"

"Of course I knew! After what he showed me! After showing me what I had always carried around inside me but never had the courage to indulge! After I learned that it's different here – this is Mars – everything is different on Mars!" Beckett began to laugh uncontrollably. It was a deep guttural laugh. His sides split with pain as he laughed and laughed. "There are no laws here!" he yelled out. "There's no ten commandments, no covenants, no restrictions, no nothing!"

Beckett rambled on in a concatenated drone. Gavin withdrew inwardly not thinking with words nor concepts. His external senses only perceived the events around him passively. It was a pure disembodiment of thought. It was then a decision was made. Within his inner reaches a deliberation had concluded. Two decisions were weighed, one against the other, and one emerged superior. A kind of legal precedent was cited and a kind of summary judgment was reached. Crossland enacted this decision while Beckett babbled.

Beckett said loudly, "Crohne, you beautiful, beautiful man!" he yelled out in a wild frenzy. "You slew them all and spared me! You chose to let me see this. Can you hear me? Can you hear me you beautiful man?"

Gavin pushed up off the floor to secure a downward angle.

"What is it you're doing?" Beckett said casually looking over at him. Gavin plainly could see the dark stain in Beckett's pants. Gavin snuffed in a clean draw of air, leveled the gun at Beckett's face and the third barrel clicked into its fitting and the hammer fell true. The crack blew his wrist back, shooting more pain up his arm. The round sped out of a cushion-like puff of black powder and flame. It struck Beckett's left cheek shattering his jaw and pushing the fragments maliciously into the soft tissue beneath his face. The force snapped Beckett's neck back almost breaking it. The bullet fragmented, echoing in his skull, defecting back into the mass of meat that held Beckett's mind. The network of synapses collapsed, interrupting the afterglow of endorphins that still pumped gallingly through his thoughts.

Gavin looked at what was left of him. Beckett's face was now contoured into the grim realization of his death. Right Honorable Francis Alabaster Beckett, Archdeacon of Bournemouth, was to preside over the christening of a new era. They had sent him here months in advance. He was to make straight the path Gavin was to make into history. Now Beckett will have to explain wet pants before St. Peter's golden gates.

"Gavin," he heard a muffled voice back in his stateroom. It was like the tiny voice of a Lilliputian had come out of a mouse hole and shouted up at him. He heard it again, "Gavin!" like a weak muffled shout. Gavin turned in a haze back towards his room. Someone was shouting through the yack-mouth. This puzzled him at first but he supposed it made sense. He looked nauseously at the weapon he held, squeezed unnecessarily so that his knuckles were white and his muscles cramped. There was at least one bullet left. Gavin set the safety and pushed the hot gun into his belt. He pushed himself into the stateroom where he heard the mousy voice.

"Gavin, Gavin, Gavin," the little voice continued until he took the ear-piece of the clapper to his ear and drew the yack-mouth to his own.

"Christien?" Gavin asked.

"Yes Gavin," came Crohne's voice over the wire. "The one who closed the airlock door after your very ill-conceived shot flew up the hall of my precious platform." Gavin turned to look up at the ceiling as if he could see through the metal walls at the Babel Tower where Crohne spent his time. Crohne laughed humourlessly. "You're not a quick learner you know? Didn't you think that third shot might have resulted similarly to the first two? Risky Gavin. I wouldn't have been able to save you then. It was everything I could do just to seal off the domicile section. So tell me, was this just the first time you've ever killed anyone? Because that was some lethal shooting. And I must inform you, Sir Crossland, that it did much more damage than end Culverton, Miser and Francis. I didn't quite get everything sealed up tight in time. I can see at least three fires from up here and if I can see three I know there are many more. Ares is burning, my fellow architect of destruction. Behold your great achievement."

Chapter 1E (15): The Lesser of Two Creations

Crohne looked down on the blazing fires that erupted about Ares Britannia, snarling blazes that lit up the portion of the blackened structures in dazzling displays. From the ovular pinnacle of his tower he could move around the complete panorama. He could see it all. He could see the blaze that was burning hot at the primary generator. If that exploded it might blow out the windows in front of him, ending his life that way. Another was burning in the Life Sciences building that hosted the largest algae vats, waste processing and water recycling. There was no need to be concerned about the sensitive balance of submersives now. There were plenty of other things that would end them far sooner than depleting oxygen. He could see the long bobbing form of HMS Daedalus, swaying a bit as the forces that rocked the platform sent resonant vibrations up the gangway but no matter.

In a leisurely motion he brought the voice actuator of the yack-mouth to his face. He spoke again to Gavin Henry Crossland.

"How often does one confront one's adversary?" Crohne asked into the voice piece. "This is a unique day for us, Mr. Crossland, in too many ways to number. A day so few may relish. An honour so very few receive. Perhaps I should dispense with the obvious so as we can make the most of our last conversation. Since it is our last, and so very unique by its nature, let's both make the most of it shall we?"

Gavin choose to remain silent on the other end.

"In all sincerity," Crohne spoke again, "I bear you no malice for ending dear Culverton. I, so like the Emperor Tiberius, brought him to my Capri to dwell with me in my Villa Jovis at the cliffs atop Monte Tiberio. He could have been my little Caligula but not so. It was inevitable that he was going to meet his fate. I suspected that the Nepali man would be the end of him but it was more fitting that he died by your hand. So much more fitting."

"How do you know that I killed him? Can you see me down here?" Gavin asked looking around him, sounding all the more defeated.

"No Gavin," Crohne laughed, "I can't see you. Of all our wondrous inventions that's not among them. But I can hear you. And I did see Culverton's body shot out into the cosmos. If I squint I think I can still see him though he looks like a shooting star now or perhaps like one of the tumbling planetoids that drew us out here in the first place. It's all so very fitting. This was really his fault you know. His proclivities were beyond concealment. I almost hoped there for a bit that we could keep it all quiet. Let you all carry out your stage play dressed up like peacocks, clap yourselves on your respective shoulders and be done with you. That is until Culverton killed Boswell. After that, I knew Sandra would be the immediate focus of his attention. When she fornicated with Lord Cholmondeley that was all too much for poor Allen. His appetites were whetted beyond pacification."

"So Culverton killed Didier's wife then?" Gavin asked.

"Oh, yes," Crohne answered, "and then I killed Didier."

"That was you?"

"Oh please, Gavin," Crohne said with an air of disgust, "you know I built the means by which I can control certain features throughout the platform. I only regret that I didn't complete the work sooner to link up with the miner's camp. We could have avoided so much if I could only have foreseen that need sooner. And, because it may not be so obvious to you, when I kill a group of unsavouries in a single act, I control the damn reaction. I show some elegance, reflecting an intimate understanding of the physics of the resulting chain reaction. Not like discharging a firearm in the domicile dome that you yourself designed!" Crohne pulled himself over to the opposite side of his tower so he could look out at the miner's side. In contrast to the central domes it was starting to go dark, the fires losing their fuel. At least the generators over there won't decay and erupt. He shook his head. He could do nothing but shake out the needless loss of it all.

"Did Royden know too?" Gavin asked.

"Oh yes," Crohne answered, "such a weak willed little man. Never have I met someone so controllable by fear. Fear was his master. He was even afraid of you though he feared me more."

"So there never was any Barabbas," Gavin stated low and long. Crohne grunted back at him in disgust.

"Beckett was Barrabas! I am so very pleased that you put a bullet in him. I hope he could see it coming. That worm disgusted me since the day you sent him here."

"Beckett?" Gavin called back his face twisted in puzzlement. "He led the miners from this side of Ares?"

"Oh Gavin," Crohne said, his high hopes for this final conversation seeping through the cracks in the floorboards. "You might as well call me Barabbas. It was all a ruse within a ruse. The only spark of brilliance Beckett ever showed. They trusted him because of his religious regalia, adorned in grace and forgiveness. We used it to keep them in line. Give them the illusion of power and control. If any of you knew what real power was, you'd be up here with me. Yet it's still not power enough. Not power enough to change the circumstances we find ourselves in now." Crohne pulled himself around the room grabbing hold of the protruding apparatus that poked out of every bare space in every direction. "That American chap, Mudgett, was the one who taught me that," Crohne said.

"The madman with the murder castle in Chicago?" Gavin asked searching his memory.

"Why yes," Crohne continued. "Though he was hardly the murderer as convicted. That hanged man, Herman Webster Mudgett, was a scapegoat for my offenses. Oh, he deserved to be hung but Herman wasn't Dr. H. H. Holmes either. That was just another name that suited me for a time. The thing about him that so impressed me was his means of secrecy. You see, when he built that murder castle he did so with very episodic groups of workers. He would hire a crew which he would mistreat in many ways at several simultaneous levels; poor wages, long hours, constantly belittling their competence, their work ethic, etc. None could guess the genius of this approach. No one group of workers knew the entirety of the design of the structure. And so I thought, how much more so could we do that here? Here along the Martian shores?" He paused to marvel at the structure around him. He could almost imagine the hands that worked the steel of these walls, that fitted the glass structures into place that tested their integrity to ensure the minimal loss of pressure.

"The workers you recruited were among the worst dregs of the Empire," Crohne continued. "They went off into space, but their families back home knew full well that they would never be heard from again. There was no way to bring them back home. Labourers sent to space only book a one-way ticket. For all intents, they were already gone, lost to a trackless void that may as well been the yawning mouth of the grave. The only hope of reunion would be in the afterlife."

"As Beckett so aptly put, there's no law up here, Mr. Crossland. The finger of the almighty may have etched the Mosaic tablets, but that finger fails to reach up here. There's no barrister to argue nor judge to hear the indictment. This is true law. Words on paper can be consumed by a flame but action is law. What one can do, not what some word imposes on him. Allen certainly was right about the gods of the Greeks. He was a man of many flaws, but of that he was most certainly correct. I wonder how the freshly reaped fields of Elysium smell this time of year." Crohne drew in a long breath and took a wandering look around his throne room. The room where his demi-godhood almost seemed true.

"But this is a mass murder-suicide," he said, "and I'm afraid it has now come to its inevitable terminus. The end I foresaw when we were told of your coming. The one consequence for which there is no recourse. I've had intimate relations with the dawn and the daughters of Olympians have lilted at my slightest gaze, and this is how it ends? The misty gown of Nix once swept about my naked ankles as she leaned to kiss my cheek. Edmund Spenser would have wept, 'Ye learned sisters which have oftentimes been to me a-dying, others to adore, whom ye thought worthy of your graceful rhymes, that even the greatest did not greatly scorn.'" A rare tear touched upon Crohne's cheek. "It is with no pleasure I do this," he said.

A gravity beyond reckoning overtook, Gavin. His thoughts were uncontrollable and feral. This could not possibly be the end of everything they'd built here. This could not possibly be his end. There were so many greater things at stake. What of the Empire? What of the Queen? What of the citizens around the entire world who fell under British rule? What of the future generation that depended on this great venture? This hope to secure Britain's place among the planets. What of his wife? What of his children? Every wild self-centred thought each bit with a pang of guilt and apprehension as the words raced through his mind. What would his very last thought be? What would be the final thrusting spark of electricity that shot between his neurons before they were snuffed in final expiration?

"See here!" Crossland shouted back at Crohne through the yack-mouth. Each breath he took like the tick of a depleting countdown. Bereft, Gavin could only weep and plead. "I have, I have nothing to say to you, man! Nothing! You sorry bastard." Shaking and sobbing, he could barely mouth the words. "I have a family! I have a place in society! I have a future! The Empire has a future and we are in what's left of it! God and all the Saints, man! I have been given a portion with the great! This is not how this ends! Do you hear me? This is not how this ends!"

He paused to gasp and gasp and gasp. He waited through the long pregnant moment, glaring at the cold brass yack-mouth, the black shadow within its neck seeming to reach down into all future time; "Christien, I beg you, please reconsider. We can save this."

The white noise that came to him through the yack-mouth was a torturous sound.

"How would you like to die, Gavin?" Crohne asked, "I could reopen that pressure door and you could join your comrades in space or you have one last bullet in that gun. If you are a man you will take your own life here with me in Ares Britannia."

Gavin cried like an infant. He considered the finely crafted weapon, the interlacing leaves that were carved up each barrel, the skillfully tooled ivory handle. The symbol of his great success. He threw it off into the air above him and it clattered off the walls. He cupped both hands around his face and wept.

Hearing the clatter of the gun, Crohne made his assumption. He removed the ear-piece of the clapper and pulled himself over to the key box he had crafted to end the miners. It was currently locked in the pattern that shut the pressure door that was keeping Gavin's section safe for the time being. The door that separated Gavin from that unholy breech in the glass at the other end of the hall. He gripped the lever in his right hand and closed his fist around the safety release. He felt the mechanism disengage allowing the lever to move freely. He pulled it briskly on a well-oiled axle toward him. Though the response was silent, he knew with intricate detail how one gear moved upon another, how springs and pressure points and hydro tubing cascaded into a finely orchestrated series of consequences.

He moved over to the window and looked down and the section of hall that ended near where the passage to the mooring docks connected to the men's side of the domicile domes. There he saw a finely dressed dying man shot off into space. He followed the form of that dead man as he joined a small cluster of others who had preceded him. Their tumbling bodies made a kind of glittering constellation that had been cast into the heavens. They were like dust now. Ashes to ashes. Their lifeless husks so much flotsam and jetsam cast into the eternal sea.

Επίλογος: The Aftermath

Crohne felt cold. It had nothing to do with his emotional state, far from it. It must be the unyielding cold of space, already sapping the heat of the remaining structures. The generators would bravely fight a last battle against the freezing onslaught, but must ultimately fail, the great chill of space beating it to final submission. There are no atmospheric effects on Phobus to help retain heat. The old place was no help to them there. In an eon's time, the ragged, oblong, twisted rock may one day pass too close to Mars and be dashed into so many asteroids. Perhaps it would form into a picturesque ring like Saturn's. Ares Britannia may one day be part of that ring and Crohne's body with it. That was a pleasing thought.

Crohne fetched his pipe from a little box bolted down by the east wall. He smoked in Babel Tower often, well at least as often as he could get his contacts on the moon to smuggle tobacco up to him. At least it was often enough for his tastes. He pulled open the drawstrings of the little pouch and packed a hand carved mishra pipe with as much as it would hold. He slipped the pouch into his vest pocket. He struck a flame from his glass lighter and drew in some long puffs. The tobacco had grown a bit stale but it was satisfying. The taste, the aroma, the warmth in his mouth was all perfectly enticing.

Did he really want to die in the tower? What would people think if they found him there? Regardless of where they found him he had to ensure that they understood what they found. He couldn't leave it to the musing of the dolts back on earth. The so called scholars who would be asked to comment about everything that happened up here. Like any of them were even capable of understanding.

He pushed off to drift up to his writing desk mounted on the ceiling. It was enormous. The broad table where he would pour over the building schematics and blueprints he received from Gavin's team. The ones he then sectioned up and modified and passed down to Allen to see them built. He unlocked one of the drawers with a tiny key and pulled out some pages. They were all written by his hand. They were lovingly written. He had thrown away dozens of iterations of this same writing until the perfect version had been committed to paper. He reread a passage to himself.

In Xanadu did Kubla Khan a stately pleasure dome decree, but did the dread Khan ever suffer the invasion of his vaulted palace? Or did the Emperor Tiberius ever suffer an invasion of his isle of Capri? Even now profane intruders are on the wing, ascending Jacob's ladder towards me. Soon after their arrival all that I have done will no longer be concealed behind the thick veil of planetary expanses. After considering these circumstances from every possible angle I see no other outcome. They will see beneath the gilded veneer. They will look upon the naked flesh of my beautiful atrocities. They will judge me and in so doing will brand me among the most prolific of villains. I will not allow them to drag me back to their planet of dregs to stretch my neck for the hangman's noose. I will burn them all in a fire of my ignition. I will vomit them from my mouth into the merciless vacuum of space.

He folded these pages perfectly into thirds and slipped them neatly into the inner pocket of his jacket. The parchment was flattened lambskin. If anyone ever found him they would be sure to find it also, even if that was decades hence.

From where he hovered, he could see the HMS Daedalus, lashed like a prize horse, pulling a bit with the death throes of the platform raging beneath it. If only a single man could manage such a liner it might have been a means of escape. Though even if possible he hardly had the skills. None of his Martian companions did. And if they had where would they have gone? Back to one of the lunar platforms on the Empire's prize vessel? No, there was no solution be found there. For him, the Daedalus was only a prison ship, one he thankfully would never occupy.

He recalled the day when he heard the news that Gavin Henry Crossland would be making his way to Ares Britannia. He could remember the face of the young British lad who bounded down the gangway from the HMS Commonwealth and personally hand delivered it to him. The lad was so proud to fulfill his charge to deliver the letter. It was tucked in with a large bundle of parcels that had all the myriad correspondence that were only intended for him and the building crew. Included there was a red envelope that was sealed around in gold leaf. Another letter was tied up with it in twine. The later was a note that Gavin wrote to him to better explain the rhetoric contained in the royal edict.

Christien, he wrote, it is my great honor to inform you that soon I will be a passenger on the HMS Daedalus and have the good pleasure of meeting you in person. With me will be a royal contingent hand selected by Her Majesty and key members of parliament. Contained herein, in the letter attached, are the instructions as per all the necessary preparations. This will be our finest hour...

It went something like that anyway. Bring a pack of useless hereditarily entitled simpletons to Phobus merely to host a ceremony. As preposterous a notion as he had ever heard and oh, with what cataclysmic outcomes. His life must end due to this indivertible act of earthly arrogance.

Taking his last looks, he had thereby seen enough of Babel tower. He slipped over to the hatch in the floor and opened it. He descended rapidly and moved out into the domes that intersected at the point where the tower had been erected.

Now, entering the domes seemed emotionally hollow to him. Ironic really, how these empty spaces were even far emptier still, devoid of any personal affiliation. No one cares what they are now. They are places without purpose. The puffs he took from his pipe were the only satisfaction to be found. Perhaps those puffs were the last satisfaction of his life? Perhaps. He wondered if there was anyone left alive on the platform. There very well could be. Like those women that Allen dragged off into the basement. If that section is still oxygenated they might yet live. Wouldn't that be a horror? To revive locked in a cramped space, still sore from the beating that drove you unconscious. What will strike them first? The stale air? The creeping cold? The fact that they are locked in rooms with no one to answer, no matter how hard they beat on the door.

Goodnight, Lady Inverness, Crohne thought to himself, at least I found you interesting.

There was a painful ringing in his ear. It wasn't real of course, more a malady of his innards. He stuck a finger in his ear canal and shook it vigorously. It was mainly due to the unstable pressure he thought. Perhaps the onset of an infection. He snuffed and realized the uselessness of this pondering. The time had come to determine where to die.

It must be a section of the platform that will remain largely intact when this chain reaction had run its course. The gates of Ares sounded right. A bit obvious of course but maybe obviousness was what this called for. The thickest struts were there. The likelihood of anything rupturing that section was low at best. Maybe waiting there would be ideal. Without a better notion, Crohne made his way. He drew himself along with an air of majesty, the reigning lord over this great fallen house.

He feared that a pressure door had closed to block his passage. Some would automatically do so to protect the station during disasters like the one happening all around him. He would have brought along a key box to open them but that would be most unwise without knowing the conditions on the other side. He certainly didn't want to be flushed out into space. His remains must be found here. Someone was sure to come up to explore the ruin one day. He must be here when it's found. It took some winding around back passages but he got there.

The gates of Ares were shut and a pressure door had fallen behind them, just as it was designed. The two flanking naked statues were there, their spears in hand. He looked up at the seal of the British Royal Astronomical Society. He read the bold plaque that was hung beneath it.

Phobus and Deimus quickly drove Ares' smooth-wheeled, chariot to him and bore him up from the wide paths of earth into his richly wrought carriage and then straight lashed his team till coming to high Olympos.

No one was coming for him. He had no sons to save him. He had no chariot to ride - or did he? The thought of the Biblical prophet Ezekiel ascending into heaven on a flaming chariot jogged his mind. His body tingled from head to toe. It was as if a spiritual being came up to him and en-wrapped him with a swirling, misty embrace.

"I was meant to be here," he said aloud. He had come to such a deep resolve that he would never leave Phobus the very thought of it eluded him. He'd believed that since the very day he arrived so many long years ago. And now it suddenly dawned upon him that perhaps this wouldn't be the last day he'd ever be here. He had never considered that after all this there could possibly be another tomorrow.

"How could I have been so blind?" he asked no-one.

He lightly slipped the precisely folded pages from his inner pocket. He unfolded them in his hands and read the line again, "After considering these circumstances from every possible angle I see no other outcome." He removed the lighter from his vest and struck a flame. He held out a corner of the page until it caught. Extinguishing the lighter he let it drift away into space. He let the pages sputter and crackle in this hand, as every word he wrote was washed black, consumed by the flame. When he could no longer hold it he let the remnants waft into the air. The hot pages danced before his face in thin films of ash fluttering about with glowing orange edges.

He turned his back on the gates and moved away. The feeling of a spiritual presence was still with him. Cherubs and Seraphs were swirling around him on bright wings singing inhumanly sweet songs. The kisses of chthonic goddesses were alighting on his lips. The ringing in his ears was the rush of the river Styx.

He moved up the passage as if he was invulnerable. Like all the destruction around him was someone else's dream. He then came to the hollowed out tube that led to a passage away from the central domes. The hall crawled like a skulking creature across the barren desolation of the Phoban surface. The doorway was wide open of course. Fate would have cast it aside had it been any other way. The rounded corners of the aperture beckoned. The unlit hallway was indiscernible, pitch black and featureless. It seemed to go on endlessly. He paused as he looked up that hallway, rich with the essence of forever.

Up that hall lay the pad that was occupied by Ares' one and only lifeboat, the one that Royden kept at the ready. To ensure that no matter what happened he'd have a means to escape. It seemed so foolish to Crohne at the time. A waste of resources that amounted to yet another variable in their living space to biomass quotient. But now it all fit together. One long string of interconnected events that led all the way back to when the Thousand Eyes tread the earth and an infant deity dared rise against the rule of his predecessors. Uncountable marching steps that led from heaven to earth and now to the moons of Mars.

Crohne closed his eyes and drew in a long breath of inebriating air laced with penetrating aether. He then proceeded down the dark hall, the dusts of all unknowable eternity swirling about in his wake.

~ The end ~

Appendix– Chronology

1766 *Mikhail Lomonosov (Russia) publishes Speculativa ex Foederibus Natura Suscipit Tempus (Theoretical treaties on the dynamic nature of time) marking the theoretical basis for pioneering space flight.

1782 *Henry Cavendish (Britain) conducts the famous "stopwatch" experiment and discovers candidus agris, or "radiant fields" that slightly alter the passage of time in small, contained areas and the dynamics of "temporal corrections" when "offset" time contradicts "natural" time.

1793 Montgolfier Brothers (France) construct first lighter-than-air vehicle.

1798 *James Watt (Scotland), the foremost pioneer in the use of steam powered engines, demonstrates that successive placements of "radiant field" emitting elements can be used as a form of propulsion. Invention of the first strahlendmach (Germany) paddle follows.

1800 Maiden voyage of the Nautilus, the first practical submersible (American design, Robert Fulton, & French construction).
Alessandro Volta (Italy) invents the electric battery.

1801 Formation of the United Kingdom of Great Britain and Ireland.
*Flight of the Universelle (France) the first manned vehicle utilizing strahlendmach propulsion
Giuseppe Piazzi (Italy) discovers Ceres, or the "dwarf planet" between Mars & Jupiter – becomes the first to speculate that natural resources may be prevalent on extraterrestrial bodies.
First Barbary Coast or Tripolitan War (United States and Sweden vs. North African Ottomans, Tripolitania, i.e. Libya and Morocco) begins, ending in 1805.
Thomas Young (England) demonstrates the wave nature of light.

1802 Napoleon declares himself Emperor of France, immediately increases investments towards the potential of manned spaceflight.

1803 Thomas Jefferson makes the Louisiana Purchase.

1804 Embarkation of exploratory journey of Lewis & Clark.

1808 *Founding of the Fanderghist Shipwright Co. (Germany), manufacturers of a multitude of personal and commercial lighter-than-air flying machines.

1809 Yellow clouds observed on Mars.

1812 War of 1812 between United States & Britain ending in 1815.

1814 *Battle of Bladensburg becomes the first major military victory (British) attributable to superiority of airships.
British troops burn Washington D.C.

1815 Napoleon defeated at Waterloo.

1819 *Tsar Alexander I, called "The Blessed," declares that Russia will be the first nation to settle in space. His successor, Nicholas I would later state that, "from above, Russia will rule below."

1821 Michael Faraday (Britain) builds electric powered motors.

1823 The United States enacts the Monroe Doctrine.

1825 Completion of the Erie Canal.
First passenger carrying railroad opens in England.
William Sturgeon (Britain) invents the electromagnet.

1826 *Flight of the Ruscosmos IV; Russians successfully launch the first animals into stable earth orbit.

1827 *Turkish Empire develops a self-sustaining, submersible vehicle that can withstand high pressure within an enclosed atmosphere

maintained by recycling concentrated hybrid plant and animal life. Historically combining the needed advancements later labeled, submersives.
*Russia suffers the "Cosmodrome" tragedy resulting in the deaths of three crewmen in the upper stratosphere (not literally space) during a test flight of the Foton 2, which promised to be the first reusable, manned space vehicle. This marks the first in a long string of space-borne fatalities.
*Number of deaths related to pioneering spaceflight: 3.

1829* *United States launches the Aquila III (utilizing Tempore Impar drive bands, departing from the paddle-wheel designs of the strahlendmachs).
On March 9th, the three brothers, Valentin, Yuri and Boris Gzhatsk (Russia) becomes the first men to enter orbital spaceflight.
*Number of deaths related to pioneering spaceflight: 8.

1831 Michael Faraday (Britain) invents electric dynamo.

1832 *Turkish explorer, Evliya Celebi, becomes the first man to spend over eighteen months beneath the ocean without resurfacing to replenish life support.

1834 *Tyneside Spaceyarde, Ltd. Newcastle upon Tyne, Tyne and Wear, England is combined from several shipwrights to form the first British commercial airship service. Boasts that they will be the first to supply commercial passenger service into space; a boast that is never realized.
Number of deaths related to pioneering spaceflight: 18.
Charles Babbage (Britain) demonstrates the "analytic engine," which becomes known as the first computer. Analytic engines become instrumental in the navigational capabilities of manned space-liners

1836 *United States becomes the first to send manned flight to the moon and the groundbreaking of Tranquility Base, the first (partially) self-supporting off-world colony.

*Alexander Von Humboldt becomes the first man to walk on the moon. He states famously, "Man has shed his bounds. Mankind is truly boundless." Rumours spread that the quote is inaccurate.
*Number of deaths related to pioneering spaceflight: 20.

1835 *Russian cosmonauts, Ivan Chersky and Vladimir Obruchev begin exploration of near earth asteroids.
Discovery that the Perseids (meaning star-like) meteor showers actually caused by comet fragments.
*First reported case of, Brickets or "space sickness." Experts from different nations begin recording a wide range of symptoms ranging from gastrointestinal afflictions, nausea and vomiting, to symptoms related to the blood such as internal infection and bleeding. Extreme cases include physical burns, neurological effects, and death.
*First multinational league meets in Rome concerning the American dominance of lunar and near-earth mineral rights.
*British industrialist, Sir John Brown, declares, "If the floating rocks about the Moon are worth millions, the rocks about Mars are priceless."

1836 *Brighton Corporation and Tranquility Base begin regular shipments of extraterrestrial resources extracted from near-earth orbital objects (NEO's). Initial shipments consist of iron and copper but interest expands greatly when objects containing silver and gold are also discovered.
*Number of deaths related to pioneering spaceflight: 26.

1837 Victoria becomes Queen of Great Britain, * declares that, "The Empire's shores border on eternity."

1840 New Zealand becomes a British colony with the Treaty of Waitangi.

1841 * The League of Outworldly Nations formed to impose basic legal framework for enforcing national affiliation, exploratory claims, and mineral rights for off-world territories. The United States reluctantly agrees to participate. Most of the nations included lack

the capabilities to implement their own space programs but make significant investments with their allies.
*Nations capable of space flight include United States, Germany, Turkey and Russia.
*Germany erects rival lunar station, the Goldene Zeitalter, at Tycho Crater.

1842 Member nations of the the League of Outworldly Nations sign the Strategic Arms Limitation Treaty, or more commonly called the Vladivostok Military Suppression Pact, a loosely written treaty that prohibits the use of firearms beyond earth orbit. This is not only specific to personal arms, but extends to the use of space-liner, platform, or colony based armaments.

1843 Isambard Kingdom Brunel (Britain) launches the S.S. Great Britain, the first propeller driven ocean going ship and the largest constructed to-date.

1845 *Turkey launches the first of a number of Platformlari, man-made platforms equipped with submersive domes that allow men to live for prolonged periods in near-earth orbits.

1846 Mexican-American War begins, ending in 1848.
Johann Gottfried Galle (German) discovers Neptune.

1851 London hosts The Great Exhibition of the Works of Industry of All Nations.
The Crystal Palace serves as a new architecture for the next age of man.
*The exhibition becomes known as the "Golden Milestone" marking the time when industrialization turned space-ward.
*Queen Victoria (Britain) unveils designs for the HMS Commonwealth the first of British space-liners that are capable of extra lunar distances.
*Russia establishes a "semi-permanent" lunar settlement, Central'noj Buhty (центральной бухты), at Sinus Medii.
*Nations capable of space flight include United States, Germany, Turkey, Russia and Britain.
*Number of known deaths related to pioneering spaceflight: 38.

1853 *Signing of the Edward Walter Maunder Agreements (In accordance with the Extra Orbital Trade Authority) with American & German Lunar Port Association to service British space-liners as they make their way to and from Mars.

1854 George Boole (Britain) writes theories of probabilities.
The Crimean War between the Russian Empire and allied forces of France, England, Sardinia and Turkey begins, ending in 1856.
*Ottoman Empire suspends space program in light of war debt and diminishing territory. *Unable to provide external support, several of Turkey's orbital Platformlari or "platforms" are abandoned. It is assumed that all Ottomanauts on-board are lost.

1855 Henry Bessemer (Britain) invents a process for mass-producing steel.
Paris France hosts the Exposition Universelle.
*Nations capable of space flight include United States, Germany, Russia, Britain and France.
*Number of deaths related to pioneering spaceflight: Unknowable.
*Number of lunar colonies: 3, United States, Germany and Russia (The Russian settlements being solely dependent on the American and German programs).

1857 The Indian Mutiny breaks out, largely sparked by the policies of the East India Company.

1858 The East India Company is abolished and India falls under British rule.

1859 Charles Darwin (Britain) publishes the Origin of Species.

1860 Abraham Lincoln elected president of the United States of America.
Jean Joseph Etienne Lenoir (France) invents internal combustion engine.
*French deep spaceflight, Diamant, launched by the Centre National d' Etudes Spatiales, lost somewhere beyond lunar orbit

and never heard from again. Becomes knows as the Ghost Ship of the Stars.

1861 Fort Sumter, South Carolina fired on by Confederate forces starting the U.S. Civil War.
*Tranquility base remains "sympathetic" to Union states and the established Federal government. Lunar official consider succession or the application for statehood, but remains a recognized District within the union. Rumors spread that lunar colonists that hail from southern states launch an organized uprising against the local authorities.
Prince Albert (Prince Albert of Saxe-Coburg and Gotha, Francis Albert Augustus Charles Emmanuel; later The Prince Consort, dies to what is believed to be Typhoid fever.

1862 London hosts the International Exhibition of 1862.
*The United States, formally the leader in pioneering space, fails to demonstrate any significant advances at the exhibition.
*Nations capable of space flight include United States, Germany, Russia, Britain and France.

1864 U.S. Union General William T. Sherman's makes his infamous march to the sea.
U.S. Confederate General Robert E. Lee surrenders the rebel army to U.S. Union General Ulysses S. Grant at Appomattox, Virginia, ending the American Civil War.
Pres. Abraham Lincoln assassinated at Ford's Theater in Washington D.C.

1866 Alfred Nobel (Sweden) invents dynamite.

1867 Paris hosts the Exposition Universelle.
*Nations capable of space flight include United States, Germany, Russia, Britain and France.
*Number of lunar colonies: 4, America x2, Germany and Russia.

1873 Vienna Austria hosts Weltausstellung 1873 Wien.
*Turkey officially announces the abandonment of their space program, content to be the sole supplier of bio-submersive

components to almost all extraterrestrial vehicles, platforms, and colonies.

1874 William Thomson, 1st Baron Kelvin (Britain) publishes the Second Law of Thermodynamics.

1876 Alexander Graham Bell (United States) invents the telephone.
Philadelphia, Pennsylvania hosts Centennial International Exhibition.

1877 Asaph Hall (United States) discovers Mar's two moons, Phobus and Deimus.
Thomas Alva Edison (United States) invents the phonograph.
Giovanni Schiaparelli (Italy) produces maps of Mars with its notable canals, i.e. "canali." The scientific world predicts that alien life will be discovered on Mars.

1878 Paris France hosts Exposition Universelle.
*Number of lunar colonies: 5, America x3, Germany and Russia.

1879 Battle of Isandlwana marks the first major conflict in the Anglo-Zulu war.
Thomas Alva Edison (United States) invents practical electric light.
*British space-liner, the HMS Aspiration becomes the first to orbit Mars and return safely.
*British Royal Astronomical Society commissions the construction of the Ares Britannia platform on Phobus.

1881 British military forces suffer the defeat at the Battle of Majuba Hill. Peace treaty is signed with the South African Republic ending the First Boer War.
Adolph Hitler (Germany) born.

1883 *Britain adds the HMS Jewel of India to her complement of vessels capable of flying between Mars and the moon.

1884 Fabian Society founded to promote socialist reformist politics and the raising of the middle class.

Establishment of the Greenwich Meridian as the "Prime Meridian" to standardize a global time tracking system.

1885 Robert Gascoyne-Cecil, 3rd Marquess of Salisbury (Britain) becomes Prime Minister until 1902.
*Dr. Christien Crohne sent to Mars as on-site architect to supervise the building of the Britain's Ares Britannia Martian lunar platform on Phobus.

1887 Queen Victoria celebrates her Golden Jubilee.
The thwarting of the, "Jubilee Plot" to assassinate the Queen by planting explosives in Westminster Abby. Attempt perpetrated by Irish Parliamentary Party under the leadership of Francis Millen of Clan na Gael.
*The Royal British Interplanetary Society proposes the development of a space-liner capable of completing commercial voyages to Mars independent of reliance on American or German installations on the moon.

1888 Herman Hollerith (United States) contributes significant advancements to the computer.
Heinrich Hertz (Germany) discovers radio waves.
Jack the Ripper brutally murders five or more prostitutes in Whitechapel area of London.

1889 Paris France hosts Exposition Universelle.
*Nations capable of space flight include United States, Germany, Russia, Britain and France.
British and Egyptian troops are victorious in the battle of Omdurman, establishing Britain's rule over the Sudan.

1893 Chicago, Illinois hosts the World's Fair.
*United States announces the commissioning of the USS Emancipator, promising to be the largest space-liner to-date and the only one capable of regularly returning those who have ventured into space safely back to earth.

1895 Physicist Wilhelm Roentgen (German) discovers X-rays.

Konstantin Tsiolkovsky (Russia) publishes article on the possibility of advancing space flight using rockets.

1896 Antoine-Henri Becquerel (France) discovers a new form of "radiance" produced by uranium.
Founding of the Royal Victorian Order of Knighthood and related titles.
*The HMS Daedalus embarks on its historic journey to Mars. Gavin Henry Crossland joins the royal compliment to the commencement ceremony on Ares Britannia.

Made in the USA
Middletown, DE
09 November 2017